THE DON

THE VALENTINI FAMILY: OATH: PART ONE

SERENA AKEROYD

Copyright © 2021 by Serena Akeroyd

All rights reserved.

No part of this book may be reproduced in any form or by any electronic or mechanical means, including information storage and retrieval systems, without written permission from the author, except for the use of brief quotations in a book review.

❦ Created with Vellum

DEDICATION

TO THE BEST mum in the world. Thank you for paying the bills, believing in having cupboards with food in them, only putting vinegar on chips, and for always, *always* keeping me safe.

Love you x

BON VINUTI A LA FAMIGGHIA!

WELCOME TO THE *SICILIAN* FAMILY, darlings.

This is the start of a whole new dynasty in New York City.

The Valentinis are not afraid to shed blood or to break allegiances in order to reclaim what's theirs, including brash New Yorkers who don't know they belong to a Sicilian yet... ;)

Let me introduce you to some names/terms you'll come across.

Fionnabhair - *Fee-on-a-bar*
Luciu - *Loo-cee-you*
Custanzu - *Cust-an-zoo*
Aoife - *Ee-Fah*
Giovi - *Gee-oh-vee*
Cèilidh - *Type of Irish dance (kay-lee)*
Buttana - *whore/bitch*
Vicchiareddu - *old man*
Bona sira - *good evening*
Duci - *sweetheart*
Bedda mia - *my beautiful*
Gilatu - *ice cream*
Figghiu ri buttana - *son of a bitch*
Porca troia - *Goddammit*

Pezz'i miedda - *piece of shit*
Miedda - *shit*
Famigghia - *family* (Sicilian spelling)
T'amu - *I love you*
Grazii - *Thank you*
Se - *Yes*
Natali - *Christmas*
Vinu russu - *Red Wine*
Capisci? - *Understand?*
Russu - *red*
Pi favuri - *please*
Cielo - *heaven*
Culu biddicchiu - *cute ass*

Hell's Kitchen, and Manhattan in general, just started to sizzle a whole lot more.

As always, **TRIGGER WARNINGS** if you're squeamish and don't like violence on the page. There's plenty of that. LOL.

Much love,
Serena
xoxo

THE CROSSOVER READING ORDER WITH THE FIVE POINTS

FILTHY
FILTHY SINNER
NYX
LINK
FILTHY RICH
SIN
STEEL
FILTHY DARK
CRUZ
MAVERICK
FILTHY SEX
HAWK
FILTHY HOT
STORM
THE DON
THE LADY
FILTHY SECRET
REX
RACHEL
FILTHY KING
REVELATION BOOK ONE

REVELATION BOOK TWO
FILTHY LIES
FILTHY TRUTH

RUSSIAN MAFIA
Adjacent to the universe, but can be read as a standalone
SILENCED

PLAYLIST

If you'd like to hear a curated soundtrack, with songs that are featured in the book, as well as songs that inspired it, then here's the link:

https://open.spotify.com/playlist/oIOdaI4u243k6n6LMDtnHP?si=1732b464f6cd4b8e

PART 1
NEW YEAR'S DAY

ONE

JEN

"FUCK ME," I snarled when his fingers dug into my ass, the tips dragging against the soft flesh, pulling the cheeks apart.

I heard a slight noise, then felt the slickness as saliva dripped down over the crinkled skin.

His thumb speared me there, the tunnel caving to his demands, conceding defeat to his invasion. He thrust in and out twice then hooked down against my pussy, making it throb with need.

His subsequent retreat had me clenching hard around the digit, but he just laughed, the sound a taunt that had my nostrils flaring with outrage.

Before I could rear up and twist around, he dipped down and bit my butt cheek. Jolting, I yelped, then when he was pressed up against me once again, I shoved my ass deeper into him, grinding against that log between his thighs that I wanted so fucking desperately.

He growled, biting harder on my flesh, raking his nails down the sides of my hips, the sensitive skin straining at the aggressive caress before, all of a sudden, he was *there*.

His goddamn tongue was against the pucker, flicking it with the flat of the muscle, then prodding it with the tip.

I almost yelped again because I hadn't expected that, but the teasing flutters felt so fucking good that he robbed me of my surprise. Before a yelp could form, he made me groan when he darted back and graced the curve of my ass with another bite.

The pain had me gritting my teeth as I pressed my hands harder into the desk I was leaning against.

The edge dug into me when his cock was back, grinding into me, teasing me with the thick fullness that I needed to be deep inside my ass.

Now.

Like he knew I was going to twist around, his hand went to the wide expanse between my shoulders, and he pressed down. Each finger felt like a steel bar as he held me in place, a place I wanted to be.

I didn't want to be anywhere goddamn else.

Didn't he know that yet?

"Stop teasing me!"

He laughed again, and I pushed back against his hold.

Then I made a stupid mistake.

Even stupider than fucking an Italian mobster.

I growled under my breath and swept my hands against the desk, dragging shit to the floor, uncaring that I tossed a laptop and only God knew what else onto the ground.

His laughter deepened.

"Little cat has claws."

"Bet your ass I do."

"I won't bet mine, but I'll sure as hell bet yours."

His thumb went back to my pucker and while he speared it into me, the other hand went to the back of my neck.

He pressed me down, shoving me until my cheek was rubbing up against the leather topper on the desk. Nails spearing the soft surface, I released a keening sound as he dug down against my pussy, making me so aware of how empty I was that I could have thrown all that stuff onto the floor again.

Skewering his thumb inside me, then corkscrewing it before he pulled out, he rumbled, "Stay there," his tone dark, deep.

Nasty.

My jaw clenched down against it, railing against the dominance I'd avoided my whole life, but when shit had hit the fan, when a friend had betrayed me, when I'd learned the identity of a stranger who was my biological father, I'd thought of one thing.

Well, two.

Sex.

I needed to forget.

Luciu Valentini.

He'd make me forget.

He'd fuck me raw and hard and—

A shriek escaped me when his fingers slid around my throat. He dug them into the soft flesh then jerked me up by that connection alone.

With my back to his front, he didn't stop until my head was resting on his shoulder. It felt as natural as breathing to raise my arms, to hug them around his nape.

His mouth, that sinful mouth, dragged along the curve of my jaw, a move I facilitated by stretching my neck to give him better access, before he spread wet bites over the length of my throat.

Sucking hard, slick and noisy, he marked me then he whispered, "Why should I give you my cock?"

Grinding my teeth again, I rasped, "Because you want to get off?"

"There are a thousand whores out there," he disregarded, "Why should I give *you* my dick?"

Though I loathed admitting it, his arrogance wasn't unfounded.

Neither was I surprised by his anger.

After all, I'd been ignoring him for over a week now.

Regular men didn't appreciate being ignored. Nothing about Luciu was regular. A man like this wasn't used to being dismissed.

When I'd overheard the O'Donnelly brothers talking about him at the disastrous New Year's party I'd just left, where they'd unwittingly confirmed my belief that he was with the Italian mafia—what we called the *Famiglia*—everything clicked and made sense.

And for all that he was dangerous and someone to avoid, his lifestyle even more so, I knew the women sniffing around him *would* be in the thousands.

That didn't take into account the bitches in his club right this second, either. Each of them would be willing to spread their legs for a man as powerful as this one.

Throw in the fact that it was New Year's Eve, with midnight long since gone, and with everyone either high or fucking hammered, he could have anyone he wanted...

But I wasn't here to stroke his ego.

I was here to get off.

"Why did you pick up my call?" I rasped, smirking when his fingers bit into my throat. Hard enough that they'd leave marks in the morning.

Fuck, I hoped they would.

"Why would you answer? You didn't have to. Not if there were a thousand whores out there who'd fuck you." I licked my lips and dared to whisper, "You want me. Not another whore. You want *me*."

He released a snarl that I felt deep in my pussy.

The tips of his fingers acted like a brand, so hot, so hard, before he growled, "Hands on the table."

I obeyed, knowing that, at long last, he was going to give me what I'd come here for.

Fingertips spearing even harder into the leather topper on the antique desk, back arched as he'd yet to let go of my throat, I felt him bend with me, leaning into me so that he covered me. The expensive silk-blend suit he wore brushed against the sensitive flesh of my spine like it was a caress.

Everything about him stank of money.

It was the only thing that should have drawn me to him, but it wasn't.

It wasn't.

I wished it were.

His lips pressed a small kiss to my shoulder before he snapped a bite around the delicate flesh there. I yelled out in pain, then shuddered when he whispered in my ear, "Don't taunt a man like me, Jennifer. We bite back." His teeth settled around my earlobe, and I shivered, waiting for him to grace me with another bite as hard as that one, but he didn't.

Instead, he pulled back, let go of me, leaving me to sag into the desk. I was half certain that he was about to let go of me entirely, about to back off, leave me like the trash I felt I was sometimes; only he didn't.

I heard drawers being pulled open, the scraping mechanism raking up against my ear drums like nails down a chalkboard.

Breath shuddering from my lips, I waited, endlessly, ceaselessly for his next move, and then he made it.

I heard a zipper being lowered.

Oh, God.

It was so loud in the quiet room. Outside, the walls vibrated from the rage of the music, the joy of the crowd. Inside, it was like a tomb, but I felt every sound as if it were an action being taken against me as he clicked open what I knew was a bottle of lube.

The splatting sound, along with a strong scent of coconut, combined with the cold chill of the liquid coating my ass had me jerking like he'd spanked me.

Then he did.

With his cock.

Christ.

His dick sloshed through the puddles of lube he'd made on my ass, some of it landing between my cheeks, some of it on the curve that was now dripping down the backs of my legs.

He was thick.

He was long.

Jesus.

My eyes almost crossed at the prospect of taking him there, of him sliding his cock home, of him finally fucking me after taunting me so much—

"A condom," I choked out at the last minute, realizing why he felt so fucking good.

Why he felt so hot—

"Are you clean?" he intoned calmly, his dick still sliding between the twin globes of my butt.

Tits heaving as they were shoved into the desk, I rasped, "I'm clean. I've never fucked without a condom—*tonight included.*"

He hummed as he pressed the tip of his dick to my pucker. He prodded me there, the tip not going deeper, just rocking against it. "I'm clean. I have bi-monthly checkups."

I blinked. "Because you have so much unprotected sex?"

"I haven't fucked without a condom in years," he rumbled, and I got the picture—he wasn't going to tell me shit.

"Then—"

"You're clean. I'm clean." The tip pushed into my ass, and I didn't struggle.

I could have.

But fuck.

My eyes clenched closed as I reared up onto my forearms and instead of pulling away, instead of running screaming for the hills, I pushed my butt back until he was filling me.

Claiming a hole that many guys had claimed before.

He took more care than I'd anticipated at first—not just slamming into me—but making sure my ass was ready, that *I* was ready before I felt the burning heat of him all the way inside me...

He pulled out, and I squirmed at the sudden emptiness.

He thrust in, and I groaned, my head bowing, my forehead rocking against the table.

Again and again, he pounded into me, and I didn't just lie there, I *ground* into him. Not just accepting what he gave me, being a passive participant, but actively encouraging him.

Reaching back, even though it meant my tits smushed into the table, I grabbed his hips, holding him inside me, and I undulated against the leather, wanting deeper, harder, pounding thrusts that I'd feel tomorrow. That I'd feel every time I sat down.

My nails dug into the silk covering his ass, and I had no idea why it was so hot that we were both fully dressed, but it was.

With a cry, I begged, "Fuck me, Luciu, fuck me hard."

He loomed over me, his front pressing me into the table, his weight uncomfortable, then he did as I asked.

He fucked me.

He ground into me.

He gave me what I needed, giving me everything I could take.

The edge of the table butted against my stomach, and it hurt, but I didn't care.

I needed that pain.

I needed the discomfort.

I needed to fucking feel.

He made me experience all those things, and I could have kissed him for it.

Not that we'd done that tonight. Not yet. Maybe never again.

A scream escaped me as his hand tunneled around my front, his fingers coming to my clit.

As he rocked into me, he caressed me there, rubbing with an insistence that spoke of a man who knew how to get a woman off.

I growled when my pussy clenched down, suddenly so fucking empty, emptier than it had ever been in my life and considering I'd never had a dick in there, that was saying something.

It was a stark contrast to the thick, burning brand of his length in my ass which was something I felt in the back of my goddamn throat.

He moved his hand down, not stopping until the butt of his wrist was rubbing my clit and his fingers—

Oh, God.

He pressed two into me, then angled his hips down, arching up higher on the balls of his Brioni-shod feet so that he was thrusting those fingers and his dick against my G-spot.

I cried out the first time I felt him pound that part, then a low keening sound rumbled from my lips as he burned me with pleasure, branding me with the scolding hot heat—

Faster.

Harder.

I screamed.

Ecstasy ricocheted through me, tormenting me, making me growl and cry and sob and *burn*.

The flames licked at me, and I loved them. I needed them to hurt. I needed the pleasure to cleanse. I needed him to fuck me like this, like we were fucking animals.

We both cried out together.

His slick seed was spent inside me as I shuddered through my orgasm, whimpering and mewling as he took me higher, higher, higher—

His teeth nipped at my shoulder before he bit down.

Harder than before.

Nastier.

Crueler.

And that sting sent me soaring, had me flying so high that I knew the drop would be brutal.

Just like everything else in my life.

Beneath me, the ground trembled. At first, I thought it was an aftershock, the intensity of the orgasm shaking the earth itself.

That was when I heard the screams.

And the gunshots.

TWO

LUCIU

THE SOUND of gunshots had me tensing up, but not with concern. Mostly just irritation.

La Notte di San Silvestro. New Year's Eve.

Was nothing sacred in this godforsaken city?

As much as I'd strived to own it, Sicily would forever be my homeland.

Catania... *Cristo,* how I missed it. There, things were done with panache. Here, it was as if the men had watched too many Van Damme movies during their formative years.

Grumbling under my breath at the disruption, I carefully pulled out of Jen's fine ass, my hands gripping the cheeks, enjoying the taut curves as I made my retreat.

"What's that?" she asked breathily, her nerves clear.

"I think you already know, *cara mia,*" I told her dryly, straightening up so I could shove my dick back into my pants.

She placed her hands on the three-hundred-year-old desk that had once sailed the high seas with one of Sicily's greatest Barber pirates, and, more importantly, had once graced my grandfather's office, then pushed up. The move made her ass look biteable which had me tilting my head to the side with enjoyment as I watched the show.

I'd just tapped that, and I wanted back inside.

I'd never known a woman who wanted anal on a hook-up before, but I wasn't about to complain even though that pussy of hers—

"You goddamn mobsters. What is it with you?" she snapped on a huff, dragging the skirt of her dress down to cover herself.

Well, if it could be called a dress.

It was more of a napkin that somehow, through magic, stayed up. I thought her nipples had something to do with how it remained draping over her, but I wasn't entirely sure. Either way, I appreciated the seamstress who'd made this delectable piece of nothing.

I smoothed a hand over her butt, tucking her into my side. She struggled, shoving at me, but I was stronger and as I hauled her nearer, I forcibly walked her over to the wall of windows at the other end of my office.

Russu was my flagship nightclub. It had funded my war against the Fieri *Famiglia* and would continue to be a mainstay of my income stream.

The place had earned me two million legitimate dollars last year, had laundered four, and had helped me outsource over six million in coke to the crowd of city slickers who needed some white powder to help them enjoy their evenings.

Fools.

"What the hell do you think you're doing?" Jen snapped, all sass and vinegar.

"I thought an orgasm would sweeten you up," I half-crooned as I brought us to a halt beside the windows that overlooked the club floor.

She scoffed, "I'm sweet enough considering there's gunfire outside—"

I waved my free hand. "No gunfire in the club. See? My security is good."

"So good that we heard the gunshots over the beats the DJ is pumping?"

"They can't hear a thing," I assured her calmly. "It's soundproofed."

She frowned. "Why?"

"Because I like to control what my patrons hear and see."

The pucker in her brow deepened as she looked up at me. "Why aren't you running out there to defend yourself? Guns blazing—"

"You Americans. So obsessed with John Wayne movies and guns."

"I'm not obsessed with either," she snarked, tugging out of my hold, but I snapped my fingers around her arm, holding her against my side.

I was used to people tensing up around me. It went with the job, but something wasn't right here.

The night I'd met her, the night we'd danced, she'd been like fucking putty in my hands.

Then she disappeared.

In this very goddamn club.

"What happened?" I rasped, peering down into those gorgeous cocoa bean eyes of hers that were raging with defiance.

"When?"

"You were coy and shy. Now, you're growling and bristling like a cat who's facing off against a dog," I told her smoothly, but I added a bite to my next words as I enunciated each one clearly, "What. Happened?"

I saw the flexing of muscles in her cheek as she clenched her jaw. "Nothing."

"Do you know what's gone down between then and now?" I reached up and traced a finger over that ticking muscle in her cheek.

"What?" she asked warily, tugging away from my affectionate gesture.

"I went from the man who was trying to become the Don of the *Famiglia*, to ascending."

I saw her flinch as she registered the title and what that meant.

I winked at her. In part, to reduce her fear, in part, to hide my rage at what might have caused her to pull away from me like she did. I knew firsthand now the havoc her ex had wreaked.

"If someone has hurt you, *duci*, tell me. I might be able to—"

"What?" She sniffed. "I'm only someone you agreed to fuck."

"Those were your terms," I said calmly. "I neither accepted nor rejected them, I just fucked you in the ass."

"Agreed. That's exactly what you did. You fucked me in the ass, and now it's time for me to go home because, apparently, I'm capable of making the worst mistakes imaginable." She stomped her foot like a recalcitrant toddler, and while it should have irritated me, mostly I found it amusing. "Fucking mobsters. I'm a moron."

My eyes narrowed at her. "You fuck mobsters on the regular?"

She grunted. "No. I don't fuck them. I make it a point not to because I like to stay alive. The gunfire makes it clear that I really am an idiot."

I tipped my head to the side as I looked down at her, recognizing I'd misunderstood what she meant.

"You're not an idiot."

I'd seen her test scores; her CPA results had set a record within the NY testing branch for a hundred percent mark on one of the most difficult sections of the exam.

Jennifer frowned. "I am. I know what you are, and I still fucking came."

"You came quite loudly."

"Are you trying to piss me off?"

"No, but apparently you're trying to piss *me* off."

"See, with ordinary men, that doesn't matter. With mobsters, you have to think about getting your throat slit when they have a temper tantrum—"

"Who said I'd slit your throat?" I rumbled, tugging her into me. I slipped one hand between her shoulders, then arched her back as I used my arm as a supportive band to keep her upright. When I dipped her down, she gasped, hair tumbling in a fall of waves that made me want to gather it in my fist, curl it about my wrist, and tilt her head more. "Hmm, *cara mia*? Who said I'd slit your throat?"

She narrowed her eyes at me, evidently hearing the threat. "I told you I'm Irish. I met you with Aidan O'Donnelly Jr. at my table. You know I know more about the mob than those fools down there—"

"Maybe the mob, but not the mafia."

Her mouth gathered into a tight purse. "Is that supposed to make me feel better, Valentini?"

"Such venom—" I rasped, hauling her back into me with a snap that had her squealing, her hands coming up to my chest. The second they collided, she shoved away, but I dragged her deeper into me, banding that arm tighter around her, not letting her worm away. "—when I just made you purr."

I twisted her around in my arms, much as I'd done on the dance floor the other week. To the sounds of techno and EDM, I'd treated her like we were back in the forties, dancing as my *Nanna* taught me and as she'd been taught by her grandmother.

With her arms crossed against her belly, the wrists on her hips, I held her in place, held her firm and tight, close to me as I pressed my face to her throat. She shivered as I kissed her there, trailing my tongue along the arch even as I shuffled her into a two-step movement that had her ass grinding against my dick.

The exquisite torture had me growling under my breath, as did the reflection of her face in the glass.

Beyond, there were five thousand patrons, each of them dancing and partying hard as they celebrated the start of yet another fucking year, but all I saw was her.

The way those almond eyes were dazed, the thick lashes fluttering in response. How that full bottom lip, so pouty and plump, was tucked between her teeth, white shards of enamel against bright red lipstick that I wanted staining my dick.

For a moment, the tension that had invaded her at the sound of the gunfire was gone. Her earlier anger as she stormed through the office door, demanding to be seen, had dissipated.

She was putty in my hands again.

This was how I wanted her.

This.

I growled as I pressed my lips to her nape, then I moved down, taking advantage of the fact the woman seriously had no self-preservation if she could wear handkerchiefs in sub-zero temperatures.

Sliding my mouth along her spine, circling each nodule, spreading up and along her rib cage, kissing everywhere I touched, teasing everywhere I tasted, moving along the curve of her waist, I savored her like she was a treat. She pressed her hands into the window, the tips streaking the glass as she arched back, and I carried on.

Down.

Down.

Down.

The handkerchief-like skirt floated around her legs, revealing streaks of cum that had seeped from her ass. My tongue flattened against the strong muscles of her thighs, tasting myself, tasting us as I moved down and along the length, cleaning her up.

"Oh, God," she whimpered, "what are you doing?"

"Making you clean again." I moved to her sit spot before I grabbed her hips and tilted her forward even more, encouraging her to press up against the mirrored glass. I carefully nudged one leg wider, then sank my face between her thighs.

The taste of her pussy was like a junkie's first hit of heroin.

It sank into my fucking bones as I flicked my tongue over and along to her clit. Just as she moaned, the hungry sound was punctuated by the sounds of more gunfire from the back of the warehouse.

The way tension invaded her was interesting. I knew from my investigation into her that she was a New Yorker born and bred. Not only was this not the first time she'd have heard it, but I knew she'd been exposed to it on a personal level.

With the moment broken, her terror now filtering the air around me, an emotion that I ordinarily lived to trigger in someone, I recognized that I didn't crave her fear.

I needed her to want me.

Standing, I went to hug her, to comfort her, but she twisted away until I grabbed her and hauled her into my chest once more.

Her cheeks, once flushed with need and warmth, were blanched, but in her eyes, there were the signs of the lady she was. A regalness overset her, like a warrior queen of old as she faced her fear, choked it down, and headbutted it rather than let it overwhelm her.

Her nails dug into my suit once more, crushing the silk as she snapped, "Don't you have to go and be a big ol' boss? Make some people regret crossing you?"

"You have an attitude problem," I told her softly, uncaring that my mouth and chin were slick with her pussy juices.

"You ain't the first person to tell me that," she snapped. "You won't be the last."

I pressed us closer together, so close that her tits smushed up against my chest. "You do know that your attitude is the reason why you lost out on that promotion, don't you?"

She tensed. "I beg your pardon?"

I smiled at her. "I have a very thorough *capo*."

"What's that supposed to mean?" Jennifer scowled up at me. "A *capo*... what is that?"

"Essentially my right-hand man." I dipped my chin. "They saw how... interested we are in each other and decided to take notes."

"Past tense, buddy. Past fucking tense."

Tutting, I told her, "Hardly, seeing as this is the present—"

"And a big, fat fucking mistake."

At her snarled correction, I retorted, "You shouldn't tell lies, *cara mia*. Not when I'll enjoy making you tell the truth."

Fear lit her eyes up. "This was stupid of me," she breathed, tension freezing her in place at the sound of more gunshots, her attention splitting for a fraction of time until she whimpered, "So fucking stupid of me."

"You are safe here," I crooned.

"I'm the exact opposite of safe," she snapped, but it was less venomous than before, and her hands stopped crushing my jacket and, instead, clung to it.

Yes, there was a difference.

Both ruined my suit, but what was damaged silk when you had an angel in your arms?

"I-I need to go."

"You need to stay," I countered, dipping my head so I could press a kiss to her lips. The second I was a half-inch away from that kiss, she whipped her face to the side to avoid the caress. It had nothing to do with the slickness still coating my mouth.

"No!" She shoved at my chest. "Get away from me. I shouldn't have done this."

I smirked at her. "We'll do this again and again, *cara mia*—"

"Don't call me that," she snapped, ignoring me aside from the endearment.

"—tonight was just the start."

Fire replaced the fear, setting the deep brown alight as she growled, "Your wife might have something to say about that!"

PART 2
DECEMBER 22ND

THREE

LUCIU

"AIDAN O'DONNELLY, it's a pleasure to finally meet you," I murmured as I stepped up to the VIP table at The 68.

A socialite's hotspot located in The Sharpe, one of the exclusive skyscrapers that Acuig Corp. had constructed over the past two decades as they transformed the Manhattan skyline, The 68 was the epitome of class, elegance, and raw power.

Within these walls, deals were made that shaped the United States itself, and none of the politicians were aware of who owned it.

Or, if they *did* know, then they turned a blind eye.

I found Americans were very capable of doing that when it was worth their while.

The heir to the Five Points' Mob stared up at me, his head tilting as he coolly took me in.

The man's rep almost went as deep as his father's, no small feat considering Aidan O'Donnelly Sr. had imprinted his level of insanity on the city for decades.

In a corner banquette, one arm resting upon the backrest, the other holding a glass of whiskey from a bottle that I knew cost nearly fifteen grand, he studied me as much as I studied him.

I took in the Prada suit, sharp, black, and slick with it, the lack of a tie, the handkerchief in his top pocket, and the fifty grand Patek Philippe on his wrist.

He took in a hand-tailored suit from Savile Row, shoes that were hand-tooled in Rome, a maroon tie made from raw silk, and my Rolex—a gift to me from my father. One of the last gifts he'd given to me before we'd stopped speaking to each other before his death.

"And you are?" O'Donnelly drawled.

I wasn't offended that he didn't know my identity. I'd gone out of my way to hide that from most of the factions, hell, from the majority of the city—the Irish Mob included. My surname had spread like Chlamydia in a whorehouse, but my identity? Tighter than a virgin's pussy.

I smiled at the Irishman and murmured, "My name's Valentini." Surprise appeared in his eyes. Not fear. *Interesting.* "You've heard of me." It wasn't a question.

"Only by reputation." His eyes narrowed. "There are sixteen guards sitting in this restaurant," he informed me. "Each one armed with more firepower than a SWAT team. If you even think about pulling out a weapon—"

My smile turned into a smirk. "I can tell you where each is sitting in the bar if you'd like? I'm well aware that you're protecting Savannah Daniels, O'Donnelly. But you mistake my reason for being here. It has nothing to do with the New World Sparrows or the exposés Ms. Daniels is releasing—"

O'Donnelly raised a hand to stop me. "Then why *are* you here?"

"To speak with you, of course."

"The last time an Italian walked into a restaurant I was frequenting, I got a call from my father and had to watch him hack some of your fellow countrymen into pieces after your play went sideways, Valentini. I have plans for tonight. Plans that don't include that."

"They weren't my countrymen."

He arched a brow. "They very much were."

"The Fieris purged the *Famiglia*," —the Italian mafia— "of all Sicilians when they slaughtered my grandfather, O'Donnelly. I'm Sicilian. *Not* Italian."

"You're telling me there's a difference?"

"Are you English?" When he said nothing, I murmured, "I think the twelve million dollars your father funnels into the IRA on a yearly basis says otherwise, don't you?"

He smirked at me. "Touché."

"The Italians are no friends of mine."

"Glad to hear it."

"I'm not here to hurt you."

"Even gladder to hear it. Although I'm not entirely sure how you got in—"

"My money's as good as anyone else's. This place functions as a business, I believe."

O'Donnelly's gaze darkened. "If you're not interested in the New World Sparrows—"

"I didn't say that," I denied. "I'm very interested. Just as every other person in the country is.

"A secret society of bent politicians and corrupt officials spanning City Hall to the nearby police precincts? That's fascinating stuff for anyone who's amused by America's dedication to democracy.

"Corruption is the basis of every single one of your dollars. People are just too naive to see that."

"And God love them for it." He tipped his glass at me in a silent cheer.

"Knowledge is power."

O'Donnelly shrugged. "Only in the hands of the few. Anyway, we all love a conspiracy theory, don't we? I'm sure there'll be a Netflix show about it soon."

"A secret society functioning within the government?" I scoffed, "Is it a conspiracy when it's actually happening? Isn't that just the truth?"

O'Donnelly raised his glass to his lips and after he took a deep sip, blandly asked, "You said the Sparrows weren't your reason for approaching me. So why are we talking about them?"

And here it was.

A move I'd been waiting ten years to make.

A move that I'd shed blood for.

That I'd sacrificed my *life* for.

A political power play that I needed to ram home, one that had nothing to do with the Senate floor or the Supreme Court.

O'Donnelly had to agree to help me.

He had to.

My father had died for this, had died because of this fucking city and its movers and shakers, and I couldn't let his death be in vain.

"The *Famiglia*. As much as I'm sure you'd like them all culled from existence, mass genocide is still something that even a rat-riddled government such as your own disapproves of.

"You and your allies chopped off the Italian mafia's head when you killed Benito Fieri—" And had denied me what I'd been working toward for over a fucking decade. "—but you never stopped to think about what would happen to its body. The Italian mafia can function without a head but they're morons without leadership."

"I don't care what the Italians do," Aidan drawled.

"We both know that's bullshit."

He stared into that fucking whiskey. "Do we though?"

"Yes. We do." I didn't wait for an invitation to take a seat, just slid opposite him. "It's bad business if the cops are sniffing over territory that butts up against yours.

"As they clamp down on the stupid moves the *Famiglia* is making, I'm pretty sure that the sanctioned actions your runners take will come under police scrutiny as City Hall tries to sweep up crime. Especially in the face of the mayor's involvement with the Sparrows."

Involvement was an understatement.

The mayor had recently been killed in his office in City Hall. Shot by a fellow Sparrow who, in turn, had been gunned down by a sniper at the scene.

And they said there was no honor among thieves.

In my experience, it was far easier to make a lot of problems go away when there was a patsy involved. Detective Craig Lacey, the dirty cop who'd killed the mayor, was probably going to be tried for every unsolved crime committed in the past fifteen years in his precinct whether he was guilty of them or not.

Land of the Free... *sure*.

My mouth tightened at the thought, but I merely said, "The Valentini family made the *Famiglia*—"

"Made it what it is? The face of that conspiracy theory you're talking about?"

I frowned. "What do you mean?"

"I mean, the *Famiglia* was hoodwinked by the Sparrows too." He took another small sip then shifted in his seat. As he did, I saw a flash of something in his face, muscles tightening, skin bunching, and having been behind a lot of men's pain over the years, I knew what it looked like.

O'Donnelly was in pain?

I knew years earlier he'd been involved in a drive-by shooting that had wrecked his leg. Every now and then, he walked with a limp, but as far as I was aware, the Irish Mob had gone out of their way to portray him as a well man.

Facial micro expressions didn't lie, however. They were the bullshit detectors I'd learned back in university and which had come in so handy during my time as the head of a faction of Sicilians who were determined to take their territory back in Manhattan. Who'd go to any length to bring down the Italian mafia and to claim it as their own.

His response to fidgeting was far more interesting than his words.

Slowly, musing upon his actions all the while, I said, "I'm not surprised the Italians were the front. That makes sense, actually. Fieri proved time and time again that he was an incompetent leader, just like his father."

"Not that incompetent," O'Donnelly pointed out. "I've had a recent history lesson on the *Famiglia*, more's the pity. I know that the Fieris butchered your family and had you running with your tail between your legs back to Sicily."

Though rage whirled inside me, the stirrings of a hurricane that I'd been controlling for ten fucking years, I merely rasped, "Would you say that the Five Points function on honor, O'Donnelly? Beneath it all, the blood and the death and the violence, is there an honor code among you?"

"As you pointed out, Valentini, my father is Irish and a devout Catholic. What do you think?"

"I think the Irish Mob wouldn't be so tight knit if there weren't some kind of mores and laws in place." When his jaw tightened, I catalogued the response. "If someone came in and decimated those rules, killed every single member of your family, I'm sure you'd retaliate."

"You're still standing. So, decimation is a little hyperbolic, wouldn't you say?"

Hyperbolic? So, the Irish heir had picked up a dictionary in his time. There went the theory they were all meatheads.

"Would you like to hear how my seven-month-pregnant grandmother almost died in the same fire that killed my grandfather?

"How she had to hide out in the wilds of fucking Idaho before they came after her again? Nearly killed her newborn son, so she had to run to Maine, then sail away on a goddamn fishing boat so she could spend the rest of her life in the Sicilian countryside?

"My goddamn queen of a grandmother, fucking mafia royalty," I spat, "having to marry an abusive farmer and be grateful for every beating because he kept her son alive? Is that what you want to hear?"

"I don't want to hear any of it. Not my monkey, not my circus because while your tale is tragic, so's mine, Valentini," he ground out. "My mother was kidnapped by the fucking Aryans, gang-raped until she was a shadow of her former fucking self and rescued by my da who came riding in like a white knight to slay her dragons." His top lip curved up in a sneer. "We've all got war stories, Valentini. That's the price we pay for this fucking life. That's the price of these goddamn suits and the watches on our wrists that'd buy an average man a car.

"Now, I have business to attend to, business that doesn't include yours, so if you'd kindly fuc—"

"Sir? I have a note for you."

The server's abrupt appearance had neither of us jerking in response. That he'd been aware of her presence as much as I was spoke of a man who lived up to his reputation.

Rumor had it that O'Donnelly Jr's signature move was to cut out his pound of flesh then rub salt in the wound… then and there, I could see it happening.

His gaze snapped to the woman who stood there, frozen in place, as he snatched the note out of her fingers. "You can go," he said dismissively, but his tone was kinder than I'd have expected.

The woman bit her lip but made a hasty and grateful retreat after she laid out a second glass for him, her fear so strong that she didn't even think to ask me if I wanted to order something.

As O'Donnelly read the note, the paper was thin enough that I could see there were three lines of text. It might as well have been an essay for how long it took him to process what he was reading.

The man wasn't an idiot. Idiots didn't use words like 'hyperbolic' in everyday sentences. Dyslexia, then?

I scanned my memory for any reference to that in my personal encyclopedia into every mob faction in NYC but came up blank.

"Problem?" I queried, as if I had a right to know.

"No."

He dropped the note on the table then poured himself another measure, as well as some whiskey into the empty glass. I half-expected him to give it to me, but he didn't. He just pursed his lips with irritation. Not at me, however. Just at whatever it was he'd read.

"Glad to hear it."

"I'm sure." His gaze scanned the restaurant, but when he came up blank, he cast me another look. "Are you still here?"

"I want your family's endorsement."

He scoffed. "What for? President?"

I didn't laugh. "What's left of the *Famiglia* and isn't either taking up room in a morgue somewhere in the city, polluting the Hudson, or wearing orange jumpsuits, is in the process of being brought under my control. However, it will take peace to look like a leader."

"Peace? There's no fucking peace in this city."

"There can be. The Italians are at war with you and the Russians. If we can draw a ceasefire, work together, we can own Manhattan once again."

"And how would you have us work together, Valentini?"

"A treaty." I shrugged.

"A treaty? What are you? The League of Nations? Is this 1918 and I just didn't fucking realize it?"

I arched a brow at that. Definitely dyslexic—the League of Nations were the precursors to the UN. The man knew history but took eons to read a three-lined message?

"Why not?" I reasoned, tone placid. "They work from time to time."

"What would we gain?"

"Territorial lines appropriately demarcated, an agreement not to undercut each other, harsh rules to keep our mutual foot soldiers in line among other such stipulations. Agreements to trade fairly among ourselves.

"We can each own our kingdom, can each make it work for us and get rich while we do it. We'd hash out the accord together." When he didn't reply, I carefully asked, "I'm assuming that the sudden influx of Bratva princesses for sisters-in-law means you have an in with the Russians?"

"When the country is at war, we make money. When *we're* at war, the only people who profit are the District Attorneys and the undertakers."

"There's no denying that," he confirmed bitterly, his jaw wiggling to the side as he studied me. "How did you get in here?" he demanded again.

"By fair means," I assured him, then, aware he wasn't going to let this drop, I continued, "Your brother has a standing reservation at this restaurant. Every evening at eight PM. When that reservation was changed to six, I knew an O'Donnelly was coming."

"So, you expected to meet with Conor?"

I nodded.

"You've got someone on the staff on your payroll?"

I laid out my hands in a placatory manner. "I do, but as of this evening, they no longer work here."

"Your transparency is... unusual."

"I wish to build allegiances, O'Donnelly, not allow more enemies to fester. When you check up on me, you'll find I don't speak falsehoods with allies."

He made a scoffing sound. "I actually believe you. Not sure if that makes you the fool or me."

"You're not a fool," I assured him. "If you know my name, you know my reputation."

"I've learned of it recently."

I bowed my head, well aware that there was an insult in there, but it spoke of how high up the ranks O'Donnelly was.

To him, I was a mosquito, a pesky gnat that was biting him in his sleep. Not for long, though. Not for fucking long.

"I could easily make an enemy out of you, but I'd prefer to make a friend."

O'Donnelly's glance lingered on me a second before something caught his attention. I let my focus drift over to the same spot and found him staring at Savannah Daniels. Her face was plastered all over the TV right now thanks to the articles she was writing on the New World Sparrows.

Disinterested, I turned to the woman with her.

Porca Madonna—who the fuck was she?

I'd seen the backs of both women as they headed over to the bathroom, had noticed that one wore a sharp suit that was more befitting a man while the other wore a dress so short it left little to the imagination.

Having disregarded her as a whore, a *buttana*, I regretted that now.

She was beautiful. *Bedda*.

Cristo, she wasn't just beautiful, she moved like fucking poetry and had the grace of royalty.

In a silvery dress made of metal plates that were sewn together, almost like chain mail of old, nothing about her was cold. It clung to every curve, revealing everything, hiding nothing, but for all that she had the body of a *buttana*, her face belonged to an angel.

She had hair like the finest espresso, rich and glossy with streaks of fire in it that the lights in the restaurant made gleam. Her eyes were almond-shaped, the irises as dark as her hair. Her nose was dainty, but the tip was slightly blunt before it led to the enhanced pout of her lips.

Red, the color of dried blood, that pouty curve had me gritting my teeth and wanting to trace the delicate line of her jaw.

With her hair tossed over one half of her face, she hid from me.

Hid.

I couldn't allow that.

I *wouldn't* allow that.

Dick hard, I stared at her, willing her to look at me. Willing that angel to see this humble soul.

Angels weren't made to be pawed; they were meant to be cherished.

Worshipped.

Even heathens like me knew that, but this angel walked toward me, and with each step, I felt the heat between us stir.

Her gaze never faltered, neither did mine, and lightning sparked into being, ricocheting between us as she moved nearer to me.

"Savannah, Jennifer, please, meet Luciu Valentini," O'Donnelly murmured when they finally reached the table.

I stared at her, seeing the dazed heat in her eyes, knowing she was burning up for me as much as I was for her. "It's a pleasure to meet you, ladies."

Moving along for her to take a seat beside me, I watched as the skirt of her ridiculous dress pulled taut, exposing more of her thighs.

"Jen, your guest sent a note. He isn't coming."

Aidan's words had irritation, followed by fear, flashing over her features. I could deal with the former, just not the latter. Why was she scared?

She didn't reply, but her hand snapped out and she grabbed the whiskey that Aidan had poured into the spare glass earlier, downing it in under five seconds.

When she started choking, I hid a laugh. "Do you need some water?"

She coughed, and her cheeks began to burn. "I'm fine, thanks," she told me even though she clearly wasn't fine.

Who was this guest who had her alternating between scared and annoyed and who drove her to drink?

Aidan had dropped the note on the table. I scanned its location and determined to pick it up when no one was looking.

"I think you just lost your bet, Jen," Savannah jibed, which made Jennifer cough again. The look that flashed between them was a combination of annoyed and amused, but it told me they knew each other well enough to tease.

"Bet?" I crooned.

"Jen keyed her ex's Ferrari," Aidan replied.

She spluttered, "He was cheating on me! What was I supposed to do?"

Some fool had cheated on her? What on earth was wrong with the men of New York?

"He cheated on you?" I repeated, stunned by the notion.

Savannah, ignoring my comment, joked, "Dump his lying ass?"

"Well, I did that afterward. Keying his car was more satisfying," she grouched, raising her hand to her nose, the move a means of shielding a rude hand gesture she shot at Savannah as she did so.

"A woman with a taste for vengeance, interesting." That stirred my blood like nothing else could.

"If the prick isn't going to show up, our reason for being here is obsolete."

Aidan's declaration had a visible effect on Jennifer. Her shoulders slouched and an air of defeat tainted the air around her.

I didn't like that look on her. She wasn't born for defeat. *She was made to conquer.*

Aidan told me, "I'll speak with my father. You have my word."

That was the first time I looked at him after Jennifer's arrival because his statement came as a surprise. Before the women had returned, I'd thought he was going to send me away, but instead, he was interested in brokering peace.

Relief had me replying, "I appreciate it. Men of their word are hard to find."

"I don't disagree. But I make no promises. You know of our reputation, so you know as well as I do that my father dances to his own beat."

My lips quirked up. "I can handle rejection. I just would like an opportunity to present myself to him. Court him, as it were."

"If you're honest with your family's intentions," Aidan declared, "then I don't see why he'll disapprove of the move. I'll be seeing him for the holidays. I'll speak with him then."

"I appreciate you marring *Natali* with business."

"It's in all our interests." Aidan's tone was cold, but it warmed up as he turned to Jennifer and said, "I'm taking Savannah home, Jen. I'll pick up your tab if you want to eat—"

My hand covered her forearm, then I trailed my finger up and along it, making goosebumps pop into being. She gasped, and it morphed, twisting into a soft moan that shot straight to my dick.

"There's no need for that. The tab is on me," I rumbled.

Aidan reached down, grabbed the bottle of whiskey, and surprised me by grinning. "An Irishman never hits up the chance for a freebie."

"And a Sicilian doesn't mind investing in his future allies," I inserted.

Savannah shot Jennifer a stern look. "Hon, do you want to stay or come up with us?"

Jennifer blinked, a little dazedly, at Savannah. Even though I appreciated that Savannah was concerned for her friend, I squeezed Jennifer's wrist gently, with just enough pressure that she knew I wanted her to say no.

Satisfaction surged inside me as she replied breathily, "I'll text you later."

It was not a good sign that I was happier about her agreement than Aidan O'Donnelly's.

"You'd better," she intoned darkly, a warning clear in her voice.

"Valentini," Aidan muttered a farewell.

"O'Donnelly."

"A pleasure to meet you, Luciu," Savannah remarked.

"The pleasure was all mine, Savannah."

As they drifted away, I snatched the note Aidan had discarded, my focus returning to Jennifer after I scanned the name on the small piece of paper.

> I won't be able to make it.
> See you in court.
> Damian Headley.

The ex. It had to be.

A ridiculous wave of jealousy unfurled inside me. One that was unnecessary, but one I couldn't help.

I leaned into her, close enough that I could smell her heady perfume, so that it was pretty much all I breathed in, and asked her, "Do you like dancing?"

"You can't dance here."

My lips curved at her breathy retort. "I know. It's staid. The Irish never could throw a party."

"I'm Irish." Her eyes gleamed with amusement.

"I have time to show you that Sicilians throw better celebrations. Without whiskey lubricating everything."

Her laughter made my heart pound as she told me, "It's a good thing you waited for them to leave before you started throwing shade at the Irish. I'm not as hardcore as Aidan Jr."

"How do you know him?"

"We're the godparents for the son of our mutual friends. Now, of course, he's dating Savannah."

"You're close?"

"To Savannah? Very. To Aidan, less so."

I trailed my finger higher along her forearm, and her gaze moved with the digit as it traced up and along to the internal center of her elbow. She watched its journey whereas I watched her. I noted when she swallowed thickly, stroking the thin, almost ethereal blue veins there, and a soft mewl escaped her when I slipped it higher up her arm, along the curve of her shoulder and back down again.

"You were disappointed your guest didn't arrive?" I inserted now her attention was split.

Her eyes darted to mine, and deep within them, I saw a peculiar panic combine with the lust I'd stirred in her. "It was my ex. He's taking me to court for keying his car. I was hoping Aidan would scare him into dropping the suit. It's a lot of money and," she sighed, "I just don't have it."

Silently, I made a promise to her—I would have this Headley drop the lawsuit. I'd even get an apology for his infidelity. She didn't have to know I'd draw blood to achieve both.

Well aware that the lighter touch would have her shivering, I hovered my fingers over the back of her hand as I traced a circle there. Goosebumps appeared, followed by the tiniest of shivers.

"Would you like to go dancing with me?" I asked her, watching her blink a few times as she drifted onto the new subject.

"Ever heard of stranger danger?" she whispered.

"You do not know who I am, do you?"

"No. I don't. Aside from Luciu Valentini. But I can guess you're bad news if you're friends with Aidan."

"I like the taste of my name on your lips," I murmured, but that she associated me with bad news was something I had to change. "There are thousands of people in this city who should fear me... but you're not one of them."

She stared into my eyes, before slowly, tipping her forehead forward in silent assent. "I'll dance with you."

FOUR

JEN

THAT EVENING

BECAUSE I WAS on the hunt for a rich husband, I knew most hotties in Midtown by this point. My position at a firm of accountants that regularly 'serviced' the Wall Street 1% meant that I should have at least come across a 'Luciu Valentini' before.

This guy, however, was new to me.

Very new.

But God, as much as I loved fresh blood, I couldn't avoid the fact that this one was dangerous.

Dangerous enough to take a seat at a table with the heir to the Irish Mob without fearing for his life...

"You have beautiful eyes, Jennifer," he told me softly, his finger moving along the curve of my chin, stealing my breath and making my heart skip a beat.

"Thank you," I whispered, entranced by his stare. Overwhelmed by it.

"Sir?"

He blinked, the fog between us fading as he turned to the server. "The check? And our coats, *pi favuri.*"

When the waiter returned, Luciu paid the check and placed a credit card inside the leather folder he'd been handed.

Taking the opportunity to study him, I took in the Rolex—an odd selection because as costly as they were, they weren't the usual choice for a mogul—and the simple diamond cuff links on his sleeves.

Because I was an old pro at this, I did a quick guesstimate on his outfit and figured he was wearing over fifty grand's worth of gear.

Minimum.

That depended on the type of Rolex, of course. Suits like the one he wore didn't come cheap, either. The hand stitching on the lapels was so tiny that, even this close to him, I had to squint to see the individual stitches.

Was it bad that I wanted to run my tongue along them?

Well, okay, not bad, just weird.

Another server arrived with our coats, and against the expensive wool of his topcoat, mine looked even more ridiculous: skimpy, as barely there as my dress, and not at all made for the weather we were having. For the first time, I felt ashamed.

Against his saturnine elegance, I was dressed like a whore.

'Everything in this life, Fionnabhair, comes at a price. Make sure someone else pays the tab.'

My mother's words haunted me, but she was right. I'd dressed this way so that if Aidan hadn't been able to scare Damian into dropping the lawsuit, I'd hoped that seducing him would make this nightmare go away.

I should have known the fucker wouldn't come. That was what I got for daring to hope.

"Come, Jennifer, let me show you how Sicilians throw a party."

My lips twitched. "Never heard of a cèilidh, have you? The Irish are good at parties."

"I've seen how you jig. We're far more romantic."

I wasn't sure if I could handle more romance. Not from this guy. I was already close to detonation and that was from a few strokes of his fingers against my elbow.

He snatched up my coat before his hands moved along my arms, dragging the nerve endings to life, making me shudder as he pressed a kiss to the side of my cheek.

"Beautiful, *duci,* beautiful."

I nearly whimpered when he moved around to rearrange the lapels of my pathetic excuse for a coat, and I let him. I actually let him because his eyes tangled with mine, and he looked at me as if nothing could break his stare. Like his end goal was the only thing that mattered...

That end goal?

Me.

He was the beautiful one, though, and drowning in a look from him was headier than walking into a room with a dozen stoners smoking pot.

I reached up, stroked his chin. With just enough of a beard for the hairs to be soft and not prickly, covering a large expanse of his jaw, shrouding the soft pink of his firm lips, he had a mouth I wanted to devour. "I hope your dances include kisses."

"That can be arranged."

He shrugged into his coat, then rubbed a careless hand over his head.

His hair was a mixture of floppy and structured, making me think he'd probably washed it, put some product in, then fixed it with his fingers. That artless look would probably take me a couple hours to achieve, and undoubtedly took him ten minutes, but I could forgive him for it.

If anything, it was hot. So hot that it didn't take much effort for him to look that good.

The man was a work of art.

A serious Mona goddamn Lisa. Just the guy version.

And those chocolate eyes? Holy Mama of Jesus.

Sweet Lord.

And whoever the hell else I could blaspheme because none of it, and I meant, not one expletive, could begin to describe how gorgeous this man was.

Those eyes.

Just...

Seriously.

It was like he was made to have me melting into a ridiculous puddle of need.

Leaving The 68 took a while because there was some kind of snafu with the elevators.

The Sharpe was one of Manhattan's latest mega-skyscrapers, so it was definitely weird that there was a problem, but I was a born-and-bred New Yorker, so I knew it was a part of city living.

Everyone got stuck in an elevator at some point. With buildings this tall, they didn't even shut them down when there was a fire because who the hell could run down eighty-four floors to escape a fiery inferno that started on the hundredth story?

When he saw the line, he arched a brow at the maître d' who scurried over to him.

"I'm so sorry, Mr. Valentini. The delay won't be long—"

Luciu passed him something, his sleight of hand artful, and the maître d' crumpled his hand around it before murmuring, "If you'd like to step this way, please?"

We moved ahead of the line, and I'd admit, I felt like royalty. Each and every glare and grumble were ignored with a stately lifting of his chin, and because I was on his arm, I mirrored him.

He owned the room.

Together, *we* owned it.

It was intoxicating.

Like a lifetime of being teetotal and suddenly discovering the joys of tequila.

The ride down to the garage took place in silence, but the second the doors opened, I felt the rush of a draft all along my spine thanks to the really shitty taste in clothes I had for a wintry evening. Luciu paused, slipped out of his winter coat, then placed it around my shoddily covered shoulders.

I didn't tell him it was unnecessary, didn't question the chivalrous gesture. Instead, I embraced it, tucking myself tighter into the folds of expensive wool, sucking in air that scented of him because he smelled divine, and the heated coat against my chilly flesh felt so damn good that it made me want to huddle into his side even more.

Once I was wearing his coat, he placed his hand at the small of my back and we strode the few steps toward a Rolls Royce. I wasn't altogether surprised to find he had a driver who was waiting at the side of the vehicle, huddled into his coat, the engine rumbling.

I let him guide me to the car, then daintily accepted his hold as, once the driver opened the door, I climbed into the backseat.

When he moved away to join me, the driver shut me in, and I was alone for a second in the expensive vehicle.

It was the first time I'd been alone all evening, and it was oddly intense. Each breath felt supercharged, and I swore it was because his coat drowned me in his scent. I'd once read about pheromones and how they were nonsense, but Luciu made a believer out of me.

The heated leather seats were warm against the backs of my cold thighs, and I relaxed, letting the heat sink into me as Luciu eventually climbed in beside me. The second he did, he pushed a button and a privacy screen popped up between us and the driver.

Expectation and, even stranger, nerves overwhelmed me.

I gulped when the engine roared, breaking into the silence that fell between us. As we began to drive out of the garage, I half expected him to haul me onto his lap or something, to let the embers that burned between us flicker into being.

But he didn't.

It grew quieter.

And quieter.

And quieter.

Jesus, it grew so quiet that I could hear my breathing. Every exhalation and inhalation sounded shaky and oh, so loud. Enough that it embarrassed me. The tension in the air, the vibrancy and energy were awe-inspiring. It made me feel as if we were in a vacuum. One that swallowed everything else up, everything that wasn't us, and made this the center of the universe.

Our universe.

I wondered if he was as aware of me as I was of him. I wondered if this was all me, if I was being stupid and crazy... then, his hand settled on mine.

A low moan escaped me as our fingers collided, skin brushing against skin, heat rebounding into heat, and as they tangled, he reached for me with his other hand, drawing me closer, nearer to him, so that his arm was around my shoulders.

It was second nature to twist a little, to rest my head against his throat, to have him encompass me in his strength, to let down my walls so he could hop inside at a moment where I felt sure I was the most vulnerable I'd ever been in my life.

I stared out onto the city, well aware that even if it were daylight, no one would be able to see in here. It made me feel our isolation more, and I loved it.

Wanted it.

Craved more.

Needed like I'd never needed before.

Then, everything changed.

It was quite accidental.

A sharp turn around a bend had us jostling into each other. Nothing crazy. But our hands slipped, and the edge of mine brushed against his crotch.

He had a hard-on.

He had a hard-on, yet he wasn't pawing at me. Wasn't treating me like I was a whore. Was holding me as if I were the opposite, in fact.

His control was lust-inducing.

His arousal was inspiring.

And I wanted both.

I wanted his control ruptured.

His arousal burned off.

On me.

I turned my face to the side, letting my lips press against his throat. His pulse bobbed as a result and as I let my tongue dart out to play, he groaned, and I felt the soft vibrations. Encouraged, I sucked down, nipping and teasing as I made my way up, soft kisses dancing against the line of his jaw where I could feel the slight bumps of stubble that would begin to grow soon.

Finally, I found his mouth. Reaching up with my free hand, I encouraged him to tilt his head downward so our lips could meet.

A whimper escaped me when they did.

It felt as if I'd been waiting a lifetime for this moment, for the meeting of our mouths, for this kiss. Time stopped still, everything in me freezing as my body processed the rightness of the connection between us.

He growled.

I felt that in my pussy.

He shifted.

His hard-on rubbed against my hip.

He tugged me onto his lap.

I spread my legs, my knees cupping him as I let our sexes collide.

I groaned as I rocked my hips, letting his cock rub against my softness, each pass nudging my clit and making me see fireworks.

At fourteen, I'd done dirtier deeds than this when I was sneaking around with Jonny MacLeod, but this was a thousand times more sinful.

When his hands relinquished their hold on me, I groaned when he slid one along my cheekbone before he slipped it down and around to cover the side of my throat.

As he did so, I didn't even care that he might have smudged my makeup. I was more interested in the way he squeezed slightly, using his hold on me to haul me into him further.

I wasn't going to complain.

With a groan, I parted my lips, and I pressed my tongue to the seam of his mouth. He immediately let me inside, and I growled, loving the wet slip and slide as we started a kiss that felt like a precursor to a dance.

His free hand went to my hips, and he encouraged me to grind into him, a little harder, a lot deeper. I cupped his face, tipping him how I wanted him, craving more, craving everything he had to give, craving everything I could take.

The price of his shoes, suit, and watch didn't matter worth a damn at that moment.

All I knew was this kiss.

Fuck.

It was like I'd been breathing tainted air all my life and this was my first inhalation of oxygen.

The taste of him was exquisite, like a drug, and I knew I was hooked, knew I'd die to get another hit.

He pulled back to nip at my bottom lip, but I didn't let him stop. I thrust my tongue back into his mouth, loving how he let me fuck him there, then I groaned when his hand shifted, ceasing to encourage me to grind into him and encouraging me to kneel instead.

His coat drifted from my shoulders with the move as he lifted up the short hem of my dress, and his fingers proceeded to rub along the crease of my G-string, slipping the fabric between my folds, before he dragged the tips over my clit.

A gasp escaped me, and I froze, pulling back so that I could breathe, but his hand on my nape held me close, so that every exhalation brushed his mouth, so that he could feel me as I could feel him.

I closed my eyes as I rested my forehead against his, then moaned long and low as he drew glowing embers into sparks of pleasure that I knew would turn into a conflagration if he took this further.

For the first time in my life, I wanted that.

I could almost *feel* his cock thrusting into me.

His dick would be the first non-silicone toy to take my pussy, and I wanted that so goddamn badly that I climaxed.

Then and there.

It was really difficult for me to get off, mostly because sex was a weapon, a tool I used to get what I wanted, but here, now, I exploded.

Detonated.

It was short and sharp and, worst of all, addictive. It surged through my body thanks to my racing heart and sank into my fucking bones.

It was delirium.

It was exquisite.

It was heaven.

My head tipped back, spine arching with the force of what he made me feel, then his mouth was on my throat, and he sucked down, hard. Hard enough to leave a mark tomorrow. Hard enough for my pulse to ricochet against his lips.

His teeth came next, and the sharp sting sent even more ecstasy slaloming through my veins. His fingers moved faster; his hand must have been a blur as he did the impossible.

A second orgasm hit me.

Like a one-two punch, it flayed me, turned my insides out and my outsides in. I felt reborn in my desire, alive with his passion.

And through it all, those teeth of his stayed buried in my throat—*I adored him for it.*

The car came to a halt long before either of us realized it. Whether the driver didn't disturb us because this was a regular act in Luciu Valentini's sideshow, or because he didn't have a death wish, I only registered that we'd stopped when my heart ceased pounding away like I'd done three spinning classes back-to-back.

"Where are we?" I rasped, turning my head to the side so I could press a soft kiss to his temple. It was slick with perspiration, but it didn't ick me out.

I didn't think anything he could do would reap that particular miracle.

Even if he had chest hair, I wouldn't care.

He could have hairy balls, and I'd probably be all over that.

Shit, this was getting serious.

His teeth dislodged from my throat in a move so seamless it made what should have been awkward totally natural. "My club," he rumbled as he softly patted my pussy as if it were a farewell, then he pressed a kiss to where he'd bitten. "*Russu.*"

I blinked. "You own *Russu?*"

"You've heard of it?"

"I've heard of the two-hundred-dollar cover charge, the VIP sections that take up most of the top floors, and that they say if you press a button, some kind of 'Ask Jeeves' dude pops up with a bottle of Cristal."

He laughed. "You've never been?"

"I've been to the club but not the lounge." I pouted. "Nobody would ever take me up there."

"Well, let's change that, hmm?"

Desire flickered through me, but this time, it was of a different variety—the gold digger scented action.

His hands grabbed at my ass. "I'll have some business to attend to, but I'll be all yours afterward."

"Okay," I agreed, accustomed to that. I was well at ease with entertaining myself.

"After, we'll go back to my place, hmm?"

I bit my lip, and while the gold digger had been awakened, it was the weird ingenue he triggered in me that answered breathily, "Yes."

Apparently, the ingenue had no street smarts whatsoever because I didn't ask where he lived or wonder about how I'd get home in the morning—I was just wrapped up in him.

He helped me off his lap like I couldn't do it myself, tucked his arm around my shoulders once more, then when I was decent, he lowered the privacy screen and said something in a delicious language that sounded Italian but wasn't.

"Give me your phone."

The order should have had me bristling, but still purring from my orgasms, I did as he asked, watching as he sent himself a message from my account.

"Just in case I need to get in touch." His top lip quirked up at the corner at my bemused glance. "If you want to check your makeup, do it now, *cara mia*."

Feeling oddly exhilarated at the way he'd taken my number—that had to mean he wanted to meet up again, right?—I quickly sorted out my hair, and a swift glance at the small mirror I pulled from my purse didn't help much seeing as it was dark, but I saw that it was okay, mussed but kind of sexy with it.

As the car started, we drove through a well-lit area, and I saw my mouth was a mess, but I was prepared for every eventuality. I grabbed a wipe, cleaned it off quickly, then turned to wipe his mouth too.

Surprised when he let me, my breath caught at the intimate move as our gazes tangled once more.

We might as well have been kissing each other, that was how raw the moment was, one that was only broken when we pulled around the building toward the front of the club.

My eyes widened in surprise as we approached the entrance, and when the car came to a halt, the door opened with a flair.

Starting to scurry out, Luciu murmured, "Wait for me."

I wasn't sure why, but I wasn't about to argue with him. Instead, I watched as he straightened up, grabbed his discarded coat and tucked himself into it, before climbing out of the door and rounding the back of the vehicle. Entranced, I watched as the paparazzi in front of the club took notice of him, and the flashes of lights were...

What the hell?

Non-existent?

Their stares, on the other hand, were *intense*.

He didn't flinch at being the center of their attention, just moved around to the door that was letting in a nasty draft, then bent down and held out his hand for me.

His saturnine beauty was even more awe-inducing because I knew him to own all this.

All this being a club that was the epicenter of Manhattan's night life.

Moreover, *Russu's* owner was a shadowy figure that rarely slithered in and out of gossipmongers' big mouths because he was a ghost...

Tonight, though, he'd be on the tip of everyone's tongue.

Because of me.

When he helped me out of the car, his hand firm around my fingers, his regard steady and heated with the memories of what we'd just done together, the cameras remained silent, but the intensity of the press's stare tripled.

While they weren't taking any photos, I was grateful I'd cleaned up our mouths because I felt sure they could see the zit I'd popped two days ago—that was the microscopic attention we were graced with.

This was the world I aspired to live in. One of fame, fortune, the high life. I wanted to reign over this sphere, to finally make a place for myself, but even as high as I'd gone with some of my exes, I had a feeling that Luciu dominated at a whole other level.

Behind our car, there were several vehicles pulling in—I heard their engines purring—but that didn't encourage the paparazzi to start taking shots.

As fear whistled through me, a peculiar warmth simmered in my veins alongside it.

This was power.

I'd seen it when I was with Aoife. The respect she was afforded as Finn O'Grady's wife was impressive.

This was the same.

But edgier.

People were outright scared of the O'Donnellys, but their fronts were a clever facade that fooled people into thinking they were turning legitimate.

Massive skyscrapers built by Acuig Corp.—the Irish Mob's corporate front—littered the Manhattan skyline, changing it and making it better. Museums were dedicated to them; there was talk of hospital wards getting the same treatment, and before O'Donnelly Sr. retired *or* died, I fully expected that he'd have a school named after him or something.

With the amount of money they were pumping into New York City, it was a wonder the governor hadn't sucked O'Donnelly Sr. off in thanks.

So yes, those who knew about the Irish Mob feared them, but Acuig meant the public was gradually getting more used to their Kennedy-esque front. The glamor, the attendances at gubernatorial fundraisers and charity foundation galas were becoming the standard feature in the society pages.

This was different.

This was raw.

This was a man who had made a reputation for himself, a reputation that these journalists were well aware of and knew to back away from.

Amid this sea of predators, each one looking to make a quick buck, uncaring of whose privacy they trod upon, whose lives they ruined in the process, they realized the biggest one of all had showed up.

I wouldn't be a reputable gold digger if that didn't make me hot.

Arousal for me didn't work the same way as it did with every other woman. It took power and privilege and wealth and position to get me wet.

Consider me moist.

I almost smirked at the thought, but instead, terrified and thrilled all at the same time, I tucked my hand tighter into the crook of Luciu's arm, weirdly proud that I was here with this man.

He tangled his fingers with mine after he smoothed his thumb over my knuckles, and as he tilted his head down, murmured, "Sorry about this."

I knew what he meant.

It was creepy, but he didn't understand how I worked.

My eyes gleamed as I peered up at him. "You have nothing to be sorry for."

A fact he more than lived up to.

As we walked down the red carpet, I felt like a queen. The tension in the air throbbed as heavy-set guys in black suits, transparent headsets tucked into their ears, monitored the crowd as if there were a terrorist lurking in the wings.

But I got the feeling this was an everyday occurrence when the boss was in the vicinity.

It wasn't my first time in *Russu*, but it was the first time I went past the second floor and was deposited on the third with a toe-curling kiss as a silent farewell.

A VIP lounge awaited me, one that was like no other because it wasn't just *any* VIP section, it was the owner's box.

Oddly enough, it reminded me of a padded cell, only everything was bright red.

So, pretty much like a padded cell that had recently seen *bloodshed*.

There was a dark red leather sofa, low to the ground, shaped like a U, with one of the loungers shorter than the other, and a dancefloor which was right in front of it.

Tiled in a red so dark it was almost black, there were recessed lights that seemed to do the opposite of their job by emphasizing exactly how dark it was in this section.

A table offset to the side housed a bottle of Cristal in a large wine bucket that was overloaded with ice, and there was even some food if I wanted to nibble on it.

I was starving, but I was used to that. Mom never had food in the house, not because she spent every cent on drugs—well, that was true too—but because she said it would stop us from getting fat.

A woman who needed to sell her body had to be perfect at all times.

I'd learned that lesson from the master, only I'd done one better—I hadn't gotten hooked on the coke that was passed around at fancy parties. But I'd grown up following some lessons: drinking vinegar to quench my hunger, and for a while, I'd even smoked to control my appetite.

My poor nutrition as a kid was why I was weedier than I'd like, but mostly it was a miracle I'd made it to this age with a set of tits worth anything.

I ignored the canapés and instead poured myself a glass of champagne.

Another woman might have been overwhelmed at being alone in a place like this, but for me, it was symbolic.

I loved it.

I loved being alone; I loved that I had the right to be here; I loved that I was two floors higher than the main dance floor, and I outright adored that I was looking down on the rest of the world.

Slipping my phone out of my purse, I switched it on to IG and took a live video, hollering, *"Russu* is where the party is at."

Flute in one hand, I shook my ass, loving the vibe and the beat of the music the DJ poured her heart and soul into as I let the camera slip and slide, showing all the best angles of the lounge.

Then I let the camera record the part that the club was famous for.

The fountains.

Spouts and turrets of water soared in a circle, and as impossible as it was, some technological wizardry had them surging high, so high that I could see the crest of the waves reaching my level, two stories up, before they fell and rose once more, perfectly synced with the beat.

But what made them creepy was the red water. A strange red. Like blood.

As if someone had bled out in the water tank and that was what danced through the air, peppering it with a fine spray that misted on my skin even here.

When I was done showing off, my cell buzzed.

I grinned, and ignoring the message, went straight to a call.

"AOIFE!"

"Wow, how much have you had to drink?" my BFF drawled.

"One glass. Oh, my God, Eef, did you see this lounge?"

"I'm used to you hitting all those swank places." She sniffed, clearly unimpressed.

That had nothing to do with her being used to the 'swank' lifestyle, more like she hated clubs with a passion.

I chuckled, guzzled down some champagne, and remarked, "Surprised you're not asleep with your mobster beau."

Aoife laughed. "You've had way more than one glass."

"I might have had some whiskey. What gave the game away?"

"Beau? Have you been reading regency romance again? Honestly, Jen, for someone who says she isn't a romantic—"

"Pfft." I took a deeper sip. "You're killing my buzz."

A buzz that had started the second Luciu Valentini's pinkie finger had connected with my arm.

"God forbid. And Jacob had a bad dream. I couldn't sleep after so I'm watching something on Prime."

"Did you start that show I told you about?"

She hummed. "I don't like witches."

I scoffed. "You're no fun."

"I'm plenty of fun."

"Witches rule."

"If you say so," she retorted, tone amused.

I leaned against the railing, staring down at the cluster of humanity. Thousands of sweaty bodies grinding together... I was so happy to be away from the perspiration and stench of body odor.

Smug, I told her, "I do say so—"

"Jen? I have to go."

"Oh, okay!" The abrupt withdrawal had me asking, "Everything okay?"

"I don't know. Finn just walked in, and he needs me. Best go, sweetheart. Talk later?"

"Sure. Or in the morning," I teased. "God knows how tonight will end."

She snorted. "I'll bet. Have fun. Night, Jen."

As she cut the call, I jolted in surprise, and, I'd admit, a teeny-weeny smidgen of concern filled me.

Just a small amount.

The Irish Mob weren't my friends or my family. I'd spent most of my life avoiding them. It was only Aoife who'd brought me into that world, and while I didn't resent it, I didn't want to get involved.

But how my heart was racing made a liar out of me.

And Savannah hooking up with Aidan Jr. was going to make things harder than ever.

Concerned about what had made Aoife's farewell so abrupt, I bit my lip, then sauntered over to the table again to pour myself another glass.

My mood was dampened but swallowing down the fine Cristal whole helped immensely.

I closed my eyes as Max Vangeli echoed around the club, and I slipped the glass onto the table so that I could raise both hands and let them swirl against one another as I moved to the beat.

That was when he slipped behind me.

I didn't jolt in surprise because I'd seen the security in this place and knew it was high grade, which meant it was Luciu.

I also recognized his scent.

That aftershave—it reeked of money.

Everything about him did.

But even better than all that, and something I'd never admit to a living, breathing soul?

His heat.

It sank into me, seeming to grind into my bones, warming all the cold places deep inside—of which there were many—going so far, I feared, as to penetrate my soul.

His fingers trailed along my belly as he cupped me there, and then his chin pressed to my shoulder for the barest second before he rested it on the crown of my head.

He dwarfed me, and I loved that as well. Even with these heels, he was like a giant, and I felt safe and cosseted, sheltered and protected.

Foolish, foolish things to feel.

I'd chide myself in the morning, but for now, I enjoyed it.

Reveled in it, even.

As his hands grew bolder, I didn't stop him, too enchanted by the privacy in this packed club.

Unable to stop myself, I lowered my arms to cup the back of Luciu's neck, content for him to hold me close, goddamn delirious about how he was holding onto me.

At that moment, after one too many flutes of champagne floating around my system, it had nothing to do with his position or his money or his power, just that he felt so fucking good.

One large hand slid upward, and I let it, spearing up to cup my breast before it moved higher, coming to rest about my throat. Loosely, but the threat was there.

A silken promise.

And I loved it.

I ground my ass into him and felt his hardness and nearly melted.

I swore that I'd have bent over if he'd have pushed me against the balcony rail. I'd let him fuck me then and there. That was the power of this moment, the freedom I felt, but something buzzed against my back.

And it wasn't a vibrator.

"*Porca troia,*" he grumbled under his breath, loud enough for me to hear against the music.

I twisted around, darted a kiss to his cheek and rasped, "Don't worry. You take it. I'll just go and freshen up."

A strange heat surged into being in his eyes, and he murmured, "When you come back, we'll dance more."

It was a command, not a statement, and I smiled at him, not coyly or enticingly, but with *joy*.

That was when I should have realized something weird was going on. Maybe he'd slipped me an edible or something because one thing I was not, was joyous.

Aoife had called me many things over the years, Savannah too, and most of them revolved around the words 'obstinate,' 'pain in the ass,' and 'strong-minded.'

And those were the kind descriptions.

What friends used to label me.

Joyous Jen wasn't a nickname that I thought was going to take off.

"I'd like that," I whispered, and though the words were too soft to hear, I knew he understood.

A wicked smile curved his lips, a triumphant one, and I was content for him to have this moment as I strutted out of the private booth and strode over to the bathrooms.

Where things got even better.

There was a private restroom which with a place this big, was a blessing.

Seriously, if the luxury of the owner's box wasn't orgasmic, this was.

I moved inside and made to lock the door, but as I did, someone shoved it open and barged in. There was a tug of war over the handle, but I lost the battle. It wasn't like I had much choice. It was either let go or fall flat on my ass.

"Excuse me!" I pretty much spat as I staggered upright, trying to stabilize myself on shoes that were more suitable for digging into a man's ass than walking on tiles. "This is the owner's restroom," I sniped.

The woman was, in a word, beautiful. She was also everything I wasn't.

She had curves on top of her curves, and a little like Aoife, she rocked them.

This woman wore an elegant black dress that covered her from head to toe. By comparison, I felt like a cheap whore in my napkin, a short, slutty outfit I'd worn in the vague hope that I'd entice my ex-boyfriend to drop the lawsuit he had against me.

She reminded me of a brunette Rita Hayworth, with the deep cutout in the bodice that revealed a set of banging tits, plump and full, enhanced by a pendant that dangled between them. With a fishtail skirt that showed off the roundness of her hips, she was hot.

And she knew it.

She was also checking me out as much as I was checking her out, and where I was awestruck by her beauty, she was the opposite.

She looked at me like I was a cheap hooker.

Then, she raised her left hand which had a simple gold band on the ring finger.

I swallowed, but I had no idea why the sight of it triggered a visceral reaction in me. As much, if not worse, than what Luciu had made me feel earlier.

"You American sluts are all the same," she rasped, and her voice was hard but husky, like she was ordinarily soft-spoken, but I'd pissed her off.

Which, considering we'd known each other less than thirty seconds, was a feat not even I thought I could achieve.

I grated on people. I knew that. But this much?

"I'm sorry if I'm using the wrong bathroom," I started, confused and embarrassed by her disdain.

Normally, I wore people's disapproval as if it were an expensive perfume, but with this woman... it was like a duchess was dressing down a servant. I felt every inch of my poverty, every inch of my shameful upbringing in the face of this glorious creature's scorn.

"This isn't the wrong bathroom. I'm the owner of *Russu*."

I blinked. "Huh?"

Great comeback. But, actually, her words comforted me.

There was obviously some misunderstanding...

"I don't think so," I told her calmly, not wanting to get into it because the woman was clearly mad, potentially drunk or high, and I didn't want to get into a catfight. "I know the owner. I just left him."

She hissed. "I know you did, *buttana*. Luciu is my husband," she snapped, and then she raised her hand and she slapped me so hard that I staggered back, and while my stiletto heels did great things for my ass, they weren't exactly stable.

As I stumbled, with so little support and the shiny tiles beneath me, I just went down. Like a house of cards. Boom.

A shriek escaped me, but before I could do anything, she was in my face, and she grabbed me by the hair then forcibly hauled me onto my feet.

"You will leave here, *buttana*. If I ever see you again, if I see you even sniffing around my husband, I *will* kill you."

FIVE

JEN

DECEMBER 23RD

FROM THE CONFINES of the safe room on the O'Donnelly compound, I'd admit that I was losing my mind.

I was only here because Aoife was taking pity on me and didn't want me to be on my own at Christmas, and now, I was just wishing I'd gone to a party or had decided to spend all day reading because *this* sucked.

We'd been minding our own business when shit had started exploding. Literally. *Exploding*.

This wasn't a Bill Nye kind of explosion. This was real life, warfare tactics.

Knowing the O'Donnellys had a safe room under their house, like this was normal, was somehow worse than anything.

They'd anticipated this.

At some point, they'd imagined this could happen.

What in the hell kind of world were they living in?

The safe room made my ex's swank penthouse look grody. This place was decorated like a Vogue photo shoot was going down in it tomorrow, but that didn't make things any better when half the women in here were trying not to stare at the clock on the wall like it held the answers to the universe. As they tried not to wonder if their husbands would be murdered in their parents' home the night before Christmas Eve.

Worse still?

Savannah's crazy ass was out there.

She'd actually elected not to come to the safe room where it was—shock shock, horror horror—*safe*.

Terrified for her, anxious for the men who were Aoife's family, wondering who the hell had sent an army to a personal, private residence, I turned to my phone for comfort.

Losing a couple of hours on TikTok seemed like a smart way to kill some time.

That was when I saw the message from *him*.

It wasn't the first time he'd texted me since I'd run away from *Russu* last night.

Of their own volition, my fingers surged to my throat, touching the mark he'd left behind.

Though shivers whispered down my spine, they were forged in anger, not lust.

Luciu: *Where are you?*

I frowned at the question. How dare he ask me that? Damn nerve.

Me: *I don't want to talk to you.*

Luciu: *You're lying.*

I scowled at my phone.

Me: *What right do you have to call me a liar?*

Luciu: *Where are you?*

Me: *Where are YOU?*

Who did this guy think he was?

Luciu: *I'm at Russu. You should come. We never got to finish our dance.*

No, because his wife had goddamn attacked me.

Should I have stuck around to suck his dick while his wife was waiting in the wings to annihilate me?

I was used to the blatancy of men. Seriously, the things they thought they could get away with beggared belief, but this took the cake.

Me: *Don't contact me again.*

I made to switch over to TikTok, but a swipe down of the menu revealed his message to me, and it made me want to hurl my phone against the wall.

If I wasn't in desperate need of a distraction from the goddamn war going on outside, I would have.

Luciu: *You know where to find me when you're ready.*

I wasn't sure he could have said anything more annoying than that. In fact, I knew it.

I'd gone home crying last night.

Crying.

Not because I'd hurt my ass when I'd been thrown down like it was a fancy WWE match, but because I'd thought—

I rubbed my eyes where tears were beginning to make themselves known again.

I'd been stupid, so stupid—I'd thought there was a connection between us.

One that was genuine and real, and worth something. I'd never felt that way before. Never felt as if I understood what all the songs were about when you met that one person who made the universe stand still for a moment.

His message just made it stand out in stark relief how much of an idiot I'd been.

And I was *not* an idiot.

Many adjectives could be used to describe me, most of them bad— flighty, sly, covetous, avaricious—but idiotic wasn't one of them.

I went into the iMessage app, made sure he knew I'd read his message, then I backed the hell out of there. Not just physically but mentally.

Fool me once, shame on you.

Fool me twice, shame on me.

Jennifer MacNeill was not a fool.

SIX

LUCIU
DECEMBER 27TH

THERE WAS no time to think. The time for thinking was gone.

In the past.

Now was the time to act.

Stan, my brother, pressed the detonator, exploding the C4 one of our men had left by the gates that led onto the Fieri compound, meaning that those curlicued gates were no more.

From a thousand yards away, the noise from the blast rang in my ears, but Stan slammed his foot on the accelerator and with a whoop, we charged forward like goddamn conquerors of old.

Behind us, fifteen SUVs drove into battle with us, in a way that made my history-loving heart crow with glee as we waded into a war that was ten years in the making.

As we drove over the busted railings like they were shards of glass, we made it onto the compound's courtyard. Bullets tore into our vehicles, doing little damage thanks to the bulletproof shell, and Stan let loose a holler as he drove into the guardhouse where the Italians were firing from.

As we collided with the small hut that was made of wood, it went down like a house of cards. The blaze of bullets from the gunfire stopped as soon as our wheels bumped into the now-dead guard on the ground.

Stan moved around the compound as if we were on the bumper cars: knocking into shit, tearing stuff down as we rode around the perimeter, checking for clusters of guards.

We knew why we were here but to get to that phase, we had to make sure that any security details on the outside were handled.

By the time we'd collided with two more huts, driven over three guards who thought they could take us with their submachine guns, the bulletproof shell was undoubtedly battered but worth the two-hundred-and-fifty K I'd plowed into each vehicle in the flotilla to prepare for this night.

"*Cristo*, what the fuck was that?" Stan rasped as a loud explosion echoed through the compound.

"More C4?" I asked him, but it was rhetorical.

Instead of wasting time guessing, I grabbed my phone and sent out pings to the driver of each vehicle and received a quick message on what was happening out front. Three men were down, and two were injured after an Italian had thrown a hand grenade at one of our SUVs.

The Italians weren't happy about a Sicilian takeover.

Tough. Shit.

As we made it back to the front of the compound, I saw the damage for myself. Three SUVs were overturned; a few others were dented and shredded from the blast.

As Stan braked to a halt, I saw the front door of the Fieri mansion had been blown in, and that our men had secured the area ahead of schedule.

Leaping out of the car, guns in hand and feeling like I was in a goddamn video game, I headed up the stairs and into the mansion.

"The council room's over here, boss," Lorenzo, one of my most trusted men, called out.

Finding him after I scanned the area, I took into account the grand entranceway that was larger than some people's homes—complete with a double staircase that arched around the room and led to a single landing. There, a painting of that fucker, Benito Fieri, and his young bride hung pride of place...

Raising my gun, I shot the fucker, and the bullet landed right between his brows.

It didn't hold the same satisfaction as killing the cunt myself, but it was as good as it got seeing as someone else had already pulled the trigger before me.

I strode over the red carpet toward Lorenzo and watched as three of our men who'd hauled a battering ram in began to break down the door to the council room.

Gunfire immediately pounded the entrance way, and Accursio and Carino took the brunt, falling back as bullets pounded their Kevlar vests.

My soldiers surged forward, one tossed a smoke bomb into the meeting room, followed by a tear gas grenade, and that turned the tide of the battle.

Within a half-hour, the remaining Rossis and Genovicos who had survived the last gathering of the crime factions in the city and were ruling the *Famiglia* now that Fieri was dead, were either plowed down or corralled.

It took two hours all in all to lay siege to the compound and to win it. To take the Fieri widow hostage. To eradicate the threats to my takeover of the *Famiglia*...

Two hours, after ten years of striving.

When I took a seat at the head of the table in the council room, a meeting place that had probably heard more war stories than the offices of the Joint Chiefs of Staff, I peered around, almost unable to believe that I'd made it.

That I'd done it.

Might was right in this world, and I'd just taken the last bastion of the Fieri reign.

There was still so much to do, so much to achieve, and the war wasn't won entirely, but this was my equivalent of planting the flag at Iwo Jima. Taking ownership of this compound was my first step as Don.

Sitting here, in this seat, was the first time I actually felt like I was worthy of that title.

Why I reached for my cell phone and sent a message to Jennifer was beyond me.

It just felt right.

Me: *I want to see you.*

In the lead up to the raid, Stan had been researching her background. She was not the type of woman I should be thinking about tangling with, but there was something about her. Stan's report be damned.

I needed to see her.

I had no idea what made her leave that night at *Russu*, but I was pissed she left when she did.

If she thought I was going to disappear, I wasn't.

But I couldn't throw away plans that were a decade in the making. I couldn't forget my real purpose for being in this fucking country in the first place.

Stan made an appearance and told me, "Cops showed up."

"Dealt with?" I asked, even though I knew the answer.

It had taken a lot of cash to make the night's events slip under the radar. I considered it an investment in our future.

Commissioner Kingston was the most corrupt bastard I'd ever had the misfortune of running into in my whole goddamn life.

He made the officials back in Sicily look transparent.

"Of course."

His face was too serious to make me think that was the only reason he'd come to me. "What is it?" If not the cops, then... what?

"Accursio's dead."

I closed my eyes. "Fuck."

"*Se*. Mancuso and Pietro as well."

Three men who'd fought with us since the beginning. Stan had gone to school with Accursio. They'd been friends since they were children.

"You okay, *frate?*" I rasped, grief for him and for Accursio etched into each word.

"No. You?"

I shook my head. "No."

We hadn't brought this war to the Fieris; they'd done that to us. But having lost more men who mattered to us, the triumph I'd felt at sitting at this godforsaken table shrank away into nothingness.

"Maybe now we can have peace," I rumbled.

"I wouldn't bet on it," was Stan's grim retort.

And I knew he was right.

"I wouldn't either," I muttered to the room itself before I tipped my head and saw the '*read*' notification on the message that I'd sent her, but there was no reply.

I should have known I was fucked over her when that had me hurling my cell at the wall...

SEVEN

JEN

NEW YEAR'S

I COULDN'T BREATHE.

I really couldn't.

Air was flowing into my mouth, but I couldn't seem to get it into my lungs.

Was this how I was going to die?

Running out of the O'Donnelly NYE party while everyone was in full celebration mode had been surprisingly easy considering I was gulping down air like a dying fish.

Or maybe they were just glad I was gone.

Did they know?

"You're Padraig O'Donnelly's illegitimate daughter, Jen, and I have the DNA test results to prove it."

Savannah had betrayed me to get those DNA test results. She'd lied about how we met. She'd lied about everything.

My cell buzzed. I almost didn't hear it with the loud raucous cheers of the crowds as they celebrated in the streets.

Luciu: *Happy New Year, cara mia.*

I stared at the message, stared at it long and hard, and suddenly, I could breathe again.

Air flowed.

My lungs sucked it up.

My back to the wall in the alley I was hiding from Savannah in, the bitter cold sinking into my bones, I stared at his message.

Me: *Where are you?*

The second I sent it, I regretted it.

Cursing myself for a fool, I huddled into my coat, but even the wicked wind chill didn't numb my panic.

Savannah, my BFF, was a liar.

My dad was an Irish mobster.

Luciu: *Russu*

Luciu: *Come dance with me? The guards know to let you in if you turn up at the club.*

Dance?

No.

I didn't need to dance. I needed something, anything, to stop this panic.

Fucking.

That would work.

I wanted to forget.

I knew he'd help me with that.

Not answering his message, I arranged for an Uber to collect me.

I needed another one of those orgasms Luciu was so good at handing out.

Stat.

PART 3
NEW YEAR'S DAY

EIGHT

LUCIU

"MY WIFE?"

Even as I boomed the question, a banging sounded at my office door.

Before I could process what the hell she was talking about—*what fucking wife?*—irritation whipped me as one of my men pounded on the door loud enough to wake the hounds of hell.

"*Trasi!*" I snarled.

When she started toward the exit, I grabbed her arm and hauled her back toward me. She struggled, her hand coming up to slap my shoulder as she snapped, "Let go of me!"

"Not until we hash this out."

"I'll hash something out," she hissed, "on your face."

As pissed as I was, as much as another *buttana* might be banished from my sight for such an insult, and a man might feel my blade in his cheek, the *focu*, the fire, in her set me alight.

She was scared.

But she was not beaten.

She was nervous.

But she was not weak.

Her strength called to me. *She* called to me.

When Giovi opened the door and made eye contact with me, I raised a hand to make him wait. "I have no wife, Jennifer."

"My name's Jen."

Technically, her name was Fionnabhair. But I couldn't pronounce that yet. The only Irish I knew who spoke Gaelic were the O'Donnellys and while I'd had dealings with them recently, asking them for a pronunciation guide on the world's most exasperating woman wasn't a priority.

I narrowed my eyes at her. "Jennifer," I enunciated carefully, forcing her to realize that I was not like everyone else, that I would not be like anyone else in her life. "You will wait for me here. You will sit that *culu biddicchiu* down and wait for me to discuss this with you."

"I have nothing to discuss," she spat. "I should never have—"

"You should never have," I agreed darkly, "because if you think that's the one and only taste of you that I'm going to have, you're mistaken."

Her nostrils flared in agitation, and in front of my soldier, she razed me with that *focu* once more, stepped into me and growled, "I'm leaving."

"You're not," I intoned before Giovi launched a flurry of Sicilian at me.

"Sir, there's an issue out back."

"I heard," was my cold retort as I stared down at her, not stopping, needing that fire banked and for her to back off.

I'd never known a woman to be so aggressive outside of my family. Maybe that was what attracted me to her. Maybe the coy shyness of before would have bored me. Seeing this other facet of her nature gave me hope.

If she saw me, the real me, maybe she wouldn't cower.

Maybe she'd get angry.

Maybe that was exactly what I needed.

"You're going to sit down, Jennifer," I rumbled, my voice low, deep, obsidian black. A warning within a warning.

A stillness overcame her, and just when I knew she was about to argue, I reached up, curled a long swathe of her hair around my hand and tugged her head back.

"Don't fight me on this, *duci*."

Her gaze darted over to the doorway, an awkward move considering the angle of her head right now, but I knew she was summing up the situation.

A different woman, another fool, might make me think she was checking out how far away the doorway was from here. Might be trying to calculate if she could make it out of my office intact.

But Jennifer?

No.

I knew she was recognizing that in front of Giovi, I had no choice but to dominate her.

Our eyes clashed and held, tension filled me, tension that invaded the room, sinking out into the atmosphere, changing it, morphing it, until, at long last, she submitted.

She sank into me, her body turning limp as she rubbed up against me.

"Okay."

The acquiescence was soft.

Her eyes, however, were hard.

I smiled, not in triumph, but in anticipation.

Something about her set my blood alight. Made me want to breathe her in. Inhale untainted air that wasn't soaked with grief, vengeance, or rage.

She was clean.

Not unstained by this world, but free from the toxins of mine in particular.

Appreciation whispered into me as I held her against me, guiding her where I wanted her to sit.

Staring up at me, a mulishness entering her gaze, I decided to make a hasty retreat before she changed her mind. I had a reputation to live up to, and Giovi was the kind of man who'd appreciate me slapping her for her insolence.

I had no desire to do that.

So, I saved her from myself. From my reputation.

I retreated before she could say a word to piss me off, before her good reason failed her and she made me look bad in front of my soldier, and left.

The second I did, keying in the code to lock her in and keep her safe, I demanded, "Who was shooting?"

"The Triads," Giovi replied.

I turned to him with a scowl. "What the hell for?"

"They must have heard about the shipment."

"Did they target the crates?"

"I don't know."

"How many were there?"

"We're still counting."

"How did they find out about the shipment?" I questioned as we strode down the hall, me following him to wherever the hell we were going.

Russu was the front of a Twenties-era warehouse that I'd redesigned into a labyrinthine fortress to ensure maximum confusion during a raid by the cops. That meant we could have been heading to any part of the edifice.

He gulped, seeming to sense my growing impatience. "I truly don't know, Don. The shooting took place out in the loading bay."

He said that like I should reward him for knowing that much.

I scowled at him. "Where are Rory and Stan? They're supposed to be all over this fucking shipment. I didn't even want to deal with the *Lobos Rojos.*"

Goddamn street gangs. I didn't care that they acted more like a corporation that dealt in illegal weapons, they were still a gang to me.

Wincing, Giovi muttered, "Don, they're your siblings. I have no idea where they are."

My scowl only deepened, and his shoulders hunched forward as a result. The fear I triggered in him was born of ten years of his working alongside the Valentinis as we sought to regain our rightful position.

Back when I was in college, when I'd worked hard to get my MBA, I'd never in a million years imagined that I'd be terrorizing what was, essentially, my very own militia.

Terrorizing a boardroom, sure. A classroom after I returned to school with a different major, definitely. But this? No.

Reaching up to pinch the bridge of my nose—Giovi didn't deserve to fear for his face just because my time with Jennifer had been disturbed by gunfire—I demanded, "The shooting is under control?"

"*Se.*"

"*Bonu.* Any deaths?"

"Not on our side. The Triads who survived have been moved into cold storage until you're ready to interrogate them."

Relieved not to have lost any more men this *Natali*, I dipped my chin before we maneuvered to the rooms at the back of the nightclub. The converted warehouse had many areas where less than legal business went down. Shit that would make the IRS sob with glee if they ever discovered them.

Not that they would.

Or, if they did, those particular agents would be having a very long walk off this very short pier.

As we ducked into one of the backrooms, I eyed the area, spying a couple of corpses on the ground. Peering at them, I asked, "You sure they're Triads?"

He frowned. "Well, they're inked like Triads. Not Yakuza."

I just hummed as I stepped toward one of them, then kicked the dead man's foot. "How many were there?"

Lorenzo made an appearance. "Half a dozen." *Thank God, someone with answers.* "These two were the only ones who died."

"The Chinese aren't usually so foolish." I narrowed my eyes at the corpse. "They sent them here as cannon fodder."

Giovi gaped at me. "Cannon, what?"

Cristo, I missed the academic world. A world where people knew what words meant. I wasn't even speaking with him in English, for fuck's sake.

Rubbing a hand through my hair, trying not to get angry because it wasn't Giovi's fault he didn't have a goddamn bachelor's degree in World History or an MBA in Business, I muttered, "Generals of old used to send in waves of foot soldiers to take the brunt of a battle, to wear down the front. It was a foolish game then, and it hasn't improved with time." I grunted at the thought. "What's their end game?"

"End game?"

With my patience about to reach the upper echelons of its limits, I grumbled, "Show me where the shooting took place."

Lorenzo chimed in, "I'll show you, Don."

Don...

Feeling the mantel of power settle onto my shoulders, I strolled with him over to the loading bay which, back in the day, had been used to offload slaughtered cattle, where I found the destruction to be minimal.

I narrowed my eyes. "Have you checked the police scanners?"

"*Sè*. Of course. No one's interested in this part of the city. That's why the club's so popular. You know that."

He wasn't wrong.

Russu was on the border between Two Bridges and the Financial District. On one of the piers, we'd gradually taken over each lot as it became available, and because *Russu* was known as a hotspot during the night, and because we were unapologetic about its past and refused to pretty up the exterior, it wasn't like the other piers with their fancy restaurants and family eateries.

This was our slice of misery in Manhattan.

The FDNY were across the water, but with the noise from the club, I wasn't sure if they'd have heard the shooting or not. Water carried sound, after all. I thought we'd have heard sirens by now, though.

Slowly, I checked out the pitch-black water that gleamed in the light from a thousand skyscrapers, scanned the ground where there were men scrubbing at bloodstains, studied the bullet holes that decorated the back wall of my club.

Mind whirring, I asked, "Did my sister transport the Anjous to our home?"

Lorenzo nodded. "She did. We got her out just as the shooting started."

Grunting again, I murmured, "Tell them to hurry with the cleanup and bring in a dozen men to transport the guns to Hoboken."

"On the barge?"

I nodded. "Do it now. *Prestu*." Quickly.

This stank of a trap.

My instincts didn't lie.

If the cops were on their way in response to the shooting, or if another wave of Triads were incoming, I wanted our newly acquired merchandise out of here.

That was why I returned to the bodies, studied their slack faces, and tried to figure out why the Triads would send men into a heavily guarded warehouse and expect them to come back alive...

NINE

JEN

MY ASS HURT.

In a good way.

Also, in a bad way.

It had been a while since I'd had an angry fuck like that, but as much as I'd feel it in the morning, I was oddly more annoyed about the aftermath of the fuck rather than the actual fuck itself.

Tonight had been irritating all round.

Okay, irritating wasn't the right word. I just didn't know how to process what I had to deal with.

Hence the sex.

The sex with a married man.

God, I was such a fool.

Because I sure as hell didn't believe him. Of course, he was married. All these fucking mafiosos were.

I guess that made me a homewrecker.

Whoop-de-fucking-doo.

My jaw worked at the thought as I sidled around Luciu's office on the hunt for a private bathroom.

If he thought I was going to stay seated where he left me, he was wrong. A slut I might be, but I didn't fetch on command. Cum was leaking from my ass, and I needed to stop that. Now.

"You're no different than me, Fionnabhair."

I could hear my mom's voice in my head.

Could hear her smug satisfaction that I was a homewrecker and a whore just like she was.

Tears didn't prick my eyes at that.

Who was crying?

Not me, that was for damn sure.

Sniffling, I found a bathroom on my first try.

Like every single one of Luciu's private areas within *Russu*, it was sleek as hell, expensively clad in a bright white marble, each vein seeming to gleam like it was shot through with silver.

I took care of business, got myself cleaned up and used toilet roll to dry off because, hey, I was a considerate guest like that.

Although now that I thought about it, the cheating prick probably deserved to dry his hands on towels that had wiped my ass...

Before I allowed the notion to bear fruit, and my temper encouraged me to be gross, I got out of there and, when five more minutes passed without his return, thoroughly bored, I headed over to the door where he'd exited the room.

That was locked.

Damn.

When I tried the one I'd entered by, I found that locked as well.

What the fuck?

The idea that he caged me in immediately made me look for an escape. Because this room had a crazy number of doors leading off it—five in total—I tried the remaining two, finding that one was locked, while the other wasn't. I stepped through it, coming across a walkway that led to eight more doors—four to each side.

I was starting to feel like Willy Wonka had built this place.

On my way to the first one, the sound of someone sobbing had chills of fear whispering down my spine. Every single one of the hairs there sprang to life like a zap of electricity had whipped me.

I froze.

I'd have walked away, would have plunked my ass onto the chair he'd deposited me in and glued myself to it until Luciu returned, pretending like I'd been there all along. Only, that was when I heard him.

"I didn't do anything! Let me out of here! There's been a misunderstanding!"

Damian.

My ex was here.

"What the fuck?" I whispered under my breath as I headed down the hallway, trying to find which one his whimper had come from.

I was enough of a bitch that vengeance made me feel no pity for him. Whatever he was here for, whatever 'infraction' he'd committed against the *Famiglia*, I was glad for it. Especially if they were beating the shit out of him.

The prick totally deserved it.

In fact, I really, really, *really* hoped they *were* beating the shit out of him.

When I heard sobbing, the feral side of my nature was piqued all the more. Plus, the racket he made had the added benefit of helping me find the right door.

Ever since he'd served me with court papers, filing an injunction against me, he'd not let me go anywhere near him. The one time he had, I'd gotten him on the phone, and we'd arranged a rendez-vous at The 68. That was the night I'd met Luciu so, *technically*, this entire situation was Damian's fault.

Terrified and excited and smug all at the same time, my hand fell to the door handle and slowly, I turned it. I was sure that it was going to be locked, but I had to try. Color me fucking stunned when I found that it opened.

The door swung in, and the first thing I saw was a guy—elbows on his knees, leaning over, a Little Debbie cupcake in one hand, his cell in the other. The second the door opened, his head darted up and away from his phone.

When he registered my presence, he murmured, "Well, look who the cat dragged in."

His accent—or lack thereof, I supposed. So neutral, yet so full-bodied it was as if he'd been around the world twice—was so like Luciu's that I knew they had to be related.

The meathead who'd interrupted us had a twang to his voice, but this guy didn't. Plus, they had the same eyes, the same Roman nose. The only difference was that Luciu was elegant. Suave. This one was a bruiser. Big and muscled, his arms and shoulders bulged through the fine linen shirt he wore.

A fine linen shirt that was dotted and sprayed with blood.

It could have been my ex's or from the gunshots outside.

Did it make me an evil person if I really hoped it was Damian's?

"Do you know me?"

The stranger who I thought was Luciu's relative, a brother, perhaps, most likely a cousin, smirked at me. "Oh, yeah, I know you."

Before I could demand to know how, Damian whimpered, "Jen, help me, please!"

It said a lot that Damian was the last guy I looked at in here. There was a stoic man in the corner, who mostly looked bored, but Damian was tied to a chair with duct tape. Hands, feet, trunk—he looked like a silver sausage that was seated upright.

Amused by the thought, I stepped nearer to him. The guy in the corner tensed up, but from the corner of my eye, I saw Luciu's relative waft a hand to make him stand down.

As I approached Damian, I took in the handsome features that had made boning the prick less agonizing, especially when he had a tendency to drop a grand here or there for me to buy a dress that was worthy of the galas and events he attended.

It irked me to realize that his blond looks were lackluster in comparison to Luciu's gorgeousness. Not that I'd ever tell Valentini that. The prick already had a massive ego. I didn't need to feed it and make it any bigger.

Peering down at Damian, I saw the ragged flesh on his cheek, flesh that had been scored with a knife. "Someone's not so pretty anymore."

He let out a sob. "You have to help me, Jen!"

His plea fell on deaf ears as I tilted my head to study the gash. It was, I'd admit, pretty obscene. I didn't know why the sight of it wasn't making me want to puke, but it actually didn't. I could see Damian's implants, for Christ's sake! But nope, no nausea. I was more satisfied at him getting his just deserts than anything else.

"Seventy thousand."

He blinked up at me with dazed blue eyes. "Huh? What are you talking about? Help me!"

What did he think I was going to do? Pull on my Wonder Woman outfit and save his ass as well as my own and get us both out of here?

Dumbass. If I was going to save anyone, it'd be my fine patootie, not this schmuck's.

Snorting, I repeated, "Seventy thousand. That's how many times you'd have to say, 'I'm sorry,' for me to even think about asking Luciu to free you. But seeing as that could take all night, I don't think you have time to earn my cooperation."

His mouth gaped.

And I wasn't talking about the slash in his cheek either.

"You crazy bitch! Are you being serious? You don't want to help me?"

I frowned. "Why would I? Forty thousand in damages to the car, and *thirty* thousand for emotional damages?" I huffed out an indignant reply. "*My* feelings were hurt, Damian."

"Your feelings were hurt?" he squawked. "You were my whore—"

Temper rattled around inside me.

I could call myself that. He couldn't.

We'd been dating. He'd had no right to cheat on me. No right—

Luciu had just cheated on his wife with me.

And *I'd* instigated it.

Fuck, maybe I *was* as much of a piece of crap as Damian's sneer said I was—

No!

Needing to shut up both him and that stupid voice in my head that sounded like Mom's, I snarled, "You have any more of this duct tape? His whining's starting to piss me off."

Luciu's relative wafted a hand at the guy in the corner who moved away from the wall and gifted me with a roll of tape.

When he made to return to his perch, I arched a brow at him and asked, "You think I'm going to cut this with my teeth?"

The other guy snickered, while the man in front of me merely glowered as I pulled out a strip of tape long enough to cover Damian's mouth.

He cut it with the end of his knife, which prompted me to say, "Hold his head still."

When he complied, I knew he glanced behind him for approval, but I was having too much fun, so I didn't argue, just waited for him to do as I asked.

Damian cried like a girl as I taped him up, making sure I stuck it nice and fast to as much of his hair as possible, then I smirked down at him and murmured, "This is what you get for cheating on me, you piece of shit." His eyes flared with a mixture of panic, outrage, and fear as he wiggled around in the chair, looking less like a sausage now and more like a human centipede.

"My brother needs to watch himself if that's your threat."

I turned back to the guy and asked, "Your brother?"

"Custanzu Valentini," he declared, his name more of a warning than an introduction.

"Expect me to curtsey?" I retorted, which earned me a smile.

"I see it takes one insane *buttana* to enchant a psychotic fuck."

"What does *buttana* mean?"

He wiggled his head. "In this instance, bitch."

"That's me." I took a step back, eyed my work, then when Damian started sobbing, I felt a little bad and asked, "Is Luciu really a psycho?"

"It depends on your definition."

"On what?" I grumbled. "The DSM?"

He smiled at me, but I noticed he didn't answer, then sat upright and leaned into the chair. It was only then that I took more than a quick glance at the room.

It was, in a word, freaky.

With its stainless-steel walls and stainless-steel floors, it looked like Dexter's idea of a wet dream. One that'd save the environment from all the plastic sheeting he needed to keep a room spic and span.

I turned my attention back to Custanzu, now I'd had extra confirmation that Luciu could be insane, and questioned, "What are you going to do with him?" Maybe he'd answer that.

"He's seen you now. Probably going to have to kill him."

Even though I didn't think they were holding onto him for shits and giggles, the bluntness of his reply still took me aback. But it was Damian's scream, though muffled from behind the tape, that had me jerking backward.

"He doesn't have to die," I muttered.

"Kind of has to now." Custanzu shrugged, not appearing particularly bothered by the prospect.

If Damian's scream had me jumping, when I heard, "Jennifer!"

booming from what I assumed was Luciu's office, I nearly scuttled back and fell onto my ex's knee.

Talk about a faux pas.

"You should probably go to him. He gets kind of pissy when he doesn't get his way." He grinned at me as he raised the cupcake to his lips and took a big bite. He hummed, the sound faintly sexual, and I wasn't sure if that was because of the cupcake or the fact that I didn't scamper away like he expected me to.

Though the squirming ex-boyfriend in the chair who was apparently going to die tonight definitely had my anxiety stirring, I rumbled, "Tough. He's not the boss of me."

"He's the boss of everyone in these parts," was Custanzu's retort. He didn't sound smug either, just matter of fact.

Okay, that was both terrifying and lust-inducing, which told me there and then that I was as bad as frickin' Aoife, my BFF, and Savannah, my ex-BFF. Both of whom were entangled so deeply with the Irish Mob that they might as well have had the Tricolour tattooed on their asses.

I mean, by anyone's standards, I was a gold digger. So Luciu being the big, badass boss was enough to make dollar signs pop up in my eyes with glee.

This, however, was an entirely different situation. This wasn't just about money. This was raw, brutal power that could get me killed. This was unprecedented.

The annoying thing was, of course, that I got a sick kick out of seeing Damian all trussed up. Demeaned and belittled like he'd done to me.

Going back to his apartment and finding him fucking a couple of hookers before demanding that I screwed the others like orgies were a part of the trophy girlfriend job description was one thing, the abuse he'd hurled at me when I refused, another.

But when he'd shoved my face in the lines of coke he'd left on his nightstand even though he knew I hated cocaine because of my mom, that was when I'd run away and had decided to key his Ferrari.

I knew what I was.

I embraced it most of the time.

But when it came down to shoving my face in it like my reputation was a steaming dog turd, and then expecting me to lick all that right up, no. Nobody was allowed to do that to me.

No one.

So yeah, I found malicious pleasure in seeing Damian like this, and I wasn't ashamed of that.

"*Pezz'i miedda,*" Luciu boomed, and I twisted around as Custanzu hollered something back.

Heavy footsteps sounded down the hallway, and when he appeared in the doorway, looking as sinful as Satan himself, I tried not to back away. The temper in his eyes seemed to make the chocolate-brown orbs glow. I knew that sounded nuts. This wasn't an episode of *Agent Carter*, for frick's sake, but damn, he was mad.

Yet it was hot.

So hot.

I knew why he was angry too.

He thought I'd run off.

Where the hell he'd thought I'd gone was another matter entirely...

"What are you doing in here, *duci?*"

The soft velvet-like timber had shivers rushing down my spine.

I hated that I reacted to him this way, but what was I supposed to do? Tell the body he'd just fucked to simmer down? The dude had licked his own cum off my inner thighs. How was a girl not supposed to get turned on when he shot her a heavy-lidded look that said he was gonna spank her silly for not staying where he'd put her?

I didn't answer his question; instead, I did something stupid.

Even more stupid than finding a mafia man's kill room.

I rasped, "You don't need to kill him."

Custanzu snorted. "Well done. You just signed his death warrant."

Grimacing when Damian screamed, I twisted back and around, only to find Luciu there, right in front of me. His hands came up to cup my chin, sliding around my jaw so that I felt harnessed in place as he snapped, "You have feelings for this *fava?*"

"You mean, like a fava bean?"

Custanzu explained, "It means dick."

Despite myself, I snickered. Something in me responding to his outrage. His *protective* outrage. "Damian does have a fava bean dick," I whispered, leaning up on tiptoe so that I was closer to him, my face nearer to his. "Not like yours."

"Didn't need to hear that."

We ignored Custanzu's grumble, and I watched instead as Luciu's eyes darkened at my words.

"I had feelings for his bank balance." Deciding to prod the bear, I licked my lips, satisfied when his gaze dropped to them. "You did this for me, didn't you?"

He didn't answer, but I knew he had.

Knew it.

And had to admit, this certainly beat getting a bunch of flowers or a piece of jewelry as a gift.

Suddenly, I understood the appeal of dating a mobster.

Aoife's wedding day had ended in a blood bath because her husband was the Five Points' money man. They'd brought war to the church where she got married, for fuck's sake. When she'd stood by him—by choice, not because he coerced her—I'd admit to thinking she was insane.

But if this was how Finn decided to treat her, it totally made sense to me now.

"You don't have to kill him," I told him. "But Damian, you'd better drop the court case or so help me God, I'll be the one cutting the other side of your cheek."

Luciu's top lip snagged upward. "I'll negotiate for his life if it means so much to you."

It didn't mean anything to me.

As cool as this was, however, I wasn't a murderer.

The same couldn't be said for the other guys in the room.

"He means bupkis to me, but like, he doesn't deserve to die."

"He cheated on you, didn't he?"

Fuck, things got even hotter between my thighs.

This dude was raking every single one of the bloodthirsty traits in my nature to the surface and giving all of them an orgasm.

It wasn't right.

No murders, Jen, I told myself. *No murders. That's taking shit too far.*

Of course, I told myself that but my body was hearing something else entirely.

"Cheaters don't deserve to die." I arched a brow at him as I made the pointed dig. "There's probably a special place in hell reserved for them, but you can't say anything because this room *is* hell's waiting room."

"You want him dead or not?" Custanzu grumbled at his brother, evidently getting bored with the conversation.

Luciu's hand tightened around my chin, and he forced my head back as he loomed over me, his breath brushing my lips, the heat drawing my nerve endings to life. "Beg for his life, *duci*."

My pussy clenched.

"You want me to beg for the cheating bastard's life?" I repeated.

He smiled at me. "Yes."

Well, consider that a lick to my clit.

Damian began sobbing at his declaration, though, which totally spoiled the moment.

When Luciu's thumb moved, arching over my mouth, dragging my lip down, I snapped my teeth around the thick pad. He smirked at me, then made me squeal as he pulled some ninja moves that had him spinning me around in his arms.

One hand stayed on my throat, holding me there, my back to his front, the other slipped around my belly, the arm banding and holding me in place.

I didn't try to squirm or wriggle away.

I was street smart.

Sort of.

You didn't run from a predator, but neither were you supposed to taunt them.

Oops.

"He's a prick, but lots of men are. You can't go around killing all the guys who cheated on me."

And there were a lot.

Which was pathetic.

Ugh.

Damian was the straw that broke the camel's back though.

Fava bean dick aside, I'd actually liked him before he'd started hitting the coke in a big way.

Bastard.

He pressed his chin to the top of my head. "How many have there been?"

"You going to tell me how many pussies you sank your dick into?"

Custanzu snorted. "You got all week?"

Luciu growled something at his brother, something rumbly and deep that had Custanzu muttering something back under his breath. The only words I understood were, 'Little Debbie.'

They talked about something else then, because the guy in the corner moved away from it and started for the door.

After he left, Custanzu got to his feet, dragged his chair behind Damian which had my ex squeaking with distress, before he dumped a serial killer's toolbox on the seat and then did like the other dude—left us to it.

"Now you tell me. Where no one but me and you can hear."

Damian and I blinked at one another because that didn't bode well for his life expectancy, did it?

"I'm a gold digger, Luciu," I whispered softly, trying to calm the situation down with the harsh truth.

Was it Damian's fault that his dick accidentally landed in a pussy?

Yes.

But did that mean he deserved to die for it?

Nope.

And it wasn't like Luciu had room to judge...

"I fuck these guys for money. So they can buy me pretty shit I can't afford. How loyal and faithful do you think that makes them?"

Luciu hummed, then he stole my breath by saying, "A queen in the dirt, begging for food, desperate for a warm bed at night, is still a queen."

Was he inferring that *I* was a queen?

Me?

I was New York City's version of trailer trash. My mom was a two-bit whore with a nasty pimp who beat her black and blue, and my dad was in the wind.

Well, until tonight, I'd thought that. I knew who my dad was now thanks to Savannah's revelations.

He was Padraig O'Donnelly.

Maybe I wasn't a queen, but in these parts, I was a lot more than trailer trash—I was an O'Donnelly.

"Look at the chair Custanzu placed behind Damian," Luciu rasped in my ear.

When his fingers tightened around my throat, I took the prompt, then winced when I saw a screwdriver on the seat as well as a small baggy of pills in the box Custanzu had left behind.

"He takes drugs," I told Luciu. "Doesn't mean he should get the death sentence."

"Drugs are my business, *cara mia*," he mocked. "If you think I'd kill a good customer then you mistake how much I'm worth. However, those aren't regular pills."

I didn't need to ask what they were.

Damian's eyes turned wet, as if he knew what Luciu was about to tell me would stop me from helping him.

He wouldn't be wrong, either.

"We found him trying to dose a girl in the VIP room. He came here and thought he could shit on my doorstep?" Luciu's laughter was mocking, but my heart sank.

This wasn't for me.

All this... it wasn't for me.

I was glad they'd protected that poor woman, but still...

Luciu made a clucking sound, one that had me jerking in his hold, then his lips brushed along the curve of my ear. "Why do you think I found him doing this, Jennifer? You think I have men watching pissant trust fund babies for fun? I had eyes on him for a reason."

My breath gusted from between my lips—he'd followed Damian for me. What else had he done? Had he had other parts of my life investigated too? "What reason?" I whispered.

"Because you feel it too."

It was in my nature to bite when I was backed into a corner, so I sniped, "So does your wife. Poor bitch."

"I already told you, Jennifer. I'm not married."

"Well, I saw her, and the ring you put on her finger."

"Whoever *she* is, she's a liar," was his silken retort. And his disinterest was clear because he snarled, "Beg for this rapist fuck's life, Jennifer."

My mind went blank, but the only thing I could think was, "He should go to jail."

When he sucked my ear lobe between his lips, my knees buckled. The only thing that kept me upright was his hand about my throat and the arm around my waist.

Unable to speak, unable to argue, but not wanting to act as my ex's executioner either, I stared at Damian a second, recognizing how fucking surreal this moment was.

That was when Luciu murmured, "Come with me."

As if he knew I was standing on shaky legs, he hauled me into his side, holding me against him as he walked me out of the room.

When we moved a door down, I came across another stainless-steel hellhole, but this time, there was a woman passed out on a sofa that looked as if it had been dragged in for this purpose. It didn't take much to figure out that this was the woman Damian had drugged.

There was a man standing in the corner again, and I eyed him. "How do you know she's safe with him?"

"Because Ricardo is honorable, and also very, very gay," Luciu retorted.

"Didn't think the mafia allowed homosexuality."

"My mafia isn't like the rest of the world's mafia. Now, look at her, and you tell me that *pezz'i miedda* doesn't deserve to die."

I winced because, at that very moment, she puked. Everywhere. It spurted out over the sofa, dripping down to the floor, spattering the area around her.

The sight and the sounds made me gag as Luciu drew me back out of the firing range of vomit, and as I gulped down air that was tinged with the scent of puke, he asked, "Did he drug you, *cara mia*? Would you even know? Would you remember? That's what I'm thinking as I look at her..."

I bit my bottom lip as fear started to churn inside me. It was a selfish fear, one that made me wonder if I was...

Closing my eyes, I shook my head, but it wasn't in answer to his question, more like at what it might mean for me.

He wouldn't believe me if I told him. And maybe he'd be right to if Damian had drugged me in the past...

I was a virgin.

Mouth, ass, and mind were definitely not, but my vajayjay was, I'd always thought, untouched.

Purposely.

Hypocritically.

Well aware I was trembling, I whispered, "I want to go home."

"No. No dice," he replied. "You have to answer. Don't you think he should die for this? For what he might have done to you?"

Damian screamed, out of the blue, and I twisted in Luciu's hold. This wasn't fun anymore. This was scary and real and...

The rancid scent of the other woman's vomit seemed to flood the air again as she hurled and the need to puke hit me too.

When Luciu's hold on me tightened, it stopped feeling supportive and started to feel like he was imprisoning me.

Furious and nauseated, I growled, "I don't know how to answer. I'm not God. This isn't my decision!"

"In my world, *I am God.* I make life and death decisions every day."

"That's your choice. In my eyes, that just makes you a monster."

"Mobster," he corrected. "And if I'm such a monster then it shouldn't come as a surprise to you that you're coming with me. Your morals are evidently dubious. I can't trust you not to go to the cops even though the fucker deserves to fry."

"I won't say anything," I rasped, staring up at him with what I hoped was anger in my eyes but what I felt sure looked more like fear.

"I don't know that for certain, do I?"

"You do! I've been around the O'Donnellys for years, and I've never said anything." When he didn't reply, I snapped, "Since when are mobsters upholders of consent? Seeing as, you know, this isn't consensual."

"I have a sister too. She could have been targeted tonight," was his flat retort. "And you wanted everything that happened in that office. You'll want everything that happens next, I can promise you that."

"I never said what we did was nonconsensual. It's this that isn't. You taking me to your fucking Dracula lair is the exact opposite of what I want," I snarled, relieved that my anger returned in a double throttle wave that drowned any fear I'd felt before.

"Police—we're here to execute a search warrant!"

The feedback from the megaphone hurt my ears which told me it was close by.

That was when I had to accept that my New Year's evening would end as crappily as it had started.

Getting arrested was really going to be the cherry on the cake.

Under my breath, as the police raid stirred Luciu into action, I muttered, "That orgasm was not worth this level of shit."

TEN

JEN

I JOLTED awake the following morning, my head aching from the night before, the ramifications of what had gone down still reverberating inside my skull even though Luciu *had* helped me get away before the cops neared.

I'd been in a mafioso's kill room.

I'd been in his office.

I'd been fucked by him.

I'd heard a gunfight between the Sicilians and the *whoever*, and then I'd almost been a part of a cop raid.

A fucking NYPD raid.

I bit my lip as I stared up at the ceiling, trying to reconcile the current state of my life.

Two weeks ago, the worst thing that had happened to me was the impending lawsuit of a jackass trust fund baby with the personality of a toddler who was pissed that I'd keyed his Ferrari.

Now, I was complicit in an abduction—that was a felony. A *federal* one. No state prisons for that crime—had somehow become entangled with the Sicilian mafia, and worse than all that?

I'd been betrayed by a woman I loved like a sister.

"You're Padraig O'Donnelly's illegitimate daughter, Jen, and I have the DNA test results to prove it."

I'd thought Savannah and I were more than best friends, but she'd lied to me.

"I knew where you worked. That's why I went to that particular accountant. I'd always stuck to my dad's before, but I wanted to meet you."

"What? Me? Why? I'm nobody." My confusion was as real then as it was now.

"It started off a certain... way, but like, we have so much in common, Jen. We're both loudmouth bitches who hate being told what to do and have really expensive shoe habits. You're my BFF for real."

Lies.

All lies.

She'd fed me crap from the beginning. Switching firms to the place I worked to get close to me. To research a story.

A fucking story on the Irish Mob.

Our friendship was founded on bullshit and falsehoods, and as much as that pained me, there were the ramifications of her confession to deal with too.

I was an O'Donnelly.

A woman who'd scraped and saved her whole life, who'd worked dead end job after dead end job just to make it through community college, yet I was somehow Irish Mob royalty.

I shook my head at the thought, unable to believe it, unable to untangle myself from the current fuckfest that was my life.

Mom had whored herself out to everyone before *and* after I was born, so me having a surprise daddy didn't come as much of shock, but that my father was Padraig O'Donnelly?

You bet your ass I was stunned.

It was early, far too early to speak, but I had the sudden need to talk to the only person who hadn't lied to me, betrayed me, or tried to hide something from me.

Me: *Aoife? You awake?*

She didn't reply, just called me. The relief that hit me was immense.

I wasn't sure what I'd do without Aoife. I'd felt that way about Savannah too, but apparently, the feeling wasn't mutual.

"Wassup, bish?" I greeted, trying to sound like my usual self and failing as I answered the call.

I knew I sounded off.

I wasn't sure if I'd ever feel *on* again.

"You sound weird."

Trust her to pick up on that in two words. "It's five-thirty," I said grumpily. "On New Year's Day, girl. What do you expect from me?"

She snickered. "You think you can pull the wool over my eyes?"

"No wool to pull. I have to work out. Do you blame me for being pissy?"

Aoife sighed. "I hate it when you run in this weather."

"I'm not. I started running in my apartment."

She fell silent. Then, "Please tell me you're joking?"

"I'm not."

"Jesus, don't you get bored?"

"Of course, but—"

Wails came down the line. "Two mins, babe, your godson is pissed at having to eat oatmeal for breakfast."

When I heard her comforting him, I smiled, especially when she started singing an Irish song I remembered hearing her mom, Michelle, sing when she was younger—'Rattlin Bog.' Aoife was just like her sometimes.

God, I hadn't thought about her in too long.

Last night was making me maudlin.

Michelle 'Ellie' Keegan hadn't been like family to me. I didn't think she even liked me that much, but she hadn't discouraged Aoife from being friends with me. And I'd always loved being around Aoife's place when I was growing up. Somewhere that was night and day to where I lived.

A home where bills weren't paid, candles were a replacement for lights, and the cupboards consisted of coffee and vinegar and, if I were lucky, ramen.

When the bastard who'd mowed her down in a hit and run had killed Ellie, it had sent Aoife and me into a tailspin. Only meeting Finn had saved Aoife from losing herself in her grief.

As for myself, I wasn't sure if I'd ever recuperate.

"How do you run in your apartment? It's the size of a postage stamp?" Aoife queried after a couple minutes.

A muffled sound came down the line and I was sure it was Jake playing 'choo choo' with a train set I'd bought him for Christmas.

I hoped he was—that fucking thing had cost me a fortune. With Aidan O'Donnelly Jr. as a godfather, a guy who could drink a bottle of fifteen-thousand-dollar whiskey without it hurting his wallet, I had some serious competition in the godparent game.

"I run from the doorway to the window in the room, along the hall to the bathroom, and then back around again."

"You being serious right now?"

It was only because I loved her that I didn't snipe, *"We don't all have rich men who love us whether we're fat or thin,"* but I didn't.

That'd be bitchy, and Aoife didn't deserve that.

Instead, I grumbled, "It's either that or go out in the snow. Which do you think is better?"

"I'm not sure," she admitted. "They both sound like hell."

"They are," I assured her, "but the snow and the wind were doing bad things to my skin. Premature ageing isn't something I can afford."

She hesitated. "Honey, you'll be ninety and still be beautiful."

Faded beauty didn't pay the bills, and when I was ninety, I fully expected to be divorced a couple of times, and alone.

Hopefully with enough alimony to keep me living in comfort in a nursing home with really hot guys giving me sponge baths.

"What happened last night?" she asked eventually, knowing me well enough that I wouldn't respond to her compliment.

We both knew what I was.

She understood, even if she often shook her head over it.

She even helped.

Finn had been strong-armed into introducing me to some of the top execs on his board of directors because of Aoife.

She'd probably never understand how much that meant to me. How much her support and help got me through some tough times.

"Nothing. The ball dropped, and I was ready to go home."

She sniffed. "I finished talking to you, Savannah came over, and the next time I tried to find you, you were gone."

"I had a headache."

"So? That James guy was there, and so were Cameron and Henry.

Do you know what I had to do to get Finn to invite them over to a family party?"

Gratitude aside, I had to laugh. "Nothing you didn't enjoy doing."

She chuckled. "Okay, no fair. Enjoying the act of sacrifice doesn't take away from the effort."

"This is true," I conceded. "And thank you. I wasn't really feeling it yesterday."

"I could tell. What was with you? Seriously, James owns a yacht, Jen. Not a little paddle boat. A frickin' yacht. We went on it in August. He was trying to impress Finn."

"Did it work?"

"Nope, takes more than that to impress Finn in business," she said with a laugh.

"Damn, what's it take?"

"You know what they're like," she drawled. "They have a bunch of ethics and morals that only make sense to them.

"Anyway, James is old money. Cameron came up from nothing. He doesn't have a yacht, but he has a really nice penthouse on the Upper East Side."

"He got the job?"

"Sure did." She grunted. "I should probably remember what his job is, but I knew that wouldn't interest you. He's on like eight hundred thousand a year without bonuses."

I loved this girl.

"Thank you for finding that out for me, Eef."

"More than welcome, sweetheart. Okay, enough stalling. What really happened at the party, Jen? Savannah looked upset when I asked where you'd gone. Plus, you weren't answering your phone all night—"

I heard her concern, felt it like a living, breathing entity, and it was like a hug. A warm embrace.

She was the only person I ever let my guard down with, so...

What did I do?

If I shared the news with her, would it go back to Finn? And if it did, would that be such a bad thing?

I knew she couldn't keep anything from her husband, mostly because he worried about her constantly. The second Finn saw her brow pucker, he was in her face, wanting to know what made her frown so he could turn it upside down.

It was sweet at the beginning. Now, I didn't know how she could stand it.

He was always trying to fix shit for her.

Aoife wasn't exactly a shrinking violet. Sure, she'd been naive and an innocent when they'd met, but we'd been raised in the same neighborhood in Hell's Kitchen.

No innocents were truly raised in that area.

If I didn't share it with Aoife, though, who the hell *would* I share it with?

Savannah had told me for a reason. What that reason was, I had yet to find out, but truthfully, I knew she'd only told me because she had to. Things were changing. Now she was Aidan Jr.'s fiancée, nothing would be the same again.

And that was before I learned of her betrayal.

"Savannah told me something last night," I whispered eventually.

"Something that had you stalking away from prey?" Aoife clucked. "Color me intrigued. I need to know more."

Rolling onto my side, I tucked my knees high into my chest as I comforted myself like I was four again.

"What was it, Jen?" she chivvied. "Spill the beans."

"She told me that how we met was a lie."

Aoife grunted. "Jacob, Mommy's boobs aren't for standing on."

"Why's he standing on your tits?"

"Because he's a monster?" Aoife joked, but I heard some kissy noises, followed by some childish giggles that made my heart skip a beat, which told me she was teasing him with kisses.

I liked Jacob.

It surprised me how much I did.

Maybe it was because I was his godmother, and kind of had to like him, especially because I saw him a lot since Aoife and him were Gorilla glued together, or maybe it was just because he was that—*Aoife's.*

"They're just sore right now so can't take as much of a pounding as usual." Aoife was pregnant again.

I chuckled though. "What you and Finn get up to behind closed doors is your own affair."

She snorted. "Hush. Okay, back to you. Why was it a lie? How could the way you met be a lie? You said you met when she came to your office. She transferred her account to your boss, right?"

The firm of accountants where I worked dealt with the finances of the rich and famous, and Savannah was definitely that. Not only was she Dagger Daniels' daughter, as in *the* Dagger Daniels who made Mick Jagger and Steven Tyler look like penny-ante rock demigods, she'd also graced New York with her face every morning on TVGM—breakfast news.

She was wealthy in her own right, so her coming to my office made sense. There were all kinds of departments under the one umbrella, but my boss's specialty was accounts and tax havens. By extension, that was my specialty too seeing as I did most of his work which he took the credit for.

"Savannah made it seem at the time like it was a happy accident. We bonded over a love of Louboutins," I mocked.

"But it wasn't?"

"No."

"She wanted to meet you?" Aoife guessed hesitantly.

"Yes."

"Why?"

"Because she wanted to get some of my DNA."

"Whoa." Aoife whispered the curse, "Are you shitting me?"

"I wish I were."

"What the hell was her problem? Why on earth would she want your DNA?"

"Because she had a working theory and she needed to confirm it." Before she could ask me what that working theory was, I whispered, "I can't believe this is even happening to me, Aoife. She says I'm Paddy O'Donnelly's daughter."

For a second, there was silence, then, softly, Aoife mumbled, "Aidan Sr.'s brother? We're talking about *the* O'Donnellys, right?"

"Yeah."

"The dead one?"

I growled under my breath. "They're all dead. That's what happens when you're an O'Donnelly."

"Not true. All Sr.'s sons are alive," she contested.

"Only for so long. Someone will blow their brains out or stab them sooner or later—"

"Jen, don't you even dare joke about something like that."

I scowled at the ceiling, but I heard her shaken tone. She was right to be shaken.

"Aoife, what did we both go through at Christmas?"

Of all the men she knew thanks to her connections to the Irish Mob, there was one rule—never set me up with a mobster.

I'd had a shitty childhood; I did *not* intend to have a shittier adulthood. In my opinion—and any rational human being's too—there was nothing shittier than being shot down on your fucking wedding day like Aoife had been.

Mobsters.

See? This was why I avoided them.

This was why Luciu Valentini was one of my biggest ever mistakes.

"We survived the holidays, didn't we?"

Survived?

She wasn't talking about bickering over the goddamn turkey here.

"*Only just.* I have no idea how Aidan Sr. even made it to fifty, never mind his ripe old age. Pretty sure it had nothing to do with God," I retorted.

Aoife released a shaky breath, and I knew why.

Neither of us had really talked about what happened over Christmas, and I knew we wouldn't, either.

Not only had the O'Donnelly compound been attacked like we were in downtown Baghdad, New York, on the whole, had been on red alert ever since its cathedral had been destroyed in an arson attack that had wiped out the centuries' old building.

Even worse?

The archbishop was reportedly inside when it happened.

I shuddered at the very idea of being burned alive, and then, my mind whispered along to Damian.

Had he perished last night?

Or had the NYPD raid saved his ass?

Did I want him to be dead?

"I want to bury my head under the covers."

"I can't blame you," was her soft reply. "But you don't have to do anything about it, Jen. You can just pretend you don't know about Paddy."

It all hinged on Damian.

On whether he was alive or dead.

If he was dead, then I didn't have to worry about a court case and the subsequent fines.

I was in debt, but it was a comfortable level. It wasn't choking me. Not yet. I was maybe four pairs of Jimmy Choos away from the chokehold.

If Damian still lived, then that was a different matter entirely.

Although... wouldn't the cops have banged on my door at some point during the night?

He'd have snitched on me in a heartbeat.

"Want to know something worse?"

"Of course."

I grimaced. "I may have had sex with a married man."

"Jesus, Jen!" Aoife barked. "What the hell?" As I winced, she muttered, "Wait. May have? How does that work? Did you have sex with him or not?"

"I did, but he said he wasn't married."

"So, what made you think he was?"

"I met his wife."

A snort escaped Aoife. "Jen, I swear, your life is already complicated without you being an O'Donnelly. How do you get yourself into these situations?"

I cringed. "I don't mean to. I really like him, Eef."

"So does his wife."

"She was really angry."

"I'll just bet she was," she retorted. "I'd have stabbed you with a fork if you came onto Finn!"

"Nice to know."

The smooth, deep baritone had me rolling my eyes, and it was only compounded when Aoife let out a soft whimper which told me she'd been kissed senseless.

I'd have grouched into her ear, but I was too used to this.

I pitied Jacob when he was old enough to get embarrassed about

PDAs, because he was gonna die when he saw how often his dad had his hands on his mom.

They were one of those sickeningly happy couples that, you just knew, would be forever until death did them part.

Bleugh.

I'd prefer to die on my own at ninety than have that.

I sniffed. "Aoife, for God's sake, if I wanted to listen to a live sex show I'd go to *Elemental*." But only after she mewled again.

Two minutes *later*.

A soft, husky laugh made itself known to me, and I huffed, well aware I'd amused Finn. Because, ya know, that was what I lived to do.

"Sorry about that," Aoife said breathily, sounding like she'd gone ten rounds on a step machine and had face planted into it.

I groused, "Would hope so."

"Are you going to talk to Savannah about what happened?"

"Why? What happened?" Finn asked.

"Never mind you," I sniped even though he couldn't hear me.

"Girl talk," Aoife soothed.

"I'm not sure I like that you three are all linked together."

Aoife chuckled. "Why not?"

"There's danger in threes."

I had to grin. "Tell him he's right to be afraid."

"I won't tell him that," Aoife retorted.

"You're such a goody two-shoes," I complained.

"You're not married. You haven't learned there are fights you pick and choose."

"Why? What do you want to fight with him about?" I queried, intrigued at the prospect.

I knew it was stupid to think they never got angry with one another, but they were so stupidly in love it was hard to imagine any harsh words ever being passed between them.

I wasn't sure if that was boring as hell or #lifegoals.

I pursed my lips at the thought, yet before she even had the chance to answer me, I had to sigh and murmur, "Thanks, Eef."

"What for?" she asked in surprise.

"Taking my mind off things."

"You should talk about it with Finn. He might help you understand."

"His loyalty is to Aidan Sr.," I denied. "I'm not about to get in the way of that. I'd lose every time."

She hummed. "Maybe. I don't think so though."

"You have to swear you won't say anything."

"I do swear." Her voice turned soft, but there was a thread of steel behind it. "Finn knows that some things we talk about aren't for his ears."

"Hence the terror of you and Savannah getting friendly too. Jen's bad enough."

"Charming," I muttered, peeved, but then I thought about it, and I smirked up at the ceiling. "Actually, I'm pretty proud of that assessment."

"She says she's proud of that assessment," Aoife repeated.

"She would be," Finn grumbled.

"You should come over for dinner," Aoife prompted, but her voice was light with her amusement. "It'll do you good. You'll be stuck by yourself otherwise."

She wasn't wrong, but I wasn't in the mood for food.

Hell, there was only one thing I was in the mood for, and it definitely wasn't good for me.

My ass twinged from the pounding it had received last night, but I'd take it again in a heartbeat.

A tone chimed on my phone, notifying me of an incoming call.

"I'd best go, babe. I have an incoming call."

"At this time?" she complained.

"You know what work is like."

"You deserve a promotion."

"I agree," I told her, even though I knew for a fact it wasn't work.

My boss was useless without me, but even he wouldn't be calling on New Year's Day.

Only because the markets were closed, though.

"Speak later, sweetheart," I told her.

"Come to dinner and bring an overnight bag!" she chimed in quickly before she cut the call, both of us knowing I'd be there before five and would probably spend the night.

I stared at the caller ID for so long that the noise of the ringtone didn't register. It only stopped ringing when my phone disconnected the call.

Then it restarted.

Was he calling at this time to hook up? To give me a heads up about the police that were about to come and arrest me?

My next-door neighbor pounded on the wall, making me jolt so hard with surprise that the bed bounced back with a loud knock.

Quickly connecting the call, I placed it on speaker as I called out, "Sorry, Mr. Yardley!"

"Who is Mr. Yardley?"

His voice, *dear God*, his voice.

Like sin and silk and sex all wrapped up in one delicious package that came bundled up with a wedding band.

Maybe.

"Jennifer," he growled, and that was even sexier. "Who is Mr. Yardley?"

The dominant snap had me flinging myself onto my back, the self-comforting fetal position no longer required, as I huffed, "Why do you want to know?"

"The dumb act might work with other fools, but not with me. I repeat, who is he?"

My lips curved. "We make noise together."

A snarl escaped him, and it shot up my spine like an electric shock.

"In my bedroom," I taunted.

When he cut the call, I smiled.

I knew exactly what he was going to do.

And married man or not, liar or not, every part of me readied myself for the tornado that was about to come my way.

ELEVEN

LUCIU

I WAS AN INTELLIGENT MAN.

Some might say I was too intelligent for the career path I'd chosen.

With an MBA and two bachelor's degrees, there were few people with my education who'd elect to become a mob boss.

Of course, at career day in school, I hadn't made that decision either.

Not until the mob had come knocking on *my* door had I chosen this path.

When the New York *Famiglia* had slayed my father, my innocent *patri*, they'd made an enemy of the Valentinis.

An enemy that had corroded their foundations for over a decade.

Yet, for all that I was an intelligent man, for all that I was a powerful and dangerous adversary, there was something about Fionnabhair MacNeill that perturbed me. Not least that she didn't use her real name...

No, something about her had me thinking about the lores I'd read when I researched my own ancestral line.

The Valentinis weren't simply immigrants to New York, peasants who'd been seeking a better life in the New World. We were founded in the House of Anjou-Valentini. We'd been royals. One of my great-great-great-grandfathers had been a prince, for God's sake.

When the Valentini queen drips in the blood of the earth, only then will the family's star continue to rise.

As Lorenzo, my driver, raced Giovi, my guard, and I over to Hell's Kitchen where Jennifer lived, I thought about those words.

Thought about them and imagined her dripping in blood.

Of course, they weren't talking about lifeblood, but the Anjou-Valentini rubies.

I could see her wearing the infamous jewels, earbobs sparkling amid the chestnut locks of her hair, the tiara perched on the crown of her head, the choker necklace that would paint her chest crimson.

I thought of the matching wrist cuffs, and, even better, imagined the anklet—a Moorish tradition that had slipped into the family line over the centuries.

Dripping in blood.

In rubies.

The family's rubies.

My dick began to ache, and that it did was a miracle considering my temper.

No, my fury was full throttle until the only red I saw was Mr. fucking Yardley's.

I didn't care that it was just past dawn on New Year's Day, didn't give a damn that my man Giovi had to break into the front entrance—if anything, I highly disapproved of the lack of a doorman. The only thing that mattered was breaking up whatever the hell was going down in Jennifer's apartment.

As I strode up the stairs, making it to her floor, I'd admit to being surprised when I saw her door was open.

Giovi's hand snapped for his gun, whereas I reached for my dagger, but as our pace changed, morphed into a stealthy stride, her head bobbed around the door.

A quick glance revealed she wore nothing but a man's shirt, which made my blood boil, and I snapped at Giovi, "Turn your head away. Guard the entrance."

"Shall I inform Lorenzo he should idle the car?" was Giovi's calm retort, like I snapped at him to guard doors every day of the week.

"Sè."

Dismissing him without another thought, I stormed forward, hauled her against my chest, then slammed the door behind me.

The second it was shut, I grabbed both sides of the shirt and tore it apart.

She laughed, and in her eyes, there was mockery and fire.

Fire.

She burned with it.

I felt the flames licking at my control, tearing at it, razing it to the ground.

I dragged the silk off her arms and proceeded to dump my winter coat onto the floor before I removed my jacket and tucked her into that.

She allowed me to do all this, of that I was well aware.

Moreover, she *dared* me to do it.

Those eyes of hers... Goddamn them and goddamn her.

What the fuck was it about her that pushed my control to the edge?

"Should I frisk your pockets? Finders/keepers?" she taunted, those flames still licking at me, daring me to snap.

This new Jennifer stunned me.

Where was the woman I'd initially met? How had she been replaced with this siren?

I couldn't complain.

For all that she'd enchanted me from the start, it was only last night that had me thinking about her wearing rubies...

Voice like gravel, I demanded, "Who's Mr. Yardley?"

"So, you don't know everything about me," she sniped. "Your investigation into me wasn't as extensive as I feared."

Damn, she had a point.

"Who is he?" I spat.

"An octogenarian who disapproves of me falling asleep to TikTok videos when our bedrooms share a wall."

The ridiculousness of my jealousy didn't even faze me. The relief was too raw.

Too real.

No blood would be shed this morning.

Instead of telling her that, I peered around the apartment and told her the first thing that came to mind, "This place is a shithole."

Her eyes narrowed with a warning that, for how my dick reacted, might as well have been her dropping to her knees and reaching for it. "It's *my* shithole."

I dipped my chin in agreement.

She'd tried.

That was clear.

The tiny room housed her bed with little space for anything else apart from nightstands with two ornate glass lamps that were probably the most expensive items in here.

The sheets were mussed, a single pillow was dented with her head. A fact that eased my temper some.

I saw a small TV fixed on the wall behind me, and a tiny window that made a jail cell's look large.

It was... a shithole.

Impeccably clean, very neat, but still a dump.

"You belong in a mansion," I told her simply, meaning every word.

She blinked at me, her mouth rounded which, naturally, had my cock twitching, and her shoulders slumped as she tucked herself tighter into my jacket.

"You didn't expect me to say that, did you?" I rumbled quietly.

"Why would I?"

"Because you don't know your worth." I tipped my head to the side. "And yes, what you find in my pocket you may keep."

Her eyes flared. "What?"

"What you find in my pocket you may keep," I repeated calmly, folding my arms against my chest as I leaned back against the door.

Taking her in, those long legs that went on for miles, the tumbled hair that draped over the Brioni jacket that looked better on her than it did on me, the way she crumpled the silk as she tucked it against her small waist... I salivated at the sight of her.

Between the folds of the jacket, her tits were plumped up spectacularly, and the desire to get my hands on them was strong.

I'd barely touched her last night, not enough to satisfy the incessant craving that throbbed in my blood whenever I was near her.

I'd never wanted to own a woman before, had never wanted to claim one, until her.

There was something about her...

She was a witch; I'd settled upon that explanation last night during the hours of interviews.

A witch who'd enchanted me. Bedeviled me. Tormented me.

I was more than okay with that, so long as I enslaved her in return.

I watched as she reached down and pressed her hand into the pocket. As she did, the lapels parted, but she wasn't ashamed of her nudity.

Why would she be?

It was a commodity to her.

I'd read the file I'd commissioned on her—from front to back, I'd devoured every word.

She was a whore.

She used her body, leveraging it to the highest bidder.

In my world, she was tainted goods.

For all that, when our eyes collided as I perused the slivers of slim curves she revealed to me, I knew the only thing that mattered wasn't the first man she'd slept with, but the last.

She eventually found the case in the inside pocket.

Frowning, she jarred it open. Frown deepening even more, she pulled out the credit card that I'd been waiting to give her. First, I'd wanted her to come to me. She had. This was her reward.

"I don't understand."

"You owe forty-nine thousand nine hundred and twenty-four dollars and fifteen cents—"

"Someone really did their homework," she sniped.

"You know that already. After last night." I shot her a smug smile. "I shall have to encourage Stan to dig deeper because you're right—he didn't tell me about Mr. Yardley."

When she sucked her bottom lip between her teeth, I saw how fear surged in her eyes.

I'd already known there was something different about her, but that I didn't like seeing that fear was the equivalent of a mountain moving in my very soul.

I craved fear in every individual I came across who wasn't related to me.

Not because I was a sick cretin, but because, in my line of work, those who didn't fear me were to be monitored as future threats.

"Is Damian dead?" Jennifer whispered, her hand sliding higher to tug at the lapels of my jacket. The move subconscious as she shielded her throat from a predator.

"Why do you care?"

"Because if he is, that makes me an accessory to murder!" she whispered on a hiss, but I knew she wanted to scream the words at me.

A feat she couldn't achieve without the neighbors hearing, I assumed.

Regardless, relief hit me.

"You care only about the crime?"

Her brow furrowed. "Are you for real?"

"I think we both know the answer to that."

"I never know what to think with you."

"Good. It means you're as twisted up as I am inside where we're each concerned. It's only fair."

"Fair?" Her scowl morphed, transformed into a glower of confusion.

"You think I storm across Manhattan for every woman who struts in front of me like a bitch in heat?" I bit back. *"Cara mia*, no."

"I take offense on womankind's behalf."

"Feel free. They're not the ones I want to own."

Her eyes narrowed and she tapped the credit card against her hand. "You won't own me. No man will ever own me."

"That's where you're wrong," I rasped. "That's just the start, Jennifer. You're debt free now—"

"He's really dead?" she interrupted before I could finish my sentence.

"He really is."

"Did the police find him?"

Did she think I was an amateur?

Maybe I was misunderstanding how involved she was with the O'Donnellys.

I'd seen from the report that she'd grown up with the wife of Finn O'Grady, the Five Points' money man.

I knew that she'd been at the family compound for Christmas, knew plenty about how close she was to the O'Grady household in particular.

Rubbing my jaw, I asked, "Do you have any plans for the rest of the day?"

"I was going to sleep—"

"Perfect. Come with me."

Waspishly, she spat, "Come with you? Is that a euphemism?"

"It can be whatever you like. I spent the remainder of the night at a police precinct. I want a shower, breakfast, and a nap in that order. I would like you to join me."

I felt her yearning, even as I knew she was going to argue with me.

Her body leaned forward, and her eyes caught and held mine before she reined herself in and shook her head. "I-I can't. I have plans."

"What plans?"

"With my best friend. She invited me for dinner."

"You can go to dinner. I want your morning."

She huffed out a breath. "You're married."

Fire snapped at the frayed edges of my temper. "How many times? I am not married! Didn't you even Google me?"

She seemed to consume my fire and hurl it back at me—the difference was that I gloried in the flames, in her heat as she snarled, "I *did* Google you. When was the last time you searched for yourself on there?"

"Never?"

"Well, whoever you pay to completely eradicate your existence on Google deserves a raise."

Ah. My lips curved. "My sister handles that. She's very good at making people disappear."

"Apparently." She mimicked my stance, folding her arms across her chest, a slice of black metal peeping out against the jacket sleeve as she clung tightly to the credit card. "I know bupkis about you whereas you, it seems, know everything about me."

"The imbalance displeases you." Her desire to know more about me, on the other hand, *pleased* me.

"You talk like you're in a Jane Austen novel. Did you know that?"

Did she mean to sound so accusatory? "I'm Sicilian. English is my second language."

"You were born there?"

"I was. I will tell you all about me over breakfast. Have you ever eaten granita for breakfast?"

Her eyes rounded. "You mean like the ice cream?"

I nodded. "It's not supposed to be eaten in winter, but I find the one joy in being an adult is that I can eat ice cream for breakfast," I told her, even though my *Nanna* would have slapped me upside the head for daring to call granita ice cream.

In my opinion, there were very few advantages to leaving the innocence of childhood behind apart from eating and drinking inappropriate items at whatever time of the day I saw fit.

When she nibbled on her bottom lip, I could see her weakening.

"I also have brioche. Freshly baked." As I studied her, I knew food wasn't her weakness, but it didn't stop me from offering it to her. Maybe it was the hunter-gatherer instinct? "For a holiday morning, wouldn't you prefer to spend it in circumstances that befit you rather than this dump?"

"This dump is my home," she said stiffly.

"This dump is a waiting room," I informed her.

She harrumphed, then, with a growl she uttered under her breath, dropped the credit card on the sheets of her unmade bed and proceeded to pull off my jacket.

Throwing it at me, I watched as, bold as brass, she dipped down to grab the shirt I'd dumped on the floor, then twisted on her heel and moved over to a thin cupboard that opened up to reveal an impressive, if overstuffed, wardrobe.

That was where the money in this place was—in that tiny closet.

It was more than apparent that she invested all her funds into clothes and shoes and purses, so she could present the image she wanted the world to see.

I wondered what she'd think if she knew that the first time I saw her, I'd dismissed her as a whore for what she wore, then when I saw her face, saw the vulnerability in her eyes, found myself entranced by her beauty.

A beauty that needed no makeup. No designer clothes or purses or shoes.

She had high walls I'd need to climb to steer her into my circle, but I was willing to put in the effort for a woman worthy of wearing my rubies.

When I found them, of course.

I watched her dress, amused by how uncaring she was as she pulled on panties and a bra, then came a slimline pair of dark jeans that highlighted her slenderness, followed by a turtleneck sweater—Ralph Lauren—in a bright red.

She topped it with a slimline tailored jacket in a navy that offset her coloring while making her look like one of the Country Clubbers and toed her feet into a pair of black, patent leather high-heeled boots.

When she twisted back around, she was dressed—preppy and pretty with it.

Then, she ignored me and made her bed. I imagined soldiers were less precise with the creases and the folds on their sheets.

Once that task was complete, the credit card having been placed very carefully on her nightstand, she demanded, "Take me to breakfast."

I slipped into my jacket, a smile curling about my lips at her command as I dipped down to grab my coat.

Porca troia, the woman had more gravitas than a queen, and she didn't even know it. It throbbed in the air waves around her as she strode toward me.

Oxygen particles fired up and burned away as she stirred the atmosphere itself with her energy.

Something that was only reinforced when, her eyes on mine at every moment, fire snapping between us, silently she dared me to mention that she was keeping the credit card...

Money had stopped interesting me a long time ago. It was something I accumulated with little difficulty, but power and respect weren't earned so easily. They were my commodity of choice.

Where she was concerned, currently, I only had money and power to back me up. In my opinion, those were the weakest two of the trio.

Without even a backward glance at the card, I opened the door for her and walked her out into the hall.

With a nod at Giovi, I pressed my hand to the small of her back as she locked the door then guided her down the stairs.

She heaved a sigh at the devastation I'd left in my wake at the front entrance. "You?"

Perhaps she wanted me to be embarrassed, but I wasn't. "Yes. It would be wise not to make me jealous, *vita mia*."

Her mouth tightened. "At any point when you were in my ass, did I call you Mr. Valentini?"

I grinned. "I think I'd remember that."

"So, why would I be fucking *Mr.* Yardley? Is it my fault that you were being irrational?"

I didn't answer. Her logic made sense. I was discovering I wasn't very sensible around her, and while I should feel ridiculous, I didn't.

Then of course, I saw the gleam in her eyes.

"Witch. You wanted me to be jealous."

"Correction: I wanted to see if I could make it happen." She smirked. "You passed that test."

Because I didn't have a comeback, I merely watched her ass as she sashayed away from me like a proud cat who'd trapped two mice with one paw.

It was hard not to be angry at being played with. But it was harder still to be angry at someone who made me feel as if I were finally living.

Those moments where jealousy throbbed through my veins like it was an entity of its own, I was a different man. One who wasn't possessed by grief, who wasn't consumed by vengeance.

"You should stay somewhere with a doorman."

"I can't afford a place with a doorman. I can barely afford this dump," she groused.

"I will have the door fixed."

She peered up at me, those cat eyes of hers slanting upward as she took me in. "You will?"

"*Se.* I am a man of my word."

"Is that supposed to be reassuring?" she complained, but I saw the smile dancing on her lips and found myself charmed by it.

"I will always reassure you," I promised her, meaning it, even if she laughed like I was joking.

I wasn't.

Guiding her to the town car that hovered beside her building while traffic veered around it with their horns blaring—even at this time of the morning on New Year's Day, New Yorkers were angry—I watched as Giovi darted out to open the door for her.

As she climbed in, like she was used to this kind of transportation, seemingly unimpressed by the luxury of having a chauffeur-driven car in the city when the state of her building said otherwise, I smiled as I turned to Giovi and ordered, "Fix the front door. And make sure that her apartment has stronger locks."

I'd seen hers. They were pissant. Any rainy-day burglar could break into them if he so chose.

I grabbed Giovi's arm after he nodded at me in understanding of my orders and made to turn away.

"Do not enter her apartment. Do not touch anything that belongs to her."

"Of course not, Don," he grumbled.

I just grunted, then slipped in beside Jennifer and closed the door behind me.

Immediately, the car began moving, and I was pleased to see that the partition was up when it hadn't been on the ride over here.

As I turned to her, a glow from one of the streetlights peeked through the windows, illuminating her, highlighting the different colors in her hair. "You look beautiful this morning."

Her head whipped toward me, and her eyes widened as she took in my honest compliment.

But she was.

Dressed up, dressed down, barely dressed or naked, she was gorgeous.

Fuck.

I wanted her.

I wanted to own her.

Even more dangerous...

I wanted her to own me.

"Do you get to be the head of the mafia by being so impulsive?" she whispered, her voice husky with surprise.

It was like she read my mind and didn't approve.

I shot her a grin. "I make many impulsive decisions on a day-to-day basis. But you are correct. It takes many years of planning to take this role. Many years of greasing the right palms and gutting the right people."

She blew out a breath. "You say these things on purpose to make me nervous."

Her accusation had me shrugging. "I don't actually. I rarely say things for effect."

She squinted. "Why don't I believe you?"

"You should. I will not lie to you. I have no need."

"You're very confusing."

"Good. I feel as if you are far smarter than you let most men see. It will serve you well to be confused by me."

Her eyes rounded. "Thank you for the compliment."

"I meant it."

"I know you did. That's why I thanked you."

I sensed her bewilderment, which made me wonder why she could be so confused.

She knew her beauty. Used it and traded on it.

I rubbed my thumb along my bottom lip, wishing it were hers, and said, "You will like my apartment."

"I won't if your wife is there," she groused.

"I have no wife," I told her calmly. "If I did, you wouldn't see her at the apartment anyway. She would be in Brooklyn with my mother in the house I have there."

"You live with your mom?"

I smiled. "No. I tend to stay in Manhattan. Stan usually lives with me though."

"Usually? Why doesn't he have his own place?"

"Until recently, he was my guard."

"Your brother was your guard? What if he got hurt protecting you?"

"He's very good at what he does."

"Why did he stop being your guard then?"

"Because I need him to do other things for me."

"Like capture the ex-boyfriends of women you want to bone."

"Yes, important tasks like that," I drawled, amused when she flushed.

"Is he dead? Really?"

"I told you I won't lie to you. He had to die."

"He should have gone to jail," she muttered, her gaze on her knees, no longer on me.

I didn't like that, so I reached forward and curved my hand about her jaw, urging her into looking at me again. "He deserved to die for even the threat of having raped you."

She gnawed on her bottom lip. "I don't know if he did." Her brow furrowed. "I think I'd know, wouldn't I?"

"It depends on how he drugged you. If he kept you drugged in the aftermath. Eased it by getting you drunk."

"Why would he go to the trouble?"

I pondered that, then asked, "Do you have anal sex with many men the first time you fuck?"

Her nostrils flared but her head tipped away from me, her chin backing out of my hold as she peered at the side of the street. "That's none of your business. I could ask you the same thing."

She'd flounced into my office last night, Giovi traipsing after her like a lost puppy before I'd dismissed him. She planted her hands on the desk, loomed over it and demanded, "Fuck me."

I'd been more than willing to oblige, but whenever I'd tried to touch her pussy, she'd backed away, arched out of my hold. Only allowing me to touch her there when I was fully seated inside her.

In my experience, women rarely offered anal sex outside of committed relationships.

Unless they were paid for it.

Having never been in a committed relationship, I'd had anal sex with few women. A hooker my father had bought for me on my sixteenth birthday, then with a woman Stan and I had shared once.

I'd been thinking of that throughout the long hours of the interviews with the cops, each officer boring me further as they tried to learn why there'd been a gunfight outside my club.

It had been tedious, a waste of time, albeit a necessary loss of minutes as my agreeing to be taken in for questioning enabled Stan to get Jennifer out of *Russu* without detection. I'd spent my hours in the precinct reliving those moments when I'd been fucking this maddening creature at my side.

"Maybe if you never offered him your pussy, he decided to take it for himself," I said, verbalizing it as softly as I could because the idea made me want to kill him again.

Slowly, this time.

Not just a quick thrust of my knife to the base of his throat.

A languorous, agonizing death...

I knew Stan wasn't happy about how I'd ended him. Not after what he'd done to Evangeline.

"I'd know if he touched me, wouldn't I?"

It wasn't rhetorical.

"You were with him for a few months, weren't you?"

"Yes," she whispered.

"This is why he had to die. I had no way of knowing if he had or not, and this was his punishment. No rapist deserves to live."

"That's a pretty strong stance."

I smirked at her. "I'm the type of guy who has a pretty strong stance on most things."

"Do you know someone who was raped?" she asked after a moment.

"I do."

"I'm sorry," was her simple reply.

I bowed my head. "Thank you."

"Who was it?"

"My sister. She was at college. I was not a Don back then."

She read between the lines. "So, you couldn't have him killed?"

"No."

"Did you when you came into power?"

"Oh, I handled him years ago. The second I came to New York and found my footing."

She wriggled on her seat. "Why is that sweet? That really shouldn't be sweet. You can't go around killing people, Luciu. It's not right."

A bark of laughter gusted from my lips at her chiding. "I wish I could listen to you, *cara mia*, but in my line of work, death goes hand in hand with life."

"I know it does," she grumbled, "why do you think I'm so scared?"

"Of me?" I asked silkily because I couldn't allow that.

A woman could never surrender if she was terrified.

"Of everything. Yesterday was a mistake, but here I am." She shook her head, looking around the town car with confusion. "I'm annoying myself by being so stupid."

"You're not stupid. You feel it too."

"I feel nothing apart from a headache and indigestion," she groused, folding her arms across her chest, inadvertently plumping up her tits.

"I think we both know that's a lie."

She sniffed. "You're in my head now?"

I surged forward, fast enough to make her jump, then I reached for the back of her neck, sliding my hand around to cup her there, fingers dipping beneath the turtleneck.

Tilting her head back, I asked, "I can own you, possess you, and claim you, and you can always say no. You will always be able to back away, but you cannot back away from the truth.

"The second I saw you in The 68, the second you saw me, everything changed. You know it, I know it.

"Do not lie to me and tell me you don't feel this, when it's as strong as a lightning bolt ricocheting between us."

She peered up at me with big doe eyes, and while her breathing came fast, I saw that her fear wasn't founded in my proximity but in my words.

I felt the change of the car's velocity, felt the shift as we approached my building, but it didn't stop me from carefully lowering my head, and with all of the tenderness she hadn't allowed me to show her last night, pressing a kiss to her lips.

A shocked, soft gasp escaped her, one that blew out long and low into a deep sigh as I moved away.

"We have arrived at my building," I informed her. "You do not have to stay past breakfast. If you do nap with me, I do not expect sex. If you stay the day, you may treat my apartment as you would your own. *Capisci?*"

Her mouth trembled, but the confusion in her eyes was more than worth it as she nodded her understanding.

TWELVE

JEN

LUCIU'S APARTMENT was like Aoife and Finn's—expensive.

Big.

Luxurious.

I loved it.

I loved every inch.

From the marble-tiled hall to the massive lounge where I could see Lady Liberty peering at me.

I loved the jewel colors of the fabrics that decorated the space because it wasn't cold and brittle, no minimalism here. In fact, if anything, it had a distinctly Aladdin-esque feel to it.

Squashy sofas, low footstools, patterned metal corner tables, colorful rugs...

It was nothing like I imagined, but it suited him.

I wasn't sure why, not when he stood there, watching me look around his home as calm as a lion who'd just eaten a whole gazelle. Yet while he presented the look of a mogul, this was distinctly old-school.

I hadn't been able to find anything on Google about him, exactly like I said, but I *had* researched Sicily.

I knew that they had a massive Moorish influence on their culture, and it was reflected in this space. Which told me more about him than he could possibly know.

He might be in New York, he might be a Don, he might kill people for a living and have a secret network of offices in an old meatpacking warehouse that housed a hotspot club, but culture mattered to him.

His heritage was an important part of his life.

Last night had been long, and I hadn't slept all that well, not in the aftermath of having been shuffled out of the odd corridor of kill rooms into a secret tunnel that took me out onto the roadside where I'd been dumped into a taxi that had sent me back to my place—which, in the grand scheme of things, wasn't exactly comforting. He wasn't wrong about it being a shithole—but for the first time, I felt like I could take a deep breath.

This felt like a home.

Sandalwood in the air, a pleasant heat that settled in my bones, deep carpets that my toes longed to curl into, and a sofa I wanted to read a Lisa Kleypas novel on...

This place wasn't to my taste, but it was divine and made me question what my taste even was.

Did I have something against beauty?

No. And that was this penthouse.

He led me toward a dining table, rich teak, carved with hundreds of tiny flowers, via an archway that had a high point and glinted with small touches of gold leaf. It could have been too much, but it wasn't. It was beautiful.

I registered that he held out a chair for me, but after watching me twist around to look at all the different little design details, he sank into the seat at the head of the table—right beside the one he'd pulled out for me.

I had no idea what made me do it, none whatsoever, but I ignored him and moved around to the opposite end and sank onto the seat there.

As I did, I caught his eye, and rather than finding annoyance within their depths at my rudeness, I found delight.

He *liked* my disobedience.

My stomach twisted at the sight, but the amusement in his expression had me relaxing back against the chair that was more like a throne.

A woman darted in, speaking a language I didn't understand. It could have been Sicilian or Italian for all I knew, but Luciu spoke to her with an authority that was unmistakable. While I was aware that I didn't understand the words, I knew he was kind to her.

That mattered.

So many of the men I dated were outright bastards to their help, but not Luciu.

I wasn't sure why I was surprised.

The woman, covered with a colorful headscarf, laughed, revealing bright white teeth before she turned to me, her smile dying somewhat, a facade slamming into place like she didn't trust me.

She was probably wise.

I wasn't a very trustworthy person.

Although Aoife clearly didn't think I was unworthy of her friendship, and I'd definitely been a pain in the ass to her over the years.

"Would you like mint tea or coffee for breakfast?"

Luciu's prompt had me turning away from the older woman with the suspicious eyes and answering, "Mint tea, please."

I sensed that he thought I'd go for coffee. Seeing as he'd had me investigated, I wasn't sure how he'd know that because I'd barely been able to go to Starbucks once since Christmas.

"Would you like eggs?"

"I'll have whatever you're having."

I might not eat most of it, but that wouldn't stop me from trying it. I loved new cuisines, and I knew that what they served in those fancy schmancy restaurants was sometimes night and day to the culture the eateries were attempting—and failing—to emulate.

When the woman scampered away, her long skirts brushing the floor, the long shirt-like dress moving with it, I turned back to my host and saw him studying me.

"She's Sicilian?"

"She isn't. She's actually Russian."

"What language does she speak?"

"She knows Italian, but we talk in her dialect."

"And you speak that?"

"I speak many languages."

That really shouldn't have been so hot.

"She has a specific dialect I picked up for her though." His mouth curved at the corners. "She didn't like you."

Amused that he'd picked up on that when men were usually clueless, I grinned at him. "A lot of women don't."

"Ah, but Alina dislikes you for a different reason, I'm sure."

"What reason would that be?"

That infuriating smile danced about his lips once again. "It doesn't matter. She'll ease up."

Would she really need to?

It surprised me that he allowed his staff to have opinions about his guests, but Luciu was full of surprises.

The most shocking thing of all? His actions, his posturing, didn't piss me off.

When he'd torn the shirt I'd been wearing off my body, my heart had raced in my chest—not with fear, like it might with another man, but with excitement.

Yet he could joke with the woman who cooked him breakfast like they were old pals.

Curious, curious.

"I met Alina when I liberated her and her daughter from a sweatshop over in Queens." He leaned back against his chair, his hands curving around the ornately carved pommels of the arm rests. "She was grateful."

"I'll bet." My brow puckered with consternation. We liked to think that those kinds of places existed only in developing nations, but they were everywhere.

And in the anonymity of the city that never slept, they could pop up wherever a man looking to make a quick buck wanted.

"How long ago was that?"

"Back in the early days. She's been with me for years."

He smiled when Alina reappeared, this time with a silver tray in her hands. Complete with two tiny glasses and a large, tarnished silver teapot that was decorated with flowers, which she placed on the table.

I watched as the two talked, the animation between them enough to make me wish I understood the language, before she poured the tea into the glasses.

The amber brew streamed out of the thin spout, with smoky eddies of steam curling from the rim.

She plunked one in front of me, after she snagged a small dish from the same tray, and on it, there were tiny cookies.

I ignored those and instead picked up the tea. The glass was hot enough to sting my fingers, but I sipped at it, enjoying the intensely sweet concoction.

Alina disappeared after chatting with Luciu, ignoring me entirely, but once she was gone, I couldn't stop myself from asking, "How long have you been in the States?"

"Ten years."

"Only ten? Your accent isn't as strong as I'd have thought." I was coming to realize that he picked and chose his accent. That was kind of cool.

Sometimes, he sounded American, other times he sounded Sicilian.

The Sicilian came out around me.

Because I tested his control?

How I hoped that was the truth...

"My mother is British. I learned English from the cradle." Sorrow swept over his expression like a bank of clouds over the sun on a summer's day. "She met my father when she was on vacation in Catania. Her first vacation as an adult. Theirs was a love match."

More grief shadowed his expression, and that he revealed that to me had me settling back against my own throne, feeling a little more at ease.

The truth was, I had no idea why I was here. Had no idea why I was chasing the devil when I knew he was bad—*so bad*—for me, but that was how temptation worked.

A man didn't give a woman like me a credit card with close to fifty grand on it for nothing.

He wanted something, and that was obvious, but when he revealed his emotions to me, it made things seem less cut and dry.

Less business deal and more...

Well, I didn't know what. I'd never been in this situation before.

Men gave me shit, and I gave them arm candy, blowjobs, and higher self-esteem.

Something told me Luciu wasn't lacking in the self-esteem department.

Which meant he was a wild card.

I tugged on my bottom lip. "You said that your mother lived in your house in Brooklyn. Not your father?"

"He was murdered," was his simple reply, but the torment in his voice told me more than his words ever could.

"Ten years ago?"

"Yes."

I swallowed. "Oh."

"Yes, that about sums it up."

"I'm sorry, Luciu."

He reached forward for the small glass of mint tea. "You didn't murder him."

"No. I didn't," I said. "I don't murder people often."

"Unless they deserve it?"

A smile danced about my lips. "Maybe not even then. My boss probably deserves it, but I somehow manage not to poison his coffee with arsenic."

"What does he do to deserve it?"

"Shoves all his work onto me, and I do it because I want a promotion."

"You handle all of his accounts?"

"I'm not supposed to, but yes. He's grown lazy because he knows how competent I am." My nose crinkled. "I'm hoping at the next quarterly review, he'll put me up for a promotion."

His head tipped to the side and, slowly, *carefully*, he asked, "Why would he promote you if you do all his work? He wouldn't want to lose you, would he? Not if he's reliant upon you for things he shouldn't be."

For a second, I could only gape at him, then I slumped in my chair. "Damn, why didn't I see that?"

"Because you're thinking like a worker. Not a boss." His crooked smile made an appearance, but it didn't make me feel any less stupid.

I tugged at the turtleneck that blanketed my throat and muttered, "I'm kinda mad at myself now."

"I'm surprised you let him take advantage of you."

The ominous gloom shrouding his voice had nerves filtering through me, especially with his choice of words, but I merely reasoned, "I'm sure that you've seen my background."

"I have. I see nothing to be ashamed of."

"I didn't go to a fancy college. I was lucky to get the job I did."

"Luck had nothing to do with it. He hired you because of your qualifications—"

"He hired me because of my tits," I drawled.

"You have a nice set of tits, that's for sure," he confirmed, tone wry. "But I don't think his bosses would have allowed him to take you on if you were completely unsuitable for the job. You're not a PA if I understand it."

"No. I'm an account assistant." *My boss just treated me like I was a PA.* I tapped my fingers against the table. "I intend on learning everything I can from him before I strike out on my own, but I need more experience first. I won't get that stuck in this same position though."

"Has he forced himself on you?"

"Why? Would you slice off his dick if he had?" I taunted, irritated by how he was dissecting my life.

"If you asked me to. If you didn't, I might just threaten to."

Though his statement, and the ease in which he offered it, left me shaken, I merely took another sip of tea. "Men often make advances. You can't slice off all their dicks. You'd get a reputation."

"I already have one. I'm known for my skills with a knife."

I had no idea why that, of everything he'd said, made me flinch, but it did.

"You have a reputation with a knife?" I whispered.

"I do."

"What kind of reputation?" But even as I asked the question, I knew the answer.

I thought back to last night, to the deep cut in Damian's cheek, and I pressed my finger to the same curve on my own face.

He nodded. "A signature move."

"Jesus," I rasped, unsure if I wanted to run away or...

Or, what?

It wasn't like I was a prisoner here.

He'd invited me. He hadn't forced me to come.

I'd gotten dressed, I'd locked my door, and I'd gotten into the car and out of it of my own free will.

I wanted to be here.

I just didn't understand why.

Was it because of what he said?

That we had a connection?

Only that logic was flawed because I didn't trust connections.

To my mind, they made people do crazy shit, and I had enough crazy in my life without adding to it.

I studied him, aware that he was studying me, awaiting my response.

"You're scared," he said flatly.

"Wouldn't you be? In my shoes?"

"No, because I already told you that I mean you no harm."

"Damian once told me the same thing, but he could have date-raped me," was my gruff retort.

"Never liken me to that bastard. I have my flaws, but that is not one of my sins."

"No, but you have a dozen others on your conscience."

"Are you Catholic?"

"No, but I was raised in the faith. Sort of."

"My files on your mother would not indicate she raised you that way."

"She was a party girl," I confirmed. "But she went to church. You did that when you lived in Aidan O'Donnelly's world."

"What ties you to him?"

"We lived in a—" My eyes widened as a singular realization struck me. One that made the hurt behind Savannah's confession pain me even more.

You're Padraig O'Donnelly's illegitimate daughter, Jen, and I have the DNA test results to prove it.

He didn't notice that I felt like I'd been speared in the belly with one of the forks on the table, just asked, "Where did you live? I have the address, but I don't think that is what you meant to say."

"He owned the building where we lived," I said dully.

Had Paddy known about me? Is that why we lived in a building owned by Acuig?

Of course, that had been back in the day. Acuig hadn't been as much of a big deal as it was now.

Their real estate portfolio in the early nineties had been small and crowded, high occupancy, high rents, small pigeonholes because they had a central location.

I reached up and rubbed at my forehead where an ache was gathering.

Mom could never have afforded a place like that, not on her own. Not with a baby.

Paddy or Aidan *had* to have known about me. They must have given her a discount on the rent or something.

I swallowed, somehow more disappointed by that than I'd have liked.

My father or uncle had known of my existence but had never acknowledged me, even though I'd been on the periphery of Aidan Sr.'s world since Aoife had married Finn.

I'd eaten at his goddamn table at Christmas dinner.

Had slept under his roof—

"*Cara mia*, what is it?"

Taken from my thoughts by Luciu's question, I turned to him and blurted out the first thing that came to mind that wasn't in relation to my family secret, "Gomez Addams calls Morticia that."

He grinned. "Yes, he does. But many Italians call their women that."

"I'm not your woman."

He just hummed. But there was a spark dancing in his eyes as Alina returned, this time with another tray loaded with food.

She came to me first, placing a dish in front of me, one that had a small brioche loaf on it. The bread gleamed a rich golden brown, and there was a ball on it, which made the entire thing look like a bun on a woman's head. Beside that, there was an ornate glass filled with a slick portion of shaved ice that was so thick and wet, it was unlike any slushie I'd had before.

She served Luciu then returned with the teapot to fill my glass, did the same for him, then disappeared back into the kitchen. At least, that was where I assumed she went.

Curious as to how to eat this when it seemed like a weird combination, I watched as Luciu ripped the top of the brioche off and scooped up some granita with it.

"Well, I didn't think that was how you'd eat it."

He pointed to the tip of the bun in his hand as he tore it off, and said,

"This is a special kind of brioche. In Sicily, they make it with Marsala wine and honey. This part is called a *tuppo,* and that's where its name comes from—*brioche col tuppo.* You eat that part first. You're not supposed to have it with mint tea, but it's my favorite."

"Why do you eat it in winter?"

"Because I can." Then, he shrugged. "Makes me think of Catania."

"You miss it?"

"Very much. I haven't been back in years."

"Ten?" I guessed.

He nodded. "Too much to do."

"That's sad. Life's too short."

"It is when it's robbed from you." His lips pursed, his jaw clenched, and his anger seemed to surge over his face, his rage transmitting itself to me as much as if I were experiencing it myself. "My father..."

"When he died, had you fallen out?" I queried softly, reading between the lines and wondering if that was the source of his guilt.

No rage like that was purely based on grief. On a desire for vengeance.

As little as there'd been on Google about him, there was plenty about Benito Fieri—the previous Don who'd inherited the seat from his father who'd reigned over the city for decades.

Fieri's time at the top was over now though. He had gone missing before he'd been fished out of the Hudson just before fall swept over Manhattan. Prior to his death, his youngest kid had gone missing, and his eldest had been shivved in jail.

Last year had really sucked if you had Fieri has a surname.

I had to wonder if their downfalls were because of Luciu.

He said that years of planning had led to this moment; those plans had definitely come to fruition this year. The only remaining Fieris in the city were wives and daughters. I'd read an article in the Times about the uptick in violence between Italian men believed to be a part of the mafia...

A lot of men who shared a surname with the previous Don now graced slabs in the morgues or were already buried, something reporters had been speculating on for the last couple of weeks.

I mimicked him, scooping some granita up with a spoon to see what it tasted like—espresso. Rich. Dark. Sugary.

Apparently, Alina and Luciu didn't believe in diabetes.

I did as he had, copying him, but I preferred the two separate, so I started eating the ice and left the brioche for after.

Well aware, that with every bite I took, he was watching me.

Contemplating whether to tell me the truth or not?

Not that I needed confirmation he'd argued with his father prior to the elder Valentini's death...

"We had a falling out, yes."

Pleased, not about being right but that he'd confided in me, I asked, "About what?"

"Do you really wish to know?"

"Why wouldn't I? You said I could ask you anything, didn't you?"

"I didn't imagine it would be about my father."

Though he drawled that, a flicker of amusement to his comment, I knew he was hurting.

Knew he was trying to make light out of it.

"I could always ask you about the size of your dick, but I've already felt it. Some questions I prefer to get the answers with my hands."

His eyes burned with the light of hellfire as he watched me spoon some granita up and slip it between my lips, his focus on my hands.

"So? Why had you fallen out?" I prompted before he thought he could bend me over the table and blanket me with some of that fire.

"He owned an accounting firm in Catania. He wanted me to take over the helm when he retired."

"And you didn't want to?"

"No. I didn't."

"What did you want to do?"

His mouth twisted as he reached for the brioche and then bit into it. A large mouthful that kept him quiet for a moment.

"I wanted to be a lecturer in college," he eventually answered when I made no move to fill the silence.

He watched me, waited for my response, and I knew he thought I'd be surprised, but I wasn't.

Having met each of the O'Donnelly sons, I knew that there was more to a mobster than the slick suit, the expensive watches, and the high-rise apartments.

Finn rode a desk now, but everyone who was raised in a Five Pointer neighborhood knew how it worked.

Wetwork first, then you rose through the ranks.

Finn had blood on his hands, as much as any other Five Pointer, but I'd seen him watching Disney movies with Jacob.

I knew he had to work out two hours a day because he enjoyed Aoife's cooking so much...

People were multifaceted.

They might kill or evade taxes for a living, but that didn't mean that was the sum total of their day.

Everyone had hopes and dreams—even if their career choice meant they robbed other men of *their* hopes and dreams.

"What would you have lectured in?"

"History."

"A specific period?"

His mouth curved. "You wish to know?"

"Why would I ask if I didn't?"

He dipped his chin. "I specialized in Sicilian history, then micro-specialized in my patrilineal ancestry."

"A patriot through and through," I commented.

"Yes."

I studied him, the tension around his eyes that hadn't abated since we'd spoken about his father, and I just had to know.

I *had* to know.

So, I asked, "May I use the restroom?"

He turned his gaze back onto me with as much intensity as I showed him.

"If you leave this room, and turn left, it is at the end of the hall. There are three bedrooms. One is mine; one is for Stan when he stays here, and the last one is empty. You will see I hide no wife here."

Unashamed about being caught out, I tipped up my chin. "Which is your room?"

He straightened, the chair scraping against the floor as he did so. "I will show you."

"You said yourself that your wife would live with your mother."

"She would if I was the kind of man who liked to tuck his possessions away," he concurred.

I had no idea why that sent shivers down my spine, but it did.

"And you're not that kind of man?"

He made it to my side, loomed over me a second, then pressed his finger to the curve of my cheek. "No, *duci*, I like to play with my toys."

My nostrils flared. "I'm not a plaything."

"Aren't you? Aren't we all with the right person?"

I shoved the chair backward, but he was there, his hand held out like a gentleman as if he expected me to help steady myself with his hold.

I ignored it and him. "Lead the way."

He smirked at my command but silently led me to a hallway, and with a docility that stunned the heck out of me, guided me to a room that stole my breath away.

It was like something from a pasha's palace.

A gorgeous antique bed that could sleep four was the focal point. There was no headboard, just scattered cushions that were beyond impractical.

It was also round.

And absolutely beautiful.

"This is like Hugh Heff was a Sheikh in olden times or something."

Luciu laughed but said nothing, just leaned beside the door as he watched me move around the room.

It was hard not to feel like I was at the center of a set of crosshairs with how fierce his focus was on me.

I liked it though. In fact, I more than liked it.

It made me feel relevant.

Alive.

Worthy of being watched.

Gnawing on my bottom lip at the thought, I shifted my attention to the bedroom, but though it was ornate, it wasn't feminine. And there were no distinctly feminine touches to appease my curiosity.

Small seating areas made out of large jewel-colored floor cushions were dotted here and there, cushions I couldn't imagine this indomitable man resting on. Little tables, made out of beaten silver, which had tiny ornaments on them that glinted in the light, were scattered around.

The rugs were old, had the patina of age on them, but were all the more beautiful for it.

The room scented of incense, rich and luxuriously sensual. The overtones of frankincense in here were warming and sumptuous.

Nothing about this apartment spoke of the man, yet when I turned back to look at him, I saw the twinkle of humor in his eyes and shook my head—*he was at ease in here.*

This, somehow, was the real Luciu Valentini.

"I would never have imagined you slept in a room like this," I rasped, surprise making my voice husky.

"Where's the joy in a soulless, white-walled room? Minimalism is for prisons. I, *cara mia,* am not in jail."

I thought about my exes, how their homes were exactly as he said —*soulless.*

White leather, white walls, white rugs. Silver finishes, sometimes black. All stark lines and chilly atmosphere.

"Maybe that's the historian in you," I replied, surprised by how enchanted I was by this place.

Then again, *Aladdin* always had been my favorite Disney movie.

Maybe one of these Persian rugs could take me on a magic carpet ride...

"Perhaps."

"Is everything in here antique?"

"Yes."

I bit my lip as I took in the panels on the wall, heavily carved, then studied the glass chandelier overhead that made little bursts of color dance around the space.

It was charming. Nothing that I could have expected and all the more delightful for it.

I twisted back to look at him. "Where's your closet?"

"Over there." He pointed, his grin making a reappearance because he knew where I was taking this.

It stunned me that he was willing to allow me this liberty.

Stunned and *pleased.*

With a sniff at his grin even though it scorched me from the inside out, I followed his guide and headed over to a heavily patterned doorway that I could have missed because it looked like a decorative panel.

Before I opened it, he murmured, "And what, *vita mia,* do you owe me when you realize you're wrong?"

I'd been calm. Enchanted by the room, comforted by it. His question changed all that. It made my heart pound. I felt my body begin to simmer like, after being left in the cold, it was finally starting to warm up.

I twisted around to face him and gave him the truth, "Whatever you want."

That hellfire made another reappearance, and I nearly staggered back against the wall, slumping into it as he raked me from head to toe with a glance.

No part of me was left untouched, every inch of me was caressed by his stare.

"Then you'd better quench your suspicions," he told me, but that rumble in his voice let me know exactly how affected he was.

Feeling like I'd been dumped in the Sahara at midday, when my ass was most definitely in frigid New York, I came across a modern kind of walk-in closet. So opposite to what was beyond this area that I had to shake my head. *This* was minimal, space-saving, but expansive.

It smelled of his aftershave.

I closed my eyes and sucked in a breath.

It smelled of *him*.

Intoxicating.

I wanted... Christ, how I wanted.

And I never wanted. Nothing aside from cash, *security,* at any rate.

Forcing myself to concentrate, I saw that it was open plan so every inch of it was available for my perusal. The compartments were filled with suits, and I didn't care that I was prying—he wanted me here—I went to the drawers, and I pulled them open, curious to see if a woman had left anything behind.

I found nothing.

Relief had never been sweeter.

"I never bring women here."

I jumped at the proximity of his voice, spinning around and finding him looming in the doorway.

"Why did you bring me then?" I rasped, hand flying to cover my heart.

To protect it?

Would any part of me be safe now that I was in Luciu Valentini's sights?

"Because I wish to sleep with you and seeing as you've made it abundantly clear that you don't like murder, I think I can sleep with you without you trying to kill me."

His words disarmed me enough to make me dissolve into laughter. "That's some logic."

He tapped his temple, his gaze on my hand still covering my heart. "I'm pretty clever when I try."

"I can see that."

"What's the verdict? Do I have a wife or not?"

"I met her," I insisted.

"And still you came to me last night." He tilted his head to the side. "Why did you?"

"Because I wanted to," I said with a huff. "It was just a hookup."

"Nothing could ever be so transient between you and me."

"That's all we can ever have," I countered.

"That sounds like a challenge, and trust me, you don't want to challenge me."

I squinted at him. "Are you aware you're a pain in the ass?"

"Yes, I'm also aware that you're likely the only person who'd tell me that. Aside from my brother and sister, of course." He smirked at me, a cocky twist of the lips. "Another reason why I want to sleep with you."

"Because I tell it how it is?"

"Yes. Although I didn't know this until last night." His perusal of me grew more intense as he said, "I liked it when you stared up at me with dazzled eyes; I liked it when you were breathy and shy around me, but I think I prefer this. Whoever pretended to be my wife has done me a favor."

My nostrils flared at his admission.

He couldn't...

No.

Impossible.

But...

He was...

He liked me?

He actually liked me?

The snarky Jen who had most people grinding their teeth. The bitchy Jen who only Aoife and Savannah had ever laughed at—and maybe Savannah had been making that up.

Very few people liked me. Men never did. They just wanted to fuck me, and I was more than okay with that.

Until now, I suddenly wasn't.

"Why would someone pretend to be your wife?" I questioned before I melted into the tiles beneath my feet.

"Because I'm a rich and powerful man. I'm also single. Why wouldn't someone try to take out the competition?"

"You know that makes you sound like a prick, right?"

He grinned. "You've felt my prick. You know I have no reason not to be confident."

I rolled my eyes, but my ass clenched at the memory of him pounding into me.

Then, of course, my pussy got involved.

"The next time you walk into my bedroom, you'll be naked," he rasped.

My shoulders jerked as I straightened up. "Excuse me?"

"You heard me." His eyes gleamed. "No clothes past the door."

Then, he did the damnedest thing.

He stripped, and it was better than that show I'd dragged Aoife and her sisters-in-law to last year.

With each item of clothing he dropped to the ground, he revealed every luscious inch of him that had, thus far, been hidden from me.

Long, lean muscles made an appearance, silken skin faintly brushed with hair.

His strength was there, corded and coiled. But it was how he moved that entranced me.

He was a predator.

I should have been his prey, but he didn't want that from me.

He didn't.

Why would he like me if he did?

I was a pretty predator, one who lulled men into thinking that I was a lot more docile than I was. One who wanted rich men to believe that I was vacant between the ears, that my one purpose in this world was to look beautiful and to be good in bed.

But Luciu saw beyond the surface.
I wasn't sure why or how, yet he did.
Which entranced me.
He saw an equal.
I wanted, so badly, to be that equal.
Reaching for the hem of my turtleneck, I started to drag it overhead. If we were going to sleep together, I didn't want anything between us either.

THIRTEEN

LUCIU

I DRIFTED off to sleep with Jen at the other end of my bed, curled on her side, tucked amid the satin and silk, her nudity adorning the sheets as much as the embroidery on the pillows thrown here and there.

I watched her watch me, both of us staring at one another, wondering what was happening.

I was not the kind of man who brought women home for naps, but this one... she needed gentling.

I'd brought a tigress into my apartment, and I needed to make sure she didn't maul me. It would take a strong man to tame this temptress. But her fear wasn't something I craved; her submission, on the other hand, was.

"When was the last time you slept?"

The question penetrated my sleepiness. I didn't expect to rest all that well with her here, but now I'd seen the state of her building, I didn't want her at her apartment. Not until the locks were changed.

"Two days ago."

"Why?"

"Work."

"Never stops, does it?"

"No," I retorted. "It doesn't." I closed my eyes. "I won't attack you in your sleep."

"Didn't think you would."

"You get any nearer to the edge, you'll fall off."

"I'm used to being at the edge. You saw the size of my bed."

I had. She wasn't wrong.

The pathetic pallet Alina and her daughter had slept on in the sweatshop where she worked and lived had been around the same size.

"Why did you bring me here, Lucius?" she asked, just as I was on the brink of sleeping.

Dopily, *unknowingly*, I whispered, "Because I want to see you dripping in *russu*."

I slept after that, my heartbeat evening out, my guard lowering in a way that it did for no one. Not even around my sister or brother who, though they were forceful creatures in their own right, needed my eye on them in case they fucked up because both were volatile and impetuous.

I had no idea what she was doing here, no idea what I was doing in bringing her here, but I knew that it felt right.

And I worked with my instincts.

So, I slept, and I knew she did too, because when I awoke, she was resting still, curled up closer to me than this morning, looking like a kitten amid the sheets.

Her hair was tangled, some of it lying over my arm, and her lashes rested on the top of her cheekbones as she slept deeply.

From this position, I noticed that the sheets had fallen down, with most of her covered up, but I could see the upper curve of her breasts, the shadows of her nipples.

When I'd stripped off, I hadn't thought she would too, but she'd joined me.

She'd come willingly to bed.

And had slept beside me.

A smile curved my lips, one that felt real and natural and whole.

"*Porca troia*, are you smiling?"

The fact that the intruder spoke in Sicilian kept my heart from stopping.

That my brother was in my bedroom, seeing what I was seeing, had me surging upright, rolling off the bed, and slamming my fist straight into his face.

"Get the hell out of here," I snarled at him, my voice as low as his had been.

He'd taken worse beatings in his time, so he didn't utter a word even though the force of my punch had him jerking back and nearly falling onto his *culo*. Quickly, I twisted around, making sure Jen was still sleeping.

She was.

Because Stan was capable of being smart sometimes, he swiftly scurried out, away from my wrath, taking the damn kabob he'd been eating and that had gone flying onto my priceless Persian rug with him, and I retreated to the bathroom where I pulled on a bathrobe.

Storming out, I followed my idiot brother and found him in the dining room where Alina had clearly been feeding him.

There was a platter with lamb kabobs on there as well as a massive serving of rice.

"What game are you playing, *pezz'i miedda*? Coming into my private quarters like that?"

He didn't bother nursing his jaw, just slumped back into his chair and forked up some rice. "Alina said you'd brought someone home with you. I wanted to see who it was."

"Alina's too nosy for her own good."

Stan snorted. "You've only just figured that out? I think she'll quit if you're going to start bringing women around here."

"Who's the fucking boss?"

"Not you?" he retorted with a smirk. "Not if you want to stop eating food like this."

I grunted as I grabbed one of the skewers on his plate, taking a large bite of the lamb.

There was no doubt about it—Alina cooked better than most Michelin-starred chefs.

I'd offered to set her up in a restaurant of her own, but she'd refused.

Her Orthodox background clashed with good sense.

Her daughter might have the balls for it, but that depended on whether or not Alina had her way—now Evangeline had hit eighteen, she wanted her married off.

Because that had done Alina so much good...

I'd managed to convince her to let Evangeline go to college, but I wasn't sure how I'd wrought that particular miracle.

I stared at Stan, wondering if he'd be okay with that, with Evangeline being tied to another man, and rather than prod the wound, asked instead, "How is she?"

"I took her to Aurora's." His jaw tensed. "Of all the women, that fucker Headley had to pick her."

I scrubbed my jaw. "I know."

"Thank God we had eyes on him."

"Agreed." I took a seat beside him and asked, "Had she stopped puking by the time you left her?"

He nodded. "Yeah. She was okay. Just woozy."

"Alina will ask where she is."

"I'll tell her. She likes Aurora."

"She doesn't. She says it's unnatural for a woman her age not to be married."

"Alina thinks every woman should be married. I don't know why, considering her husband was a bastard."

"Culture."

We rolled our eyes at each other, not in mockery, just in shared misery.

Alina was a pain in the ass as a housekeeper. She didn't understand that her opinion and mine didn't have to be in accord, but I didn't mind.

Not really.

My men would think me weak by accepting how she spoke to me, but I'd seen her in that shithole, clutching at her daughter like she was a teddy bear, terrified we were there for Evangeline...

My jaw ached at the memory.

What a fucking world we lived in.

I grabbed Stan's glass and took a deep sip of *vinu russu*—red wine.

Because it enhanced the rich spices of the lamb, I finished it off, placing it down and watching as he loaded it up with more from the open bottle at his side.

"You slept all day?"

"Yes."

"I heard everything went well with the cops."

"They couldn't find their assholes with a magnifying glass," I sniped. "It was mostly posturing."

"I'm surprised you let them take you in."

"A distraction was required. And you know the DA has a boner for me."

"Didn't stop them from making a full search," he pointed out, but he was smirking as he said it.

"No, but they didn't find the offices, did they?"

He shook his head. "Piu said they were untouched."

"Of course they were. I designed them that way," I said drolly.

My offices were tucked within secret openings in the building that were only made possible because Russu was based in an old warehouse.

I'd constructed the club from the ground up within its grim interior and that had come with a customized office area that the Feds wouldn't find if I handed them the key to the door.

The *Castello dii Donnafugata* in Ragusa, back home, had given me the inspiration.

The ancient fortress had been constructed by a baron with a taste for secrets and playing pranks on his guests—enemies and allies alike—as a stone labyrinth was the only exit from the edifice.

I missed home. Fuck. Here, everything was so, so... *new*.

"Then why the need for a distraction?" Stan grumbled, breaking into my wistful thoughts.

"Because Jennifer and Evangeline had to get out of there."

His eyes darkened at that, turning measured as he stared at me over the rim of his glass. "I can't believe you brought her here."

"I want her."

"And what big brother wants, big brother gets."

It wasn't a question.

"Not always. We both know that."

"When do we take over the Fieri compound? Are we still on track?"

"Three weeks. I gave the widow Fieri until then to clear out."

"Everything in there belongs to us anyway," he pointed out.

"Fieri's wife doesn't," I drawled. "Her wardrobe is of no interest to me, and whatever crap he had there that she wants, she's welcome to."

"Don't you want that Rembrandt? Could see you getting a boner the second you caught sight of it."

Lips twitching, I told him, "It's not to my taste, but the price tag is." What it represented—*triumph*—gave me the boner. "I locked it in the council room after you drove..."

"You can say it. *After I drove Accursio's corpse to* Russu."

I shot him a look, saw the pain in his eyes before he shielded his expression from me and took an overlarge bite of kabob.

When I didn't say a word, he changed the subject. "You locked all the artwork away?"

"Most of it. She didn't mind. She's twenty-three. She's more interested in the jewelry. When she saw I wasn't going to take that, she was more than happy to accommodate me."

"Stupid bitch."

"She had some nice pieces. Benito was generous."

"Why else would she be with him?"

"This is true."

"You sure the amber wasn't there?"

"I'm sure."

He grunted then forked up some rice. "I've begun mapping out the layout of the cemetery."

Interest piqued, I asked, "When can we hit it?"

"I think a few weeks. With the city being on high alert and a lot of places on lockdown because of that looting over in the Bronx, it'd be smarter to make our moves there."

Pondering his words, I plucked at my bottom lip. "I want that ring."

"I know," he soothed. "We'll get it."

"It's important."

"You're preaching to the converted," he groused. "Anyway, that's just one phase. Aurora says she thinks she knows where we can get our hands on the anklet."

"She told me yesterday."

"Cufflinks, cravat pin, necklace, tiara, arm cuffs, anklet, two sets of rings, and ear bobs. Never been so fucking interested in jewelry in all my life." He scratched his jaw. "I'm pretty sure it's a load of old bollocks."

My nose crinkled at the very British cuss word. "You've been spending too much time with *Matri*."

"She misses him."

"It's his anniversary."

"Well aware," Stan said gruffly. "*I miss him.*"

"Me too." I reached for his glass of wine and took a deep sip.

Losing men after *Natali, Patri's* anniversary… we had so much family to grieve.

"When we have the collection back together, I'll feel better," I muttered.

"It's nonsense."

"No true Sicilian would say that."

"I'm half-British."

"And I'm not?" I countered. "You and I both know curses make Sicily go around."

"True. Why else do you think I'm going along with this crap?"

I grunted, aware he was being difficult because it was easier to give me shit than to grieve the death of his friend. "Don't come into my bedroom again."

He reached up and rubbed his chin which was already starting to bruise. "Don't worry, I won't. I just thought Alina was bullshitting me."

"When have you ever known her to do that?"

"You never bring women here," he pointed out.

"There's a first time for everything."

He shook his head. "I don't get it."

"You don't have to."

"I do. The timing is terrible." His eyes narrowed. "She's a *buttana*."

"Call her that again, and I'll do more than punch you," I warned.

I saw the flash of temper in his eyes. "Fuck you."

"How would you feel if I slighted Evangeline?"

"She has nothing to do with this. There's a big difference between some slut you've taken a liking to—"

He didn't have a chance to finish the sentence. I grabbed his collar, hauled him over to me, and snapped, "What did I just say?"

Before he had a chance to back talk me, we both stilled as the gentle sound of footsteps padded down the hall. She was nearer than I thought though because her movements made themselves known to me and, a second later, she was there.

Jennifer saw me, hands clutching at my brother's collar, the threat of fratricide clearly etched into my expression, and her eyebrows surged and fell as she moved toward the table.

She'd pulled on her jeans and turtleneck, and I almost wished she'd picked up my shirt and had used that to cover up instead.

Maybe I'd give it to her so she could sleep in it tonight.

The beast that flickered to life when she was around purred with approval at the prospect. And equally raged at the idea of her wearing the one I'd torn off her this morning.

"Do you always fight over food?" she asked, her voice still sleepy.

"We're Sicilian. Fighting is in our nature," was Stan's careless retort.

He wasn't wrong.

Jennifer peered between us then commented, "That must be tiring."

She had no idea.

And where that thought whispered from, I truly didn't know.

"It is when you're fighting a losing battle," Stan replied. "But we won ours."

Triumph flashed in his eyes, and I felt it and celebrated with him.

Ten fucking years of striving, of sneak attacks, of undermining Goliath with the strength only of David...

But here we were.

I reached for the wine glass again and asked, "Would you like something to eat?"

"No. I'd better go. I have my dinner plans, remember? I slept later than I intended."

I tipped my head to the side. "I remember. I'll dress and drive you—"

Her cheeks flushed. "No, that isn't necessary. I'll just grab an Uber."

Stan snorted. "Yeah, because that's what all mob wives use."

"I'm not a mobster's woman, never mind a wife."

I wanted to argue about the first point, but I thought it was futile.

For the moment.

She wasn't mine.

Yet.

But Stan knew me too well.

She would be.

And that was why he was acting like he'd been attacked by an army of mosquitos.

I got to my feet and told her, "I will drive you."

Her scowl made a reappearance. "Do you always ignore what people want?"

"Don't think your ex was asking to have his face sliced open," Stan pointed out, prompting me to slap him upside the head.

"Shut the fuck up," I rumbled, wincing when I saw Jennifer's tension begin to creep up.

"He deserved everything he got," Stan said without compunction. "If it weren't for you making my brother chase you, we'd never have stopped him in time from hurting Evangeline." He snatched the glass from me, tipped it to her, then took a sip. "Thank you for that if nothing else."

Jennifer blinked at that. "You knew that girl?"

"She's Alina's daughter. She was there with her friends, and only because Alina trusted us to keep her safe," I said, regret lacing my words. "Her guard failed us."

Dread whispered across her expression at Stan's comment, and Jennifer swallowed. "Is he dead too?"

Stan cracked his knuckles. "Wishes he were dead, but no. Not this time."

"You have no idea how crazy you sound, do you?"

Stan smirked. "It's just getting started."

I wasn't surprised when she jumped to her feet, but Stan grabbed my arm as I made to take after her. "Best way, brother. If you want her, then she needs to know the lay of the land."

"You're a prick."

"I'm a realist. Best for her to figure *miedda* out now rather than later."

I jerked my arm out of his hold and snapped, "Give me your phone."

He did as I asked, acting intelligently for once, unlocking it before he passed it to me.

I connected a call with Lorenzo, ensuring that the car would be ready for her by the time she made it to the front entrance.

He was under orders not to take no for an answer from her.

A quick text to Giovi reassured me that the upgrades to her apartment's security were completed.

"She has your dick in a vise."

I glared at him. "Fuck you."

"She does." He shook his head. "I don't get it. She's like any other American *buttana*—"

"Watch your words," I hissed.

He shrugged. "I'll let you beat my ass if it saves you from making a fool out of yourself."

"She's stronger than she looks."

"She's a whore," he repeated, like I wasn't understanding him. "I worked on her file, Luciu. I helped make the list of all the fuckers she's skimmed for cash."

I knew he wasn't wrong. I knew she was exactly what he said she was. But everything could be made to be past tense.

Once upon a time, I'd been destined for a lecture hall.

Now, I sat here, my hands drenched in blood, the skull and bones of my enemies underfoot, ruling over my segment of New York City's underworld.

Our pasts were the stepping stones we'd walked upon that led us to today.

It was today that heralded the start of the future, and whatever he said, I wanted her to be in mine.

A woman like her... she was made for a man like me.

I knew it. Whether Stan thought I was losing my touch or not, I knew Jennifer was strong enough not to crumble under constant contact from my overbearing nature.

She fought fire with fire.

Stan might be content with an ingenue for a woman, but I wasn't.

I needed someone with guts and courage.

She just needed a helping hand to find her path.

"You're too old to have a crush," Stan bitched at me.

"You're too old for Evangeline," I sniped back, but it shut him up.

Knew why as well.

Because I spoke the truth, but he wanted her anyway.

Just as I did with my Fionnabhair...

FOURTEEN

JEN

"WHAT'S WITH YOU TODAY?"

I peered up at my boss and tried not to grimace when he glowered at me.

If he thought he looked frightening, then he was wrong.

Very wrong.

He reminded me of a petulant baby.

In fact, no.

It was the kid in that movie *Boss Baby*—that was who he reminded me of.

Dressed up in a sharp suit, his shiny bald head with sparse tufts of hair adding to the effect, he was about as impressive as a jar of peanut butter that had been sitting in the sun all day.

"Nothing's wrong with me, sir. I've been busy," I told him calmly, even though I knew exactly why he was pissed at me.

While I was doing my job, I wasn't slogging my guts out. Hadn't been for two weeks, ever since Luciu had made me see the light of day.

"The directors want to see files on the Daniels' account."

My mouth tightened at the reminder.

I hadn't spoken with either Luciu or Savannah since New Year's.

Savannah kept trying to call me, and I kept on ignoring her.

I guessed this was how she was going to try to trap me into talking to her—through work.

Exactly how she'd ensnared me in the first place.

Bitch.

As for Luciu, I didn't know what the hell his game was.

I knew that I had new locks on my door. My front entrance had security lights installed on the portico roof that were brighter than floodlights. I knew that the credit card had the amount of money on it that he'd promised me, thanks to the login details to the account he'd texted me.

But I hadn't seen him since New Year's Day.

I'd say he was gone for good, but did a man really drop fifty grand on a woman and then leave?

Did a man come to a woman's apartment on New Year's Day locked and loaded with a credit card that would wipe out every cent of her debt if he was just going to disappear afterward?

Did he keep dropping off little gifts for someone he didn't intend on seeing again?

I didn't think so.

Not unless he was the Pope, and even then, the bastard would want my eternal soul in exchange.

Nothing, after all, in this life came for free.

"Jennifer, you need to start performing better or we'll have to have a word with human resources," my boss intoned grimly, like I was supposed to be scared.

But I wasn't scared. I was pissed off. And my level of pissed-offness was only increasing.

Every day I came here, every day I worked my ass off, and all so that he could take the credit for the tax havens and corporations I worked hard to set up, while he got the kudos and I had to stay in this dead-end position.

Because I was pissed, I wasn't as diplomatic as I could be when I declared, "I'm fulfilling the terms of my contract, sir. You and I both know that I've been doing work that should be handled by you.

"I'm also certain that if the directors knew the responsibilities you'd been giving me, they wouldn't be happy. And I wouldn't be the one being blamed—you would be."

I had him.

Jason knew it.

And his mouth curved up into a sneer as he hissed, "Just work harder."

I shot him the bird as he stormed away, well aware that my coworkers acted as witness to the act.

I shared an office with six other account assistants, and the atmosphere here was competitive so it was a risky move, but I was past caring.

Not because the fifty grand in my account would pay off my debts, because debts easily ran up in a city as expensive as this one, but because I was tired of being bossed around, tired of dangling at the end of a guy's finger.

For years, Jason had taken advantage of me, for years I'd let him.

What had it gotten me?

No promotion, no perks. Not even a damn raise.

I was still on my entry salary, even though he kept promising me more at every quarterly review.

By this point, I figured I could take a job with Finn. I knew Aoife would pull some strings for me. I didn't even care that it meant working for a mob front because, right here, right now, I was sick and tired of this.

Of everything.

Of where I lived and how I lived. Of the fear a bunch of cops would turn up to have me arrested for conspiracy to commit murder, that Luciu would make an appearance, and, worse still, that Savannah would.

That she'd tell me she had informed her fiancé about my biological father.

That, now, the whole O'Donnelly clan knew about me and who I was. And, worse still, they didn't give a damn.

I stared at nothing for a second, self-pity filling me when I rarely let that happen. There was plenty of shit to be down about, but I didn't see the point in letting it get to you.

Lately, that hadn't been my mantra though.

I grabbed my cell phone the second lunch came around and tucked myself into my coat.

As I did, I headed out of my office, refusing to stay in and work like

I'd been doing before the holidays—that had a lot to do with not being able to afford Starbucks thanks to the expensive Christmas gift I'd bought Jake though—but it had also been because I wanted to impress the jackass.

As I slipped out of the door, however, I saw him.

And Luciu saw me.

Like he'd been waiting.

But he couldn't have been.

My heart leaped into my throat before the traitorous thing went down.

All the way down.

Down and down and further still until I could feel the throb of it in my core.

And that was the rub.

My reaction to his wanting me.

Men wanted my body all the time.

I rarely wanted theirs in return.

But him, I did.

I really did.

I tilted my head away from him, needing to break the zap of energy that linked us together, scurrying away before I did something stupid like think about texting him later.

Because he was standing with one of the directors, I doubted that he'd leave them to rush after me, but it didn't stop me from practically running down the hallway toward the bank of elevators.

When I made it to the foyer, I released a relieved breath and strode outside, heading to the Starbucks a block away rather than the nearest bar like I'd have preferred.

I even treated myself.

That was how riled up I was inside.

Instead of a zero-calorie cold brew, I downed a caramel macchiato, not even replacing the milk for nonfat, just guzzling down the calories, finding myself wishing, oddly enough, for a sip of that mint tea Luciu's bitchy cook had served me.

When I returned to the office a half-hour later, I didn't see him.

But on my desk, there was an envelope.

A small one. The color of blood—the guy really had a fixation with red—and it had a little bulge in it.

I knew it was from him. Just like I'd known when they started turning up on my desk.

Who else would be leaving me expensive gifts? My boss? Jackass Jason? *Ha.*

As I unfastened it, the sixth gift in two weeks, I found a single earring inside.

It was a stud, but when I raised it to the light, I knew what I was seeing.

A diamond.

A carat.

I licked my lips at the sight before I placed it back in the envelope and tucked it into my pocket.

What the hell was his game?

"Jennifer?"

I twisted around, not in the mood for my boss's BS, but when I saw Aidan O'Donnelly Jr. standing there, my brow furrowed into a deeper scowl. I forgot where I was, who I was with, I simply saw Finn's best friend, Savannah's new boyfriend, which meant he was a pain in my ass that I didn't want to be dealing with right now.

"Aidan?" I groused. "What are you doing here?"

Jason the Jackass sniffed. "This is most irregular."

"With as much money as my fiancée and I are going to pump into this place, I think you can withstand some of our 'irregular,'" Aidan dismissed without even a glance at him.

My boss's frickin' boss, one of the directors, stood behind Aidan, and I shot Mr. Crawford a nervous smile.

"Mr. O'Donnelly Jr.," there was a distinct reprimand in that, seeing as I'd called him by his first name, "would like to speak with you in conference room three."

I dipped my chin but glared at Aidan. He merely shot me a grim look by return, then held out his arm, indicating I should act as the guide here.

I stormed toward conference room three, a room no one at my pay grade ever entered, and barged in.

Aidan moved into the space behind me, and as I twisted around to look at him, I saw him shut the door, very firmly, in the Jackass' face.

Lips curving at the sight, I quickly turned my head away so he couldn't see before I shuffled toward the bank of windows that overlooked Madison Avenue and faced him once my arms were folded over my chest.

"What are you doing here, Aidan?"

"I want to know what happened between you and Savannah."

"She didn't send you to intimidate me?"

He scoffed, "Not sure anyone could intimidate you, Jen."

Call me simple, but that cheered me up. You had to fake it until you made it, right?

"It's been known to happen."

"I doubt it." He leaned against the conference table, and I saw some relief lighten his expression as he took the weight off his knee.

Aoife had lost a spleen in the drive-by shooting on her wedding day—Aidan had to have a knee replacement.

I remembered that day so well that it often gave me nightmares.

"What is it, Jen?" Aidan asked softly, seeming to sense that my mind had drifted.

"You're telling me she didn't let you know why I stormed off at the party?"

"No. I didn't even know you'd left until she came to me in tears." He scowled at me. "I don't like seeing my woman sobbing her heart out, Jen."

I narrowed my eyes back at him. "I apologize for the inconvenience, Aidan, but let me throw this out there... Maybe she shouldn't have betrayed me? I'm the one who was hurt, not Savannah."

"She said as much, but she wouldn't say why," he conceded grimly. "I don't like seeing her so upset—"

"Are you the emotion police? What the hell is it with you Irish fucking mobsters? Women are allowed to feel things, you know? We don't need our men to always fix shit for us."

"I love her," was his soft reply. "I want to make sure she's happy."

"You ever thought that that isn't your job?" I countered.

"You weren't raised the way I was."

Whose fault was that?

I pursed my lips. "She betrayed me."

"You said that already."

"That's why we're not talking, and that's why I have no desire to answer her calls."

"You're not much of a friend, are you, Jen? One mistake and you cut her out of your life like this?"

My temper surged into being with all the power of a flash flood. I straightened up and spat, "I don't have to explain jack to you, Aidan."

"That's where you're wrong," he growled. "You're not leaving this conference room until you've explained what the fuck is going on."

He'd pissed me off enough that I felt reckless, so I threw down the gauntlet and I drawled, "Once you open this can of worms, Aidan, you can't close it back up."

"I think I can deal with whatever bullshit has made you two fall out." His head angled to the side. "What did she do to hurt you?"

"She lied."

"About what?"

"I thought we were friends by chance. A love of Louboutins," I mocked. "I thought it was just one of those happy coincidences, but it wasn't. She engineered it."

"She engineered meeting you?"

I bowed my head. "She wanted to get some of my DNA—"

"What?"

"Yeah, I had the same reaction," I mocked.

"What did she want to test it against?"

"Your uncle's DNA."

He stilled. "Which one?"

"Padraig."

"A paternity test?"

Our gaze met and held as I nodded.

"Jesus." He read between the lines. "You're my cousin?" He pulled a face and a bark of laughter escaped me when his first response was: "I'm so glad we never fucked."

"Me too," I admitted.

I wasn't sure what I expected from him—a hug? A 'welcome to the clan' speech, but it wasn't, "Your friendship wasn't a total lie."

"You find out I'm your cousin and that's all you have to say?" I retorted, stung.

"What do you want me to say? I just need to fix this so Savannah doesn't look so fucking heartbroken.

"She misses you. She goddamn loves you. Whether it started off rocky doesn't mean it's like that now."

"How do you know that? What she did was fucked up."

Money worries were a constant in my life. Debt was as much of a BFF as Aoife. I didn't believe that she told me so I didn't have to worry about money anymore. Savannah never did anything without a reason, one that usually helped her career.

And that was what hurt.

That she put her career before me.

I said as much: "Aidan, she told me now for a reason. I don't know what that is, but she weaponized it." I shook my head. "I can't trust her."

"If you saw how devastated she is, you'd know you're wrong."

"Well, I'm devastated too, and getting you to fix her problems isn't going to endear her to me."

"She doesn't know that I'm here."

"She was already pulling strings. I had to get the reports on her account together for a meeting.

"I wasn't playing ball by answering her texts and calls, so she was going to pressure me where I work." I scoffed. "Real nice thing for her to do.

"You saw what Mr. Crawford was like when I called you by your first name. No way in fuck would I be able to ignore her if she brought our argument inside this building."

His hands moved to cup the side of the table. "You're right. I'll tell her not to force the issue."

"Thank you."

"Who's your mom?"

"Why?"

"I want to run this by Da."

"Why? What good would that do?"

He scowled at me. "You're an O'Donnelly, Jen. You're also Padraig's only child. When he died, he had assets. That's your inheritance."

For a second, I just looked at him, then I stunned us both and said, "I don't want anything from him."

FIFTEEN

JEN

I MADE it home a lot later than I'd have liked. I was trying to have a better work-life balance ever since Luciu had told me that a promotion was never going to be on the cards when my boss could use me, but tonight, I'd had to resolve a couple of issues with a new client's paperwork as I set up a tax haven for him in the Cayman Islands.

The local government didn't appreciate the fact he went by only one name.

I had no idea how his legal documents even allowed that, but Martinez was the only name on the contracts and the licenses and the birth certificate.

I knew wealth allowed for a lot of crazy shit to happen. Palms could be greased, and doors could be opened and banged close, but I'd never seen anything like this.

Neither had the Cayman Islands.

It was going to take a lot of capital to make them look the other way —capital, i.e., *bribes*—and I'd spent half the night trying to find out how much it would cost to get them to green light the documentation.

Wasted time.

I was tired and stressed and aggravated by Aidan's visit and, I'd admit, horny.

I was never horny.

Ever.

I knew I was using sex as a distraction but seeing Luciu before lunch hadn't helped.

Damn, why did he have to be so hot?

And generous.

So goddamn generous.

I placed the red envelope he'd left at my desk today beside the others. Each one housed a gift that I'd have given a tit for before, but I wasn't sure of his game.

There were no notes, no messages to indicate that he was trying to wheedle his way into my life.

Much like with the credit card, he simply gave with no parameters.

Which meant he was either generous or crazy.

As I stared at the six envelopes I'd propped up on my tiny kitchen table, trying to decide which it was, my cell buzzed.

When I saw 'Mom' make an appearance on the caller ID, I groaned under my breath.

I swore, the woman had a sixth sense for when I was rolling in it.

She never got in touch unless she wanted something, and she had the luck that I usually felt bad enough to give into her because I had it.

A part of me wondered if she had me watched, but she was poorer than me and had a fucker of a pimp who labeled himself her boyfriend—as if they'd waste the time of day on me.

It rang a few times, but unlike Luciu, she gave up faster. Until she rang again.

When Mr. Yardley banged on the wall, I rolled my eyes because it was on vibrate.

For a guy who was approaching a century, he had a sixth sense where technology was concerned. Either that or super sensitive hearing aids.

Because I didn't want to deal with her tonight, I switched off my phone. It wouldn't be the last I heard of her, but I'd hit my bullshit limit for the day.

I headed for the tiny bathroom, got undressed, and showered before I wandered back into the main room.

As I picked up my dinner—a banana—I moved over to the red

envelopes, feeling them call me over like they were enchanted or something.

Opening each one up, I let the contents fall onto the table and stared at them.

Some were expensive, some weren't.

I picked up the small pieces, trying not to be charmed.

There was the earring from today, a '68' in diamonds, a Times Square ball, a tiny champagne bottle, then a bright blue nazar—an evil eye—and, finally, a little mask that I'd had to Google. A Moorish head. A woman with a crown topped with fruits that were picked out in gemstones.

This was beyond generous—this had thoughtfulness behind it.

And that was even more dangerous.

Intoxicating too.

Hot and sweet?

Annihilate my heart now.

I swallowed as I grabbed a thin necklace from the small box I had that housed the minimal jewelry I owned, and pulled out a simple chain.

I wasn't sure why tonight was the night I threaded them onto a necklace, but I did then placed it around my neck before I headed over to the bed.

As I slipped between the sheets, I set an alarm on the bedside clock seeing as I wasn't about to switch on my cell for anyone—a clock I only owned for the times when my mother called—and I turned out the light to stare up at the ceiling.

The city was noisy, the apartment building was too. My mind whirred, work chasing after thoughts of Savannah, of my biological father and, of course, Luciu.

Agitated and fitful, a good half-hour passed as I tossed and turned.

Eventually, I gave up and did the dumb thing—reached for my cell phone, turning it on again when I should have been sleeping.

Then I did something I hadn't done all week—I checked my messages.

He hadn't sent anything, not even an acknowledgement of the gifts he'd left, and I hadn't thanked him. Not because I was ungrateful but because I didn't know what to say.

As I lay in my lonely bed, in my shitty apartment, I thought about the glorious grandeur of his rooms. I thought about the scent of incense in the air and the rich silks that felt so good against my skin.

That would feel even better when he was on top of me, creating friction as he thrust into me.

Closing my eyes at the thought, I sucked in a breath then did something stupid.

Crazy.

Reckless.

Exhilarating.

Me: *Send a car to my place.*

His reply was pretty much instantaneous.

Luciu: *It will be there in fifteen minutes.*

Like any sane woman, I darted out of bed and pretty much dove into the bathroom. Only, as I stared in the mirror, I didn't feel like putting on a full face of make-up. It was eleven thirty, I was tired, but I wanted... God, I just *wanted*.

Maybe it was the strange side of my nature that Luciu brought out in me, an odd type of rebellion that made me act like a teenager, but I decided I wouldn't dress up.

If he wanted me as much as the insanely expensive gifts indicated he did, then he could take me as he found me.

It didn't stop me from using one of my goodies though—a lubricating suppository that came complete with a luscious dose of CBD oil.

Once inserted, I knew that by the time the car showed up, my butt would be ready to par-tay.

Shaking said butt once I'd put my contacts in, I pretty much danced over to the closet and found myself presented with my first major problem.

Dressing down wasn't something I did.

How could I?

My appearance was my best asset.

Pissed at the foiled plan, I grabbed a pair of jeans and a workout hoodie. The jeans might have cost four hundred dollars, but the workout hoodie said athleisure... Would that confound him enough?

I tugged at the sweater, wishing it weren't Dior, but I looked sort of dressed down. Expensive, but definitely not the kind of outfit I'd ordinarily wear for a booty call.

Certainly nothing like the first time we'd fucked at any rate.

I dragged off the charm necklace and laid it down on my nightstand, then just as my butt started to feel the intended effects of the CBD oil, and things started to get interesting down below, the buzzer sounded.

"On my way," I declared into the intercom.

The only sneakers I had were a pair I worked out in, so I wasn't going to wear those. Instead, I pulled on some boots. Ready now, I grabbed my cell phone, dragged my arms into my winter coat, and was out of the door when a thought occurred to me.

I'd enjoyed sleeping with him. Not the fucking. The sleeping.

I'd more than enjoyed the fucking, but the actual closing my eyes and lying in that big bed with him, feeling safe—how stupid was that?—I'd enjoyed it.

And it was late... Maybe he'd be okay with me spending the night?

Before I could second guess myself, I darted over to the closet and selected a simple black dress that I quickly rolled so it wouldn't need ironing in the morning, a red jacket that I folded as best as I could and tucked them both into a larger purse with my wallet.

I'd feel underdressed in the morning, but that was that. At least I'd be ready for work if I spent the night.

As I locked my door, the anticipation in my blood was hard to ignore. It had nothing to do with being horny, nothing to do with the CBD, and everything to do with the one massive rush to the head that was Luciu Valentini.

I knew he was dangerous. I knew he was a lion just waiting to maul me, but if I made it out alive at the end of it, I got the feeling I'd like the mauling.

Jeez, what those lips could do...

Smirking to myself, I left my building, saw the car waiting, the driver huddled in his coat standing by the backseat door.

As I rushed over to him, I apologized, "I'm so sorry for making you wait."

His brows lifted in surprise at the apology, but he ducked his chin and opened the door for me.

Was I disappointed that Luciu wasn't there waiting on me?

Yes. I'd admit it.

But as I placed my things on the seat at my side, I decided not to hold it against him.

He owned a nightclub. Nightclub owners tended to work, ya know, at night. That meant he was at *Russu,* but he was going to leave it for me.

Or maybe he wasn't.

Maybe he was going to have me dropped off there for another fuck in his office before he had the same driver return me to my apartment.

I studied the roads, trying to see if they mimicked the route we'd taken on New Year's Day. When we did, the relief that hit me told me a lot more than I was comfortable handling.

I didn't want to catch feelings for a mobster, but maybe it was already too late for that.

Maybe they'd been caught.

With every weird thing he did, maybe he ensnared me more in his net.

Which, to be frank, made me like those fools who owned lions and tigers and let them roam around their mansions...

I wasn't just waiting to be mauled, I was asking to have my arm ripped off.

Or, in this case, my heart broken.

I reached for my phone to see if he'd messaged, but he hadn't. Instead, I started to compose a text to my mom, telling her to stop calling me because I was having financial issues of my own and had an upcoming lawsuit to deal with—she didn't need to know that the defendant was dead.

Nobody knew that yet, as far as I was aware.

When we rolled up to his building, I'd deleted and restarted the message to her four times. Angry with myself, I shoved my phone back in my purse, wishing I were capable of avoiding her manipulation but knowing it was a lost cause.

I was pathetic where she was concerned.

I knew it, owned it.

That I had cash to spare when she was fucking shady guys to make rent twisted me up inside, but that wasn't on me.

I was relieved to get out of my headspace when the car came to a halt, to get into the swanky elevator that took me up to the top floor of the mega-skyscraper, where anticipation flooded me.

Maybe it was a little more desperate than before, but I'd take that over feeling anguish about my mom's current situation.

When the doors opened up, he was there, waiting for me. A stillness about his body that made me think all that power was coiled and charged, just ready to snap.

Something had happened.

I caught that in his expression.

Something bad.

A few drops of blood dotted the forearms that were exposed as he'd raised his cuffs to his elbows. The white silk shirt gleamed against his olive skin, but there was a micro spray of blood there too.

Had he killed someone?

Or had he just cut someone?

Just.

Christ.

I knew I was getting in over my head, but when I looked at him, and he registered my fear, he did the damnedest thing.

He crooned, "Come to me, *cara mia*."

Fuck.

Fuck.

I was so screwed.

Licking my lips, I took a hesitant step into his foyer, but as I did, his scent seemed to hit me, eradicating the ocean smell from whatever they pumped into the elevators. The second it did, I was more than a goner.

I launched myself at him. Bag dumped to the ground, phone falling forgotten to the tiles, mom pushed aside, worries about coming across as too eager shoved away.

All that mattered was getting my hands on him.

He caught me.

Of course, he did.

I knew he would.

I knew that, for as long as we were together, he *always* would.

His hands cupped my ass, and I snagged my thighs around his lean hips and though his fingers dipped into the curves, his focus was on my mouth—catching it with his own, thrusting his tongue between my parted lips.

A shaky sigh escaped me as I slipped my arms around his neck, holding him close, needing more, wanting to climb into his fucking skin.

I felt him start to walk, but I didn't give a damn, just groaned and moaned into his mouth as his tongue played with mine, supping from me, tasting and tempting, eating me up like I was a piece of cake he wanted to finish.

My hips bucked, rocking into him, and when I felt his hard-on against the thick denim gusset, I nearly moaned in disappointment, needing more contact but aware that my winter gear wasn't about to allow for it.

He pulled back to nip at my bottom lip, then rumbled something in Sicilian that was pretty much a stroke of his tongue to my clit. I had no idea what the hell he said, but I didn't care.

At that moment, I knew Luciu was a miracle on two legs.

He could talk me off.

I knew it.

I just fucking knew it.

I tightened my thighs about his hips, shoved up against him, and rasped, "I want you to fuck me."

He grunted in Sicilian, which made me wonder if he even knew he wasn't speaking English.

And wasn't that even hotter?

I reached up and tried to snag his mouth with mine, tugging him in for another kiss, but he angled his head to the side, then dragged his cheek along mine. I could feel the faint bumps that came from the shadow of a beard, but when I felt the slick glide of his tongue along the line of my jaw, my arms tightened around his neck as I arched my back, my head falling too, his lips drifting down to my throat where he supped at the tender, exposed flesh.

As he nipped and sucked, he seemed to trip every single nerve ending I had there. I knew it would leave a mark, but I didn't care. I didn't have it in me to care. It felt too good.

It was so me-centric.

So focused on me.

I didn't have to entice or tease or turn on.

He was turned on.

He was ready.

Luciu knew what he wanted, even more, he was sensual. Inherently sexual. Leaving me feeling like I didn't have to stroke his ego like I would with my exes, coo over the size of his mediocre cock, or tell him that I'd orgasmed even though a kindergartner had more finesse with an eraser than he did with his hand down my pants.

This was sex.

Not a transaction.

That felt better than I could imagine.

I squirmed against him, then groaned when his teeth gripped a sliver of skin between them. Hard enough to hurt. To mark. I could pretty much feel blood pulsing up there, starting to stain the flesh a rosy red.

Whimpering, I felt myself being lowered, and I tensed before I realized we'd made it to the bedroom.

When he pulled away, I reached for him, not wanting him to go, but he shushed me, straightened up, and then began stripping. When I started to as well, he grabbed my hand, shook his head, then said something else.

You guessed it—*in Sicilian.*

I blinked at him, feeling the rumbles of that oddly aggressive accent in my pussy, and watched him drag off his tie. I studied his hands as he unfastened the buttons on the beautiful piece of silk that was his shirt, found myself enthralled by the sound of the zipper lowering, and was entranced as each item seamlessly disappeared to the floor.

In a room full of beautiful artifacts, he was the most beautiful thing of all.

Coiled power, seething anger, tender touches—that particular combination didn't make sense, but in him, it did.

He stood there for a bare second, reminding me of a conqueror of old, before his hands went to me. Carefully, he tossed off my winter coat, then surprise lined his expression when he saw my hoodie, but he didn't say anything, just helped me out of it—because I really needed the help—then growled when he saw I wasn't wearing a bra or anything underneath.

I cast his cock a glance, licking my lips when I saw how he'd been hard before, but now he was dripping precum.

Groaning, I was eager to taste for myself, but he didn't let me. His hands snapped out, the fingers diving for the button on my fly before he dragged my jeans off.

I almost grinned when he grunted at my forgotten boots, but shortly after, I was bare on the sheets—the silken sheets on his sinful bed, surrounded by luxurious cushions that made me feel like a dragon queen sitting among a treasure hoard of jewels.

And he looked at me that way.

Like I was something to be worshiped.

When he loomed over me, I half expected him to dive in for another kiss.

I wasn't wrong.

Just... the area of my lips and the kiss was.

In a smooth move, he snapped my legs apart, wide enough for the tendons to strain with the action, and then he was between them.

The noises he made, dear God.

Head tipping back, I screamed, "Oh fuck!" as he went at me like an animal. Lips and teeth and tongue, all of them working against me, working to please me, to grant me what few men had even cared about.

He played my clit like he was a virtuoso, supping and licking, suckling and teasing. It shot through me, ricocheting with all the kickback of a dozen bullets through my system, prompting me to dig my heels into the bed then surging up onto them so I could shove my cunt harder against his mouth.

That was when his eyes flashed open and ours collided.

That bolt of lightning bounded between us once again, echoing back and forth, but with each pass getting stronger, stronger, never weaker. Instead of gradually disappearing, it flared to life, booming into being so that every particle in the air around us was turbocharged. A roaring tsunami intent on laying devastation in its wake.

All the while, he feasted on me.

Wet, slick noises came from that area that should have made my cheeks tinge with pink, but I felt no shame. I didn't worry about having to please him—no, this was for me.

And he loved it.

I saw it on his face.

He devoured me, insisting on my pleasure, wanting to own it and me.

I was there for that. All in.

His tongue slipped down, thrusting into my slit, and I jerked in surprise when he rubbed his nose against my clit. Fuck, he was a beast, and I wanted to be ravaged.

My back arched as his relentless pace had pleasure growing wings inside me, and when I came, it was a transcendental moment.

So glorious and beautiful because it was for me.

At that moment, I recognized this was better than the solitaire earring.

Better than the credit card.

Sure, it didn't have a monetary value, but value came in different forms, and attention and focus and care were three such forms that were, I recognized, *priceless*.

In the madness that was this man, I was at the eye of his storm.

I froze, each muscle locking, each limb tensing up as my orgasm soared through me like the best of adrenaline highs. I rode those waves like the boss ass bitch I was, then when I sank back down, he was there, on top of me.

His mouth was wet.

I had one rule in the bedroom—no vaginal sex. Everything else was open season, but no one had just eaten me out to the extent that he had. His lips and jaw and chin gleamed with my juices. I should have been repulsed; instead, his ferocity drove me wild.

I tipped my head forward and much as he'd done in the hallway, let my tongue drag along his jaw. I used the flat of my tongue though, not the tip, going so far as to travel around his mouth, nipping the pad of his chin too.

His dick was hot against my pussy, and he rocked his hips as I cleaned him up. The growls and grunts that escaped him made him sound like the animal I'd just compared him to, and I was here for that as well.

The bestial noises had my pussy clenching down, the gnawing emptiness deep inside an ache I couldn't ignore.

When our mouths finally collided, he arched so that he could thrust a finger into my pussy. I yelped because he'd moved fast and his finger was thick, and because I needed to nip this in the bud, I pushed forward, surging upward so that I could twist us around so that I was on top.

A little surprised when he let me, I straddled him then grabbed his hands and placed them on my tits.

"*Mia*," he rasped under his breath, making me shiver with need.

I grabbed his cock and slipped it through my folds, going down, and down, pressing the tip to my asshole.

He stared up at me, something in his eyes, a mixture of confusion and need—but he didn't ask or argue—as I did what I was used to, let him sink into my ass.

I'd grown used to it over the years, so much so that I enjoyed it. Even if I didn't always get off, I liked how tight it was, I loved how each thrust was hard won, and I loved that it usually had men climaxing faster and harder, meaning they'd stop pawing at me sooner. Plus, the CBD worked wonders for relaxing me.

But this was so different. Like all the other times had taken place in the dark of night and this was the light of day.

As my body accepted his into mine, I didn't stop until my asscheeks were resting against the tops of his thighs.

When I looked down at him, I had to admit that I'd missed out on so much when he'd fucked me from behind and fully dressed.

"Damn, you're hot."

"I think I'm the one who is looking at fire, *duci*," he rasped, and Fionnabhair 'Jen' MacNeill blushed.

I'd say it was an impossible phenomenon, but was it that when it had happened before with him?

Pressing my hands to his chest, I made a circling motion with my ass before I arched up, beginning to ride him at a crazy slow pace.

His pupils turned to pinpricks, his nostrils flared, and his hands dug into me where they settled, biting into my hips, urging me to move faster, but I wouldn't.

Couldn't.

All the while, my hair fell around us in messy waves, my tits ached for the feel of his mouth or hands, but equally, I liked his fingers where they were. It wasn't like he was grounding *me*, but himself.

I felt his control snapping at the edges.

Felt it quivering like the beast I knew he housed in his soul, and though I knew it was madness, I wanted that to rain down on me.

I loomed over him, dragging my tits against his chest, savoring the hardness of his muscles, the strength of a man who used his body for labor and didn't just work out in a gym, and I hovered my mouth above his before I parted mine and quickly nipped his bottom lip.

A storm raged in his eyes.

"*Cara mia*," he intoned grimly, darkly. *Ferociously.*

I loved it.

And what sealed the deal?

He rasped something else in Sicilian, the tone just as grim and as dark. He could have been telling me he was about to cut me up into a million tiny pieces, but I didn't think so.

Not when he looked at me that way.

"This makes no sense," I whispered.

"The best things in life never do," was his husky retort, and then he helped me.

He urged me into moving, using brute strength to shift me on his lap, while he arched his hips up and fucked me even though I was in the position of control.

A guttural groan slipped from my lips as I pushed my forehead into his, and I savored the sensation of him taking over, of him doing all the damn work, but the lack of friction against my clit was a massive problem.

I surged upward so I could drop one hand to the nub and the other went to my nipple. As I caressed them both, I felt how wet I was, and that rare wetness had everything to do with this man and what he did to me.

"Are you going to come for me, Fionnabhair?"

I gulped at the sound of my hated name slipping from his sinful lips, but, nostrils flaring, I nodded and focused on my release as he pounded into me from below.

I wished I'd let him take over, wished that I hadn't tried to control this scene because I wanted to feel his weight on me, covering me, holding me down.

Moaning, I let my head fall back as I rubbed my clit, but he had me whimpering by slipping a finger into my pussy again. The thick digit rubbed against his cock as he pressed backward.

He grabbed ahold of my hand, and I let him, thinking he was moving it aside so he could caress my breasts, but he didn't—he dragged it to his face and then he sucked one finger into his mouth.

I mewled. The sound was pathetic, but what that one touch did to me packed more of a punch than when I rubbed my clit.

He sucked it between his lips, added extra suction, before pulling back and, with another growl, biting down on the pad. How that triggered me, I had no idea, but it worked. The pleasure from his cock and his heat and his thickness combined with the mischief my hands were up to had me shooting higher than before.

I screamed.

Long, loud, pained and delirious, overwhelmed and needy.

It seemed to sink into the walls, a fitting place for the cries of a woman who had always been a slave to men for their wallets, but in here, felt more like a sheikha with a pleasure slave of her own.

But what made everything so much better was when a groan escaped him too, and when, rather than using me like I was an overlarge Fleshlight, instead, he rolled up, grabbed the back of my neck and hauled our foreheads together once again so that his cries and mine, our breaths, our pleasure-loaded gasps were mingled and entangled.

I knew then, at that moment, I'd never felt closer to another human being, and if I wasn't going through the orgasm of my life, that would have scared the living crap out of me.

Instead, I was happy.

Happy when I knew happiness wasn't meant for people like me.

THE NEXT DAY

JEN: *You didn't have to do that.*
    Luciu: *Received today's gift, I see.*
    Jen: *Are you into findom or something?*
    Luciu: *nn*
    Jen: *Huh?*
    Luciu: *Non. I'm not into findom. Lol.*
    Jen: *You're going to keep using Italian with me, aren't you?*
    Luciu: *Sicilian.*
    Jen: *Did you know you sound hot when you speak Sicilian?*
    Luciu: *Se.*
    Jen: *Big head.*
    Luciu: *I'm big all over.*
    Jen: *Har-har-har-har*
    Luciu: *I'm sad you don't know this already.*
    Jen: *Sad's coming on a little strong, wouldn't you say?*
    Luciu: *But you don't know how hard we Sicilians feel things.*
    Jen: *I do, actually. Lol.*
    Luciu: *;) She has a sense of humor.*
    Jen: *He has some nerve using the third person with me.*
    Luciu: *I have several.*

Jen: *I have to go to the gym, but I just wanted to say thank you. I love the earrings.*

Luciu: *You'll like tomorrow's gift even more.*

Jen: *I will?*

Luciu: *You will.*

Jen: *I'll take a picture.*

Luciu: *Grazii.*

A DAY LATER

JEN: *I'll be the Gomez to your Morticia. Hahaha. You're nuts.*

Luciu: *Does that mean you like it?*

Jen: *Of course I do! I love the little Addams' family house charm too.*

Luciu: *One day, I want to see you in a long black dress like she wore.*

Jen: *Is this some kind of fetish?*

Luciu: *You're obsessed with my kinks, aren't you?*

Jen: *There has to be something wrong with you. Aside from the killing people thing.*

Luciu: *Oh, that thing? Lol.*

Jen: ^^

Luciu: *I have to go. You can text me whenever you want. I will always make time for you.*

Jen: <3

LATER THAT NIGHT

JEN: *I can't sleep.*
    Luciu: *You could come to my apartment.*
    Jen: *Maybe tomorrow.*
    Luciu: *Have you eaten?*
    Jen: *Yes. I've read a book. Watched TV. Nothing works.*
    Luciu: *I have a solution.*
    Jen: *I'm sure you do.*

SIXTEEN

LUCIU

I WASN'T sure if she'd pick up the phone, but I was pleased when she did.

"*Bona sira, duci.*"

I heard the smile in her voice as she greeted me, "Good evening, Luciu."

The way she pronounced my name was enough to give me a boner, but considering my circumstances, I decided it was best to keep it under control.

Watching Stan beat the living shit out of a soldier who preferred it when the Fieris ruled over the *Famiglia* was entertaining, but I'd already seen him work off his frustrations on three others who'd been conspiring against us.

My lips curved at the mere thought.

My mother would call me arrogant.

I called me smart.

"Thank you for calling."

"You're welcome," I drawled. "I'd prefer to end the night with your voice than one of my soldier's."

"I think that's a compliment."

"Trust me, it is," I joked.

"Soldiers... is what you call them?"

"Among other things."

I had an army—she needed to accept that.

Georg Hegel had once said that we learned from history that we learned nothing from history, but I didn't agree.

I learned.

I'd studied for years, had dedicated my life to understanding how war was waged back in the eighteen hundreds.

I knew how to win a war, even more importantly, I knew how to broker peace and sometimes, that involved breaking heads and rattling cages.

Fortunately for me, Stan had a taste for this kind of work.

I was more strategic with the way I wielded my own temper. Stan had a lot of guilt to burn off, understandable considering the Fieris had only learned about our father and us because of his misspent youth, so brute force was more his style.

As for me, I liked how a knife could be an extension of my arm, and how cuts and scars lasted a lifetime where bruises were only temporary.

One couldn't forge a new empire on temporary.

Scars were visual stamps of an individual's past.

Anyone who wore the demi-Cheshire Cat grin was a visible enemy of mine, and I never forgot.

Would never forget.

Once an enemy, always an enemy.

Having left my brother to his fun, I retreated to my office and murmured into the extended silence, "You should visit *Russu*."

"I have work tomorrow," she said dryly.

I'd read her file. I knew how she targeted rich men, but I found it interesting that a woman like her, beauty but with brains, had chosen the path she had.

It made me determined to find out why and how she was like that. Made me want to know every goddamn thing about her.

The stacks of files I had on her provided me with the information, but not the details. Knowing she was best friends with Savannah Daniels and that they'd had a falling out wasn't enough—I wanted to know the minutiae of their argument. The files didn't tell me what her favorite book was or where she'd gone on vacation as a child.

I wanted more.

I longed for it all.

I craved her.

A man like me wasn't born to crave. We owned. We possessed. But Jen... she was as fleeting as a butterfly. I had no intention of pinning her to a piece of card so I could stare at her whenever I wanted, but pinning her to my desk? Pinning her to a bed, to a shower wall, a breakfast table?

Yes, they were all in the cards.

"You enjoy your work?"

"I thought you were going to start up phone sex, not discuss my career options."

My lips curved. "Maybe I'd like both."

"You never say what I think you'll say."

"I imagine that's a good thing."

"It's annoying."

Her confession had me barking out a laugh. "Because you can't control me?"

She huffed. "Yes."

"Your previous boyfriends were all dumb fools?"

"They were rich. A lot of them self-made. So they can't all have been idiots," she grumbled.

They were more than fools—imbeciles for letting her go.

I rubbed my hand over my jaw as I stared over my nightclub, wondering why the sense of ownership, of pride in having built this up from nothing wasn't there tonight.

Normally, I found great satisfaction in it, but not so much today.

Weeding out rats, finding those who didn't like that there was a *Sicilian* family in charge now was growing wearisome.

Throw in the situation with the family jewels—not the ones between my legs—then the fact that the Chinese still hadn't retaliated after we'd taken their men and dumped their corpses on the front step of the house belonging to Zhao, the Dragon Head of the Triads, and I was more than ready, I recognized, to head out.

The question was, would she be my end destination?

"You're quiet for someone who wanted to talk on the phone."

There wasn't an accusation there, more curiosity.

"You're curious about me?"

"I think we both know that's an understatement," she drawled.

"Do we?" I queried, brow furrowed.

"Yes. What are you thinking about if it isn't phone sex?"

I thought I'd called with that in mind as well, but my pensive state made me question things.

"That it's an unusual feeling to have achieved everything you've been striving for."

"Show off."

I laughed. "Hardly."

"Well, I haven't achieved dick, so I can't tell you that things will work out for themselves in time because I don't know."

"You gained a degree," I pointed out.

"I did. I worked hard for it too." She heaved a sigh. "But I'm not doing what I want."

"No? What do you want?"

"Well, I should clarify. I'm doing what I want, just not where."

"Explain?"

"Do you know Finn O'Grady?" she asked carefully.

"I do. He's the money man for the Five Points."

She hummed. "You know he's Irish Mob, okay, good. Well, I was still at school when he met my best friend. They're married." A laugh drifted from her lips. "It's weird that you don't know this already. Although, I guess it could be in my file."

"You visit with her a lot," I excused.

"I notice you don't apologize for having me investigated."

Men like me didn't apologize. "I'm sorry for invading your privacy."

I sensed her hesitation. "I didn't expect you to say that."

"I can apologize for the action, but I don't have to feel bad for it."

"Never let it be said you're not honest." She laughed.

"I told you that I would always be honest with you within reason."

She huffed. "Anyway, when Aoife and he started... I don't know if you could call it dating. One minute, they didn't know each other and the next, they were getting married. But when he first cropped up, I was at school, and I worked at Aoife's tearoom.

"I knew he was in the Irish Mob, but when I learned what he did, I'd admit, I was fascinated. I took longer to graduate because I took some specialist courses."

"In tax evasion?"

She chuckled. "Legal tax evasion. Have you read this file on me from cover to cover?"

"Three times."

"I didn't know I was so fascinating."

"I think we both know that's a lie."

"Luciu," she rasped, but I heard the pleasure in her voice.

"Fionnabhair," I crooned, loving how her breath hitched.

"I hate that name," she told me, much as she'd told me before.

"It suits you."

She sighed. "When I was little, nobody could pronounce it."

"You earned a nickname?" I guessed.

"Flea."

I snorted. "Like the insect?"

"Yes. I have no idea why I'm telling you that."

"Because I'm interested, and you wish to talk?"

"Maybe. I'm feeling exposed. Expose yourself."

More laughter tripped from my lips. "If I were there, I would."

"I'm sure," she purred. "But seeing as you're not, you can just tell me something private."

My smile died as I admitted, "I feel like all the private information on me is sad."

"Maybe. My past has sad parts too. They all make us into who we are."

"Very true." I scoured my brain for a happy memory though. I'd had a long day, and I wanted to hear her laughter not feel her pity. Truthfully, I'd had a fantastic childhood in a wonderful country that I missed. "Remember I told you my mother is English?"

"I do."

"My very English grandfather could never pronounce my name. Or Stan's for that matter. He could manage Aurora, though he was the one who nicknamed her Rory." I chuckled softly, pleased by the memory because I hadn't thought of him in too long. "We used to spend a part of the summer with him and my grandmother.

"It was quite idyllic. They lived by the coast, at the top of a cliff, and we used to race down to the beach every day when the weather was fine. Which, because it's the UK, is rare. Even in summer.

"Grandfather would follow us, grumbling about us being Sicilian heathens, but he always allowed us to drag him into the water, always played cricket with us."

"Wait, is this why Stan is called Stan?"

"Yes," I said dryly. "He tried, but he could just never pronounce the name right."

"What did he call you?"

"Luc." My lips curved. "I haven't been called that in a very long time."

"Not even by your brother and sister?"

"No. They've always been able to pronounce my name," I teased, happy when she laughed.

"When I first heard yours, I was scared about saying it wrong too. I kept thinking I was going to call you Lucy Liu. You know, the actress?"

I smirked. "Wouldn't be the first time it was butchered by an American."

"May I call you Luc?"

"You may. Just not in bed."

"Maybe there won't be another time in bed."

"Oh, *cara mia*, we both know that's a lie."

"Arrogant," she chided.

"Smart," I countered, amused at that particular choice of adjective considering it ran adjacent to my earlier thoughts. "You know you wish I were in bed beside you."

"You'd take up too much room."

"You could go to my apartment. I wouldn't want to disturb your rest."

"You wouldn't take up that much room."

"Would you like me to come tuck you in?" I teased.

"No. But you could talk me off."

The statement had a rumble starting in my chest that made me feel like a fucking animal.

What was it about her?

How the hell did she make me feel like a primal fucking creature that forgot all sense of decency and purpose?

I scrubbed a hand over my face. "I'd prefer to slide into that pretty pussy of yours rather than think about your fingers filling you."

Her gulp was audible. "I think I'd prefer that too."

"Fionnabhair?"

"Yes, Luc?"

"Why do you always instigate anal sex?"

"Do you really want to know the answer to that?"

"Wouldn't have asked if I didn't."

"You know how to kill the mood."

"I know how to bring it back."

"You'd better," she groused. "And if I tell you something sad, then I want something sad from you as well."

"Agreed." I shifted away from the view of *Russu*, and instead, slipped into my seat and rocked back, mentally preparing myself for whatever she was about to say.

If whoever hurt her was still alive, they wouldn't be for long.

"My mom had a lot of boyfriends when I was young. Mostly, they left me alone, thank God. If I felt unsafe, I used to run to Aoife's place. She lived really close by so it wasn't a problem."

"They touched you?" I snarled, straightening up, muscles locking as the ramifications of her words hit home.

"No, no," she replied quickly, before muttering, "I don't mean like that. They used to beat her. She always knows how to pick the violent ones."

"She lives still?"

"Like you don't already know."

I just grunted—*I knew*. Her mom was a hooker, and her pimp was a sketchy Russian who had ties to the Bratva. I didn't think the money from his woman's whoring went to the brotherhood, but I'd yet to establish what his links were aside from his having a brother in their ranks.

"One boyfriend did try to hurt me though. I was seventeen and made the stupid mistake of trying to take a shower in the bathroom—locked door and everything. Dumb, right?"

My nostrils flared with outrage. "He... touched you?"

"No. Well, yes. He tried to. He slipped on the water and hit his head on the toilet after we...fought."

"I hope it killed him."

"It didn't. Mom was furious with me," she said sadly. "I stayed with Aoife for a while after that."

"I'm relieved you had a safe place to land back then."

"Me too," was her hearty reply.

"What did he do to you?"

"He said I was just like my mother. Always asking for it." She sucked in a breath. "Back then, I wasn't like I am now. I was different. Not shy or anything, but cautious.

"I was dating this kid at school, and I was pretty sure I loved him, but I'd seen Mom's boyfriends change overnight so I didn't exactly trust men.

"When he called me a whore, told me I was like her, I made my boyfriend wait until senior prom for us to have sex for the first time. He cheated on me before that happened."

"The *figghiu ri buttana* didn't deserve you."

Her laughter was soft. "Thank you for the vote of confidence. It's funny, but it doesn't hurt so much right now. As far as last year, I'd get all teary-eyed over it like an idiot."

"He hurt you."

"Yes. He did. But he was just a kid, and I was..."

"Why are you telling me this, *vita mia*? Not that I don't want to know, but why?"

"Because it became this big thing in my head. A stupid kind of ridiculous logic that made me feel better about myself.

"When you told me Damian could have raped me, the first thing that slipped through my mind was that all these years, I'd never let a single man inside my pussy for a reason, to own my fucking virginity, to hold it up like a trophy or something, and Damian... Well, that had been stolen from me too."

Tension filled me. "You've never had sex? Vaginal?"

"No. Not consciously, anyway."

The bastard that I was, the possessive, jealous, covetous fucker roared with satisfaction...*and* fury.

It made me doubly glad that I'd killed that cunt for even the possibility of having taken what was mine.

Mine.

I'd said it before, but now the word slammed into me.

Like a punch to the gut.

A hit to the head.

Virgin or not, gold digger or not, she was mine.

But for all that it came as a shock, it settled in my bones like I should always have known this. Like I was a fucking idiot for not having picked up on this important fact sooner—

"Luc?"

I heard the hesitancy in her voice and understood it.

If I sounded like I was angry, then so be it. I was. Just not at her. "You will choose when you grant me the gift of your virginity, Fionnabhair," I told her gruffly.

She paused at my words, then bitterness leaked into her voice as she muttered, "I might not have anything left to gift."

Fuck, I wished I'd thrown Damian into the sty at the pig farm the *Famiglia* owned, alive. Wished that I'd allowed him to feel the animals eating him, while I watched the realization of his predicament form in his eyes, overtaking his sanity—

"It will be a gift because *you* are a gift," I corrected her firmly, not willing to let her drag herself down.

"I'm not, Luc. I'm really not." She heaved a sigh. "This got grim, fast."

Though the tension in me made my muscles feel as if they were on the verge of cramping, I managed to grate out, "It is my turn to share a sad tale, is it not?"

"Yes," she rasped. "If you still want to."

"Why wouldn't I? I'm a fair man."

She hummed. "Not sure everyone would agree with that."

"People who work with me, who work for me, who enter my world know the harsh reality. You don't reach this position by being kind."

"I'm entering your world, Luc," she said. "Does that mean I'm fair game?"

Her point stung. "I will always keep you safe."

"You can't promise that," she retorted immediately. "Did you hear about what happened with the O'Donnellys just before Christmas?"

Unsure of what she meant, I didn't answer immediately.

Was she talking about how I'd gifted the O'Donnellys the Archbishop of New York? How I'd brought him to them ready for them to kill for what he'd done against the middle son?

Was she talking about the aftermath? An aftermath I'd undoubtedly triggered?

Manhattan's Cathedral was burned to rubble now because of me.

Because of the steps I'd taken to reach this point. This moment, this position.

I'd bartered with the Irish for peace so that I could approach the *Famiglia* with a token of strength. With no leadership, nobody of authority in power, the Italian mafia had been crumbling into dust.

At war with both the Irish and the Russians, they had no choice but to accede to me when I took control of the Fieri compound and promised them a ceasefire.

Most complied with that ceasefire, but there was still some dissent within the ranks. As if to underscore my point, I heard a scream from within the corridor where Stan was at work.

Clearing my throat, I asked, "What happened?"

"You know the New World Sparrows?"

A snort escaped me. "Do I? Aren't they on every news channel around?"

"Well, yes," was her prim retort, "but I don't know what news channel you listen to, do I? Is it one of those stupid ones or one of the smart ones?"

I laughed. "Touché."

"They targeted Savannah. Did you know that? Because of her exposés on them?"

Savannah Daniels had exposed the Chief Justice of the Supreme Court as being a part of the underground society who had riddled its way through the United States' government like it was a block of cheese.

City officials, senators, gubernatorial candidates... The Sparrows had infiltrated every part of American society, staining it with its corrupt taint.

It was one thing to be a part of a brotherhood of criminals, to profit on illegal acts. It was another thing entirely to pretend to be the face of law and order but to commit crimes against humanity that not even I would perpetrate...

"I saw her interview on TV," I confirmed. "I know she was targeted."

"They blew up the gate to the compound. They stormed it, Luc." I heard the tendrils of fear in her voice. "We were shoved in a safe room, but Savannah refused to go. She's like that. Crazy."

"You disapprove?"

"Hell, yes, I do. You're supposed to keep your butt from getting killed, not hurl yourself into the fire." She harrumphed, the sound loaded with enough disapproval that my smile widened. "I saw their safe room, Luc. It was insane. We could have stayed down there for weeks, and it was furnished like it was a part of their house."

"It is for them," I told her.

"Do you have one in your house?"

I sighed. "Yes. For my mother."

She fell silent. Then, "It scares me."

"Nothing in this life is safe, *cara mia*," I told her quietly. "The cathedral burned, shootings happen, bombs go off, and life carries on. Are you going to walk away from something..."

"From something?" she prodded when I hesitated.

"From something beautiful," I said thickly, "out of fear?"

"You think it's beautiful?"

"I know it is. I don't... you know what I told you, Fion—"

"Okay, we need to stop this. Call me Fi. I can deal with that. If you're not going to call me Jen or Jenny, then call me Fi."

I chuckled. "As my Celtic princess wishes."

She huffed. "Shut up."

"Am I wrong, Fi?" I demanded arrogantly. "I told you I don't date—"

"This isn't dating," she interrupted again.

Wasn't it?

"Not like regular dating," She conceded after a few seconds. When I stayed quiet, she grumbled, "It's still good. Just odd."

"I like odd."

"That comes as no surprise. Okay, I didn't mean to get deep. Carry on with your show and tell story."

"I'll get deep with you one day, Fi," I half-growled, aware that her breath caught at my words. "But—" The need to see her tonight was imperative though. Whether she knew I was there or not. "I won't pressure you."

"That's a lie if ever I heard one," she said drolly. "But I'll take your BS with thanks and hug it tight."

"As long as it's between your tits, I can stand for that."

"I'll make sure to titty fuck the hell out of it. Do you want to know something hilarious?"

"Of course."

"People get her name wrong."

"Who?"

"Savannah."

"She's Dagger Daniels' daughter," I drawled. "How do they get it wrong?"

"I don't know. I read about it once—The Mandala Effect. Anyway, it really pisses her off."

"If I meet her again, I shall use a different name to greet her."

She chuckled. "You'd do that for me?"

Didn't she know I'd do worse things for her? *Had* done worse things for her?

I didn't bait the bear, just hummed. "Of course."

When she snorted, I smiled but it faded as she prompted, "Your turn for story time."

"*Patri*, my father, he wanted me to take over the family firm."

"I remember. That's why you got your MBA."

I grunted. "Yes. But when I enrolled in another course, he was furious with me. We didn't speak for three years."

"Three years?" she blurted out, her surprise clear. "Three? Wow, that's a long time for a guy who lives with his mom."

I had to grin. "She lives with me."

"If you say so."

"I do. But yes. He was a stubborn man."

"I wondered where you got that from."

I clucked my tongue, even though I was pleased she found a likeness between us.

I let my desk chair swing from side to side as I thought about my *patri*. A strong man, and an indomitable one, but loving. Kind. Just difficult when it came to business. "He wanted me to conform and—"

"I could have told him you're not one of the world's conformists. You're a rebel with a cause, Luc."

"I wasn't back then." My smile was sad even though she couldn't see it. "When he died, we were still estranged. I was living in the UK, at a university there. I was a Rhodes' scholar, but not even that was good enough for him." How did that still have the power to hurt? My voice turned gruff as I rumbled, "The day I got that call..." A shaky breath escaped me as I rocked back in my seat. "I was devastated. Mother hasn't gotten over his death to this day, and I know our whole family hasn't either."

"Does being Don bring you closure?"

"I thought it would."

"But it doesn't?"

"No."

For a moment, all I could hear was the gentle soughing of her breaths before she whispered, "Do you have any regrets?"

"No."

"None at all?"

"Aside from the wish that I'd had a chance to call him before he died? No. Everything happened that led me here, to this time, to this place. I have to believe that happened for a reason."

I didn't want to think that it had gone down this way because it was supposed to lead me to her, but I couldn't get away from the mental image of her dressed in the Anjou rubies.

I could see it so clearly. Her head held high, neck erect and straight, shoulders back as she stood tall, doused in rubies like a fucking queen...

My dick ached with the power of what that imagery did to me.

It was better than anything Sports Illustrated could cook up.

"Thank you for telling me that, Luc."

"There are plenty sadder stories out there," I murmured, scanning the report in my in tray. I flipped through the pages, looking at a *vicchiareddu*, an old man, who'd been in prison for far too long and for a crime the poor bastard hadn't even committed. *That* was sad.

"Most origin stories are grim," she pointed out.

"Knowing this, are you still frightened of me?" I rasped, needing to know and needing that answer to be no.

She hesitated, but slowly said, "No. Only, please don't give me a reason to be scared of you."

"I'll try my best not to."

"I guess that's all I can ask." She sighed. "I'm going to go to sleep."

"Okay."

"Night, Luc." Her voice was so husky that it added to the ache in my dick.

"Rest well, *duci*."

I'll see you later.

SEVENTEEN

LUCIU

THREE DAYS LATER

I PULLED on the death mask, smirking at Stan's idea of a joke.

Moorish heads were a symbol of Sicily, so while the masks shielded our identities, they didn't exactly hide our nationalities.

Still, as I looked at him and he looked at me, both of us cracked up.

And when we turned around to face our crew, spying more of the iconic faces, I decided Stan's idea of a joke was in good taste.

The masks depicted a Moor, one with heavy brows, a full and thick beard, rounded cheeks, and a wide forehead, but Stan had come into his own with a crown that was topped with basil leaves—a symbol of good luck.

Legend had it that a Moor had fallen for a Sicilian woman, but when she'd learned he had a wife and family in his homeland, she lopped off his head to keep him with her forever and planted basil leaves in his skull.

Never let it be said that Sicilians weren't a passionate race.

I came by my skills with a knife organically.

"Who knew you were capable of whimsy?" I mocked as we jumped into the Range Rover and set out for Green-Wood cemetery.

"I'm capable of many things," Stan retorted with a sniff. "You just underestimate me."

My lips curved as we neared the long driveway that led to the famous steepled gates that guarded the cemetery and had done for centuries.

"Hey, pass me a cupcake."

"Now? Seriously?" I rolled my eyes. "Where are they?"

"Glove box."

Finding a six-pack of Little Debbie cupcakes in there, I laughed and hurled one at him.

Hand on the wheel, tearing the packet with his teeth, he dove into the cupcake as we pulled up, a ways down the lane.

A guy came out, wearing a security guard's uniform. Stan flashed his lights, then we heard the creaking of the gates as they opened up.

It was pretty cloak and dagger, very Cold War in its approach but I wasn't about to complain when, with the guard letting his flashlight beam at us as a prompt, we set off again.

My heart quickened as we passed through the gates, and in the dead silence of the graveyard, I found myself praying that Fieri had been buried with my family's relics because if he hadn't, I didn't want to have to set up a fucking hunt for those as well.

He'd been wearing them at the last public event he'd been photographed at—the funeral for that fucker of a son of his.

I rarely let myself feel anxiety because there was no place for that in my world. A strong front, an impervious facade kept my family and me alive, and that mattered more than my concern, but in this, I *was* anxious. I had feelers out across the goddamn globe for the Anjou-Valentini jewels, and I didn't need to be hunting down forty-million-year-old pieces of amber too.

The rubies were rare enough to leave a trail. The amber pieces were a family legacy. Nothing special. Ridiculously expensive but not unique enough to stand out on the black market.

A needle in a haystack.

While I was in the dark as to the location of the Fieri fucker's grave, Stan knew where we were going, but I felt his tension like it was my own.

We both knew what this meant.

Sicilians believed in curses, our folklore and legends were a part of our culture as much as the sunlight in summer was. Whether we were rational and logical beings or not, we believed in superstitions enough that we knew not to mess with them.

While I didn't think the House of Valentini hinged on whether my future wife wore the jewels or whether I sealed my personal missive with the house crest which adorned the signet ring, I preferred not to risk it.

This grunt work wasn't for the likes of Stan and I, but it spoke of how important these pieces were to us that we were willing to get our hands dirty in the worst imaginable way.

My grandfather had been the first Valentini who'd been without them and look what had happened to him.

I reached up to rub my jaw, but when I did, I came across the latex mask. "I'm ready for this to be over," I muttered, tugging at it and grimacing at the slick perspiration it left behind.

Stan heaved a sigh. "Agreed."

In the dark, with no lighting thanks to the late hour, our headlights were the only source of illumination in the entire cemetery.

That meant when we saw her, sitting there as if she were on a throne, the first thing Stan and I did was reach for our weapons.

But, as we neared, I saw that she was sitting on the butt of a submachine gun, the nose of which she'd burrowed into the ground.

"Like it's a fucking stool," Stan rasped, his mind on the same track as my own.

A goddamn *expensive* stool.

As he braked to a halt, I asked, "You know her?"

"No."

She didn't squint at the full force of the glare from our headlights, but I saw how she'd covered her face in paint.

It reminded me of those contour lines I'd seen Aurora put on her face when she was going out in warpaint. But this was a little like Dali had reached her brushes first.

"She's messing with face recognition software," Stan whispered, even though I could pretty much guarantee it was impossible for her to hear us.

I dipped my chin. "More comfortable than wearing masks, I suppose."

"If you do it on the regular."

"I'll deal with her," I told him grimly, starting to open the door, but he grabbed my hand.

"No! This could be a trap. You're the Don now—"

"Exactly. I'm not about to stay behind my desk just because I'm at the top of the tree." I said it loud enough for the men in the back to hear.

It was important they knew I was still going to get my hands dirty—that hadn't changed with my promotion to the head of the *Famiglia*.

Italian Dons allowed their soldiers to be cannon fodder.

Sicilian Dons didn't.

I shrugged off Stan's hold and jumped out of the van. As I did, the woman's shoulders straightened slightly, but she didn't reach for a weapon or even pull the submachine gun, which had to cost over twenty grand, out of the ground. Her blatant disregard for it spoke of an ease with weapons that told me she didn't need them to get the job done.

Arm her with a straw, and she'd probably be deadly.

Cautious, and rightly so, I moved toward her, my booted feet crunching on the snow-covered grass when I saw that her hand was tipped out, something settled on her palm in a silent offering.

I also saw what she'd done.

In the shadows, beyond the puddled glow from our headlights, Fieri's casket was out on display.

The top had been destroyed, and his pungent, putrid stench was filling the air, whacking me in the face as I approached it.

"That bacteria will kill you."

"I've been inoculated against worst germs than what a corpse can excrete." Her voice was cool, calm, emotionless. "You're the Don."

I arched a brow—not that she could see that behind my mask. "I'd be a fool to admit to that, wouldn't I?"

She hummed. "I recognize your voice. You're fortunate the cameras here don't pick up sound."

Thanks to Stan having staked out the area over the past couple weeks, I knew she wasn't lying to me.

"Does it matter if I'm the Don or not?"

"It matters. Seems you've got more guts than this one. Died a coward's death. Tossed in the Hudson." She smirked. "I don't think you were behind his death."

"No. We," I stressed the pronoun. "weren't. If we were, then we wouldn't be here." I eyed the casket and, trying to stay calm, kept my voice free of inflection as I stated, "You've been graverobbing." What the hell was her game?

"Just got there before you did."

Miedda.

Had she found the Valentini amber?

My heart rate pitched at the prospect.

"Why? Who sent you?"

"A friend of yours."

"Didn't know that I'd had enough time to make friends with anyone in the community." Plus, her helping me out seemed more like a fucking power play than a favor.

Was Aidan O'Donnelly Jr. behind this?

"Oh, there are always people out there, watching. You've gained a lot of interest over the period of your very short tenure, Signore Valentini." She got to her feet, and her eyes danced over to the van.

I lifted a hand to stay the men. "If you pull any sudden moves, I can't promise my brother won't put you down."

"I'd like to see him try, but I appreciate the warning."

"Maybe it was a threat."

"Maybe it was, but I don't think so." She smiled. "I come bearing gifts. No reason for you to get your hands dirty."

She passed over a Ziploc bag, and my heart both soared and sank as I saw the three pieces floating in a filthy solution. The stones were coated in it, grim and gore, rotting flesh, but I saw the tiniest glint of silver.

"It's only alcohol. His body was a mess from being fished out of the water anyway. It's not a pretty sight in the coffin."

I let the liquid slosh around the pieces of jewelry as I raised the ring to the light. It was difficult to see but I knew what was missing—the 'V' that had been inscribed on there.

Once upon a time, my grandfather used the ring as the indentation in a wax seal on letters.

Now, an 'F' stood pride of place.

It made sense. Logically, I knew Fieri would have done that, but it still hurt to behold.

I thought about what *Nanna* had said before she died, the importance she'd stressed on finding these pieces, and I tucked the dirty jewelry into a pocket before I turned my attention to the woman.

"You have a name?"

"I have many names."

"Don't we all," I mocked.

"Some are more interesting than others," she agreed. "I've heard that you like to make your victims smile."

Despite myself, my lips curved. "I do. In pain, there is beauty."

She huffed. "Not sure they'd concur, but that's an intriguing way of looking at it." She slicked her finger along her cheekbone, mimicking the cut I was growing famous for—the half-Cheshire Cat grin. "You should squirt lemon juice on there. Makes it even more painful if you're looking to create more beauty."

"Wouldn't it begin to cauterize the wound?"

"Worth the initial sting though. That'll have them crying."

"Tears aren't something I crave."

"No? What then?"

"I wish to make a memory." More than that, *a legacy*.

She tipped her head to the side, and slowly, she held out her hand, but this time, angled to the side, and I knew why.

I slipped mine into hers. "Luciu Valentini."

"Dead To Me."

"Ahh, infamy is something we both appreciate, I see."

"I like to make a memory too. Take them out with a smile on their face. Just a different kind to yours."

"Should I be concerned that a 'friend' has sent you to me—you, a known CIA operative who gives her marks gifts before they die?"

"I don't send this kind of gift." She hitched a shoulder. "They don't want you dead. In fact, they want you very much alive."

"And you're not going to tell me who they are?"

"No." She grinned. "Where would the fun be in that?"

She twisted back to the gun and dragged it out of the ground, while keeping the muzzle down. I could feel the tension back in the car, heard the click of a bunch of safetys and the lowering of the windows on the Range Rover, but I knew she meant no harm.

At least...

"If I open the bag, will it emit a neurotoxin?"

"I told you. I have no wish to kill you. Today, it doesn't suck to be you."

I blinked at that then watched as she headed away, much as if she were at a catwalk show, heading deeper into the darkness like this was midday and we were in Central Park.

I watched the sashaying of her hips, not because they were mesmerizing but because I wanted to see if she was about to make a swift turnabout, and when the darkness swallowed her up, I felt the relief overtake me.

I hadn't feared for my life, but when a man set out to rob a grave, only Christ knew how the evening would end.

"Who the fuck was that?" Stan barked in my ear, making me jolt because I didn't realize he'd left the car.

"Dead To Me."

"That nutcase bitch who sends a gift bag to the dudes she's gonna kill?"

"She kills women too," I pointed out wryly. "I don't think she discriminates."

"Feminism for the win," Stan grumbled. "What did she give you?"

"The jewelry." I handed the Ziploc bag to him. "They're there."

I wandered over to the mausoleum where the open casket lay askew at the foot of the steps that led to the entrance, glanced at the rotting corpse of the son of the man who had killed my grandfather, pinned the crime on my great-uncle, and who had had my grandmother running across the ocean with her tail between her legs fearing for my father's safety.

This man had killed my innocent *patri*, had taken away the love of my mother's life, made my grandmother die of a broken heart, and had set me on a path that I'd never wanted, had never asked for.

Becoming the Don wasn't supposed to have been my future, but instead, it was all I'd ever know.

Until I managed to die of old age or until an enemy slayed me to take my throne—much as this fucker had passed.

Was I looking at my future?

Or would I be one of the lucky ones who died with his family around him?

Was anyone ever really that fortunate?

"What is it?" Stan asked, stepping up behind me.

I heard the men in the car getting out and wandering over, clearly wanting to see for themselves what was going on, and I didn't chide them.

Every man here was Sicilian.

They'd fought with me.

They'd lost brothers and uncles and fathers and grandfathers just as I had.

We all had a vendetta against the Fieris.

I hadn't intended on doing this, but seeing as Dead To Me had taken away my satisfaction in uncovering the body on my behalf, I reached into my pocket and pulled out a box of matches.

Because he knew me too well, Stan murmured, "Marcu, grab the gasoline from the van."

"How big of a burn do you want, *capo*?"

"Enough to tarnish Green-Woods' pretty reputation," I rumbled.

"Let's make some memories," Stan concurred, inadvertently repeating what I'd told Dead To Me, cackling as Marcu rushed over with the petrol can, which he proceeded to slosh all over the corpse of our enemy.

We hadn't taken his life, and that stung. It meant our vengeance was still unsettled. But as we basked in the flames for a handful of seconds before we drove off to evade the sirens that would be incoming shortly, I felt a semblance of peace settle in my soul.

We were one step closer to our end goal.

And apparently, we'd picked up a friend.

Funny how peace felt like heartburn, wasn't it?

EIGHTEEN

JEN

AFTER ANOTHER TWO calls from my mother, calls which I somehow managed to ignore even though the guilt was still worming its way through my system, I fell asleep at long last after sinking back a glass of wine.

I hated wine, but I drank it at times like these. Cristal was more my thing, but that didn't make me sleepy, and after a day like today, I needed sleepy.

Work had been hell with my boss blaming me for Martinez's lack of a first name which was causing havoc in the Cayman Islands, and then with my mother still calling me, I was starting to feel trapped.

I knew where I'd feel free, but Luciu was a silken promise taunting me with every breath he took.

Finding solace in him was just asking for trouble...

Wasn't it?

I went to bed with him on my mind because thinking about him was a lot nicer than worrying about Mom and getting angry about work, so when I woke up and I saw him, at first, I was pretty fucking sure I was dreaming.

Bleary-eyed and dopey, I almost rolled over and went back to sleep, but I heard him sigh.

And that sigh sank into my bones.

I gave him my attention again, registered that he was sitting at the table, watching me, and as my pulse raced in my ears, I let out a short, sharp, surprised scream.

Like he had the volume on his hearing aid turned to max for just these moments, Mr. Yardley banged on the wall between us, making me jump.

Who didn't jump? Not at my scream or the banging on the wall?

My midnight visitor.

Hand falling to cover my heart which was getting more of a workout than when I went running, I rasped, "You shouldn't be here."

"I wanted to see you."

His words triggered a peculiar flicker of heat that began throbbing in my core. The soft ache came as a surprise—especially as my heart was pounding so hard it made me feel nauseated.

I rolled upward as he asked, "Are you wearing the charms?"

It took me a second to figure out what he was talking about—his gifts. They hadn't stopped coming since we'd slept together again.

I wasn't a 'one and done' kind of lay, at least.

"Yes," I told him huskily.

"You weren't wearing them last night. Or the night you came to my apartment."

Still dazed by his presence, my voice was more groggy than demanding as I groused, "How do you know I might be wearing them?"

"Most of the envelopes are empty."

"Maybe I threw them away."

He cocked a brow at me. "You've left them leaned up against that lamp for days."

A soft, shocked breath escaped me, then I wanted to smack myself. What about his behavior came as a real surprise? Really? Truly?

"How many times have you done this?" I demanded.

I knew he was cray-cray jealous, ridiculously possessive—I'd learned that when he'd smacked his brother when he thought I was still resting that first time I slept in his bed—but this was different.

Right?

"Three. Since our call the other night."

"Why?" I felt fear start to chime into being like a death knell that had me wishing he weren't between me and the front door.

My red alert button had been smashed and had informed the cops in the tri-state area that I had a nutcase in my apartment.

"Because when you look at me, you don't see a mark."

That jerked me out of my growing fright. "What?"

"Don't demur," he said calmly, talking like frickin' Mr. Darcy again. "We both know I speak the truth."

"Have you ever seen the movie *Twilight*?"

He paused. "No." I heard the laughter in his voice. "I, a thirty-six-year-old man, have never watched Twilight. Does that come as such a surprise?"

"You could have watched it with a girlfriend. Most girls were obsessed with it when they first came out."

"I don't have girlfriends."

I snorted. "You have girlfriends."

"I didn't say I was a virgin, *cara mia*," he drawled. "Just that I've never dated. I've never needed to."

"Ever?" I squinted at him with disbelief because Stan had indicated Luc was a Ladies' Man. Capitalization required.

"No. Never."

So, he was a fuckboi. I really did have a type.

His gaze was measured as it settled on me though. Calm. Level. A message hidden in the depths, one that made my heart pound.

Needing to change the subject, I blurted out, "Edward, he's a vampire, sneaks into Bella's room every night to watch her. Just FYI, it's creepy as fuck."

"Maybe for the person sleeping."

"No, Luciu, for the whole world." I clicked on the lamp on the nightstand, squinting as it revealed him in, dammit to hell, all his glory.

He wasn't wearing a suit, which was unusual. Instead, he had a black sweater on, black pants, and black boots.

And he looked *fine*.

Better than fine.

So good you could spoon him up.

Not that I told the insaniac that.

"You trying to look like a cat burglar? Or is this the outfit you wear to sneak into a woman's apartment?" I sniped, wondering why the air of danger around him was more turbocharged than normal.

And why it was like a lock in a key that made me want to lift the covers and invite him into my bed...?

Now who was the lunatic?

"I have a key." His lips curved. "I don't sneak into anywhere."

"I'm a light sleeper." You had to be in this part of the city. "You snuck in, or I'd have woken up."

"Semantics."

I grunted. "Oh no. This isn't a case of poh-tay-toh, poh-tat-toh."

"I have no idea what that means."

"Never mind," I said with a huff. "That's beside the point. You're in my apartment, Luciu. Without my agreement."

"We both know I mean you no harm."

"That doesn't matter." I swallowed, then insisted, "This is creepy."

"Perhaps." He tilted his head to the side like he was trying to understand the strange behavior of a wild animal.

Was it really so strange not to want to wake up to find him sitting in my room, for God's sake?

And why, though I wanted to slap him upside the head, was I fighting a smile?

"Did you like today's gift?"

I narrowed my eyes at him. "Are you changing the subject?"

He laughed. "Yes."

"Don't do this again," I groused, aware I sounded snooty. "It's fucking weird."

"How else will I see you?"

I huffed. "Are you for real?"

"I'm very real. We lead busy lives, *vita mia*. I find peace in watching you sleep."

"It's weird, Luciu. We could just go on a date."

"You've been screening my calls."

That had me stiffening. "How do you know that?" And dammit, I had.

Waking up with him had been too good.

Dangerously good. Enough that I couldn't repeat it. Not immediately.

Sleepy mornings after with smiles and kisses weren't meant for women like me.

"How do you think?"

"That weird guy with the monobrow? I thought I saw him at Starbucks, dammit—"

"Can I show you something?"

I scowled at him, aware he was changing the subject again. "If it's long and gets hard when you prod it, no."

A snort escaped him. "I don't need to show you my dick, Fi. Although, you bring it up often enough in regular conversation for me to suspect that you miss it."

It was my turn to grunt. "Yeah, yeah, you keep telling yourself that."

He wasn't technically wrong.

I brought up his cock more than he did, but in my defense, it was a nice cock.

And life was all about the technicalities.

"What do you want to show me?" I grumbled, well aware that I was going to dig myself into a deeper hole if I didn't jump out of this one.

He got to his feet, then raised his arms in a way that told me he meant no harm. Only, I believed him without him having to do that.

If a man was to be judged on his actions, I could say that Luciu was a fucking freak.

But he was a gentleman with it.

Did that make the weird stuff he did better or worse?

He took a seat on the side of the bed and passed me something from his pocket.

When I saw the Ziploc bag, I squinted at it, then I fumbled blindly for my glasses.

After I slipped them on, he made a soft, clicking noise with his tongue that had me peering at him.

"I didn't realize you wear glasses."

He hadn't? I'd have thought he knew my prescription by now.

"Only after I get ready for bed," was all I said.

His eyes roamed my face, and I was pretty sure that he explored it far more than Magellan had done the Earth.

He mapped every crevice and every nook, devouring me more thoroughly than any part of me he'd plowed.

It was intoxicating.

Everything about him was.

I didn't know how he achieved that, just that he did.

Nipping a tiny chunk of my bottom lip between my teeth, squeezing down hard on it, I raised the Ziploc to eye-height and frowned. "Amber?"

"Yes."

The liquid the stones were in was brown and pink and all kinds of disgusting. Like shit slurry.

"What's it in?"

"Alcohol. I changed it twice. Sorry."

That had me blinking at him. "So, this is clean by comparison to how it was before?"

"Yes."

"Where did you get them?"

His lips twitched. "You should think carefully about the questions you ask me, Fionnabhair."

A soft breath whispered from me at his utterance of my name. A name he'd said when we were having sex. A name I hated but that, on his lips, made shivers dance down my spine.

"I hate being called that. I thought we'd agreed on Fi."

"We did. But sometimes I wish to call you by your full name. Jen," he scoffed. "A beautiful name for sure, but Fionnabhair's the name of a Celtic princess. Why would you be simply Jen when you could be that?"

"I never thought of it that way."

He hummed. "You Americans never do. The past means nothing to you."

"Haven't spent much time on TikTok, have you?" I chided. "People do all kinds of shit to preserve our history in America."

He wafted a hand. "Not like in Sicily."

I almost asked him why he was here if he liked it so fucking much in Sicily, but hell, I wasn't sure a single O'Donnelly had ever stepped foot in Ireland, but they identified more as a patriot of the motherland than the homeland.

Pursing my lips at the thought and wondering if all mobsters were hypocrites, I asked, "You'll tell me the truth if I ask you a question?"

"Ordinarily, I'd say yes. But in this instance... Within reason."

"What reason?"

"Plausible deniability."

I knew what that meant. "For my safety or yours?"

"A mixture of both."

I studied the jewelry and asked, "It matters to you?"

"The House of Anjou-Valentini was an ancient royal line in Italy. The Valentinis are direct descendants."

Whatever I might have expected him to say about the bag of crap with silver bits inside it, it wasn't *that*.

"Jesus! You're, like, a prince?"

He smiled a little. "Hardly. But once upon a time, my ancestors were. These are the relics of that past. There's a set for the eldest son of the line and his wife. I think there were others, but they were lost a longer time ago than the sixties."

"Amber for the husband?"

"Sè. Rubies for the wife." His smile died. "'*When the Valentini queen drips in the blood of the earth, only then will the family's star continue to rise.*'"

"What's that?" I whispered, wondering why shivers rushed up and down my spine.

"Something my grandmother told me when I was younger."

I thought about what he'd said the first time I lay in bed with him: *I want to see you dripping in* russu.

I'd initially thought he meant blood, and hadn't that been a nice way to go to sleep? But now, I wondered if that was what he'd meant.

Russu was red, or so Google had told me. Rubies were undeniably red. And weren't they the blood of the earth?

While terrifying, his sleepy words hadn't induced me to climb out of his bed at the time. Not when I'd been able to...

Jesus.

I'd watched him sleep too.

I was in on this creep factor crap.

"Where did you get these?" I repeated, even more curious now and eager to switch mental gears.

"Sicilians are superstitious by nature, did you know that?"

"Wikipedia told me as much."

"You googled my country?" He sounded pleased, so I just huffed.

"Once."

His eyes gleamed with delight. I was almost sad when that delight began to fade. "They say that a Valentini who reigns without these is a Valentini who will not reign for long."

"Who told you that? Your grandmother?"

"*Se*." He eyed the jewels. "When Benito Fieri murdered my father, she survived him by five days."

Stunned, I whispered, "She died of a broken heart?"

"Decades of protecting him from his past, tucking herself away in a farmhouse in Sicily when the Italians butchered her husband, finding shelter for them both in the bed of an impoverished farmer who didn't deserve her, and all for those bastards to get him eventually." I was used to seeing fire in his eyes, but this was a different kind entirely. This wouldn't just burn a person; it'd cremate them where they stood. "Her heart couldn't stand it." His words were far softer than that look.

"I can't imagine her grief," I rasped and, unable to stop myself, reached out for his hand.

As our fingers tangled, he tightened his about mine, then murmured, "She gave me the same story my grandfather had told her on their wedding day.

"With *Patri* dead, and how he was murdered," he tacked on, sounding choked for the first time which told me his father hadn't endured a pleasant death, "she knew they'd found us. She knew we were in danger too."

"What story did she tell you?"

"For the wedding reception, he draped her in jewels. A tiara, a necklace, a ring, cuffs at the wrists, an anklet, and earbobs."

"She must have looked amazing."

"She looked like his queen."

"You have pictures?"

"We do. They're at my home in Brooklyn."

"One day, I'd like to see them," I admitted softly, and it was then that I recognized how he looked at me—always with heat. But at my request, an inferno blazed into being. An inferno that surpassed the incendiary storm of moments before.

He nodded. "I'll get them out so you can see them."

"Thank you."

"He told her the story of the Valentini queen, and how there was no king without her."

Wow.

Heart fluttering a little, I tipped my head to the side. "Were they in love?"

"I think it was an arrangement but either she fell for him fast or she fell in love with his memory. As a farmer's wife, her life was not easy. As my grandfather's wife, she'd never have had to lift a finger—she was bitter."

"Understandable."

"She was strong. A good woman. Stubborn. She could have chosen a different path, but she didn't." His interest drifted back to the bag in my hand. "She reminds me of a certain someone I know."

My cheeks did that thing they only did around him—*turned pink*. "Did your grandfather lose these? Why are they so dirty?"

He scratched his jaw. "*Nanna* said that they were stolen. Have you heard of the Camorra?"

"No."

"They're Sicilian transplants too. Their territory is in LA."

"Are you friendly?"

"We used to be. My grandparents visited their territory to celebrate a wedding. *Nanna* wore the family's finest... but there was a robbery at the place they were staying. A few men were killed, and the jewels were stolen and broken into separate lots."

A gasp escaped me. "The Camorra were in on it?"

"So the story goes."

His noncommittal tone had me frowning. "You don't think so?"

"No. I think Benito Fieri's father was behind it. I think he caused dissent between the Camorra and the *Famiglia* who were always allies so that when he took down my grandfather, the Camorra wouldn't retaliate."

"Jesus. It's like something from a book."

"I wish it were," was his gruff rejoinder.

"Me too," I said with a wince. "I'm sorry, Luciu."

"It's done. In the past."

"But you're still living by their mistakes. Your life has been dictated by their actions. That's a burden no child should have to bear."

"Perhaps."

With his gaze on the bag, I reached forward to tilt them toward the light. I saw murky amber with that famous inner glow, I saw tarnished silver, and one stone had some kind of etching on it. But the alcohol solution it was drowning in was a disturbing color. Not just brown, but oddly red too.

As much as I'd enjoyed story time with a Don, curiosity and concern entwined as, slowly, I asked, "Where did you get these, Luciu?"

He caught my eye and slowly, calmly, told me, "From Benito Fieri's casket."

THE FOLLOWING DAY

LUC: *I saw these and thought of you.*

Two hours later

Fi: *You know, at some point, I want to read this file you have on me seeing as you know that I love roses.*

Luc: *You like to keep a man waiting.*

Fi: *It's one of my talents.*

Fi: *Scared I wouldn't answer?*

Luc: *Maybe.*

Fi: *I'd ask how you know that, but I know you or one of your creeps, at least, still have eyes on me.*

Luc: *Stan did.*

Fi: *He's your brother, but that doesn't make him less of a creep.*

Luc: *This is true, lol. I'll tell him that.*

Fi: *I don't think he likes me.*

Luc: *He doesn't have to.*

Fi: *One minute, there's someone at the door.*

Five minutes later

FI: *You didn't have to.*

Luc: *You don't really understand the concept of gifts, do you?*

Fi: *I guess not. Thank you. I didn't know I wanted FroYo. Or roses. They're beautiful. And the FroYo is delicious.*

LUC: *One day, you'll taste gilatu in Catania. Then you'll never want to eat FroYo again.*

Fi: *You shouldn't talk like that. I might not want to go to Catania.*

Luc: *Only a madwoman wouldn't want to go to Catania.*

Fi: *Maybe I'm a madwoman. I'm talking to you, aren't I?*

Fi: *Though you did have FroYo sent to my door, so I guess I'm not that crazy.*

Luc: *If you'd met Nanna, you'd know what crazy is.*

Fi: *In the blood, is it?*

Luc: *Lol. As she got older, she gave less of a damn. Saw her holding a knife to the throat of a man who was trying to sell her encyclopedias once.*

Fi: *That must have been hard not getting them to press charges.*

Luc: *It was definitely something I was glad my father had to deal with.*

Fi: *You really miss him, don't you?*

Luc: *I really do. Enjoy your FroYo. If they didn't include the freeze-dried raspberries, tell me.*

Fi: *Why? What will you do? Cut off the server's hands?*

Luc: *That can be arranged. See, you're bloodthirsty too.*

Fi: *Pfft.*

Luc: *If they hadn't included them, I'd have sent you more. I can be civilized too. ;)*

Fi: *I need a file on you. How am I supposed to learn anything about you if I don't have one?*

Luc: *Just ask me. I'll answer.*

Fi: *Anything?*

Luc: *Anything. Just remember, you might not like what I have to say.*

NINETEEN

LUCIU

THE KNIFE SLIPPED through the soft flesh of the Triad runner's cheek as I peered into his eyes, demanding in Mandarin, "Why did your Dragon Head attack us?"

As far as I knew, they were the only faction in the city who weren't out for our blood.

Though Yang moaned, his eyes were filled with hatred. I didn't expect him to like me after I sliced and diced his face, but how close-mouthed these fuckers were was starting to piss me off.

The last Triad in our warehouse, we'd held this bastard since New Year's, and he'd yet to break.

I'd already made ground meat of his cheeks, but seeing as they'd begun the tedious process of healing, instead, I carved them up again, watching with grim distaste as the prick remained silent.

Jamming my sleeves higher up my forearms, I pressed my hands to the armrests of the chair where he was duct-taped into place and told him, "Silence does you no good. You're a dead man whether you help us or not, but we can keep this up for quite a long time." I shot a smirk at Stan. "Maybe you should bring out the IV drip. Let's pump him up so we can drain him dry."

Yang's nostrils flared, his blood-soaked, dirt-streaked, sweat-mottled face turned pale beneath the dirt, but he rasped, "I know nothing."

"Bullshit," Stan muttered, at the same time as I said, "So, you are in possession of a voice. You must know something," I continued. "Why were you sent in on New Year's?"

I had a feeling it was just to cause mischief. To get the cops heading over to the club so they could raid it.

Did I smell the act of 'caponing' in full bloom?

It was possible, that was for sure. I was new to the position of Don, but I'd been leading my merry band of men for a while now.

In some circles, I'd gained a rep and though there were plenty of dirty cops in my pocket, with the city up in arms with all the crap that was going on politically in this country, it made sense to target a new would-be leader of the Italian mafia.

But if I was right, that meant the Triads were in cahoots with the NYPD, and I couldn't see that.

For them to have struck on New Year's, that meant they either had beef with the *Lobos Rojos,* the gang from whom I sourced my weapons, or they'd heard about my taking Damian Headley, Jen's ex. If that was the case, then he was more than just a fuckboi bastard who needed to die.

Interesting.

Rolling with that theory, I intoned, "Damian Headley."

The second his eyes flickered with recognition, I hummed, then I reached over and with a flick of my wrist, sliced his throat.

As he sputtered and blood gargled out of the wound I'd just made, I backed away from the arterial spray, then leaving him to die, moved out of the kill room and into the hall toward the end of the corridor.

Stepping inside, I began to undress because wetwork came with the clue in the title—it was wet—and dumped my clothes in the furnace that churned along at all hours of the day and night.

With my clothing being incinerated, and my shoes set aside to be cleaned, I slipped into the room off this one in my briefs, moved over to my locker, gathered more clothes together before I began showering off any other blood that might have landed on me.

It was a very industrial set up, but I didn't need marble in here. I needed it to be easily cleaned of DNA. Caponed was one thing, being indicted on a murder charge was another.

As I cleaned up, I heard movement out there and knew it'd be Stan.

"He could have had more to say."

I didn't reply because I didn't answer to him, and he knew it.

"Fuck, Luciu. He might have known more!" he growled after a couple minutes of silence where only the tap-tap of water hitting the tiled floor and the sloshing sounds of soap made themselves known.

"He told me what I needed to know, *frate*," I replied after I finished up and grabbed one of the towels, using the Sicilian word for 'brother' to make a point and shut him the hell up. "Now, unless you have a fascination with dick, get out of here so I can get changed in peace."

"What did that *pezz'i miedda* have to do with anything? Why did you mention him?"

"Stan, you possess a functioning brain. You might waste it on weed sometimes, but your mind is sound. Figure it the fuck out."

His brow furrowed. "This all started on New Years'."

"Yes." I growled under my breath as I headed over to the vanity and began shaving, letting my little brother figure things out for himself.

Stan was smart, but he rarely applied anything other than his fists to a given situation. It was sad considering his leanings toward academia before *Patri's* death.

As I shaved, he kept throwing postulations at me, suppositions and calculations, until his conclusion and mine were of the same accord.

"What the hell could the Triads want with a weasel like that fucker?" he groused, his voice turning hoarse with rage.

"I don't know, but we need to work it out and fast. If they're willing to send men after him…"

"I always knew that *buttana* was trouble," he groused under his breath.

With my jaw half-covered with shaving foam, I twisted around, grabbed him by the shirt collar, and shoved him against the wall. "How many fucking times?"

It took less than a second for his head to collide with the tiles, but even though that collision had to have hurt, he snarled, "Fuck. You."

"I told you to watch your fucking mouth where she's concerned."

"And look at the goddamn mess she's rained down upon us."

"As always, you're too busy fucking thinking with your mouth than processing the facts with your brain." Mostly because my temper was more hair-trigger than his own, which meant that he knew to keep it under control where I was concerned. "My investigation into Jen is the only reason we spared Evangeline from that *figghiu ri buttana's* end goal.

"Something you were grateful for on New Year's. So, instead of cursing her and calling her a whore when I've warned you about that, you should be goddamn thanking her.

"You need to get this crush of yours under control if it makes you lose your head like this. Anyway, Evangeline doesn't need to be dealing with it."

His nostrils flared, and he bit off again, "Fuck. You."

I smirked. "You pissed at the fact I called it a crush? Or the fact that you want something you can't have?"

"Fuck. You."

"This conversation is turning boring," I said with a chuckle as I let him slide his feet back to the ground after I pinned him in place. Before I turned back to the vanity, my chuckle waned, and I stared him square in the eye and rasped, "Watch yourself."

Cursing under his breath, he stormed out, leaving me in peace at long fucking last.

Finishing up, I splashed on some aftershave before I started to dress again. Pulling on my suit, I headed on out and found my shoes as impeccably clean as they were the day I bought them.

Sliding into those, I felt my skin tingle with warmth from the furnace which raged on as it burned my blood-spattered gear, and when I moved down the corridor, I found that Yang was already being handled as well.

A quick tilt of my wrist showed me the time on my Rolex, and I hummed as, after a quick visit to the safe in my office, I left via the warehouse part of *Russu*.

Lorenzo was waiting, the engine idling, and as I ducked into the backseat, I sighed when I saw Stan was there, his face turned away from me, looking out onto the river rather than at me.

I was more than fine with that.

Catching up with the messages I'd received while I dealt with Yang, my brows rose as I drifted through an interesting one.

"A contact says an ancient tiara has entered the market in a jewelry store specializing in antique pieces in Aspen."

Not even that exciting news had Stan doing anything other than shrugging.

I rolled my eyes at his juvenile sulk but quickly told my contact:

Me: *I'll arrange a visit. Make sure the item isn't on display until I arrive.*

Lockhart: *Of course, Mr. Valentini.*

The Anjou necklace, the item we'd regained on New Year's Eve, was still being tested for authenticity. But if we had that and the tiara, those were the largest pieces, and having them checked off the 'shopping' list would come as a massive relief.

With that dealt with, I sent out some emails to cops in our payroll, asking some questions about the Triads and others about Damian Headley.

By that time, we'd made it to Jen's apartment, and as I climbed out, I was surprised when Stan did as well. When he stepped onto the sidewalk, I frowned at him. "What's your game, *frate*?"

He shrugged. "Just want to hang out with my older brother. Not a crime, is it?"

"You know full well I'm going to Jen's."

"Maybe I think it's time we break bread—"

"The only thing she'll want to break is your goddamn nose if you sneer at her the way you do around me." And I wouldn't fucking blame her. Hell, I'd even applaud her if she landed a hit.

His top lip quirked up into a smirk. "I think I can handle myself."

"You just can't handle your mouth."

"You sound like *Matri*."

"No, I sound like everyone who's ever known you. Aurora says the exact same goddamn thing so don't make out like this comes as a surprise."

He shot me a sneer, but I blanked him, choosing to open the front door and go inside.

"What a fucking dump," Stan groused.

He wasn't wrong.

I grimaced as I headed up the stairs, every fiber of my fucking being hating that Fi lived here in this grody palace of dubious charms.

"Not ideal," I agreed.

"When are you moving her out?"

"Who says that's what's going down?"

"You? Whenever you talk about her, you get moon-eyed." He clucked his tongue. "It's pathetic."

"You're pathetic," I retorted. "Mooning over an eighteen-year-old."

"She's in college."

"So?"

He just grunted. "I leave her alone."

"Until when? You can pounce?"

The only reason he hadn't been sitting at Evangeline's side while she recuperated from the drugs she'd been doped with was because his thirst for blood made him need to see Headley suffer.

It was right then, right there, that I realized the difference between my feelings for Fi and his for Evangeline.

In those circumstances, I'd have stuck to Fi like glue, then when she was better and no longer in need of me, I'd have gutted the motherfucker.

There would be no chain that could tether me, nothing that could stop me from unleashing a world of hurt on whoever thought they could hurt my woman.

Mine.

Was this what love felt like?

As if your feelings weren't your own? Like they hinged on someone else's safety? Their wellbeing?

I frowned at the thought, falling silent as I let myself into her apartment, Stan traipsing along after me, although he headed deeper into her space.

Pulling out my regular seat, I waited for her to arrive home. Not that I sat here often in the light of day. Instead, the night usually cosseted me, shadowing me as I watched over her.

I'd watched *Twilight* two nights ago and had to admit, that Edward boy *was* creepy.

It should have discouraged me from visiting again but sometimes, in the silence of the night, the sighing breaths of a woman who mattered to you, the world at rest, a man could hear his thoughts.

Thoughts of a present that was long in the making.
Of a past that would never be.
Of a future that could be worth more than the present.

I plucked at my bottom lip as Stan rummaged through the kitchen drawers, aware that Fi would be here soon.

It didn't take long. Barely five minutes.

Because these shithole walls were paper goddamn thin, I even heard her raised voice.

"No, Mom, I won't. I don't have any to give."

Curious, I tipped my head to the side. She might have changed the login details to the account I'd given her, but I knew for a fact she hadn't touched a dime of the money within it.

She had money.

She wasn't touching it.

An odd gold digger—not that that came as much of a surprise. Most things about Fionnabhair were distinctly unusual. It was probably why I liked her. She never did what I thought she would.

I sat beside her bed while she slept, and when she awoke to find me there, she didn't call the cops—she gave me a lecture on *Twilight*.

I gave her a set of charms and a pair of flawless diamond earrings—she wore the charms, but the earrings remained safely in the pouch.

"Look, I've told you to stop calling me. If I had something to give you, I would. You should leave him. No normal person would stay with him when he was threatening you with that kind of—" A snarl escaped her. "I don't have time for this. I have a late-night meeting I need to get to. Please, if I had it to give, I would."

Brow furrowed, I heard her mutter, "Bye," then there was a clunking sound. She didn't immediately open the door, but I heard her sigh and whisper, "Fuck," under her breath before there was the distinct rattle of keys.

As she walked in, she jolted in surprise at the sight of me, her hand flopping onto her chest before she scowled. "I think you should give me my keys back."

I smiled at her. "Why would you want me to do something like that?" I reached into my inside pocket and handed her an envelope.

She squinted at it, then huffed, before she twisted around and closed the door. When she clicked the lock, she turned back to me, and then, yet again, she surprised me.

She slipped out of her high heels and padded over to me with bare feet. One hand moved to my knee as she leaned over to press a soft kiss to my lips.

"Hello, Luc," she whispered.

Deep in her eyes, I saw something that hurt my soul—*sorrow*.

Because of her mom?

"Hello, Fi."

She gave me another kiss then backed away, ignoring the red envelope entirely.

See? Unusual.

The apartment was so small that I didn't have time to warn her about Stan before she was already in the kitchen—her scream of fright had me wincing, as did the instantaneous banging on the wall from the neighbor.

"Yes, Mr. Yardley!" she hollered. "I know. I'm sorry." Then she stormed back into the room and snapped, "Why don't you just bring all the Italian mafia with you, Luc?"

"She calls you Luc?" Stan grumbled, moving behind her.

"We're Sicilian," I corrected her. "Not Italian."

"Semantics. Everything is semantics where you're concerned."

Stan grunted. "Are you North American or South American? Mets or Yankees?"

"I'm a citizen of the world, and I hate basketball."

I laughed. "Even I cringed at that, and I hate baseball."

She winked at me before she glowered at Stan. "Who said you could raid my kitchen anyway?"

"You have no food in there to raid," he complained. "How is it a kitchen without any food?"

"You don't look this good by eating," she said with a sniff.

My lips twitched at Stan's look of horror. "You have nothing in there," he repeated.

"I eat out. I don't do cooking." She scowled at him before she demanded, "What are you doing in my apartment anyway?"

"I wanted to get to know you better?"

"Why?" was her wary reply. "You don't need to know me. I don't need to know you. The fewer Sicilians I know the better. I have enough on my plate with him." She tipped her thumb at me as she stormed over to her closet.

"She has more clothes than Rory," Stan rumbled, eyeing the overfilled space.

I nodded. "I know. Wait outside. I'll bring her out. We'll grab some food."

"I'm sure *Matri* would love to meet her," he mocked.

"I'm sure she would," was my calm reply. "But not tonight."

He stared at me for a long moment. "You want them to meet?"

I gave him another nod which had bewilderment flickering into his eyes then back out again.

With a shake of his head, he did as I asked and left, so I got to my feet and walked over to her. She was changing, and beneath her skirt, she had a silk slip that clung to her hips in a way that made me want to crush it in my palms.

Fuck Stan for being here, or I would've.

Instead, I comforted myself by hauling her back against my chest, banding one arm beneath her tits and the other, I splayed over her stomach. "I like getting a kiss as a welcome," I whispered in her ear.

"You're turning domesticated."

"So are you," I retorted as I sucked on her earlobe. At her shiver, I murmured, "We're going out to eat."

"I'm tired—"

"You need food."

"I already ate."

"Salad," I scoffed. "You need pasta."

A sigh hiccupped from her lips as I nipped the tender morsel of sensitized flesh. "O-Okay," she agreed, more amicably than I imagined.

Exactly what I needed.

"I can help your mother if you want me to."

She immediately tensed. "Leave it, Luciu."

Luciu.

Now I'd heard Luc on her lips, I preferred it that way.

"Fi," I said softly, "I can handle things."

"So can she. She doesn't have to stay with him. He whores her out," was her bitter snarl. "Can you imagine staying with a man, thinking you love him, when he puts you through that?"

"All the more reason to help her—"

She pulled away, but her head jerked to the side in a physical rejection of my words. "I've been through all this with her many times. She won't help herself."

I reached for her again, holding firm when she tried to back into the tiny closet even more. "The offer is there. What kind of man would I be if I didn't at least ask, hmm?"

Fi stopped struggling at that, and the slump in her shoulders told me she wanted to help her mother but knew it was futile.

In all honesty, I knew it was too.

Women in those situations either died in them or ended up killing their partners to escape. Alternatively, if they were fortunate, the man would die of natural causes, and then they'd mourn them...

Grimacing at the thought, I pressed a kiss to the crown of her head, pleased when she twisted around and huddled into me.

"I hate saying no, but she'll take everything I have to give and it's never enough."

"She's done it before?"

"Every couple years, she wipes me out. Sorry, you didn't need to know any of this."

"Why didn't I?"

She didn't answer but surprised me by saying, "Don't call me Fi in front of other people."

"Why not?" I asked calmly, prepared to argue.

"Because..." She pulled back to look up at me, a pucker appearing on her brow. "It's a secret name." Her chin tipped up. "I won't call you Luc in front of anyone else again."

My lips curved, but I bowed my head and kissed her like we had all the time in the world when we probably had five minutes because Stan was a slave to his stomach.

As she slumped into me, her body molding against mine, her curves filling all the hard lines of my form, I took her mind away from the situation.

Then, when Stan started banging on the door, I pulled back with a sigh.

Satisfied with the hazy desire in her eyes, anything to replace the sorrow of before, I murmured, "Wear the earrings I bought you, hmm?"

She nodded. "Where's my gift again?"

I smiled and reached for the envelope in my pocket then handed it to her.

Sometimes her predictability was as satisfying as her volatility.

TWENTY

JEN

A WEEK LATER

"NHL FANS WERE STUNNED *this morning with the news that Liam Donnghal, captain of the Montreal Mounties, and the star who led his team to victory in last year's Stanley Cup Finals, was kidnapped in the early hours—*"

"Another shitty day, another shitty dollar," I muttered under my breath as I switched off the morning news and slipped in my earrings.

The carat solitaires were so big they had tiny rainbow reflections darting on my skin when the light refracted on the facets.

I loved them.

I loved, even more, the additions to them that Luciu had gifted me.

Triangular in shape, the lacy filigree detailing was embedded with more diamonds and hooked onto the solitaire so you could wear them 'up' or 'down.' It was like smart/casual to dressy in the blink of an eye.

Well, a rich person's blink.

I wasn't averse to the five-star treatment.

A couple weeks of being courted by a Sicilian Don was, I'd admit, addictive.

If a tad unique.

Somehow, red envelopes made an appearance on my desk, and last night, I'd found a gown laid out on my bed.

I'd have been pissed if it wasn't Alexander McQueen's haute couture line.

Even better?

Beside the bed, there'd been a pair of stiletto Louboutins.

If he'd have rubbed my clit, I don't think I could have squealed harder.

The man knew how to shop, and I was just greedy enough to take everything he had to give without demurring.

A shark-like smile curved my lips as I left my apartment and began the journey to work.

My mood had improved since I'd let Luciu into my life. Savannah's betrayal still stung, but Luciu was so confounding it didn't leave me much time to dwell.

We hadn't seen each other since we'd gone to dinner with his brother. I knew it wasn't because of the argument Stan and I had had about the stock market over the best tortellini I'd ever eaten.

A fact I knew because even though the restaurant's patrons had been glaring at our raised voices, Luciu had sat back, watching us both, his fingers rubbing along the seam of his lips so he could hide his smile.

So, we hadn't seen each other since just because it hadn't happened. He'd been busy with only God knew what, and I'd been content to speak with him on the phone or over text.

And when I said speak, I meant we had more of those phone conversations that lasted for hours.

I'd almost caved in last night and gone to his apartment when I'd gotten the dress, but Aoife had called me, inviting me out for lunch today, and I'd curbed my impulses.

A lifetime of running after men had gotten me nowhere.

Taking it slow with Luciu seemed to be working better for me.

I didn't want to be a Carrie with my Mr. Big. I wanted to be Fi, maybe even Fionnabhair... he probably had no idea how much of a compliment that was.

Work was boring, Jackass Jason sniped at me for not doing his job, and I coasted it until noon when I escaped five minutes early to get to my lunch date on time.

As I made it to the restaurant, I saw Aoife before the maître d' could even seat me.

I also saw Savannah.

Though I stiffened up with irritation, I saw that Aoife was pissed too, and because she was a redhead, the signs were easy to spot.

As I'd known her my whole life, I knew them easily, but anyone with frickin' eyes could see it too.

She turned bright pink, her eyes gleamed like glass, and the curls in her hair bobbed with every toss of her head, making her look like they were steaming as she bristled with temper.

She wasn't happy Savannah was there.

Neither was I.

But that meant Aoife hadn't wanted her here and wasn't forcing a meeting on me.

I was tempted to run away, to back off, but Savannah was a fucking journalist—dogged persistence was in her goddamn DNA.

I didn't sit down when I reached the table, even though the maître d' tried to seat me, but I rested my hands on the back of the chair and intoned, "I don't want you here."

Savannah's mouth wobbled. "Jen, I can't tell you how sorry I am—"

"So you should be. What you did was disgusting. It's one thing to try to hop on the bandwagon for a fucking story, Savannah, but to pretend to be her friend too?"

"I didn't pretend to be her friend! At first, I was just trying to get close to her." Savannah shook her head. "I don't have to explain myself to you; I have to explain myself to Jen." Her focus shifted onto me. "I swear to you, I intended just to grab a strand of your damn hair and that was that. But then we got talking. You liked the same stuff as me, and—"

"And what? You wanted to see if I ever found out the truth about my biological father? So you could document it or something? For posterity?" I scowled at her. "I think you should just leave."

She got to her feet, but she didn't walk away. "Jen, you were a story. I make no bones about that. I came clean because I wanted to make it right, but I didn't have to—"

"That earns you dick," Aoife retorted.

"Aoife, this has nothing to do with you."

"She's practically my sister, Savannah. Bet your ass your lying to her and stealing her DNA as part of research into the O'Donnellys, which by the way is freaky as hell, has something to do with me. You hurt her, you hurt me."

I wasn't going to lie—Aoife's defense hit something inside me that was like a bomb to the foundations of a building, and that building was gonna go down, but I didn't want Savannah to see that.

She'd hurt me.

She'd fucking wrecked me.

I thought we were BFFs, thought we had each other's backs, but all the time, she'd been lying to me? Hiding shit from me? How was I to know she didn't mean any harm with what she was keeping from me?

After all that, she thought a simple sorry was going to be enough to make up for years of lies?

Because I wanted to cry, from Aoife's defense and Savannah's actions, I forced myself to say, "Savannah, you don't get to decide when or if I'm ready to forgive you."

She blinked, and I saw the tears forming in her eyes. Ignoring what I said, she whispered, "I miss you."

I missed her too.

That was the goddamn rub.

Aoife and I were sisters, she was right about that, but we had our own preferences about stuff that just made us individuals.

Aoife loathed shopping. She was uncomfortable with her body so heading out for clothes wasn't a pleasure for her. She loved baking, and she considered a great night out to be heading to a fancy restaurant or going to see a show or a play. Finn had even gotten her into opera, for fuck's sake.

Me? If I could shop every day for the rest of my life, I'd die happy. Spending a man's money was my idea of the best time and just looking at what Aoife baked gave me a fat ass and I couldn't afford that when I wanted to leverage that ass for Louboutins.

I hated the theatre, if I had to watch a musical with Aoife again it would end with me stabbing myself in the eye, and if she ever dragged me to watch an opera, I'd have to stab *her* in the eye while the Fat Lady sang.

Savannah and I were on the same page.

She loved shopping and gossiping. We both inhaled liquid lunches that morphed into dinners before we headed to nightclubs, and horror movies were more our thing than shows.

She didn't roll her eyes when I documented my whole life on IG and usually helped me take the best picture where Aoife would scoff and get bored after one shot.

I'd known Aoife all my life, so Savannah couldn't be considered a sister, not really, but she'd been on the way to becoming that.

Because I didn't feel like lying, I told her, "I miss you too, but that doesn't change anything. You broke something that might be irreparable, and I have to figure out if it's worth trying to fix it or if I want to call it a day."

Her mouth wobbled again, and the tears in her eyes were genuine as she stared at me like I'd just shoved a knife in her gut.

Then, she surprised me.

She sniffled but straightened up. "I really hope you give me a second chance, Jen."

Savannah didn't wait for me to reply, just twisted around and came face to face with the maître d' who waffled, "Ms. David, please come with me."

I didn't even have it in me to grin at his getting her name wrong because, for once, she didn't correct him. Just strode out of the restaurant without a backwards glance.

I knew why too.

So she could cry in private.

Savannah was like me—we didn't do tears.

We were boss ass bitches who had careers. Manhattan was a man's playground, their territory, and it didn't make weak career women. Not when sharks were hovering around every second corner just waiting to tear into our asses.

With her gone, however, I could slump into a puddle of goo as I pretty much melted into the dining chair.

Aoife's hand snapped out and grabbed mine. "I'm so sorry, Jen, I didn't know—"

"Did Finn tell Aidan about our lunch date?"

"Maybe? By accident?" She grimaced. "He doesn't know why you've fallen out. Just that you have. I don't think he'd push it though. He knows you scratch when pissed off."

Though I felt drained and, dammit, sad, my lips twitched at that. "Does he think I'm a cat?"

"An evil cat." She nodded. "It's quite a compliment from Finn."

"What are you? A Persian?"

"Oh, no," she said with a grin. "I'm a Siamese."

My eyes flared wide. "Are you a yowler, Aoife?"

She chuckled, her grin bright but coy. "That would be telling."

My amusement waned as my thoughts turned back to Savvie. "Am I being hard on her?"

"Nope." Aoife snorted. "It was creepy. Some shit is easy to forgive, other stuff less so. You had it right on the money—it isn't for her to decide when to forgive and forget, that's on you."

I was a pretty decisive person. It was not only in my nature but part of the career path I'd chosen. But, in all honesty, with the people who mattered to me, I knew I had blinders on.

Mom was a toxic piece of trash but I never changed my phone number so she couldn't call. Savvie had hurt me, probably more than Mom had in years, but a part of me had wondered if I was overreacting.

Relieved we were in agreement because it took away some of the power from the stupid voice in my head that told me I should be grateful for a friend like Savannah, I nodded.

"Did the maître d' get her name wrong?"

Pleased she'd noticed, I smiled. "He did." Before she could continue, I asked, "Finn knows we're eating at Avocat, doesn't he?"

She rolled her eyes. "Yes."

"Does that mean I can order Cristal?"

"It does. So long as you don't mind going back to the office drunk."

She grinned. "I might live it up as well."

"A virgin mojito for you?" I mocked, but I leaned over to squeeze her hand to tell her I was teasing. I held onto her fingers longer than I needed to, but she got it.

Squeezing back, she let me hold onto her as she joked, "I think I'll go hardcore and have a virgin Long Island Iced tea."

Grinning, I raised my spare hand to wave over the waiter. "Let the good times roll."

TWENTY-ONE

JEN

NOT UNSURPRISINGLY, I was feeling a little woozy by the end of the meal.

Having absorbed more alcohol than calories, I considered it a great lunch. But that wasn't me casting shade at Avocat's chef. The guy had enough skill to somehow make a green salad taste good, so he was worthy of a sainthood in my humble opinion.

With zero carbs lining my stomach, that meant the Cristal went straight to all the good spots. So, when I plunked my butt in a cab, I sent an email to my boss, explaining that I'd eaten something bad and that I was puking my guts out.

Unfortunately for me, his email came back within seconds.

Really? You skip out for lunch early and you expect me to believe that you've been hit with food poisoning this fast?

See me tomorrow with a sick note from your doctor.

What a jerk.

Still, I didn't have to go back to the office. That had to count for something.

Wondering if Luc had a doctor he could bribe into giving me a sick note, I started humming, loud enough for the taxi driver to give me the side-eye in the rearview mirror.

By that time, however, I was outright singing Duran Duran's 'Save A

Prayer' under my breath, and he was humming along with me, so when we made it to my building, I tipped him for being a good sport before I hurled myself out of the taxi and made my way to the front door.

The new one Luciu had installed was crazy secure, with a gazillion locks clicking into place with the twist of my key.

I wasn't sure how the building owner felt about him making unsolicited improvements, but something told me he didn't have much of a choice.

Luciu was a rogue. The police didn't matter, laws didn't count, and he roamed around like he was above it all. Apparently, I'd spent too much time with the O'Donnellys because that wasn't exactly the turn off it should have been.

As a result of Luciu's attitude about the law and property ownership, residents of my shithole building actually had some protection now.

The security lights were blinding at night, the new intercom system didn't cut out like the old one had when it decided to be a pain in the butt and just stop working period, and the door was stronger even though the new lock worked with my old key.

As I let myself into my building, then headed upstairs, my buzz didn't die, just grew a little stronger and in a different direction.

Luciu.

He took up a lot of my thoughts, a lot of my feelings, and that had nothing to do with the Cristal and everything to do with how he treated me. How my security was a priority of his.

Did he know what that did to a woman?

When I made it into my apartment, I even found myself sighing at the sight of an envelope on the bed.

He'd used his key.

I shouldn't like it, I really shouldn't, but I twisted around to seek him out, kind of hoping he was still here. Sad to say, I didn't even get a whiff of his aftershave which had me pouting.

It was official—he'd made me as crazy as him.

With a smile, though, I kicked the door closed, reached forward, and grabbed the envelope. Because the walls were paper thin, I heard the buzzer sound in Mr. Yardley's apartment in my periphery, but my focus was on the letter.

A few days ago, he'd sent me a picture of the signet ring that had once been decorated with an 'F' and which now had a large 'V' on it, and I saw that the envelope was sealed with a wax puddle that was embossed with that same letter.

He used wax seals?

Damn, the guy really was my Sicilian Mr. Darcy.

Because, again, I was crazy, I darted over to my pathetic kitchen and grabbed a knife to flip up the seal so that I could keep it.

As I raised the flap, peeling it off and placing it on my nightstand, my doorhandle twisted.

I spun around, half expecting it to be him, but what I got was a much uglier, much meaner face.

My mom's boyfriend.

"What the fuck are you doing here?" I snarled, cursing my stupidity in not locking the damn door.

Where these red envelopes and Luciu's gifts were concerned, I was turning into a magpie that was obsessed with all things red instead of silver.

"Your mom's been trying to get in touch with you," Vlad rumbled, stepping forward with all the grace of a cow in stilettos.

As he lumbered toward me, I saw how his fists were curled into tight balls, and I tipped up my chin as I rasped, "I know. I ignored her on purpose."

Sadly, telling Mom no hadn't gotten her to stop calling me.

"We need money."

My eyes bugged. "And what about this palace I live in makes you think I have it?"

He sneered at me. "You think I'm a fucking moron?"

"Yes, actually, I do."

Okay, so that *was* the Cristal talking because Vlad was terrifying with those ham-like fists of his, a throat as thick as my thigh, and a head that looked like it had gone two rounds with a dump truck and had somehow beaten the machine.

"Those earrings will help pay our rent," he remarked, then he held out his hand.

He. Held. Out. His. Hand.

Like he actually expected me to give them to him.

My one-carat solitaire diamonds.

That Luciu had gifted me.

He hadn't made me suck his dick for them.

Hadn't asked so much for a kiss in thanks.

He'd *gifted* them to me.

Because he wanted to.

He. Wanted. To.

I stared at Vlad, and though this wasn't the first time he'd hit me up for cash, I knew it would be the last. Luc would see to that.

"You should leave. I have nothing to give to you. These are fake."

"I am not so stupid as you think." He tapped his nose. "I have seen your mark—"

"He isn't a mark," I snapped, unsure why that was so important I had to reiterate it.

"You are in love with him?" he cackled. "Of course you are. All MacNeill females must be fools." His tone turned bored. "You know what will happen to your mother if you don't do as I ask."

The last time, she'd ended up in the ER, and I'd had to scrounge together three thousand dollars to pay for her medical bill.

Jaw clamping down, I groused, "Beating her up won't make me suddenly have cash in my bank account."

I screamed when his hand snapped out and he dragged the earring from my lobe, pulling it through the flesh, uncaring that I sobbed with pain.

As he palmed it, the diamond gleaming red, Vlad shoved it in his pocket then, with a lurid grin, lurched forward, all the grace of a predator on his side.

It was then I knew.

He wasn't just here for money.

His hands imprisoned me in a brutal hold that would only end in one position if I didn't act first—on my back, him between my legs.

He manhandled me like I weighed nothing and to this roid-addict, I probably didn't.

His dick leaped to life, a thick bulge at my hip as I struggled, and he got off on it.

Vlad had always made me feel uneasy, but he never tried anything with me.

Until now.

His fingers were everywhere at once, squeezing my breasts, pinching my sides as he twisted me around so that my back was to his front. I kicked out, legs flaying, trying to stab him in the in-step with my heel, but the fury was aimed at myself.

I'd left the door open because I'd seen a pretty trinket on my bed.

I was furious with myself.

So furious.

It outweighed my fear, and maybe that would save me.

Before, I'd always cowered, had always just hidden away at Aoife's to avoid my mother's men because they were always so much bigger than me, and so much more of a threat.

But today, I was angry.

Today, I was outraged.

After weeks of being treated as if I were a goddamn lady, I was back to being tossed around like I was a whore.

I refused to feel that way. Point blank refused.

And I had a means to an end.

In my hand, I still held the knife that I'd used to open the letter.

I was going to use it for a different purpose.

When he squeezed my breast, I struck out, managing to graze his temple with my fist as he growled in my ear, "I think I should get you out on the streets. I'd sure as fuck earn a lot more than I would with your old hag of a mother."

My temper surged because our thoughts ran parallel in a way that made me shiver with revulsion.

I was tall enough in my heels for my head to be at chin height with him, so I shoved back, putting all my force into it, pushing into him so that he staggered. His hold tightened, but he was unstable on his feet. I twisted just as his hands went for my throat, closing around it, nostrils flared as I saw the fury in his eyes.

That was when I struck.

For a second, we both stared at each other in surprise. Then, he frowned as his head wobbled, chin pulling back when he tried to look down at the table knife that was sticking out of his throat like it was a toothpick I'd stabbed into his fingertip.

"Bitch," he growled, surging forward, arms high like he was still going to go for my neck.

Only, this time, not to strangle but to snap.

You didn't stop until you'd killed a wasp because everyone knew it'd come and sting you, but a hundred times more aggressively than before...

Vlad might be a massive wasp, but the principle was the same.

I snagged the knife, pulled it out, then watched as his eyes widened, turning glazed as blood spurted out of the wound. It was like something from an SNL skit. Like a red water fountain. A shocked sob escaped me when I realized it actually looked like the water display in *Russu*.

My sob broke in two, my breathing turning hard and laborious as a panic attack beckoned. He came at me again, though, unbelievably, so I aimed and managed to strike him once more...

Oh, God.

The gurgle he made.

I'd never forget it.

As he sank to his knees, I darted out of his path before he could take me down with him, and in stunned silence, huddled in the corner far away from him, I watched his blood pour onto my floor.

As he died.

As the man I'd murdered, my mother's pimp, faded into nothingness.

For endless seconds, I just sat there. Iced over. Staring. The heat and jollity of my lunch with Aoife was a thing of the past. I felt cold, so cold. Like I'd never get warm again.

When the crimson puddle moved ever nearer to my feet, that was the moment I had to act.

I had to unfreeze.

I did the only thing that made sense in my adrenaline-high, post-Cristal buzz.

I texted Luciu.

Me: *You got your wish. I'm covered in russu.*

TWENTY-TWO

LUCIU

AFTER A SITUATION this morning with the Triads that we were in the process of handling—another five had turned up, *armed,* at *Russu*—I'd decided to visit Zhao, the Triads' leader, for answers.

First, I dropped off a gift at Fi's place before Lorenzo began the drive over to Chinatown. As a result, I was five minutes away from her apartment when I received her text.

When she'd told me that she was covered in *russu*, I'd had him turn the car around because there was no misinterpreting that.

Unless she was talking about *vinu russu*—red wine—but I was pretty fucking sure she wasn't.

When I called her after I received her text, she mumbled something about her Cristal buzz dying, but she sounded more than drunk, she sounded shell-shocked.

I was pretty certain that I didn't breathe easily until I made it to the neighborhood I'd left a couple minutes earlier, and even then, I was on red alert.

Russu. Blood.
Whose blood?
Who could have hurt her?
An O'Donnelly?
It had to be.

I had no idea why she was home early, but *home* was where she was supposed to be safe. I had cameras in the hallway to monitor her, but she wasn't due back there for another couple of hours, was supposed to be at work so the man I'd set on her was at *Russu* helping torture Triads for information.

Because my interest in her hadn't become widespread news, I'd thought she'd be safe, no guard required. *Yet.*

Fuck.

Fuck!

When we made it into her building, Giovi and I tore our way up the stairs toward her floor and found her door open, just a sliver. When I walked in, I saw something I never wanted to see again in my entire fucking life.

She was huddled in the corner of her shithole of an apartment, her arms wrapped around her legs as she stared at the corpse on the floor.

The only thing that would have made this worse was if she was rocking herself, but just as I thought she was having some kind of breakdown, her eyes clashed with mine.

My heart stuttered in my chest.

Literally stuttered.

Death and blood and all the various aspects of it were a common part of my business. I'd killed more than my soul could ever atone for, to the point where the most I felt about coming across a dead body was the irritation at having to clean the damn thing up and scrub the place for DNA.

As I looked at the chasm that separated us, within the tiny confines of her apartment, it was massive.

My life and hers... so different.

So not meant to collide.

And then she looked at me.

There was no fear in her eyes, neither was there panic.

A calm resolve filled them that sent a quick blast of pleasure along my spine.

She was frozen, but not petrified.

The first time always stunned, especially when the adrenaline high faded.

Rage filled me when I saw the state of her ear, but I banked it, even as I made that injury my priority.

Eyeing the blood on the floor, I turned to Giovi and ordered, "Wait out here."

His gaze drifted over the corpse. "*Se*, boss."

Shutting the door in his face, I stepped around the body when I sensed she was incapable of standing on her own.

Was she more injured than she appeared?

"Come, *cara mia*." I held out a hand for her. "I shall have this sorted. We need to get you cleaned up."

She swallowed. "He tried to hurt me."

"Whether he did or not, you have your reasons," I told her, no judgment to my voice. I beckoned her again. "Leave behind what you don't need for tonight. I'll have someone come by and gather your things together."

Her gaze shifted, brow puckering as a distance appeared between us that was nothing to do with feet and inches.

"Where am I going?" she whispered with a frown, shock clearly setting in.

Was she letting herself react because I was here?

Because she knew I'd keep her safe?

"You're going to come and stay with me for a while," I told her softly. "But tonight, we're going to Aspen."

Her eyes widened. "Aspen?"

I cast a look at the bed where I'd left the sheath of documents and saw that it was open, but most of the papers were still in the folder. "You didn't read them?"

"I didn't get the chance," she whispered.

Gritting my teeth as I bit back the need to check her over, I reached down and helped her onto her feet.

"I don't need help," she rasped, jerking away from me. "I'm okay."

This woman—as regal as an empress.

My goddamn empress.

"Of course you are," I told her blandly, watching as she wobbled now that she was standing. My eyes drifted to her earlobe. "You did what had to be done."

Her mouth tightened, but before she started to walk away from me, she reached for my hand once more, squeezed my fingers in silent thanks, then whispered, "I knew you'd come."

She didn't let me answer. Darted over, instead, to the bathroom where she had a two-minute shower.

While she cleaned up, I peered down at her attacker and had to admit to being inordinately satisfied that the fucker had fallen on the knife. It stuck out through the nape of his neck in a way that had to have triggered excruciating agony before he passed.

Bonu.

The water turned off, and she moved out into the bedroom again, then headed into the closet where I heard her pulling on some clothes.

I called out, "We'll get you some things in Aspen."

"Okay," she replied, but there was little excitement in her voice.

That this fucker had stolen her joy aggravated me like nothing could.

Squatting down, I hummed when I saw she'd used a table knife—the dulled tip would have triggered immense pain as well.

The move would have required a brute force that came as a pleasant surprise. I hadn't realized she was as physically strong as she was.

"Where will you take him?"

The whisper was as loud as a scream to me.

"Pig farm," I told her without lifting my head, aware she was watching me.

"A pig farm?"

"Yes. They eat everything but the oink."

A shrill laugh escaped her. "That isn't how you're supposed to use that phrase."

I shot her a quick, wry grin. "I know. But I knew it would make you laugh."

When our eyes met, she swallowed.

"I'm sorry I-I brought you in on this." She reached up and rubbed her damp forehead, her laughter having died out like it never existed. "I didn't think to call the police."

"Why would you, *duci*? I am here to fix these things for you."

She gulped. "Are you? Truly?"

It was one of those moments when you had to step up or step back, but I'd had no say in the matter of stepping back since the moment I'd met her.

I'd been all in from that first night.

"Truly. My men will clean this place up, and you won't know he was ever here."

Her bottom lip pulled taut in a way that I recognized was her version of biting on the tender morsel. Though her mouth was constantly painted red, she never had the color on her teeth, and how it tautened led me to believe she pinched a sliver that wasn't visible.

More painful too.

"You shouldn't have to—"

"There is no 'shouldn't' between you and me," I chided her, letting my gaze drop back to the man.

Face twisted to the side, he was staring blindly ahead, his hair saturated with the blood that had surged from his veins from her attack...

Of course, that was when he blinked. Just the tiniest of movements of his eyes.

I ran a hand over my chin, uncharacteristically unsure of what I should do next. Did I tell her? Did I just let him die without mentioning that he was still alive? Barely, and probably impossible to spare from death—

That was when he groaned though. A whisper soft noise that she heard.

When she dropped her bag, the thud had me shooting her a look, and there was terror and disgust and hatred converging into one mass that I didn't have time to pull apart.

"He's the walking dead, *vita mia*," I told her. "Do you want to leave him like this? Or do you want me to end him?"

Her mouth trembled. "How long—"

I was no doctor, but a quick glance at the floor had me guesstimating he'd lost around four pints. Halfway drained, then.

"He's in shock now. Maybe a couple more minutes?"

I'd thought she'd slashed his carotid, but maybe not if my guesstimate was right. Shooting her a look, I saw she was frozen, so I took the matter out of her hands.

Pulling the bastard's head up by the hair, I tipped it back, grabbed the knife, and stabbed it straight into his carotid.

With his heart weakened by blood loss, the arterial spray was minor, but he took his final gasping breath as I stared straight into the *figghiu ri buttana's* eyes and smiled at him as he died for real this time.

I got to my feet and eyed her bag, the wet hair, and the new outfit. "Is that enough?"

She didn't answer, her gaze not on the body, but the blood. "How will they clean this?" she whispered under her breath.

"Best not to ask, *duci*."

I stepped around her, moving into the kitchen to clean up before checking my clothes for blood. My coat was clear, but it'd need destroying just in case some had penetrated the weave. I saw a few spots on my shoes, a couple on my cuffs, so the shirt would need destroying as well.

I cleaned my shoes, then I rolled up my cuffs to keep them hidden for the length of the journey home, then returned to her side. She was still staring at the blood, so I gently touched her elbow, but she flinched like I'd thrown her across the room.

Wishing that I'd been able to cause the *pezz'i miedda* worse pain instead of simply silencing him, I asked again, "Have you packed enough, *duci*?"

Her voice was faint. "Yes, for tonight."

That was a battle I'd be fighting in a few days' time—she wouldn't be returning here.

Not again.

Softly, and to get her talking, I queried, "Did you leave the dirty clothes behind?" I'd seen the neat pile she'd laid on the toilet seat.

"Y-Yes."

"Good. They'll need to be destroyed."

I earned a nod before she stared down at the corpse again.

"H-He—" Her mouth quivered.

"What is it?"

"He took my earring."

"I'll make sure it's found. I'll get you another pair, *vita mia*."

When she graced me with a shaky nod, I stepped closer, careful not to further disturb the scene, then after tucking her into her winter coat, I reached for the bag, grabbed her hand with the other, and carefully tugged her along and away from the body.

Once she was standing free and clear of it, I paused, murmuring, "Raise each foot so I can see the soles of your boots."

She stared at me blankly but did as I asked—the only red on them was a choice by the designer.

Nodding, I checked my own again then guided her out of the room.

Giovi was waiting, his stance one of high alert as he sought out more threats.

"Deal with it," I told him, confident that he'd secure the scene.

Leaving him behind, quietly, we walked to the stairs and descended them.

We made it outside where Lorenzo was standing huddled into his coat beside the car. Eddies of steam unfurled around the fender, and he held the backdoor open the second he saw me, keying me into the fact that Giovi had texted him to prepare him.

I guided her over to the backseat before handing him the bag. While he placed it in the trunk, I seated myself then raised the privacy screen.

She was still, so still as I reached for my cell phone and sent Stan a message.

Because he didn't approve of her, even after our meal together, I knew he'd be irritated at our involvement in this, but he could kiss my ass because this was *my* business.

Fi was my business.

Stan: *She's more trouble than she's worth.*

He had no idea what she was worth. Not to me, at any rate.

By the time Lorenzo was diving behind the wheel, the matter was under control. Stan was sending men to help Giovi remove the body, for cleanup, and to help gather her belongings. I wasn't happy about them seeing her wardrobe, but it couldn't be helped.

As the car started and we headed out, she moved closer to me even though her face was tilted away.

"Don't you want to know who he was?" she whispered, her voice so low it was hard to hear.

"Do I need to?"

Her head whipped around to the side. "You don't care?"

"I care. But he's dead and is no longer a danger to you." My lips curved. "I always knew you were a tigress."

"You—"

"That was all you. I simply made the situation more palatable for you."

Her forehead puckered, relaxed, furrowed once more before she whispered, "His name was Vlad. He's my mother's boyfriend. *Was*," she corrected.

I'd read about that prick. The one associated with the Bratva.

I rubbed my chin but didn't chide myself too much. Identification wasn't easy when a man's face was pressed against the floor and the rest was splattered with blood.

"He hurt you."

It wasn't a question. She'd told me that in her apartment, and I believed her.

"He did. But... not enough to deserve that. At least, I don't think—"

"You reacted to something he said, Fi," was my calm, non-judgmental reply. "What did he say?"

She hesitated before finally admitting, "That he should whore me out. That he'd earn more money with me than with my mother." Her mouth firmed and for the first time, she looked less shaken and more angry. "He was going to rape me."

I gritted my teeth as the rage that flooded my veins had more of a punch than a pack of C4.

Fingers tightening around my cell phone, to the point of pain, to the point where I was sure it would crack under the pressure, I snarled, "Then he deserved it."

With one hand clenching down on the phone, committing violence against the device, I carefully reached over to clasp her chin.

Tilting it down, I pressed a kiss to her temple and whispered, "I am proud of you, *duci*."

She pushed her forehead against my jaw and stayed there for the rest of the drive.

It was a step forward.

A step closer to what I wanted.

What I craved from her.

Which, in the here and now, I recognized was nothing more, and nothing less, than all she had to give.

TWENTY-THREE

JEN

IT HAPPENED IN A DAZE.

One moment I was home, giddy as I started to open Luc's gift, the next Vlad's blood coated my hands, the next I was at Luciu's apartment, my ear being patched up, then I was at the airport, being whisked away to Aspen on a private jet.

As I sat there, staring out at the endlessness of the night sky, Luc paced back and forth as he spoke in guttural Sicilian. Unsure about what he was saying, unsure that I wanted to know, I just kept my gaze on the sky.

My mind wasn't on the sheer luxury of the Falcon jet, which I knew had to cost around fifty or so million—a fact that would have made me cream my panties a few short weeks ago—nor was it on the luxurious interior which made me feel like we'd been flying in an aerial Ferrari for the past few hours... it was on that moment where I'd made the decision to kill him.

To eradicate Vlad.

A man I barely knew.

A man who whored out my mom.

A man who'd abused her and who'd mistreated her.

He'd done it for years.

I hadn't thought to kill him before.

What had changed?

Was it witnessing what Luc had done to Damian?

Was it seeing how easily a life could be taken? That murder could be covered up like a zit with concealer?

Or was it knowing that Luc would have my back?

That he'd help me in the aftermath?

A worthless piece of humanity could be removed like the trash they were when you had a mobster who'd clean up the mess you made...

The thought had me swallowing then tipping my head away from the window to look at him. As I did, I caught him watching me.

The hunger in his eyes might have scared me this morning. But then, I was a different person this evening, and that was how he looked at me.

Like I was different.

Like the Jen of this morning was no more.

And he wasn't wrong.

Did I look like Fi to him? Or weak?

Ignoring the throb in my earlobe, I sucked in my cheeks and gnawed down on the flesh to the point of pain, watching him watching me, feeling my pulse slow and a bizarre calm take the place of my odd, contemplative state of mind.

He continued talking with whoever was on the line, but he didn't take his attention from me, and at that moment, I felt our connection flood to life between us.

I had no idea what was going on here, no idea whatsoever. Some things couldn't be labeled, after all.

Shouldn't be, in some circumstances.

When I'd met the woman who'd called herself his wife, well, that had only cemented matters—I thought I'd never see him again. Then, Savannah had told me about my biological father, and the only person I could think of drowning myself in was him.

The man who'd stolen my breath across a crowded restaurant.

I knew he'd steal it again. I knew he'd rob me of the betrayal of a best friend, knew he'd decimate the memories of a Christmas weekend that had been close to devastating in its aftermath, and knew he'd take me for what I was, no judgment, because I'd thought that was what he wanted too.

No strings.

But then, as I looked at him now, I knew I'd been fooling myself.

A man didn't devour a woman the way he had if it was without strings.

No.

A man didn't covet a woman the way he did if he didn't crave every part of her.

No.

This man wanted me.

And though he'd learned some horrible truths, it didn't stop him from looking at me like that.

With his eyes on me, I straightened up. I knew there was another ninety minutes left to the flight, and I—

God.

I just needed him.

I'd already seen the bedroom at the back of the jet and though joining the mile high club had never been a life goal of mine, in that moment, I wanted to knock it off my newly formed bucket list.

Feeling his gaze on me like it was his hands literally shaping my ass, I padded, barefoot, to the end of the corridor and to the room where I proceeded to strip off.

I needed him.

Inside me. Filling me. Taking me. Robbing me of thought again. Breaking the cycle.

I might have no gift to give him. Damian could have stolen that from me, and maybe I'd never know. It wasn't like hymens were pieces of concrete that crumbled during penetration, was it? But this was the first time in my head. In my heart.

The first time that actually mattered.

I'd fucked and sucked, jacked off and done countless things to a guy to keep him happy, but this was different.

As a result, my behavior wasn't the same.

With another man, I'd have displayed myself on the bed, I'd have had my legs spread wide, my fingers in my pussy, the lights on bright.

I kept it dark, and I clambered beneath the sheets the second I was naked.

My ear hurt, my body ached, and I had bruises from Vlad, but that didn't take away from what I needed to happen tonight.

Hearing his brisk voice, still in that strange language I didn't recognize, next came his footsteps, and I saw him in the light from the hall where he was in shadow.

The call cut, he tossed his cell on the ground, and then I heard rustling as he stripped off.

Without a word, he joined me in bed. Unerringly, we both took the sides we had when I slept at his place that first time.

When he rolled over to face me, he didn't reach for me, just murmured, "*Cara mia?*"

"*Mon cher.*"

A soft chuckle escaped him. "We will have to watch that together at some point."

"I'd be down for that," I whispered, shuffling closer across the cold sheets to approach him.

My nakedness brushed along his, and his hand settled on my waist before sliding over my hip to settle at the bottom of my back. He tugged me tighter into him, his dick rubbing against my belly, a wet mark making the passage of his cock sliding over the flesh easier as it pulsed to the beat of his heart.

"You're frightened, *vita mia*. You have no need to be. I will keep you safe."

That was the crazy thing. "I know you will."

In the dim shadows of the room, I saw his head tip to the side. "Why so pensive then, hmm?"

"I just killed a man." I cleared my throat. "In the immortal words of Freddie Mercury, I put a gun against—"

He chuckled. "You stabbed him. You didn't shoot him. But it was done very well."

"Well, it was more by luck than management," was all I could think to answer.

Neither of us were talking as if I'd just killed somebody.

But in this world of his, was murder really that big of a deal?

Wasn't it more a strategy?

Each life that of a piece on a chessboard?

That wasn't a nice way of thinking about life, though, so I pressed my forehead against his throat, relaxing into him, loving that we were both naked and raw, both physically and emotionally. I needed that. I needed to feel like there was no artifice between us because I was about to trust him with me, and I didn't know if I could do that if all our cards weren't on the table.

"I didn't spend any of your money," I whispered.

"I know." His hand shuffled higher, tangling with my hair where he petted me like I was the tigress he'd called me earlier.

"How do you know?" I queried in confusion.

"I have ways of knowing most things. You probably shouldn't ask or be surprised."

My eyes ached with how hard I rolled them. "Mr. Phantom of the Mafia."

He snickered. "I hide behind no mask."

"You don't need to when the city's paparazzi purposely avoid you."

"Is that an accusation I hear?"

"No. I just... where's the accountability?"

"In my head and heart."

I huffed. "And you think that's enough?"

"Probably not, but it isn't my fault everyone's scared of me."

"Actually, I think you'll find it is," I said with a chuckle, amused that he believed his own bullshit, oddly charmed by it too.

"You're not scared?"

"Of you?"

"Of yourself," he said calmly. "You have no need to be scared of me. We have discussed this already. You can think the things I do are creepy, but there is no need for fear."

"I don't think we *have* talked about this. Not exactly."

"You just haven't been paying attention."

"If you say so."

"I do."

I thought about his question and replied, "I'm scared of how easy it was."

"If it's any consolation, it took four hours to clean your apartment," he said dryly. "It wasn't exactly easy."

"Sorry."

"I didn't say it for that. I just meant that these things are difficult. Being thorough takes time."

"Did you really send his body to a pig farm?"

"Of course. Where else?"

I blinked. "Well, there's a river outside."

"The Hudson is polluted enough without that scum there." He heaved a sigh. "I wish I'd dealt with matters myself. I should have ignored you when you told me to leave things alone. I knew about your mother's situation—"

Though he was right because this could have been avoided, I was oddly pleased that he'd listened to me. "Have you ever had to hit rock bottom?"

"No. But I believe I edged pretty close to it after my father's death. His passing... hurt."

I rested my hand on his arm and squeezed gently.

"I haven't been in my mother's dire straits, but no matter how low she sinks, she never hits rock bottom. Even thinking about trying to help her is useless until that point.

"I guarantee that when Vlad doesn't come home, she'll wobble a little, sob some, hate on him, but she'll go out and find another prick who'll treat her worse..." I sighed. "There's no helping her. I stopped trying years ago."

"Today was avoidable."

"In a sense, it was, but not entirely." I huddled into him. "Vlad, unfortunately for me, has been around since my early twenties. When Mom was struggling, I let her move in with me for a short while, but he came as part of the package." I sucked in a breath then admitted, "One day, I got back early from work and saw this guy coming out of my bedroom.

"Mom was sobbing in my bed because he'd done something to her—" To this day, I didn't know what. "Vlad was furious. Not because she was someone he loved who'd been hurt, but because his merchandise wasn't ready for the next customer." I rubbed my forehead against his chest. "His temper was mean, always ran hot, so it was only by chance that he didn't see me standing in the kitchen. If he had, I probably wouldn't be alive either."

"He killed him?"

"Yes." I sucked in a breath. "I've seen a few people die. Drive-bys, shootings. Beatings, brawls. People even died at the O'Donnelly compound at Christmas. We didn't see them, but that doesn't mean we didn't know it happened." His hand started to move up and down my spine. "That that kind of violence could unfold in my apartment was horrifying. Especially because he would have done one of two things if he'd spotted me: kill me or terrify me into staying quiet and then blackmail me by saying I was just as guilty as him."

"In the moronic laws of the land, he would have been right. Conspiracy to commit murder packs as hefty a punch as a murder charge."

"Yes." I gulped.

"What happened?"

"He had a friend come and help him with the body. I tried to get Mom to leave him, but she wouldn't, so I grabbed my things and got out of there." I released a breath. "I-I guess that's why I feel better."

"Because he isn't a threat to you anymore?"

"Yes. I didn't realize until now that I was always just waiting for him to turn up at my door and explode in my face. I was right about that. He did."

He clucked his tongue. "You're wrong. He *did* turn up at your door, but *you* exploded in *his* face. You protected yourself."

"I could have, *should* have, called the cops." I shuddered, realizing that there just hadn't been the time for that.

I hadn't even had time to barricade myself in the bathroom.

"And what would have happened? You'd have been hurt before they even sat their fat asses in a cop car. Your neighborhood isn't the best, *duci*. You'd have been at the bottom of a list of their priorities.

"No, you had no alternative but to save yourself. I'm proud of you for doing that. I'm just sorry I let you down."

"How did you? You're my..." I hesitated over the word, so I didn't settle on one. "Well, you're not a babysitter."

"I had eyes on your building. I could have helped. It kills me that you might have gotten hurt worse than your ear." He rubbed his chin over my hair. "But you broke your routine. Came home early. I didn't anticipate that when you work such long hours."

"Why did you have eyes on it?"

"Because you live in a shitty neighborhood and your building isn't safe."

"If I were living in a place like yours, would you have eyes on me?" I didn't even need a light to know he was smirking. "You're full of bullshit." My voice was lighter than it should have been considering the subject.

"Ahh, *vita mia*, you wound me."

I snorted. "I'm sure."

"Why were you home early from work?"

Tension slithered up my spine. "Savannah and I had an argument. She tried to force my hand at lunch, and I decided that drowning my woes in Cristal was a smart way to get over it."

"What kind of argument?" he inquired.

"Does it matter?" Desperate to change the subject, I asked, "You have eyes on me at work too, don't you?"

"A colleague of yours owes me a favor," he demurred.

"They're how you get the envelopes on my desk, aren't they?"

"They are."

"Who is it?"

"I have people everywhere who owe me something. Money, a favor..."

"So, you collect people."

He hummed. "In a city like New York, *owning* people gains you power. Not collecting them."

I shivered because he wasn't wrong.

A thought occurred to me. "Is this your jet?"

"Yes. Earned with ill-gotten gains." He sounded amused. "Are you going to go all moralistic on me?"

"No. I help people evade taxes for a living," I drawled. "I just wondered if you'd leased it or something."

"I travel a lot."

"You do?" Damn, did I sound disappointed?

"I do." His hand was suddenly at the back of my neck. He gathered my hair in his grasp then tugged back, just enough so that his mouth could trail along the sinews of my throat. "You're going to come with me, aren't you, *vita mia*?"

I quivered at the husky rasp in his voice but before I could answer, he shifted then pressed a kiss to my mouth with an unerringness that made me think he had mapped out my face so he knew how to reach my lips at any given moment and angle.

The silly thought made me smile, and he rumbled, "You taste even better when you're smiling."

God.

How couldn't I melt when he said things like that?

When his voice was deep and dark and like gravel?

Ugh.

I relaxed even further into him, and it was crazy that I could do that after his admission he had eyes on me, but that he wanted me to travel with him had hope flickering into being. Making what I wanted to do feel so right, so perfect, so natural that it merely affirmed what I knew to be true already—I trusted him.

Scary, scary, scary.

But he robbed me of even the whisper of fear by kissing me, treating me gently, tenderly, *softly*. I was used to passionate kisses, tongue-fucks, but this was as if he knew I'd lowered my walls for him, as if he were well aware I'd chosen the moment I wanted to be with him like this.

Maybe it was the Sicilian in him that cherished this, cherished me, where an American probably wouldn't, but that was how I felt. *Worshipped*.

The way he tasted me and savored me, kissed and caressed, his hands everywhere, calloused fingers drawing my nerve endings to life, undid me.

After this afternoon, the hard biting of Vlad's digits into my flesh that had left bruises behind, how he'd pawed at me...

Maybe I shouldn't crave this, but I did. I craved Luc. I craved how he made me feel, how he appreciated me for me, never griping at the stunts I pulled or the shit I said.

He liked me.

And right now, I needed more of that.

When he pulled back, I moaned in disappointment until Luc pressed open-mouthed kisses down my throat again, over my breasts, stomach, sinking further and further. His lips were making every inch of me stir to life as the tiny nerve endings on my body reacted as if he were sucking on my clit, not just on parts of the body that weren't even supposed to be erogenous zones.

I moaned when he circled my navel, nipping the firm flesh of my belly before lathing my hip bones with the flat of his tongue. He pressed a kiss to each, then trailed further down until his nose was rubbing against my bare mound.

Then he whispered something in Sicilian, the vibrations of the words making me feel as though they were thundering through my pussy.

"You know what's going to happen tonight, Fionnabhair?"

I swallowed. "You're going to fuck me."

His chuckle was soft, but lethal. All the more deadly for it, and I was there for that. Along for the damn ride. "Oh, no, *cara mia*, I'm going to make you mine."

A soft whimper escaped me as his mouth dropped to my clit, and he ravaged me and savaged me and mauled me and feasted on me. I luxuriated in every move he made.

Growling under my breath, I hitched my legs higher, pressing my thighs to my stomach as I spread them wider, letting him have access to every part of me.

And why wouldn't I?

He was so good at giving head that holy crap, I'd be a fool not to let him have his way with me.

The sounds he made, the noises that came from my cunt, there was no shame, only pleasure here, and it made me eager to please him. I'd been selfish with him until now, which was a complete turnabout and spoke of how oddly I behaved around him. I was programmed to give, never to think about taking, and yet, here was a man, one many might consider a monster, giving without thinking about receiving.

As he sucked on my clit like he was starved, his fingers slid into my pussy, stretching me much as he had last time, but this felt different.

I knew what was about to happen, logically, and I actually wasn't nervous—how could I be with all the sex I'd had in my life?—but it was strange not to think about turning over, twisting aside, and shoving my ass in his face.

Men loved the forbidden, and I gave it to them so easily that they never thought to question, just snapped at the chance to take what a lot of women wouldn't give.

Anal sex wasn't exactly taboo, but my exes had acted as if my butt housed El Dorado.

Not for the first time around him, my pussy clutched at the digits inside me, and I rocked my hips, needing him, needing more because this felt so damn good, yet I craved everything.

Every. Thing.

With a growl, I surged up, and my hands slipped into his hair as I tugged on the thick onyx locks that slid across my palms like silk. I grabbed and pulled as I snarled, "I want you inside me."

He surged onto me without another word, his weight settling atop mine like he was born to be there, and though his dick pressed against my pussy, he made no move to shove it inside me.

His mouth went to mine, his tongue slipping between my lips, thrusting so that I had no alternative but to taste myself on his.

"See how good you taste, *bedda mia?*" he half-growled before he slid that slick morsel roughly against mine, thrusting hard and fast, taking my breath as if he could steal my soul.

That was when he reached between us.

That was when I felt the tip of his dick against my slit, and I rocked my pelvis up, curving my body so that he could slide in easier.

The feel of him there—*indescribable.*

New.

I didn't dare think what that might mean, but it felt tight and hot and frickin' crowded, but not painful. Or maybe my pain tolerance was different than it might have been when I was younger after Pap smears and years of anal sex. This just felt good.

But definitively new.

My eyes clenched tight as my head rocked back, digging into the pillows as I writhed beneath him, but he didn't let me go. His mouth stayed fused to mine, and he stayed like that until his dick was all the way in.

The second I felt his abs against mine, I lifted my legs and raised them so I could dig my heels into his butt. He bit down on my bottom lip, nipping fast and fierce, before he rasped, "Mine."

A shocked cry escaped me at his declaration, but it seemed to fill all the cracks in my confidence. I might seem confident AF, but I really wasn't. In some things, sure, but like anyone, I had my issues. Luc's words seemed to shore me up and buoy me at the same time.

He whispered words in Sicilian to me as he pressed our foreheads together, and it was the most intense but natural thing in the world for us to stare into each other's eyes, even though it was dark inside the room, as he took me higher than the mile high club.

This was a different stratosphere.

My pussy clutched at him, hungrily gripping him, eager for everything he had to give as he started to rock harder and faster into me.

I came with a brittle cry that felt like it shattered into a million pieces amid the sound waves the second it was let loose. This battered me. It suffocated me. Pulling me under only to haul me back out from wave after wave of pleasure.

Ecstasy rattled through my veins like a pure hit of heroin, but when the wildness shot through him, when he bucked against me and started fucking me, it was even better than before, which was when I knew the truth.

He wasn't wrong.

I was his.

But he was also mine.

TWENTY-FOUR

LUCIU

"WHO'S SHE?"

I stared at her with narrowed eyes as I sank into my seat at the table in the restaurant—an empty restaurant.

One of Aspen's busiest eateries was closed at midday for a reason. The man in front of me, a man who went by one name only, had hired the entire place to show me the rubies.

"I'm his bodyguard," the Latina woman said with a sneer.

"She's my wife."

They both spoke simultaneously which had me frowning. "Is this some kind of joke?"

"No," the guy replied, rubbing his chin as he shot his wife a sour look. "She just forgets which comes first sometimes."

"I don't forget, but when you're sitting in front of New York's new Don, I have my priorities."

Definitely married.

Almost amused at their bickering, especially with the woman seeming to sense that she shouldn't fuck me around, I tipped my chin at the man. "She has a point."

"I don't think you'll be scarring my face today," the man denied, letting me know that news of my skills had somehow made it down to South America.

When Stan had proposed working with the *Lobos Rojos,* he'd investigated them thoroughly. That meant I knew more about them than the IRS.

The original founder of the gang, Martinez, had emigrated to South America to be with his bride whose appearance, not unsurprisingly, was very different than the 'wanted' posters I'd seen of her.

Martinez, his tone almost boastful, continued, "Eva's talents are as strong as yours in that field."

"Good to know," I told him calmly, even though my guards were anything but calm at my back. "What I'd like to know is how you got involved in this, Martinez? I thought you were busy sunning yourself in... where was it?" I mocked. "Uruguay?"

"Ecuador," he corrected with a soft smile that, a few years ago, wouldn't have boded well for my jugular remaining where it was.

"Yes, I think I remember that little issue you had." I cast his wife a glance. "What was it that has you on the FBI's Most Wanted? Separating a cop from his head?"

She sniffed. "He deserved it."

It took a strong man to throw away his entire world for his woman, but that was what Martinez had done for his wife. Now that I'd met her, I could see the attraction. She was beautiful, of course, but in our world, beauty was a commodity.

Eva Martinez née Kingston was fierce.

Men like us found that magnetic.

I thought about Fi in her shithole apartment, sitting in the corner, staring at what she'd done... then I thought about how she'd accepted me into her body last night, trusting me when she'd been slapped in the face with the ultimate proof that men weren't to be trusted.

Yes, a fierce woman was a worthy partner.

I rapped my knuckles against the table. "I'm sure he did. So, why are you back here? This is a huge come-up in comparison to Bed-Stuy," I drawled.

"We recently learned that the Sparrows were driving the push for Eva's arrest." Martinez shot me a bland smile. "With their power over the country waning, I thought it a good time to come back home for a visit. See how things had changed in my absence."

"Not that much that decapitation is no longer a crime, sadly. The state of the laws in this country is abominable."

"You could always fuck off back to Sicily," Eva pointed out with a grim smile.

"So, she's a patriot," I mocked.

Martinez raised a hand, snagging Eva's in his and holding onto it firmly. "My wife has a trigger temper, Valentini. I'd remember that if I were you."

"Then we're evenly matched. Now, I traveled halfway across the country because I believed I was about to be purchasing something of interest." I was going to kill Lockhart for wasting my time and bringing me into a potentially dangerous situation. "Is there a reason you dragged me here?"

Martinez pursed his lips as he leaned forward, settling his elbows on the opaque glass table. "I have a deal for you."

"I'm all ears."

"I know you're dealing with the *Lobos*, and this is—"

"You provide good stock."

"I left Juan in charge for a reason. He's a strong leader." His head tipped to the side. "I can do one of two things. Eva," he directed without turning his head. She placed a briefcase on the glass. "I can give you this or work out a deal for some free merchandise that'll make it your way over the next couple months..."

"What's the deal?" I demanded, settling back in my seat, trying to appear relaxed when that briefcase could house a gun or a bomb.

"I've got it on good authority that your woman is friendly with Savannah Daniels."

I blinked.

This was about Fi?

A part of me wanted to snarl at him for bringing her into this but hearing him call her my woman felt right.

The label would protect her where little else could, while also endangering her.

I guessed I'd better get used to the scum of NYC knowing that she was tied to me.

"What about it?" I questioned.

"Eva's situation, as you mentioned, is dicey. I'd like to take away the threat."

Eva unclicked the latches, then shoved the briefcase at me.

I tensed but when they didn't make to run out of the room, I tipped it open and found myself staring at the Anjou tiara.

I'd been chasing after these goddamn jewels for years, keeping shit on the downlow until I made my name, but now that I was the Don, I'd started scoping further afield, uncaring who knew about my interest.

I had the money.

I wanted what was mine.

"This a joke?" I rasped, aware my voice was husky, but this was a long time coming. They still needed to be authenticated, but that could happen the second Rory had her hands on them.

"No. No joke. We want to come home," Martinez murmured. "It's time."

I shot him a look and saw that Eva was leaning against her husband slightly. Studying her, I took in the pale cheeks, the slightly rounded—

"Going to be a father?"

"I'm going to be a mother, actually," Eva sniped.

Martinez smiled. "You can understand our position."

"I can. But Savannah Daniels..." How to explain? And with the tiara so close, I had no desire to short sell the situation. "I'll pay for the tiara."

"I don't want money for it," Martinez replied. "I want a deal."

My mouth tightened. "That might not be workable."

"You need to find a way to make it happen," he said gruffly before he tossed an envelope at me.

When I opened it, I saw a lab report from the same lab we were using in New York.

"You've been thorough." I stared at the certification of the gems, wanting to be uneasy that his investigation into me had been so detailed, but I couldn't find it in me.

The Anjou tiara was here—within reach.

Entranced, I ran my fingers over the crest of the jewels.

With a band of Princess-cut rubies and diamonds running around the base, six larger ruby cabochons, each one between sixty and eighty carats, were rimmed with round-cut diamonds, with the largest of the rubies at the center before tapering down. Every crevice was stuffed with diamonds or white gold filigree work that made it incredibly heavy.

I'd read reports about how my female ancestors had often had issues with wearing it for a full day of events, and I could see why.

I felt the weight in more ways than that too; I sensed the gravitas of the tiara as I placed it in my hands, resting it on my palms as I stared at a chunk of my family's history. An intrinsic piece upon which our fortunes could rise or fall.

"I'll make it happen."

Martinez shot me a smile. "You can take it with you."

"What?" I demanded.

"Don't worry," Eva rasped. "I know where you live. I can come and collect it if you let us down."

"I don't deal well with threats."

Her smile was deadly. "Funny thing that—neither do I."

"It might take some time," I countered.

"You have a deadline," Martinez drawled.

"Twenty-nine weeks," Eva confirmed.

"I want her to give birth in Cedar-Sinai."

I nodded. "I understand." And I did. Impending fatherhood made a man take drastic steps. "Why not approach the O'Donnellys themselves? Savannah Daniels is going to be an O'Donnelly soon enough."

"We haven't dealt well together in the past." Martinez sank back into his seat and pressed the tips of his fingers together as he rested them on his stomach. "Aidan Sr. is a madman."

"And he's married to me," Eva drawled, "so he knows a lunatic when he sees one."

I flickered a glance at her. "I'll do all I can."

"I know you will," Martinez rumbled, the warning clear.

Returning the tiara to the special padded bed within the briefcase, I closed it. "Pleasure doing business with you, Martinez. May it reoccur in the future."

Martinez just nodded, but I caught Eva's eye and for a second, we just stared at each other, taking one another's measure.

By the end, she was glowering, and I was smiling before I turned on my heel, motioned at Giovi to start moving, and walked out of the restaurant.

Something whistled by my ear just as I made it to the door, the metal vibrating as the tip of the knife buried itself in the doorframe. I reached up, grabbed the hilt of the stiletto blade she'd hurled at me, then waggled it overhead before I pocketed it.

Honyaki steel? *Porca troia*, I was keeping it.

TWENTY-FIVE

JEN

AFTER WAKING up to an empty bed, I'd admit, I was pouting.

I sure as hell wasn't happy about him doing a disappearing act, even if he'd brought me to an apartment in the center of Aspen that made five stars look cheap.

Everything, and I meant everything, was black.

Black on black on black.

I actually liked it because with the pops of color that were dotted here and there, everything stood out like it was neon: the copper fittings in the bathroom, the cerulean blue fixtures in the bedroom, the silver in the kitchen, the bronze in the living room.

Everywhere I went, it was calming and soothing on the eyes, and I'd admit, I'd never considered myself emo at school, but I totally understood the appeal of black outside of a little black dress that was for sure.

I snatched the shirt he'd discarded on the floor last night, and while I'd intended on picking it up to fold it and place it in the laundry basket, I couldn't.

Hating myself for lifting the collar and sniffing at it—fuck, he smelled good—I slipped it over my shoulders and buttoned it up.

Drifting into the bathroom, I looked at myself in the mirror and winced at the Band-Aid that covered the tiny stitches on my earlobe. It was both too big and too small and my hair had been catching on it all night.

Not wanting to deal with that just yet, not when it was already aching without me prodding at it, I put my contacts in then wandered into the kitchen for coffee.

The twinge between my legs as I walked gave me hope.

Hope that Damian hadn't stolen something from me.

Hope that Luciu was a kind of first.

I should have known Damian was bad news with how much coke he snorted, but that was Manhattan, those were the circles I ran in. Even old money's bank accounts were being drained dry by drugs in the city, so when I caught him with white powder around his nose or track marks on his arms, it was normal.

"Girl, you're crazy," I muttered to myself, only just realizing how dangerous it had been for me to wreck his Ferrari like that when he was always hopped up on drugs.

Grimacing and *grateful* he'd been put to death by the Sicilians—yes, I'd done a 180 on that particular subject—I grabbed my coffee cup once it was full and doused it with creamer I found in the fridge.

I had a coffee ratio.

Mornings—black.

Afternoons—black.

Bad days—Starbucks' lattes, full-fat milk.

Lazy days—more creamer than coffee.

Today was a lazy day. Tomorrow I'd have to deal with my boss, but Luciu, being Mr. Organized, had managed to get me a sick note from the doctor who'd stitched up my ear yesterday afternoon.

Still, that was tomorrow's problem, and a problem it would be from all the texts from Jackass Jason.

Today, however, I was in denial, and I got to check out Aspen.

Wandering over to the wall of French doors, I leaned against one and stared out onto the city ahead. It was like something from a movie, dusted with pure, white snow that could have been icing sugar on gingerbread.

I'd never been here before. Had never left New York. I suddenly saw the whole world open up to me if Luciu meant it about taking me with him when he traveled.

He'd mentioned Catania... I'd love to go. Especially when it was warm and sunny and the air scented of lemons and spray from the ocean.

A soft sigh drifted from my lips at the thought as I stared out at the winter wonderland ahead of me.

Did mobsters ski?

I had no desire to go skiing.

Hoping that Luciu didn't, I twisted around when someone cleared their throat. Of course, I'd thought I was alone, and after yesterday, that meant I upended the entire fucking mug of coffee down my front.

Gasping as the hot liquid splashed me, I snarled when I saw it was Stan. "You're lucky I put in more creamer than coffee."

Plucking at the drenched shirt, I stormed over to the sink and started patting down the white silk.

"What are you doing?"

I shot him a glower. "Trying to stop it from staining."

"He has a million shirts."

"I'm sure that's an exaggeration," I retorted, ignoring him as I carried on trying to clean it up.

"Not a million, then, but a lot. Don't worry, just throw it away."

My mouth gaped. "This is silk. That's sacrilege!"

His lips twitched. "If you say so."

"What the hell are you doing here?"

"Luciu asked me to watch over you?"

"Why?" My brow furrowed. "Am I on suicide watch? Because if you think I'd kill myself because of that prick—"

Stan cleared his throat. "No. More like if you went shopping, he wanted someone with you."

"I don't want to go shopping." A shocked breath gusted from my lips before I repeated, "I don't want to go shopping."

"Okay, you don't have to—"

"Jesus, is this what suicidal feels like?" I gasped. "*I don't want to go shopping*, Stan—"

"I don't think that's suicidal," he drawled, smirking as he said it.

"You don't understand. I always want to shop."

He grunted. "Maybe yesterday did affect you."

I was glad Vlad was dead, though, wasn't I?

I told him that.

"You did good. I had a file on him after I looked into you. Wasn't a nice man."

"Understatement," I said bitterly, trying not to cringe at what he must have found out about me when he was looking into my past.

No wonder he looked at me like I was trash sometimes.

Turning away from him, I carried on with the dabbing even though I had a feeling it was useless.

"Honestly, Jen, you can leave it," he said softly, stepping over to the kitchen island where I was.

Didn't mention the island before, did I? Didn't mention it was all marble and glossy and definitely somewhere you could have sex on, did I?

"I didn't mean to stain it." I rubbed harder. "What are you doing here anyway? I didn't see you on the jet." We'd boarded alone. At least, I thought we had.

His hand came out and enclosed my wrist to still my movements. "Luciu made me fly coach."

My lips curved. "Made you, huh?"

"Yes. Punishment."

"For what?"

"To be fair, I think he'd have put himself in coach too but you were on the jet."

I cast him a glance. "He's upset about Vlad?"

"Understatement. He'd be here now but the meeting... it was unavoidable."

"I'm a big girl. I can handle waking up on my own," I lied, as if I hadn't just been griping about waking up alone.

Our eyes clashed, and I knew he was aware I was lying. "That first time is always difficult. It gets easier."

I gulped because while I'd have preferred for him to have been talking about my first sexually, I knew he wasn't. Yes, that was how little I wanted to talk about the man I'd turned into a corpse.

"I don't want it to get easier," was my waspish retort as I dragged my wrist from his grasp and moved deeper into the sink so he wouldn't see my pussy when I lifted the flaps of the shirt, rested them on the counter, and scrubbed even harder.

"It will. This life... I'm surprised you haven't had to defend yourself before."

"Most people don't go around killing guys who piss them off."

"Most people aren't on the fringes of the factions. As far as I can tell, you've blurred with them all."

"What? I haven't."

"Vlad was linked to the Bratva," he intoned, making me gape at him. "You were raised in O'Donnelly territory. Now you're mixing with the Italians. And the Chinese, well, we're still not sure what kind of business Headley had with them, bu—"

"Damian wasn't with the Triads," I scoffed, even though a part of me registered how right he was.

Especially with the O'Donnelly part.

Crap on a cracker.

"He was. Somehow, between us taking him in the club and killing him, the Triads discovered that and sent soldiers in." At my confusion, he murmured, "You know what games he was playing?"

"You're not talking Call of Duty, are you?"

His lips didn't twitch. "Did he play that?"

"He... well, he used to have it on the TV a lot."

"But never played?" His eyes narrowed.

"No. I never saw him pick up the controller."

"You can stop rubbing the silk. You're not supposed to get it wet anyway."

"Shit." I knew that already.

The soggy shirt clung to my belly, but because he was right that the silk was a lost cause, I grabbed a sponge and loaded it with dish soap so I could clean the floor where drops of coffee had spilled.

Mouth twitching as he watched me, Stan pointed out, "I never imagined he'd fall for a woman like you."

"Is that a question or a statement?"

I felt his eyes on me. "A statement."

I tipped up my chin and met his gaze stare for stare. "One of a kind, that's me."

"Apparently," was all he said, his hand snatching my wrist again as I made to move away from the sink. "Just don't think you can screw him over—"

"Custanzu."

We both jerked at the bark, heads whipping to the side to see Luc standing there, his expression like stone.

Stan's nostrils flared as he backed up. Immediately. Hands raised. "She needed the warning."

"No," Luc rasped. "She didn't. Get the fuck out of here and do *not* touch her again."

The aggressive, protective possessiveness shot straight between my legs as if he'd shoved his hands between them.

Stan grunted, but then barked something in Sicilian. Luc replied in English, "She didn't need warning. She's mine. You touch her, you're touching me. Remember that. She might freeze up when you try and immobilize her, but I fucking won't."

Temper had Stan storming out like a toddler in the middle of a tantrum. Which pretty much summed things up, seeing as the entire episode couldn't have taken more than forty seconds, but between Stan's hand coming to my wrist again and him leaving, I was drenched.

And not because of the water on my shirt either.

Luc had turned to watch his brother leave, but I dragged off the damp fabric, letting it plop to the ground, and swooped in. Prowling forward, I pushed him into the wall, grabbed his hands when surprise had him dropping the briefcase he was holding, and pinned them at the side of his head.

He smirked as I surged onto tiptoe, my lips fusing to his to steal away the smug smile, fingers tightening around his, clamping him in place, needing to reward him for his protectiveness, his possessiveness, his crazy-assedness.

I was here for that.

So fucking here.

I ground into him, mound rubbing against his dick as I slipped my tongue between his lips, kissing him, owning him, fucking loving him and how he treated me.

I'd been waiting for this for a lifetime and just hadn't known it.

Simply hadn't expected it.

But he looked at me like I was worthy, and though I'd never needed a man to define my worth, that Luc felt that way lit me up from the inside out.

I knew what I was, knew my flaws and my strengths. Knew I was a decent person, a solid best friend. But Luc didn't see any of that. It was like he saw something in me, something I couldn't. Maybe it was my soul...?

I pulled back to nip on that full bottom lip before I flickered my tongue against his once again, rasping, "I didn't like waking up alone."

"I'll make sure I wake you up in the future before I leave," he rumbled, a warning flaring to life in his eyes that I should have heeded but couldn't.

"That means I'm going to wake up with your face between my thighs?"

"More often than not."

Pussy clutching at the emptiness now it knew what it felt like to be full, I groaned under my breath before I loosened my grip on one of his hands and reached between us to rub his hard cock. But that wasn't my end destination. I slid further down, touched myself, gathered my wetness, then reached up and painted his lips with my juices.

"Don't lick them," I ordered.

His nostrils flared, and I hoped that all he could scent was me and my need. "You're bossy first thing in the morning."

"No, I'm not, just want to treat my man, that's all."

His jaw clenched. "Your man?"

I felt no hesitation, no shyness or vulnerability as I nodded. "Mine."

"Good," he grated out.

"I'm about to be very, very good," I asserted before, with a final squeeze to his fingers, I pulled my hand free and slipped to my knees, my fingertips tracing down his length as I kneeled before him.

Unfastening his pants to grab a hold of his cock wasn't the easiest thing in the world, but I was careful and when he popped free, I peered up at him, saw the rich man, the dangerous man, the elegant businessman, the shadowed soul who crept into my bedroom at night and watched me sleep, and as I did, I recognized one thing.

Each one belonged to me.

I parted my lips, letting them suckle the tip of his shaft before I worked my tongue to gather saliva so I could drench him in it.

"Oh fuck, *vita mia*," he growled under his breath, his head tipping back against the wall as I treated him how he deserved.

His was one of the few uncut dicks I'd come across, but I jacked him off as I fluttered the tip of my tongue against the slit in his cock then sucked on the mushroom-like head, before nipping the flared edges with my teeth. He hissed as I moved down it, sucking along the thick vein before nuzzling his balls and sending little licks their way too.

Fluttering here, flicking there, I treated him how he treated me—giving me everything he had.

He deserved no less in return.

That was why I wasn't mad about Stan's comments.

Luc deserved to have someone watching his back. I was glad he had that. Now he had two people to do that for him because I wasn't going anywhere.

Yesterday had affirmed that.

In more ways than one.

When I moved back and began the slow slide down his shaft, gripping him at the base until I acclimated to his length, he released a guttural groan that I felt in my core.

I saw his hands were splayed, clinging to the wall, but he stayed still, hips not rocking, and I knew I had to rupture that control of his.

I wanted to see him burn because I needed to dance in those flames too.

Groaning when I felt the flood of precum in my mouth, I worked faster, sucking him harder, taking as much as he had to give. Then, when I knew he was near because his hips made the tiniest twitch, I pulled back and sucked on the tip. *Hard.* Long drags that had him cursing under his breath—his English in the wind.

When he growled and came, I let the slickness of his seed fill my mouth, taking everything he had, letting it bubble at the corners of my lips. That was when his hand gripped my jaw, but his fingers were carefully located so that he didn't tug on the wound on my ear.

Like he'd spoken the words into my mind, I showed him my cum-drenched tongue.

His lips tightened before he stunned the shit out of me by dropping to his knees in front of me, hands still claiming a firm hold on my cheeks, before he kissed me.

He. Kissed. Me.

With my mouth full of his cum.

I almost fainted.

I nearly melted into the ground because this was the hottest thing I'd ever experienced—a man who wasn't afraid of the dirty side of sex, of what his and my body did when they were aroused.

That he loved every aspect of sex, in all its nasty glory, made how he devoured me afterward even more intense. It was like he was a pleased god I'd just given an offering to.

His tongue thrust against mine, hungry and hard, and for a second, I just let him, until I fought back too.

We kissed on the floor like we were angry with one another, then he pulled back and he whispered something in Sicilian that was directed straight at my clit.

Jeez, I needed some attention now.

When he moved back, I was almost disappointed, but then he reached to the side, and I heard the clicking of the locks on the briefcase.

Frowning in consternation, I watched what he was doing, then gasped when I saw it.

A tiara.

A real-life motherfucking tiara. Like what Princess Kate would wear.

It was huge.

And the diamonds were not only the size of my pinkie fingernail when I didn't have acrylics on, the rubies were like quail's eggs.

He held it like it was sacred to him, and for the first time I understood what he meant.

When he said I want to see you dripping in *russu*, *this* was what he was talking about.

He turned back to me, the tiara in his hands, and then he did the damnedest thing.

He placed it on the top of my head and rasped, *"Bedda mia."*

TWENTY-SIX

LUCIU

I HAD no choice but to fuck her with the tiara on.

I fucked her in the hallway, after I got her off twice because my balls were still drained from that blowjob to end all blowjobs, and then I carried her into the bedroom, kissed each and every bruise that bastard had left on her arms and breasts, then I made love to her in there as well.

This time slower, watching how the tiara toppled slightly, tangling with her hair in a way that would make her want to slap me later, but it was like a wet dream come to life.

Her fire and mine were meant to burn together.

As I thrust my cock deeper into her, so fucking deep that she should have felt it in her throat, I rasped, "You're going to wear them all. One day, you'll wear them and nothing else for me."

A gasp escaped her, and the noise sank into my bones. With her head thrown back, her eyes closed, I leaned down, notched my mouth to the expanse of throat she exposed and sucked, careful with her injury, wanting the love bite there, the mark. Wanting to see it tomorrow and the day after and to think of this moment. To think of her in the Anjou tiara.

When her pussy clutched at me, rippling around me as she came for a third time, I tightened my hold on our bridged fingers and trailed my lips along to her ear and whispered, "Would you like that, *vita mia?*"

"Y-Y-Yes," she cried brokenly, even though I knew she had no idea what she'd just said yes to.

My grin formed, forged in need and lust and triumph, and I fucked her harder, needing her to give me everything, needing to claim this pussy, to make her crave me, to have her tied to me in so many goddamn ways nothing could part us, never mind some ridiculous divorce laws.

When I had the Anjou ring...

Yes.

That's when I'd propose.

That's when I'd make this formal.

With that ring on her finger for a fucking lifetime.

The thought triggered my climax, and I poured my seed into her, well aware of the ramifications, well aware of what might come, and knew that I'd better hurry my ass and find the damn ring because I didn't intend to stop until she was round with my child, until she was mine in all the ways under the sun.

I called out as I came, her name on my lips, loving the sound of mine on hers as she exploded into sobs for a fourth time, and as I rested on her, for a moment, I knew peace.

Freedom.

No whispers of the past, no shame or guilt or fear or concerns for the future.

Just a delight in the present.

And it was beautiful.

The silence I found in the harsh breaths we took, in the pounding of her heart and mine, it was a song of its own, and I rested with her, needing that and more.

Always more where she was concerned.

We woke up when my cell rang, and I knew why. The jet was fueled and ready to fly tonight, and I silently promised her another visit to Aspen as I woke her up by nuzzling my nose along the line of her jaw and whispering in her ear, *"Cara mia, it's time to leave."*

I'd never grow tired of watching her awaken, and I savored those moments as her nose crinkled, as she squinted and pulled faces before consciousness made her aware.

She huffed when she saw me watching her and muttered, "You know it's creepy when you do that."

Not a question.

"Then I'll be a creep." I smirked. "*Your* creep."

With her eyes closed, she grinned at that, wide and big and so honest, so true that my heart fucking soared. She hummed. "My creep."

"You're going to hate me in a minute."

"Why? What did you do?"

"Your hair—"

She reached up and felt for the tiara. "Shit," she grumbled, but then she smiled again. "Worth it. Where did you find it?"

"I didn't. Someone else did and leveraged it." I wasn't going to hold this back from her, make some kind of intrigue out of nothing.

"What kind of leverage?"

"Someone knows about your ties to Savannah Daniels."

She tensed. "Someone?"

"A gang."

Her eyes flared wide. "Is Savannah in danger?"

I wondered if Savannah knew what she'd done when she'd hurt Fi... Tossing away a friend who thought of Savannah first before she did herself.

"No," I crooned. "She's safe."

"Then what's to leverage?"

"Somebody would like you to persuade her to write an exposé on them."

She blinked. "In exchange for the tiara?"

"Yes."

She blinked again. "Luc? That tiara has to be worth twenty million dollars or something. Those rubies—"

"More to a bidder interested in antique jewelry," I inserted.

"How rich are you anyway?"

"Stinking."

She huffed at my smug smile. "Okay, so you could have bought it?"

"Yes, but they wouldn't sell. They wanted me to do them this favor. Or should I say they want *you* to do them this favor."

"Why didn't they ask her? And why would they be willing to drop twenty million on this?"

"Because twenty million is chump change to him? Because twenty million is worth his wife's freedom?"

Her eyes were dazed as I dropped a kiss to her lips. "What's his wife done?"

"Everything she's accused of," I said wryly and began to unfurl her hair from the tiara, being careful with the locks that were in a tangle close to her wound.

"What's she accused of?"

What did I tell her? I'd learned a lot from our investigation into the *Lobos Rojos* before we'd gotten tangled up with them in business.

From how Martinez's wife had once been an undercover cop, to how she'd infiltrated the gang, to how, eventually, Martinez had followed her to the non-extradition country of her choice when arrest warrants had been served for her.

I knew that before she'd become a cop, she'd been abducted by a serial killer and she, and his final victim, were the only ones to make it out alive.

And I knew that when that serial killer had been released from jail on a DNA lab fuck up—one that meant he'd been identified as a dead prisoner when he was very much alive—Martinez had paid the Whistler, the famed sniper, to have him killed.

"She was..." I heaved a sigh. "She was an undercover cop, and the authorities tried to jail her for the crimes she committed during that time."

"That isn't fair," she protested.

"Life rarely is."

"How will an exposé help?"

"I imagine they'd like her to tie it to a New World Sparrows' conspiracy," I told her as, finally, I released the locks that had clung to the tiara.

She reached for it then as she tilted it here and there in the afternoon light, letting the facets catch the rays, before she shot me a look. "Not sure a favor is worth twenty million, but...Savannah owes me one."

"You'll do this for me?"

She nodded. "Only if I really get to wear it."

"Who else would I let carry this crown?" I rumbled.

A second before she joined our mouths, she murmured, "My Italian Darcy."

I slipped my tongue between her lips then pulled back and corrected, "Sicilian."

TWENTY-SEVEN

JEN

DRESSED in an outfit that had miraculously appeared in the apartment after I showered, tucked into so many layers I was toasty warm as I boarded the plane, I took a seat on the buttery leather recliner and sighed with delight.

I'd never get sick of flying this way.

This was more than just style. This made a jet as accessible as a car, and though it was always the small planes that seemed to crash in the news, I'd deal with the risk to travel in this kind of luxury.

But my first taste of it looked set to be marred.

As we descended and the plane hit the runway, I saw flashing lights in the distance.

My brow furrowed. "Luc?" I pointed to what were clearly cop cars.

The place was lit up because it was night and, duh, this was a runway, but the flashing lights made it more like a Christmas scene.

Luc frowned as he leaned forward and saw what I was seeing. Immediately, he dragged his cell phone out and barked something into it when whoever he called answered.

A small pit of dread began to form in my belly the nearer we got to the cop cars, and I longed for the pilot to take off again, to get us out of here because...

They were here for me.

I knew it.

Somehow, they'd found out about Vlad, and I was going down for murder.

Shit, I couldn't be someone's bitch. I wasn't made for it. I always back talked, and I'd end up losing my teeth for it—

"It's okay, Fi," Luc crooned, reaching for the hands that I'd clamped down to the armrests like they'd melt into the metal and that would stop them from taking me. For all that his voice was soft, though, I saw the tightness of his expression and recognized his irritation as he explained, "That was my *consigliere*. They're here for me."

My mouth dropped open just as the red, white, and blue seemed to take up everything in my vision, flooding the small windows of the jet, dancing along the furniture as if it were a pretty light show.

"They're here for you," I repeated blankly.

He nodded. "I told you I'd keep you safe, and I always will." His gaze turned distant, and exasperation hit him as he growled under his breath. "Stan is flying coach, but my men are in the front and will take you back to my apartment. You don't have to worry. Everything will be sorted."

I licked my lips, unable to comprehend what he was telling me. "They're going to arrest you?" I spluttered.

How did that make sense?

I was the murderer—

Well, we both were if we were going to be technical.

Reaching up, feeling dazed and lost and scared when, before, I'd felt on top of the world, I half-listened as he spoke to me, telling me I'd be safe, that I didn't need to worry—

"WHAT ABOUT YOU?" I shouted after a good thirty seconds of his reassurances. I twisted in my seat and grabbed his arms, shaking him as I snapped, "What the fuck about you?"

When the usual fire blazed in his eyes, I knew I'd pleased him, but I didn't give a damn about that now. He snagged my chin with his hand. "*T'amu*, Fionnabhair."

I gulped because I didn't need a translator to tell me what he was saying.

It was madness.

Sheer craziness.

Utter insanity…

"I love you too."

The inferno blazed harder as he rasped, "All will be well," and he kissed me.

He said it like I should have faith in him, said it like I should believe him, and though people had let me down over the years, I chose to do that. I chose to have faith.

Until the doors to the jet opened.

Until the sight from the top of the stairs was even more chaotic; when what felt like a million lightbulbs flared to life as the press made themselves known to us.

Until I saw *her* standing there.

I grabbed Luc's hand, on the verge of telling him that the woman who'd told me she was his wife was clearly with the NYPD, but it was too late—he was walking down the stairs like a welcome party was awaiting him, not a bunch of cops.

As the flashes from the cameras blinded me, I felt one of the guard's hands grab my arm and hold me back, keeping me in the shadows of the doorway.

Before I could pull free of his hold, that was when I heard Luc's Miranda rights being read to him, that was when I saw the man I loved being handcuffed and hauled into the back of a cop car.

And when, with a single glance between us, his gaze unerringly finding me in the shadows, he was driven off, leaving me behind. Prey to the predatory press who converged upon the jet like the carrion-eaters they were.

READ THE LADY HERE: **www.books2read.com/ ValentiniTwo**

AUTHOR NOTE

Hey there, lovelies!

How's you?

Ready for THE LADY?

You can grab it here: www.books2read.com/ValentiniTwo

Trust me, you don't want to miss out!

And for a **massive release day giveaway celebration**, be sure to join my Diva reader group: www.facebook.com/groups/SerenaAkeroydsDivas

For those of who you research these things, ;), I took some creative liberties with the Camorra, who actually originate in Campania, not Sicily.

With that being said, many thanks to Salvatore Platania and his lovely wife, Lida, for introducing me to the joys of the Sicilian dialect. They got these words to me while they were traveling to Sicily, and I so appreciate their taking the time out of their vacation to help me bring this authenticity to the Valentini *famigghia*. I hope you loved the dialect as much as I do. So many confusing letters stacked together, lmao.

As always, thank you to Anne and Norma for putting up with me and my shitty deadlines. SMH, I'm a fucker. I know. Readers, you should thank them too lol. <3 They pulled some loooong hours editing/proofreading to get this to you on time. And thank you to Anne as well for the 'V.' I'm still in love with their logo. Haha. Cynthia, darling, thank you for the help with the giveaways. I think I'd go nuts without you. LOL.

Many thanks to the lovely ladies at GMB (Kylie, Jo, and Alicia) and Social Butterfly PR (Sarah and Shan) for all their help in getting THE DON out into the world.

To Letitia at RBA Designs and Gel at Tempting Illustrations for the beautiful cover and promotional teasers. You made this book look sooo purty.

To my Posse and the many bookstagrammers who have shared the promo material for me. THANK YOU. Truly. For helping spread the word.

To my wonderful Divas, for always being my safe space.

And to you, darling reader. For making this happen. For letting me be me, and for enjoying the madcap universe I created.

Much love,

Serena

xoxo

Ps. If you're new to my books, read on to enjoy the first chapters of FILTHY, the first novel in my FIVE POINTS' MOB collection.

THE CROSSOVER READING ORDER WITH THE FIVE POINTS

FILTHY
FILTHY SINNER
NYX
LINK
FILTHY RICH
SIN
STEEL
FILTHY DARK
CRUZ
MAVERICK
FILTHY SEX
HAWK
FILTHY HOT
STORM
THE DON
THE LADY
FILTHY SECRET
REX
RACHEL
FILTHY KING
REVELATION BOOK ONE

REVELATION BOOK TWO
FILTHY LIES
FILTHY TRUTH

RUSSIAN MAFIA
Adjacent to the universe, but can be read as a standalone
SILENCED

The VALENTINI FAMILY

START THE FIVE POINTS' UNIVERSE FROM THE BEGINNING...

FILTHY

FINN

Obsessive habits weren't alien to me.

They were as much a part of me as my coal-dark hair and my diamond-blue eyes. Ingrained as they were, it didn't mean they weren't irritating as fuck.

As I rifled through the folder on the table in front of me, staring down at the life of one pesky tenant, I wanted to toss it in the trash. I truly did.

I wanted not to be interested in her.

Wanted my focus to return to the matter at hand—business.

But there was something about her.

Something. . .

Irish.

I was a sucker for my own people. When I was a kid, I'd only dated other Irish girls in my class, and though I'd become less discerning about nationality and had grown more interested in tits and ass, I'd thought that desire had died down.

But Aoife Keegan was undeniably, indefatigably Irish.

From her fucking name—I didn't know people still named their kids in Gaelic over here—to her red goddamn hair and milky-white skin.

To many, she wouldn't be sexy. Too pale, too curvy, too rounded and wholesome. But to me? It was like God had formed a creature that was born to be my downfall.

I could feel the beast inside me roaring to life as I stared at the photos of her. It wanted out. It wanted her.

Fuck.

"I told you not to get those briefs."

My eyes flared wide in surprise at my brother, Aidan O'Donnelly's remark. "What?" I snapped.

"I told you not to get those briefs," he repeated, unoffended. Which was a miracle. Had I been speaking to Aidan Sr., I'd probably have lost a finger, but Aidan Jr. was one of my best friends, as well as a confidant and fellow businessman.

When I said business, it wasn't the kind Valley girls dreamed their future husbands would be involved in. No Manhattan socialite, though we were wealthy as fuck, would want us on their arm if they truly knew what games we were involved in.

My business was forged, unashamedly, in blood, sweat, and tears.

Preferably not my own, although I had taken a few hits for the Family over the years.

"My briefs aren't irritating me," I carried on, blowing out a breath.

"No? You look like you've got something up your ass crack." Aidan cocked a brow at me, but his smirk told me he knew exactly what the fuck was wrong.

I flipped him the bird—the finger that I'd have lost by showing cheek to his father—and he just grinned at me as he leaned over my glass desk and scooped up one of the pictures.

That beast I mentioned earlier?

It roared to life again when his eyes drifted over Aoife's curvy form.

"She's like your kryptonite," he breathed, tilting his head to the side. "Fuck me, Finn."

"I'd rather not," I told him dryly. "Now her? Yeah. I'd fuck her anytime."

He wafted a dismissive hand at my teasing. "I knew from that look in your eye, there was a woman involved. I just didn't know it would be a looker like this."

I snatched the photo from him. "Mine."

My growl had him snickering. "The Old Country ain't where I get my women from, Finn. Simmer down."

Throat tightening, I grated out, "What the fuck am I going to do?"

"Screw her?" he suggested.

"I can't."

He snorted. "You can."

"How the fuck am I supposed to get her in my bed when I'm about to bribe her into selling off her commercial lot?"

Aidan shrugged. "Do the bribing after."

That had me blowing out a breath. "You're a bastard, you know that, right?"

Piously, he murmured, "My parents were well and truly married before I came along. I have the wedding and birth certificates to prove it." He grinned. "Anyway, you're only just figuring that out?"

I shot him a scowl. "You're remarkably cheerful today."

"Is that a question or a statement?"

"Both?" The word sounded far too Irish for my own taste. My mother had come from Ireland, Tipperary to be precise—yeah, like the song. I was American born and bred, my accent that of someone who'd been raised in Hell's Kitchen but, and I hated it, my mother's accent would make an appearance every now and then.

'Both' came out sounding almost like 'boat.'

Aidan, knowing me as well as he did, smirked again—the fucker. "I got laid."

Grunting, I told him, "That doesn't usually make you cheerful."

"It does. I just never see you first thing after I wake up. Da hasn't managed to piss me off today."

Aidan was the heir to the Five Points—an Irish gang who operated out of Hell's Kitchen. It wasn't like being the heir to a candy company or a title. It came with responsibilities that no one really appreciated.

We were tied into the life, though. Had been since the day we were born.

There was no use in whining over it, and Aidan wasn't. But if I had to deal with his father on a daily basis? I'd have been whining to the morgue and back.

Aidan Sr. was the shrewdest man I knew. What the man could do with our clout defied belief. Even if I thought he was a sociopath, he had my respect, and in truth, my love and loyalty.

Bastard or no, he'd taken me in when I was fourteen and had made me one of his family. I'd gone from being his kids' friend, the son of one of his runners, to suddenly being welcome in the main house.

All because Aidan Sr.—though I was sure he was certifiable—believed in family.

I shot Aidan Jr. a look. "Was it that blonde over on Canal Street?"

He rubbed his chin. "Yeah."

Snorting, I told him, "Hope you wore a rubber. I swear that woman has so many men going in and out of her door, it should be on double-action hinges."

He scowled at me. "Are you trying to piss me off?"

"Why? Didn't wear a jimmy?" I grinned at him, my mood soaring in the face of his irritation. "Better get to the clinic before it drops off."

Though he flipped me the bird as easily as I'd done to him—I was his brother, after all—he grumbled, "What are you going to do about little Aoife?"

I squinted at him. "She's not little."

That seemed to restore his humor. "I know. Just how you like them." He shook his head. "You and Conor, I swear. What do you do with them? Drown yourself in their tits?"

Heaving a sigh, I informed him, "My predilection for large tits is none of your business."

"And whether or not I wore a jimmy last night is none of yours."

"If it turns green and looks like a moldy corn on the cob, who you gonna call?"

"Ghostbusters?" he tried.

I shook my head, then pointed a finger at him and back at myself. "No. Me."

Grunting, he got to his feet and pressed his fists to the desk. "We need that building, Finn."

"The business development plan was mine, Aid. I know we need it. Don't worry, I won't do anything stupid."

He snorted. "Your kind of stupid could go one of two ways."

That had me narrowing my eyes at him, but he held up his hands in surrender.

"Fuck her out of your system quickly, and then get started on the deal," he advised. "Best way."

It probably was the best way, but—

He sighed. "That fucking honor of yours."

I had to laugh. Only in the O'Donnelly family would my thoughts be considered honorable.

"If I'm fucking someone over, I want them to know it," was all I said.

"That makes no sense."

"Makes for epic sex, though," I jibed, and he shot me a grin.

"Angry sex is always good." He rubbed his chin, then he reached over again and flipped through the photos. "Who's the old guy to her?"

"To her? Not sure. Sugar daddy?" The thought alone made the beast inside rage. I cleared my throat to get rid of the rasp there. "To us? He's our meal ticket."

Aidan's eyes widened. "He is?"

I nodded. "Just leave it to me."

"I was always going to, *dearthái*r." He tilted his chin at me, honoring me with the Gaelic word for brother. "Be careful out there."

"You, too, brother."

Aidan winked at me and, with a far too cheerful whistle for someone whose dick might soon be 'ribbed for her pleasure' without the need for a condom, walked out of my office leaving me to brood.

The instant his back was to me, I stared at the photos again. Flipping through them, I glowered at the innocent face staring back at me through the photo paper—if only she knew.

Hers was a building in Hell's Kitchen. Five Points Territory. One of many on my hit list.

Back in the 70s, Aidan Sr., following in his father's footsteps, had bought up a shit-ton of property, pre-gentrification, and it was my job to either sell off the portfolio, reconstruct, or 'improve' the current aesthetics of the buildings the Points owned.

This particular one was something I'd taken a personal interest in.

See, I was technically a legitimate businessman.

This office?

I had views of the Hudson. I could see the Empire State Building, and in the evening, I had an epic view of the sunset setting over Manhattan. This office building, also Points' property, was worth a cool hundred million, and I was, again technically, the CEO of it.

On paper?

I looked seamless.

The businessman who sported hundred thousand dollar watches and had a house in the Hamptons. No one save the Points and my CPA knew where the money came from. I liked that because, fuck, I had no intention of switching this pad for a lock-up in Riker's Island.

Still, this project cut close to home, and the reasoning was fucking pathetic.

I'd never admit it to any of the O'Donnellys. The bastards were like family to me, and if I admitted to this, they'd never let me hear the end of it.

Extortion?

I usually doled that out to someone else's to do list. Someone with a far lower paygrade than me, someone expendable. But the minute I'd heard of the troublesome tenant who was refusing to sell her lot to us? After not one, not two, not even three attempts with higher prices?

Five outright refusals?

The challenge to convince her otherwise had overtaken me.

See, I liked stubborn in women.

I liked fucking it out of them.

Throw in the fact the woman's name was Aoife? It had been enough to get me sending someone out to follow her.

If she'd been fifty with as many chins as she had grandchildren, she'd have been safe from me.

But she wasn't.

She was, as Aidan had correctly stated, my kryptonite. All milky flesh with gleaming auburn hair that I wanted to tie around my clenched fist. Her soft features with those delicate green eyes that sparkled when she smiled and were like wet grass when she was mad, acted like a punch to my gut.

Now?

My interest hadn't just been piqued.

It had fucking imploded.

Yeah, I was thinking with my cock, but what man, at the end of the day, didn't?

I'd just have to be careful. Just have to make sure I put pressure on the right places, make sure she'd bend and not break, and the old bastard in the pictures was my key to just that.

See, every third Tuesday of the month, Aoife Keegan had a habit of traipsing across Manhattan to the Upper East Side. There, at three PM on the dot, she'd enter a discreet little boutique hotel and wouldn't leave until nine PM that night.

Five minutes after she arrived and left, the same man would leave, too.

At first, when Jimmy O'Leary had told me that Senator Alan Davidson was at the hotel, I hadn't thought anything of it.

Why would I?

Senators trawled for donations in fancy hotels every fucking day of the week. It was the true luxury of politics. Sure, they made it look real good for the press. Posing in derelict neighborhoods and shaking hands with people who did the fucking work . . . all while they lived it up large with women half their age in two thousand dollar a night suites.

My mouth firmed at that.

Was Aoife selling herself to the Senator?

The thought pissed me off.

I couldn't see why she'd do such a thing. Not when I'd looked into her finances, had seen just how secure she was. But maybe that was why. Maybe the Senator was funneling money to her.

The only problem was that the lot Aoife owned—did I mention it was owned outright? Yeah, that was enough to chafe my suspicions, too, considering she was only twenty-fucking-five years old—was a teashop in a small building in a questionable area of HK.

I mean, come on. I loved Hell's Kitchen. It was home. But fuck. Where she was? What kind of Senator would put his fancy piece in *that*?

My jaw clenched as I studied the Senator's and Aoife's smiling faces as they left the hotel. Separately, of course. But whatever they'd been doing together, it sure put a Cheshire Cat grin on their chops–that was for fucking sure. Jimmy being a dumbass, hadn't put the two together, had just remarked on the 'coincidence,' but I was no fool.

How did I know they were together in the hotel?

Jimmy had been trailing Aoife for four months—told you I was obsessive—and every third Tuesday, come rain or shine, this little routine had jumped out, and when Jimmy had picked up on the fact Davidson had been there each and every time, I'd gotten my hands dirty, bribed one of the hotel maids myself—and fuck, that had been hard. Turned out that place made even the maids sign NDA agreements, but everyone had a price—and I'd found out that my little obsession shared a suite with the old prick.

My fingers curled into fists as I stared at her. Butter wouldn't fucking melt. She was the epitome of innocence. Like a redheaded angel. Could she really be lifting her skirts for that old fucker? Just so she could own a teashop?

Something didn't make sense, and fuck, if that didn't intrigue me all the more.

Aoife Keegan had snared one of the biggest, nastiest sharks in Manhattan.

She just didn't know it yet.

***

Aoife

"We need more scones for tomorrow. I keep telling you four dozen isn't enough."

Lifting a hand at my waitress and friend, Jenny, I mumbled, "I know, I know."

"If you know, then why the hell don't you listen?" Jenny complained, making me grin.

"Because I'm the one who has to make them? Making half that again is just . . ." I sighed.

I loved my job.

I did.

I adored baking—my butt and hips attested to that fact—and making a career out of my passion was something every twenty-something hoped for. Especially in one of the most expensive cities in the world. But sheesh. There was only so much one person could do, and this was still, essentially, a one-woman-band.

With the threat of Acuig Corp looming over me, I didn't feel safe hiring extra staff. I'd held them off for close to six months now. Six months of them trying to tempt me to leave, to sell up. They'd raised their prices to ten percent above market value, whereas with everyone else in the building, they'd just offered what the apartments were truly worth. Considering this place wasn't the nicest in the block, that wasn't much.

Most people hadn't held out because, hell, why wouldn't they want to live elsewhere?

Those who were landlords hadn't felt any issue in tossing their tenants out on the street. The tenants grumbled, but when did they ever have any rights, anyway?

For myself, this was where my mom and I had worked to—

I brought that thought to a shuddering halt.

Mom was dead now.

I had to remember that. This was on me, not her.

My throat thickened with tears as I turned to Jenny and murmured, "I'll try better tomorrow."

The words had her frowning at me. "Babe, you know I'm not the boss here, right?"

Lips curving, I whispered, "I know. But you're so scary."

She snickered then peered down at herself. "Yeah, I bet I'd make grown men cry."

Maybe for a taste of her. . . .

Jenny was everything I wasn't.

She was slender, didn't dip her hand into the cookie jar at will—the woman had more willpower than I did hips, and my hips seemed to go on forever—and her face looked like it belonged on the cover of a fashion magazine. Even her hair was enough to inspire envy. It was black and straight as a ruler.

Mine?

Bright red and curly like a bitch. I had to straighten it out every morning if I didn't want to look like little orphan Annie.

I'd once read that curly-haired women straightened their hair for special events, and that straight-haired women curled theirs in turn, but I called bullshit.

Curly-haired women lived with their straightening irons surgically attached to their hands.

At least, I did.

My rat's nest was like a ginger afro. Maybe Beyoncé could make that work, but I sure as hell didn't have the bone structure.

"I think grown men would cry," I told her dryly, "if you asked them to."

She pshawed, but there was a twinkle in her eye that I understood.... She agreed with me, knew it was true, but wasn't going to admit it. With anyone else, she might have. She had an ego–that was for damn sure. But with me? I think she figured I was zero competition, so she felt no need to rub salt in the wound, too.

I plunked my elbows on the counter and stared around my domain as she bustled off and started clearing the tables. It was her last duty of the day, and my feet were aching so damn bad that I didn't even have it in me to care.

This owning your own business shit?

It wasn't easy.

Not saying I didn't love it, but it was hard.

I slept like four hours a night, and when I wasn't in bed, I was here. All the time.

Baking, cooking, serving, and smiling. Always smiling. Even if I was so sleep-deprived I could sob.

Jenny's actually a life saver.

My mom used to be front of house before.. . .

I sucked down a breath.

I had to get used to thinking about it.

She wasn't here anymore, but just avoiding all thoughts of her period wasn't working for me. It was like I was purposely forgetting her, and, well, fuck that.

She'd always wanted to have a teashop. It had been her one true dream. Back in Ireland, when she was a little girl, her grandmother had owned one in Limerick. Mom had caught the bug and had wanted to have one here in the States. But not only was it too fucking expensive for a woman on her own, it was also impossible with my feckless father at her side.

I didn't want to think about him either, though.

Why?

Because the feckless father who'd pretty much ruined my mother's life, wasn't the only father in my life. My biological dad hadn't exactly cared about her happiness, but once he'd come to know about me, he'd tried. That was more than could be said for the man who'd lived with me throughout my early childhood.

"You look gloomy."

Jenny's statement had me blinking in surprise. She had a ton of dishes piled in her arms, and I'd have worried for the expensive china if I hadn't known she was an old pro at this shit. Just as I was.

We could probably earn a Guinness World Record on how many dishes we could take back and forth to the kitchen of *Ellie's Tea Rooms*. I swear, I had guns because of all that hefting. My biceps were probably the firmest part of my body.

More's the pity.

I'd have preferred an ass you could bounce dimes off of, but, when it boiled down to it, there was no way in this universe I could live without cake.

Just wasn't going to happen.

My big butt wasn't going *anywhere* until scientists could make zero calorie eclairs and pies.

"I'm not glum."

"No? Then why are your eyes sad?"

Were they? I pursed my lips as I let the 'sad eyes' drift around the tea room. I wish I could say it was all forged on my own hard work, but it wasn't. Not really.

"I was just thinking about Mom."

"Oh, honey," Jenny said sadly, and she carefully placed all the dishes on the counter, so she could round it and curve her arm around my waist. "It was only seven months ago. Of course, you were thinking of her."

"I just—" I blew out a breath. "I don't know if I'm doing what she'd want."

"You can't live for her choices, sweetness. You have to do what you think is right for you."

I gnawed at my bottom lip again. "I-I know, but she was always there for me. A guiding light. With Fiona gone and her, too? I don't really know what I'm doing with myself."

This business wasn't something that made me want to get up on a morning. It was my mom's dream, her goal. Every decision I made, I tried to remember how she'd longed for a place like this, but it wasn't my passion. It was hers, and I was trying to keep that dream alive while fretting over the fact my heart wasn't in it.

"I think you're doing a damn fine job. You have a very successful teashop. Your cakes are raved about. Have you visited our TripAdvisor page recently? Or our Yelp?" She squeaked. "I swear, you're making this place a tourist hotspot. I don't think Fiona or Michelle could be more proud of you if they tried."

The baking shit, yeah, that was all on me, but the other stuff? The finances?

I'd caved in.

I'd caved where my mom had always refused in the past.

With the accident had come a lot of medical bills that I just hadn't been able to afford. Without her help, I'd had to take on extra staff, and out of nowhere, my expenses had added up.

Mom had been so proud of this place, so ferociously gleeful that we'd done it by ourselves, and yet, here I was, financially free for the first time in my life, and I still felt like I was drowning because my freedom went entirely against her wishes.

"Is this to do with Acuig? I know they're still pestering you."

Jenny's statement had me wincing. Acuig were the bottom feeders who wanted to snap up this building, demolish it, and then replace it with a skyscraper. Don't get me wrong, the building was foul, but a lot of people lived here, and the minute it morphed into some exclusive condo, no one from around here would be able to afford to live in it.

It would become yuppy central.

I'd rejected all their offers to buy my tea room even though I didn't want the damn thing, not really. Mostly I wanted to keep mom's goals alive and kicking, but also, it pissed me off the way Acuig were changing Hell's Kitchen. Ratcheting up prices, making it unaffordable for the everyday man and woman—the people I'd grown up with—and bringing a shit-ton of banker-wankers and 1%ers to the area.

So, maybe I'd watched Erin Brockovich a time or two as a kid and had a social conscience... Wasn't the worst thing to possess, right?

"Aoife?" Jenny stated, making me look over at her. "Is Acuig pressuring you?"

I winced, realizing I hadn't answered—Jenny was my friend, but she also worked here and relied on the paycheck. It wasn't fair of me to keep her hanging like that. "They upped the sales price. I guess that isn't helping," I admitted, frowning down at my hands.

Unlike Jenny who had her nails manicured, mine were cut neatly and plain. I had no rings on my fingers, and wore no watch or bracelets because my wrists were usually deep in flour or sugar bags.

I spent most of my life right where I wanted it—behind the shopfront. That had slowly morphed where I was doing double the work to compensate for Mom's loss.

Was it any wonder I was feeling a little out of my league?

I was coping without Fiona, grieving Mom, working without her, too, and then practically living in the kitchens here. I didn't exactly have that much of a life. I had nothing cheerful on the horizon, either.

Well, nothing except for next Tuesday, and that wasn't enough to turn my frown upside down.

The money was a temptation. I didn't need to sell up and start working on my own goals, but that just loaded me down with more guilt and made me feel like a really shitty daughter.

Jenny squeezed me in a gentle hug. But as I turned to speak to her, the bell above the door rang as it opened. We both jerked in surprise—each of us apparently thinking the other had locked up when neither of us had—and turned to face the entrance.

On the brink of telling the client we were closed for the day, my mouth opened then shut.

Standing there, amid the frilly, lacy curtains, was the most masculine man I'd ever seen in my life.

And I meant that.

It was like a thousand aftershave models had morphed into one handsome creature that had just walked through my door.

At my side, I could feel Jenny's 'hot guy radar' flare to life, and for once, I couldn't damn well blame her.

This guy was . . . well, he was enough to make me choke on my words and splutter to a halt.

The tea room was all girly femininity. It was sophisticated enough to appeal to businesswomen with its mauve, taupe, and cream-toned hues, and the ethereal watercolors that decorated the walls. But the tablecloths were lacy, and the china dishes and cake stands we used were the height of Edwardian elegance.

Moms brought their little girls here for their birthday, and high-powered executives spilled dirt on their lovers with their girlfriends over scones and clotted cream—breaking their diets as they discussed the boyfriends who had broken their hearts.

The man, whoever the hell he was, was dressed to impress in a navy suit with the finest pinstripe. It was close to a silver fleck, and I could see, even from this distance, that it was hand tailored. I'd seen custom tailoring before, and only a trained eye could get a suit cut so perfectly to this man's form.

With wide shoulders that looked like they could take the weight of the world, a long, lean frame that was enhanced by strong muscles evident through the close fit of his pants and jacket, then the silkiness of his shirt which revealed delineated abs when his bright gold and scarlet tie flapped as he moved, the guy was hot.

With a capital H.

"How can we help, sir?" Jenny purred, and despite my own awe, I had to dip my chin to hide my smile.

Even if I wanted to throw my hat into this particular man's game, there was no way he'd choose me over Jenny. Fuck, I'd screw her, and I wasn't even a lesbian. Not even a teensy bit bi. I'd gone shopping with her enough to have seen her ass, and I promise you, it's biteable.

So, nope. I didn't have a snowball's chance in hell of this Adonis seeing *me* when Jenny was in the room.

Yet. . . .

When I'd controlled my smile, I looked over at the man, and his focus was on me.

My breath stuttered to a halt.

Why wasn't his gaze glued to Jenny?

Why weren't those ice-white blue eyes fixated on my best friend's tits, which Jenny helpfully plumped up as she preened at my side?

For a second, I was so close to breaking out into a coughing fit, it was humiliating. Then, more humiliation struck in a quieter manner, but it was nevertheless rotten—I turned pink.

Now, you might think you know what a blush is. You might think you've even experienced it yourself a time or two. But I was a redhead. My skin made fresh milk look yellow, and even my fucking freckles were pale. Everything about me was like I'd been dunked into white wax.

But as the heat crawled over me, taking over my skin as the man looked at me without pause, I knew things had rarely been this dire.

See, with Jenny as a best friend, I was used to the attention going her way. I could hide in the background, hide in her shadow. I liked it there. I was comfortable there. Sometimes, on double dates, she'd drag me along, and even the guy supposed to be dating me would be gaping at Jenny. As pathetic as it was, I was so used to it, it didn't bother me.

But now?

I just wasn't used to being in the spotlight.

Especially not a man like this one's spotlight.

When you're a teenager, practicing with your mom's blush for the first time, you always look like a tomato that's been left out in the sun, right?

I was redder than that.

I could feel it. I could fucking feel the heat turning me tomato red.

When Jenny cleared her throat, I thanked God when it broke the man's attention. He shot her a look, but it wasn't admiring. It wasn't even impressed.

If anything, it was irritated.

Okay, so now both Jenny and I were stunned.

Fuck that, we were floored.

Literally.

Our mouths were doing a pretty good fish impression as the man turned back to look at me.

Shit, was this some kind of joke?

Was it April 1st and I'd just gotten the dates mixed up again?

"Ms. Keegan?"

Oh fuck. His voice.

Oh. My. God.

That voice.

It was. . . .

I had to swallow.

Did men even talk like that?

It was low and husky and raspy and made me think of sex, not just mediocre sex, but the best sex. Toe-curling, nails-breaking-in-the-sheets sex. Sex so fucking good you couldn't walk the next day. Sex so hot that it made my current core temperature look polar in comparison. Sex that I'd never been lucky to have before, so I pined for it in the worst way.

Jenny nudged me in the side when I just carried on gaping at the man. "Y-Yes. That's me." I cleared my throat, feeling nervous and stupid and flustered as I wiped my hands on my apron.

Sweet Jesus.

Was this man really looking for me while I was wearing a goddamn pinafore?

Even as practical as they were, I wanted to beg the patron saint of pinnies to remove it from me. To do something, anything, to make sure that this man didn't see me in the red gingham check that I always wore to cover up stains.

And then I felt it.

Jenny's hand.

Tugging at the knot.

I wanted to kiss her. Seriously. I wanted to give her a fucking raise! As I moved away from the counter and her side, the apron dropped to the floor as I headed for the man whose hand was now held out, ready for me to shake in greeting.

There are those moments in your life when you know you'll never forget them. They can be happy or sad, annoying or exhilarating. This was one of them.

As I slipped my hand into his, I felt the electric shocks down to my core. Meeting his gaze wasn't hard because I was stunned, and I needed to know if he'd felt that, too.

From the way those eyelids were shielding his icy-blue eyes, I figured he was just as surprised.

It was like a satisfied puma was watching me. One that was happy there was plump prey prancing around in front of him.

Shit.

Did I just describe myself as 'plump prey?'

And like that, my house of cards came tumbling down because what the hell would this man want with me?

I was seeing things.

God, I was so stupid sometimes.

I cleared my throat for, like, the fourth damn time, and asked, "I'm Ms. Keegan. You are?"

His smile, when it appeared, was as charming as the rest of him. His teeth were white, but not creepy, reality-TV-star white. They were straight except for one of his canines, which tilted in slightly. In his perfect face, it was one flaw that I almost clung to. Because with that wide brow, the hair so dark it looked like black silk that was cut closely to his head with a faint peak at his forehead, the strong nose, and even stronger jaw, I needed something imperfect to focus on.

Then, I sucked down a breath and remembered what Fiona had told me once upon a time. When I'd been nervous about asking Jamie Winters to homecoming, she'd advised me in her soft Irish lilt, "Lass, that boy takes a dump just like you do. He uses the bathroom twice a day and undoubtedly leaves a puddle on the floor for his ma to clean up. I bet he's puked a time or two as well. Had diarrhea and the good Lord only knows what else. Just you think that the next time you see that boy and want to ask him out."

Yeah. It was gross, but fuck, it had worked. Her advice had worked so well I hadn't asked anyone out because I could only think of them using the damn toilet!

Still, looking at this Adonis, there was no imagining *that*.

Surely, gods didn't use the bathroom.

Did they?

"The name's Finn. Finn O'Grady."

My eyes flared at the name.

No.

It couldn't be.

Finn O'Grady?

No. It wasn't a rare name, but it was a strong one. One that suited him, one that had always suited him.

I frowned up at him wondering, yet again, if this was a joke of some sort, but as he looked at me, *really* looked at me, I saw no recognition. Saw nothing on his features that revealed any ounce of awareness that I'd known him for years.

Well, okay, not *known*. But I'd known his mother. Our mothers had been best friends. And as I looked, I saw the same almond-shaped eyes Fiona had, the stubborn jaw, and that unmistakable butt-indent on his chin.

At the reminder of just how forgettable I was, my heart sank, and hurt whistled through me.

Then, I realized I was *still* holding his hand, and as he squeezed, the flush returned and I almost died of mortification.

CHAPTER 2

FINN

GOD, she was perfect.

And when I said perfect, I meant it.

I'd fucked a lot of women. Redheads, blondes, brunettes, even the rare thing that is a natural head of black hair. None of them, not a single one, lit up like Aoife Keegan.

Her cheeks were cherry red and in the light camisole she wore, a cheerful yellow, I could see how the blush went all the way down to the upper curve of her breasts.

She'd go that color, I knew, when she came.

And fuck, I wanted to see that.

I wanted to see that perfectly pale flesh turn bright pink under my ministrations.

Even as I looked at her, all shy and flustered, I wondered if she was a screamer in bed.

Some of the shyest often were.

Maybe not at first, but after a handful of orgasms, it was a wonder what that could do to a woman's self-confidence, and Jesus, I wanted to *see* that, too. I wanted a seat at center stage.

My suit jacket was open, and I regretted it. Immensely. My cock was hard, had been since we'd shaken hands, and her fingers had clung to mine like a daughter would to her daddy's at her first visit to the county fair.

Fuck.

Squeezing her fingers wasn't intentional. If anything, I'd just liked the feel of her palm against mine, but when I put faint pressure on her, she jerked back like she'd been scalded.

Her cheeks bloomed with heat again, and she whispered, "Mr. O'Grady, what can I do for you?"

You can get on your fucking knees and sort out the hard-on you just caused.

That's what she could fucking do.

I almost growled at the thought because the image of her on her knees, my cock in her small fist, her dainty mouth opening to take the tip. . . .

Shit.

That had to happen.

Here, too.

In this fancy, frilly, feminine place, I wanted to defile her.

Fuck, I wanted that so goddamn much, it was enough to make me reconsider my demolition plans.

I wanted to screw her against all this goddamn lace, which suited her perfectly. She was made for lace. And silk. Hell, silk would look like heaven against her skin. I wouldn't know where she ended and it began.

When her brow puckered, she dipped her chin, and that gorgeous wave of auburn hair slipped over her shoulder.

If we'd been alone, if that brassy bitch—who was staring at me like I could fuck her over the counter with her friend watching if I was game—wasn't here, I'd have grabbed that rope of hair, twisted it around my fingers, and forced her gaze up.

Some guys liked their women demure. And I was one of them. I wasn't about to lie. I liked that in her, but I wanted her eyes on me. Always.

It was enough to prompt me to bite out, "Can we speak privately?"

She jerked at my words, then as she licked her bottom lip, turned to look at the waitress. "Jenny, it's okay. I can handle the rest by myself. You get home."

Jenny, her gaze drifting between me and her boss, nodded. She retreated to a door that swung as she moved through the opening, and within seconds, she had her coat and purse over her arm.

As she sashayed past—for my benefit, I was sure—she murmured, "See you tomorrow, Aoife."

Aoife nodded and shot her friend a smile, but I wasn't smiling. There were dishes on every table. Plates and saucers and tea pots. Those fancy stands that made any man wonder if he could touch it without snapping it.

Aoife was going to clear all that herself? Not on my fucking watch.

When the bell rang as the waitress opened the door, I didn't take my eyes off her until it rang once more upon closing.

Aoife swallowed, and I watched her throat work, watched it with a hunger that felt alien to me, because, God, I wanted to see my bites on her. Wanted to see my marks on that pale column of skin and her tits.

Barely withholding a groan, I asked, "Do you often let your staff go when you still have a lot of work to do, so you can speak to a stranger?"

Her cheeks flushed again, and she took a step back. "I-I, you're not —" Flustered once more, she fell silent.

"I'm not what?" Curiosity had me asking the question. Whatever I'd expected her to say, it hadn't been that.

She cleared her throat. "N-Nothing. You wished to speak with me, Mr. O'Grady?"

My other hand tightened around my briefcase, and though seeing her had made my reason for being here all that more necessary, I was almost disappointed. There was a gentle warmth to those bright-green eyes that would die out when I told her my purpose for being here. And her innocent attraction to me would change, morph into something else.

But I could only handle *something else*.

Some men were made for forever.

But those men weren't in my line of business.

I moved away from her, pressing my briefcase to one of the few empty tables. I wasn't happy about her having to do all the clearing up later on, and wondered if Paul, my PA, would know who to call to get her some help.

There was no way I was spending the rest of the night alone in my bed, my only companion my fist wrapped around my cock.

No way, no fucking how.

I paid Paul enough for him to come and clear the fucking place on his own if he couldn't find someone else.

I wanted Aoife on her knees, bent over my goddamn bed, and I was a man who always got what he wanted.

In this jungle, I was the lion, and Aoife? She was my prey.

I keyed in the code and opened my briefcase. The manila envelope was large and thick, well-padded with my documentation of Aoife's every move for the past few months.

It had started off as a legitimate move.

I'd wanted to know her weaknesses, so I could put pressure on her and make her cave to my demands.

Now, my demands had changed. I didn't just want her to sell the tea room we were standing in, I wanted her in my bed.

Fuck, I wanted that more than I wanted to make Aidan Sr. a fucking profit, and Aidan's profit and my balls still being attached to my body ran hand in hand.

Aidan was an evil cunt.

If I failed to deliver, he'd take it out on me. Whether I was his idea of an adopted son or not, he'd have done the same to his blood sons.

Well, he wouldn't have taken their balls. The man, for all his psychotic flaws, was obsessed with the idea of grandchildren, of passing it all on to the next generation. He'd cut his boys though. Without a doubt.

I knew Conor had marks on his back from a beating he refused to speak about. Then there was Brennan. He had a weak wrist because his father had a habit of breaking *that* wrist.

Without speaking, I grabbed the envelope and passed it to her.

She frowned down at it and asked, "For me?"

I smiled at her. "Open it."

"What is it?"

"Leverage."

That had her eyes flaring wide as she pulled out some of the photos. A gasp fell from her lips as she grabbed the photos when she spotted herself in them, jerking so hard the envelope tore. Some of the pictures spilled to the ground, but I didn't care about that.

Leaning back against one of the dainty tables once I was satisfied it would take my weight, I watched her cheeks blanch, all that delicious color dissipating as she took in everything the photos revealed.

"Y-You've been stalking me. Why?"

The question was high-pitched, loaded down with panic. I'd heard it often enough to recognize it easily.

I didn't get involved in wet work anymore. That wasn't my style, but along the way, to reach this point, I'd had no choice but to get my hands dirty. Panic was part of the job when you were collecting debts for the Irish Mob. And the Five Points were notorious for Aidan Sr.'s temper.

He wasn't the first patriarch. If anything, his grandfather was the founder. But Aidan Sr. was the type of guy that if you didn't pay him back, he didn't give a fuck about the money, he cared about the lack of respect.

See, you owed the mob and didn't pay? They'd send heavies around, beat the shit out of you, and threaten to do the same to your family, and usually, that did the trick. You didn't kill the cash cow.

Aidan Sr.?

He didn't give a fuck about the cash cow.

Only the truly desperate thought about borrowing money from Aidan, because if you didn't pay it back, he'd take your teeth, and your fingers and toes as a first warning. Then, if you still didn't pay—and most did—it was death.

Respect meant a lot to Aidan.

And fuck, if it wasn't starting to mean a lot to me. The panic in her voice made my cock throb.

I wanted this woman weak and willing.

I wanted it more than I wanted my next breath.

Ignoring her, I reached for my phone and tapped out a message to Paul.

Need housekeeping crew to clean this place.

I attached my live location, saw the blue ticks as Paul read the message—he knew better than to ignore my texts, whatever time of day they came—and he replied: *Sure thing.*

That was the kind of reply I was used to getting. Not just from Paul, but from everyone.

There were very few people who weren't below me in the strata of Five Points, and I'd worked my ass off to make that so.

The only people who ranked above me included Aidan Jr. and his brothers, Aidan Sr. of course, and then maybe a handful of his advisors that he respected for what they'd done for him and the Points over the years.

But the money I made Aidan Sr.?

That blew most of their 'advice' out of the window.

The reason Aidan had a Dassault Falcon executive private plane?

Because I was, as the City itself called me, a whiz kid.

I'd made my first million—backed by the Points, of course—at twenty-two.

Fifteen years later?

I'd made him hundreds of millions.

My own personal fortune was nothing to sniff at, either.

"W-Why have you done this?" Aoife asked, her voice breathy enough to make me wonder if she sounded like that in the sack.

"Because you've been a very stubborn little girl."

Her eyes flared wide. "Excuse me?"

I reached into the inside pocket of my suit coat and pulled out a business card. "For you," I prompted, offering it to her.

When she turned it over, saw the logo of five points shaped into a star, then read Acuig—in the Gaelic way, ah-coo-ig, not a butchered American way, ah-coo-ch—aloud, I watched her throat work as she swallowed.

"I-I should have realized with the Irish name," she whispered, the muscles in her brow twitching as she took in the chaos of the scattered photos on the floor.

Watching her as she dropped the contents on the ground, so she was surrounded by them, I tilted my head to the side, taking her in as her panic started to crest.

"I-I won't sell." Her first words surprised me.

I should have figured, though. Everything about this woman was surprisingly delicious.

"You have no choice," I purred. "As far as I'm aware, the Senator has a wife. He also has a reputation to protect. I'm not sure he'd be happy if any of those made it onto the *National Enquirer's* front page. Not when he's just trying to shore up his image to take a run for the White House next election."

She reached up and clutched her throat. The self-protective gesture was enough to make me smile at her—I knew what the absence of hope looked like.

There'd been a time when that had been my life, too.

"But, on the bright side," I carried on, "this can all be wiped away if you sell." As her gaze flicked to mine, I added, "As well as if you do something for me."

For a second, she was speechless. I could see she knew what that *something* was. Had my body language given it away? Had there been a certain raspiness to my tone?

I wasn't sure, and frankly, didn't give a fuck.

There was a little hiccoughing sound that escaped her lips, and she frowned at me, then down at herself.

"Is this a joke?"

"Do I look like I'm the kind of guy who jokes, Aoife?" Fuck, I loved saying her name.

The Gaelic notes just drove me insane.

Ee-Fah.

Nothing like the spelling, and all the more complicated and delicious for it.

"N-No," she confirmed, "but . . ."

"But what?" I prompted.

"I mean . . . you just can't be serious."

"Oh, but I am." I grinned. "Deadly. You've wasted a lot of my time, Aoife Keegan. A lot. Do you think I'm normally involved in negotiations of this level?"

Her eyes whispered over me, and I felt the loving caress of her gaze as she took in each and every inch of me. When she licked her lips, I knew she liked what she saw. I didn't really care, but it was helpful for her to be eager in some small way—especially when coercion was involved.

Aidan had called it bribery. I preferred 'coercion'. It sounded far kinder.

"No. That suit alone probably cost the mortgage payment on this place."

I nodded—she wasn't wrong. I knew what she'd been paying as rent, then as a mortgage, before some kind *benefactor* had paid it all off. Free and clear.

"I had to get my hands dirty, and while I might like some things dirty...," I trailed off, smirking when she flushed. "So, as I see it, we have a problem. I want this building. You don't want anyone to know you're having an affair with a Senator. Or, should I say, the Senator doesn't want anyone to know he's having an affair with someone young enough to be his daughter..."

If my voice turned into a growl at that point, then it was because the notion of her spreading her legs for that old bastard just turned my stomach.

Fuck, this woman, the thoughts she made me think.

Because I was startled at the possessive note to my growl, I ran a hand over my head. I kept my hair short for a reason—ease. I wasn't the kind of man who wasted time primping. It was an expensive cut, so I didn't have to do anything to it. Even mussing it up had it falling back into the same sleek lines as before—a man in my position had to look pristine under pressure. And very few people could even begin to understand the kind of strain I was under.

The formation of igneous rock had less volcanic pressure than Aidan Sr.

She licked her lips as she stared down at the photos, then back up at me. "And you want me to sell the place to you, even though this is my livelihood and the livelihood of all my staff, and then sleep with you?"

Her squeaky voice, putting suspicion into words, had me crossing my legs at the ankle. "We wouldn't be doing much sleeping."

Another shaky breath soughed from her lips, then, those beautiful pillowy morsels that would look good around my cock, quivered.

"This is crazy," she whispered shakily.

"As far as I'm concerned, all of this could be avoided if you'd just sold to me a few months back. Now you have to pay for my time wasted on this project."

"By spreading my legs?"

Another squeak. I tsked at her question, but in truth, I was annoyed at her using those same words I had to describe her with that old hypocrite of a Senator.

I didn't move, though. Didn't even flex my arms in irritation, just murmured, "Small price to pay. And, even though it's ten percent above market price, I'll stick to the last offer Acuig gave you. Can't say anything's fairer than that."

She shook her head, and there was a desperation to the gesture as she cried, "I need this business. You don't understand—"

"I understand that some very powerful and very dangerous businessmen want this building demolished. I understand that those same powerful and dangerous men want a skyscraper taking up this plot of land. I understand that a four hundred million dollar project isn't going to be put on hiatus because one small Irish woman doesn't want to go out of business . . ." I cocked a brow at her. "You think I'm coming in hot and heavy? These kinds of men, Aoife, they're not the sort you fuck around with.

"Take my check, and my other offer, before you or the people you care about are threatened." I got to my feet and straightened my jacket out. "This suit? These shoes? That briefcase and this watch? I own them because I'm damn good at what I do. I'm a financial advisor, Aoife. Take my word for it. You're getting the best deal out of this."

She staggered back, the counter stopping her from crumpling to the floor. "You'd hurt me?"

"Not me," I repudiated. Not in the way she thought, anyway. "But the men I work for?"

Her gaze dropped to the one thing she'd retained in her hand—my card. "Acuig," she whispered. "Five in Gaelic."

My brows twitched in surprise. She knew Gaelic?

"The Five Points." Her eyes flared wide with terror. "They're behind this deal."

I hadn't expected her to put one and one together, but now that she had? It worked to my advantage.

Nodding, I told her, "Any minute now, there'll be a team of housekeepers coming in here to clear up for the night." When she gaped at me, I retrieved the contract from my briefcase, slapped it on the table, and handed her a pen as I carried on, "I suggest you let tonight be your last night of business."

What I didn't tell her, was that my suggestions weren't wasted words. They were like the law.

You didn't break them, and, like any lawmaker, I expected immediate obeisance.

***

Aoife

SO, the beautiful man just happened to be an absolute cocksucker of a bastard.

Still, this couldn't be real, could it?

The dick could have anyone he wanted. Jesus, Jenny was panting after him like a dog in heat. She would have gone out with him if he'd so much as clicked his fingers at her.

But he'd had eyes for me.

Like he wanted me.

He thought he'd bought me. Or, at least, bought my silence, and yeah, to some extent he had. But . . . why buy me, why not just drop the price on the building if he wanted me to pay for the time he'd wasted on me?

The arrogance imbued in those words was enough to make me pull my hair out, but that was inwardly. I was a redhead. I had a temper. But that temper was mostly overshadowed by fear.

Senator Alan Davidson wasn't my boyfriend, my lover, as this dick seemed to believe. He was my father, and as Finn O'Grady had correctly surmised, he was aiming for the White House.

How could I put that in jeopardy?

My dad was a good man. He'd made a mistake one summer when he'd come home from college, one that only some careful digging by his campaign manager had uncovered. Dad himself hadn't known of my existence, not until his CM had gone hunting for any nasty secrets that could come out and bite him in the ass.

This had been five years ago when he'd run for Senator. Now, Dad's goal was the presidential seat, and I wasn't going to be the one who put a wrench in the works.

When Garry Smythe had approached me back then, I'd thought he was joking. I was out on the street, heading home from work. At the side of me, a black car had driven in from the lane of traffic, just to park, or so I'd thought. As he'd held out his hand with a card, one of the car doors had opened up, and I'd been 'invited' inside.

Had I been scared?

At first.

But when Garry had told me my country needed me, I hadn't been sure whether to laugh or tell him to fuck off. He hadn't shuffled me into the car, though, hadn't tried to coerce me. He'd just asked if I'd voted for Senator Alan Davidson in the elections, and because he was one of the only politicians out there who wasn't a complete douche, and that was the name printed on the card in my hand, I'd shuffled into the back of the car.

Where the Senator himself had been sitting.

Now, when I thought about that day, I realized how fucking naive I'd been to get into the back of a limo for such a vague reason. But I'd been fortunate. Alan *had* been waiting for me. Waiting to tell me a story that still shook me to my core.

I'd made a promise to my dad that I wouldn't tell anyone. He'd offered me money, and I hadn't accepted it. I guess I should have, but back then, I'd been haughty and proud, and because the good guy I'd thought him to be hadn't been so good when he tried to buy my silence, I'd told him to fuck off. I'd been disappointed in him, frightened by the lifelong lie I'd been living, and equally hurt that the man who'd sired me was just concerned that I was a threat to his campaign.

I'd walked out of that car never expecting to see my dear old Dad ever again.

Then, the day after he'd been elected, he'd been sitting in the booth of the cafe where I worked part-time to get me through culinary school.

Seeing him, I'd almost handed that table off to one of the other waitresses, but I hadn't. Not when every time I'd passed the table, he'd caught my eye, a patient smile on his lips, one that said he'd wait for me all day if he had to.

Ever since that second meeting, I'd been catching up with him every three weeks.

And this bastard thought he could use our limited time together against my father? The one politician who could make a difference in the White House? One who didn't have Big Oil up his ass, a pharmaceutical company sucking his dick, or any other kind of corporation so far up his rectum that he was a walking, talking lie?

No.

That wasn't going to happen.

Which meant I was going to have to sleep with this stranger.

Before this conversation, hell, that hadn't been too disturbing a prospect. Because, dayum, what woman wouldn't want to sleep with this guy?

Even with an ego as big as his, he was delicious. Better than any cake I could bake, that was for fucking sure.

More than that, I knew him.

And I now knew that the life Fiona would never have wanted for her son was one he'd been drawn into.

The Mob.

The Five Points were notorious in these parts. Everyone was scared of them. I paid protection money to them, for God's sake. I knew to be scared of them, and having been raised in their territory, it was the height of stupidity to think paying them wasn't just a part of business.

Still, Fiona had never wanted that for Finn, and her Finn was the same as the one standing before me here today. In my tea room, which looked far too small to contain the might of this man.

She'd be so disappointed. So heart-sore to know that he was up to his neck in dirty dealings with the Five Points, and as he'd pointed out, the cost of his shoes, his clothes, and his jewelry, was enough to speak for itself.

If he wasn't high up the ladder in the gang, then I wasn't one of the best bakers of scones in the district.

Like Jenny had said, I had five star ratings across most social media platforms for a reason. I was good. But apparently, this man wasn't.

Before I could utter a word, before I could even cringe at how utterly sorrowful Fiona would be about this turn of events—not just about the Five Points but what her son was making me do—the door clattered open.

Like he'd predicted, a team of people swarmed in.

Finn motioned to the floor. "Want anyone to see those?"

With a gasp, I dropped to my knees and collected the shots, stuffing them back into the envelope with a haste that wasn't exactly practical.

Two shiny shoes appeared before me, followed by two expensively clad legs, and I peered up at him, wondering what he was about. He held out his hand, but I clasped the photos to my chest.

"You're making more of a mess than anything else, Aoife." His voice was raspy, his eyes weighted down by heavy lids.

For a second, I wondered why, then I saw *why*.

He had an erection.

An erection?

I peered around at the staff, but they were all men. Not a single woman in sight, well, save for the seventy-year-old with a clipboard who was barking out orders to the guys in what sounded like Russian.

So that meant, what?

The erection was for me?

The blush, the dreaded, hated blush, made another goddamn appearance, and to cover it, I ducked my head, then pushed the photos and the envelope at him.

For whatever reason, I stayed where I was, staring up at him as he calmly, coolly, and so fucking collectedly pushed the photos back into the torn envelope—it was some coverage. Better than none at all, I figured.

Being down here was....

Hell, I don't know what it was.

To be looked at like that?

For his body to respond to me like that?

It was unprecedented.

I'd had one sexual experience with a boy back in college, and that had not gone according to plan. So much so I was still technically a fucking virgin because, and this was no lie, the guy had *zero* understanding of a woman's body.

Craig had spent more time fingering my perineum than my clit, and every time he'd tried to shove his dick into me, he'd somehow managed to drag it down toward my ass.

I'd gotten so sick of him frigging the wrong bits of me, that I'd pushed him off and given him a blowjob. It had been the quickest way to get out of that annoying situation.

Yeah, annoying.

Jenny, when I'd told her, had pissed herself laughing, and ever since, had tried to get me to hook up with randoms, so I could slough off my virginity like it was dead skin and I was a snake. But life had just always gotten in the way, and I'd had no time for men.

Shortly after *that* had happened, we'd lost Fiona. Then, I'd graduated, and after, Mom and I had set up this place thanks to some insurance money she'd come into after her husband had died. It had been crazy building the tea room into an established cafe, and then mom had passed on, too.

So, here I was. Still a virgin. On my knees in front of the sexiest man on Earth, a man I knew, a man whose mother had half raised me, one who wanted me in his bed as some kind of blackmail payment.

Was this a dream?

Seriously?

I mean, I'd been depressed before Finn O'Grady had walked through my doors. Now I wasn't sure whether to be apoplectic or worried as fuck because he wasn't wrong: you didn't mess with the Five Points.

God, if I'd known they'd been behind the development on this building, I'd have probably signed over months ago.

The Points were. . . .

I shuddered.

Vindictive.

Aidan O'Donnelly was half-evil genius and half-twisted sociopath. St. Patrick's Church, two streets away, had the best roof in the neighborhood and the strongest attendance because Aidan, for all he'd cut you into more pieces than a butcher, was a devout Catholic. His men knew better than to avoid Sunday service, and I reckoned that Father Doyle was the busiest priest in the city because of Five Points' attendance.

"I like you down there," he murmured absentmindedly.

The words weren't exactly dirty, but the meaning? They had my temperature soaring.

Shit.

What the hell was I doing?

Enjoying the way this man was victimizing me?

It was so wrong, and yet, what was standing right in front of me? I knew he'd know what to do with that thing tucked behind his pants.

He wouldn't try to penetrate my urethra—yes, you read that right. Craig had tried to fuck my pee-hole! Like, *why?*

Finn?

He oozed sex appeal.

It seemed to seep from every pore, perfuming the air around me with his pheromones.

I hadn't even believed in pheromones until I scented Finn O'Grady's delicious essence.

It reminded me of the one out of town vacation we'd ever had. We'd gone to Cooperstown, and I'd scented a body of water that didn't have corpses floating in it—Otsego Lake. He reminded me of that. So green and earthy. It was an attack on my overwhelmed senses, an attack I didn't need.

With the envelope in his hand, he held out his other for me. When I placed my fingers in his, the size difference between us was noticeable once more.

I was just over five feet, and he was over six. I was round and curvy, and he was hard and lean.

It reminded me of the nursery tale Mom had sung to me as a child— Jack Sprat could eat no fat, and his wife could eat no lean.

Did it say a lot for my confidence that I couldn't seem to take it in that he wanted *me*? Or was it simply that I wasn't understanding how anyone could prefer me over Jenny?

Even my mom had called Jenny beautiful, whereas she'd kissed me on the nose and called me her 'bonny lass.'

Biting my lip, I accepted his help off the floor. My black jeans weren't the smartest thing for the tea room, but I didn't actually serve that many dishes, just bustled around behind the counter, working up the courage to do what Mom had done every day—greet people.

I wasn't a sociable person. I preferred my kitchen to the front of house, hence the jeans, but I regretted not wearing something else today. Something that covered just how big my ass was, how slender my waist *wasn't*.

Ugh.

This man is blackmailing you into his bed, Aoife. For Christ's sake, you're not supposed to be worrying if he likes the goods, too!

Still, no matter how much I tried, years of inadequacy weighed me down as I wiped off my knees.

"Do you have a coat?" he asked, and his voice was raspy again. "A jacket? Or a purse?"

I nodded at him but kept my gaze trained on the floor. "Yes."

"Go get them."

His order had me shuffling my feet toward the kitchen, but as I approached the door, I heard his strong voice speaking with the old woman with the clipboard: "I want this all cleaned up and boxed. Take it to my storage lot in Queens."

With my back to him, I stiffened at his brisk orders. *Was I just going to let him do this? Get away with it?*

My shoulders immediately sagged.

Did I have a choice?

If it was just him, just Acuig, then I'd fight this, as I'd been fighting it since the building had come to the attention of the developer. But this wasn't a regular business deal.

This was mob business, and it seemed like somehow, I'd become a part of that.

FML.

Seriously, FML.

TO READ MORE, Filthy is free on KU: www.books2read.com/FilthySerenaAkeroyd

FREE BOOK!

Don't forget to grab your free e-Book!
Secrets & Lies is now free!

Meg's love life was missing a spark until she discovered her need to be dominated. When her fiancé shared the same kink, she thought all her birthdays had come at once, and then she came to learn their relationship was one big fat lie.

Gabe has loved Meg for years, watching her from afar, and always wishing he'd been the one to date her first and not his brother. When he has the chance to have Meg in his bed—even better, tied to it—it's an opportunity he can't refuse.

With disastrous consequences.

Can Gabe make Meg realize she's the one woman he's always wanted? But once secrets and lies have wormed their way into a relationship, is it impossible to establish the firm base of trust needed between lovers, and more importantly, between sub and Sir...?

This story features orgasm control in a BDSM setting.
Secrets & Lies is now free!

CONNECT WITH SERENA

For the latest updates, be sure to check out my website! But if you'd like to hang out with me and get to know me better, then I'd love to see you in my Diva reader's group where you can find out all the gossip on new releases as and when they happen. You can join here: www.facebook.com/groups/SerenaAkeroydsDivas. Or you can always PM or email me. I love to hear from you guys: serenaakeroyd@gmail.com.

ABOUT THE AUTHOR

I'm a romance novelaholic and I won't touch a book unless I know there's a happy ending. This addiction is what made me craft stories that suit my voracious need for raunchy romance. I love twists and unexpected turns, and my novels all contain sexy guys, dark humor, and hot AF love scenes.

I write MF, menage, and reverse harem (also known as why choose romance,) in both contemporary and paranormal. Some of my stories are darker than others, but I can promise you one thing, you will always get the happy ending your heart needs!

Printed in Great Britain
by Amazon